ALSO BY OWEN KING

We're All in This Together: A Novella and Stories

Who Can Save Us Now? (co-editor)

DOUBLE FEATURE

A NOVEL

OWEN KING

SCRIBNER

New York   London   Toronto   Sydney   New Delhi

SCRIBNER
A Division of Simon & Schuster, Inc.
1230 Avenue of the Americas
New York, NY 10020

First Scribner hardcover edition March 2013

SCRIBNER and design are registered trademarks of The Gale Group, Inc., used under license by Simon & Schuster, Inc., the publisher of this work.

For information about special discounts for bulk purchases, please contact Simon & Schuster Special Sales at 1-866-506-1949 or business@simonandschuster.com.

The Simon & Schuster Speakers Bureau can bring authors to your live event. For more information or to book an event contact the Simon & Schuster Speakers Bureau at 1-866-248-3049 or visit our website at www.simonspeakers.com.

DESIGNED BY ERICH HOBBING

Manufactured in the United States of America

1   3   5   7   9   10   8   6   4   2

Library of Congress Cataloging-in-Publication Data is available.

ISBN 978-1-4516-7689-1
ISBN 978-1-4516-7691-4 (ebook)

This book is dedicated to the inspiring,
irreplaceable women in my life.
ZJBK
KTB
NRK
TJFSK
&

in memory of Sarah Jane White Spruce,
12/7/23–5/14/07

DOCTOR
(to Guido, the director)
Well, what are you working on now?
Another film without hope?

—Federico Fellini, Tullio Pinelli,
   Ennio Flaiano, Brunello Rondi, *8½*
   (dialogue spoken by Roberto Nicolosi)

CONTENTS

DOUBLE FEATURE

The steel-on-steel whisk of the curtain rings scraping along the rod seemed to come from the sky, and for the last seven or eight seconds of his dream, Sam Dolan found himself turning in a circle, searching for the source of the sound, but there was no one else in the vast parking lot. "Samuel!" bellowed an unmistakable voice. "Samuel! I must speak to you!"

Sam opened his eyes and recoiled at the rectangle of white light. He threw his hands out to block the brilliant autumn morning cascading through the revealed window. Something was wrong. "What is it? What's happened?"

A shadow grew, grew and grew, its mountainous shoulders overwhelming the bright frame. Booth stepped closer. His eyes were wide, his peppery beard tangled and wild, as if he had been rending it.

"What?" Sam's pulse was in his fingers and his toes, behind his eyes, under his tongue. He was afraid.

"Samuel, my son." His father cleared his throat and held up a sheaf of pages. "I have some notes for your script."

PART 1

PREPRODUCTION

(2002–2003)

1.

The script was for a film called *Who We Are,* a drama set at Russell College, the small liberal arts school in northern New York where Sam had matriculated. The partly autobiographical story had been his senior thesis. Central to the design of the work was the way it compacted time, by means of a trope that Sam privately considered so ingenious he sometimes broke into cackles just thinking about it.

At the break of day, the narrative's half dozen or so main figures are callow eighteen-year-old freshman, but as the film advances—through parties and drugged-out drum circles, couplings and arguments and pranks—they age at a super-accelerated rate, encapsulating all four years of college in a single Spring Festival, the annual daylong bacchanalia that was the inebriated topper on every red-blooded Russell undergraduate's year. At sunup of the following morning, finally partied out, the characters are grown-up seniors on the verge of graduation, with different haircuts and thinner faces and better clothes, yet in every significant way no more prepared for the real world than when they started.

While most readers of *Who We Are* found it funny in places, it was an essentially lyric piece that Sam felt spoke to the mad, arrested quality of those four years and, in general, of what a desperate thing it was to be young and free and American.

One character, Rachel, is a buttoned-down suburban honor student when we meet her in the morning; when we leave her, four years later, she is a fully committed member of an ecoterrorist cell; through the first quarter of the movie, Hugh drinks beer after beer, backslaps everyone in sight, climbs on every available chair and tabletop to make ribald acclamations to his friends; by the last fifteen minutes or so, Hugh has stopped going out altogether, developed a policy of conducting communication exclusively via the Internet or speakerphone, become too indolent to bother dressing himself, and just lies on his couch, gloating aloud about the energy that his old companions are wasting while he is relaxing; another, Florence, renames herself Diana, and then Aurora, and then Divinity, before finally going back to Florence—the bright, gifted arts major who woke up that morning gradually transforming into a grim scold, her final project an installation of a Dumpster filled with words carved from piss-soaked foam blocks: EMPATHY, TRUTH, INTEGRITY, and so on; a gold-chain-wearing high school football star when we meet him, Brunson discovers his homosexuality during the first twenty minutes of the film, begins to treat his shame and anxiety with crystal meth around the forty-minute mark, and shortly afterward disappears completely right in the middle of a scene, at which point everyone ceases to refer to him except in the past tense; Kira spends the entire movie holding hands, only the person with whom she's holding hands keeps changing, and they're always arguing about that other person's lack of faithfulness; she becomes angrier and angrier until she literally bites her last lover and rips a chunk of flesh from his cheek.

In a typical scene about midway through, Roger, the ostensible leader of the group, abruptly breaks up with his girlfriend. Initially a humorous skeptic, by the film's latter stages, Roger has become so chronically dubious that he refuses to believe his own mother when she calls, sobbing, to inform him that his father has suffered a fatal aneurysm. "Nice try," he says, and hangs up on her.

Several of the screenplay's characters were modeled on real people: Roger, for instance, was Sam's stand-in, and most of the things that happened to Roger—like the phone call scene—were semi-fictionalized versions of events from Sam's own life. Another key player, Hugh, was plainly based on Sam's best friend, Wesley Latsch, who had in reality, over time, winnowed his direct human contact to the bare minimum, and become so resolute in his fecklessness that there was a kind of integrity to it. Claire, Roger's girlfriend, was a dead ringer for Sam's actual college girlfriend, an indefatigably good-natured young woman named Polly Dressler:

EXT. NORTH FIELD PARKING LOT—MIDAFTERNOON
The group comes to Roger's Saab. Behind them, in the meadow and on the hillside, the festival continues—people

jumping up and down in the bouncy castle, a juggler with devil sticks, the rotating Ferris wheel, etc.

> CLAIRE

Slurpee time!

> HUGH

T-minus Slurpee!

Roger unlocks the car with a CLICK, as Claire pulls on the passenger-side door with a CLACK. Claire has pulled the handle too soon.

Roger opens his door and climbs in. Claire pulls again on the handle of the passenger-side door, to no avail. Hugh stands with her.

Roger stares at Claire through the dirty glass. Roger's Radiohead T-shirt is now a Wilco T-shirt. Claire's glasses are gone, and her hair is different.

BACK-AND-FORTH THROUGH THE PASSENGER WINDOW:

> CLAIRE

Let me in! I want Slurpee!

> HUGH

Slurpee motherfucker!

> ROGER

No. It's over. I can't do this anymore, Claire.

> CLAIRE

What?

> ROGER

I can't be with you. You're a handle-puller.

CLAIRE

What?

ROGER

I'm sorry, but we're through.

CLAIRE

Why are you being such a jerk? I just want to get a Slurpee and have an enjoyable day.

ROGER

I could never love a handle-puller. I mean, it's proof that we don't fit.

CLAIRE

Are you serious? This is not funny, Roger.

ROGER

It's not that you're impatient, it's that you want more from life than I do. You want to get going. You want your Slurpee right away. You're a handle-puller, Claire. You pulled.

CLAIRE

Yes, but I didn't mean to!

ROGER

It's too late.

She starts to cry and gives Roger the finger.

HUGH
(to Claire:)

No Slurpee for you.

Hugh raps on the window, and Roger lets him in. They pull away a moment later, abandoning Claire in the parking lot.

A Volvo pulls into the empty space. Bertie, the Welsh exchange student, climbs out, unloads his guitar. Claire, in fresh makeup now, face completely dry, runs over and leaps into his arms.

In truth, Polly dumped Sam. And she was the one who pointed out that their ambitions weren't especially compatible. Polly wanted to have a career and a family and a house and lots of affairs with men whose discretion she could trust. Sam's only real ambition was to make a movie. Beyond that, he conceded that he didn't have much in mind for the future.

But it was true that Polly was a handle-puller. This fact was important to Sam.

The breakup had also taken about two years, which was the beauty of the conceit: the compression of such a development brought it into greater relief. What Sam meant to convey was that minor troubles and lingering dissatisfactions—say, one man's deep-rooted irritation at his girlfriend's blithe impatience toward car-door locking mechanisms—often added up to personal shifts with massive consequences.

Taken as a whole, no one who read the screenplay for *Who We Are* denied that it was clever in its composition, original in its pattern, and ruthlessly unsentimental in its conclusions. It was also "a bit portentous," according to Sam's father, Booth Dolan, the B-movie mainstay famous for his stentorian blink-free performances in such films as *New Roman Empire, Hellhole, Hard Mommies, Hellhole 2: Wake the Devil, Black Soul Riders,* and *Hellhole 3: Endless Hell,* who, without invitation, had fished a copy of the script from Sam's laptop bag.

"Portentous?"

After waking him, Booth had trailed Sam to the bathroom, lingered outside while Sam took a leak, and followed him down to the kitchen, maintaining a running critique of the script throughout. The general theme seemed to be that he found *Who We Are* too serious. Sam disagreed; he felt that it was exactly as serious as it needed to be. In addition, he wasn't thrilled about having his work assessed by an intrusive old fat man before he'd even had coffee.

"Let me put it this way," said Booth. "I don't find much in the way of generosity in the story. I'm worried that the irony is perhaps too thick."

Tom Ritts—a wealthy contractor, Booth's best friend, and Sam's god-father, at whose house both Dolan men were staying—had thoughtfully made them a pot of coffee before leaving for work. Sam went to the counter and poured some into a Ritts Design & Construction coffee mug. "Maybe I like my irony thick."

"Irony is so easy, though, Samuel. It's so simple to pull out the rug and make everything bleak and awful. Isn't it more interesting to try and dig down into the hard dirt and scrape out that precious nugget of possibil-ity? Of redemption? Of humor? Of hope? Cynicism is the predictable route. Now: something hopeful! That would shock an audience, knock them back in their seats." Booth stood in the middle of the kitchen as he delivered his homily. He was dressed in a gigantic pair of sky-blue paja-mas. A big man in his youth and an enormous man in these later years, he had the legs of a monument and the torso of a snowman. Sam was tall, but his father towered over him. "Certainly, there are many amus-ing moments, but it leaves an acutely bitter taste. You should at least give your characters a chance at happiness, don't you think?"

Sam thought his father was completely wrong, about everything. He thought, I don't like you very much. He thought, It's too early in the morning.

A part of Sam wanted to yell, to just yell unintelligibly, until his father shut up and went away. He had to concentrate hard on maintaining a tranquil front. With exaggerated care, he set his brimming coffee mug on the counter. "Hold on, Booth. Just—hold it."

For as long as he could remember, Booth had been Booth. Sam was aware that people found it off-putting that he called his father by his first name—that it came off as severe or pissy or both, which, admittedly, it pretty much was—but to call him Dad would have felt like giving in.

"You know—" Sam searched for a way to concisely summarize the man's gall. To commit adultery was one thing. To break promises to your children was another. To do the things that Booth had done in movies—to rant and to brood and to stalk around like a tin-pot dicta-tor on thousands of movie screens—was another. But to be guilty of all these trespasses, and then to carry yourself as though you were a seri-ous person—The Most Serious Person—was something else altogether.

It wasn't as though he had expected Booth to like the script, let alone understand it. *Who We Are* was about the hard reality of how quickly the days sped up, how suddenly you weren't a kid anymore. Booth's movies had nothing to do with reality. They had to do with killer rats and the car-wash mafioso and the outbreak of werewolf attacks in ancient Greece. It annoyed Sam that he was annoyed by his father's opinion, which was a meaningless opinion, and which he could have predicted.

There was so much he could have said, and wanted to say, and there was Booth in his gigantic pajamas with that look of concern, as if he were not only entitled to offer his critique but actually cared. The words and the arguments became jammed up somewhere in Sam's chest. "Who asked you, anyway? And why the fuck are you going through my laptop bag?"

Booth made an innocent face. "I was going to write you a nice note and put it in there."

"What was it going to say?" asked Sam immediately, eager to catch him.

"That I was proud of you! You're a college man now."

"Booth. Who looks in a bag to put in a note before they've even written the note?"

"I needed paper to write my note."

They stared at each other. The clifflike brow that hooded his father's eyes gave him a haunted aspect. It also made him invincible in staring contests.

Sam broke away and snatched his coffee mug from the counter. A splash of hot liquid fell across his hand and fingers. He hated feeling like this, like he was a son and Booth was a father and they were arguing about whether curfew was eleven or twelve. It was embarrassing. "You know what? I want to go and drink my coffee now."

"Samuel, I am not trying to offend you!" The exclamation was drafted in Booth's Voice, the resonant declamatory tone that he adopted to lend credence to things that were ridiculous, such as killer rats and the car-wash mafia and the werewolves of ancient Greece. "I am trying to help!"

His father blinked, very slowly, and in spite of all his experience, Sam found himself swayed to consider whether this once the man might mean what he was saying. The hot coffee dripped over his hand and plinked onto the floor. Around them, the machine guts of Tom's house ticked and hummed.

"Samuel." Sam's father cleared his throat, shook his head, and lifted the hem of his pajama shirt to absently swish a finger around in the gray-haired nest of his belly button. "I am your father, and I only want the best for you"—Booth glanced down at the small meteor of hair and lint that he had mined from his navel, momentarily considered it, then carefully placed the artifact on the kitchen counter—"and that means that, above all else, I must be honest."

Honesty had, in the twenty-two years of their relationship thus far, not proved the slightest burden to Booth. He had taken every "chance at happiness" that he ever wanted—fucked anyone he wanted, said whatever he wanted, left whenever he wanted.

"What?" asked Booth, reading the look on his son's face. "What is it?"

What was it? It was everything about him.

"That," said Sam, and flung out a hand to indicate Booth's gut.

"All right, all right." His father dropped his shirt and put up his palms. "All better?"

His father claimed that the edge in their relationship dated from their earliest meeting, in a hospital room in Poughkeepsie, New York, in 1979. A nurse had handed him a bundle containing his son and, Sam's father would recall, "You peered up at me with your little scalded face, and you did not cry, did not make a single peep. You were enrobed in a kind of rough brown cloth, such as an extra would wear in a biblical production—you resembled a leper, a tiny leper. And you made no fuss at all, just squinted at me with those fierce blue eyes. You looked aggrieved, terribly aggrieved."

At this point in the telling, he would inevitably pause, taking the theatrical hesitation that could be so persuasive on the stage or the screen and so irritating in person. Booth's delivery seemed to suck up the entire atmosphere, stealing away even the air that was already in your lungs. Sam had been gagging for years.

"It was," his father would at last declare, frowning greatly, "most disquieting."

The story was undoubtedly an exaggeration if not an outright fabrication. Booth had been in the business of cheap entertainment for so long that he had gone native. In his telling, everything was a sensation, a shock, a crisis, a betrayal, amazing bad luck, or an unforeseeable confluence. When Sam was younger, his father had let him down. Now that Sam was older, his earlier self's stupidity mortified him: how could he have expected anything else from a man who relished any opportunity to tell strangers that his infant son looked like a leper? Booth's fallaciousness was right there all the time, as inherent as the nose on his face.

In 1969 Booth Dolan had produced, directed, written, and starred in *New Roman Empire,* a no-budget horror movie about hippie teenagers brainwashed by a cornpone Pied Piper. It was a naked allegory wherein Booth's character, Dr. Archibald "Horsefeathers" Law, appeared as the wicked hand of Nixonian politics, sending dazed hippies to their deaths à la Vietnam. It had been a modest success on the drive-in circuit and to this day maintained a certain cachet, primarily among B-movie superdorks. (It was telling, Sam felt, that along with their enthusiasm for Booth Dolan, this breed of cinephile could be relied upon to have an encyclopedic knowledge of all the monsters that had fought Godzilla, Ed Wood, and women-in-prison films.)

Booth had parlayed the minor triumph of *New Roman Empire* and his performance as the charlatan Dr. Law into a career spent mugging and shouting in the lowest category of B-movies. His particular, gassy flair had spiced clunkers from virtually every genre with bathos: horror, western, blaxploitation, sexploitation, sci-fi, fantasy, animation, and any combination thereof. A daylong retrospective could begin with the Nixon-era paranoia of *New Roman Empire* (1971); continue on to *Black Soul Riders* (1972), in which Booth played a racist judge named George Washington Cream and adopted a chicken-fried Southern accent to say things like "Wuhl yer an awl-ful buh-lack wan, ain'cha?"; followed by *Rat Fiend!* (1975), infamous for its utilization of miniature sets in order to make normal rats look gigantic, and featuring Booth's performance as a grizzled "sewer captain" with a "sword plunger"; going next to *Hard Mommies* (1976), wherein Booth's car-wash mafia messes with the wrong group of PTA moms in belly-baring tank tops; and, as the main feature, *Devil of the Acropolis* (1977), arguably the crowning example of Sam's father's artistic offenses, for his portrayal of Plato as an expert in werewolf behavior (as well as a howling example of Hollywood's regard for historical accuracy: Plato is killed by the werewolf in the second act); then put a bow on the day with the first episode in the *Hellhole* trilogy (1983), the title of which said everything a person needed to know, except maybe that Booth's character, Professor Graham Hawking Gould, was a "satanologist."

Even such a condensed list of Booth Dolan's inanities threatened his son with the promise of a crushing migraine. The idea of an expanded two-day retrospective, meanwhile—including such milestones as his father's voice-over turn as Dog, an all-knowing talking cloud, in what had to be the nadir of druggy cinema, *Buffalo Roam*, about a Nam vet leading a white buffalo to the Pacific Ocean; as well as Booth's role as a lovable ass-squeezing brothel owner and leader of cowboy prostitutes in *Alamo II: Return to the Alamo—Daughters of Texas*—held lethal implications. Sam would rather have killed himself or someone else—Booth, hopefully—than suffer through such a sentence.

While the old man's star, such as it ever was, had faded in the late eighties before pretty much winking out completely in the nineties (along with the majority of the B-movie production houses), the earlier films in particular continued to play on cable. To this day, on the highest movie channels, the ones that are all gore and tits and robots, a black-haired Booth can still be found battling evil with a plunger.

The acorn of Tom Ritts's mansion was a four-room Sears kit house that dated from the fifties. Since the contractor had purchased it in the eighties, he had expanded it, horizontally and vertically, by a room or two every year, and now it had more rooms than anyone cared to count. Tom's ability to build, indeed, had outpaced his wherewithal to furnish. Only a potted plant or a single folding chair occupied the newest six or seven rooms. Bats and squirrels had a knack for getting trapped in the less trafficked wings of the mansion, where they expired of thirst or starvation, to be discovered as webby, desiccated corpses months later. From the exterior, the building looked like something that a very intelligent and precise twelve-year-old might have built from LEGOS. It was a grandiose hobby for such a humble-seeming man. ("None of the choices on pay-per-view sound very interesting, and the next thing I know, I've got my measuring tape out and some drafting paper, and I'm planning a new bathroom or something," he once said apologetically to Sam. "It passes the time. Maybe someday I'll have a family and we can play hide-and-seek.")

The house had gone as far backward as it could. Perched above a steep embankment and upheld by cement pillars, a redwood deck extended to the edge of the property, where the forest cropped up and the land became the town of Hasbrouck's. On a clear morning like this one, the view was glorious; the rustling canopy of orange, red, and yellow swept away for miles, to the umber-colored shapes of the mountains.

Sam leaned against the balustrade and inhaled the crisp air and, as he released the breath, attempted to exhale his irritation along with it. A grand, towering sugar maple stood before the deck. On a branch just a few feet from the deck's railing, a bluebird perched in a resplendent tuffet of leaves and twittered. Sam had a dismal recollection of the anthology horror film *A Thousand Deaths*: Booth had played a barbarian chieftain and bitten the head off an obviously rubber pigeon, which had produced a geyser of fake blood from its neck and drenched his face in syrup.

"But I am being honest! You must admit that the whole story is heavy. There is, throughout, a sort of funereal drumbeat." Booth refused to give up. Showered and dressed, he had tracked his son to the deck and sidled right up beside him, almost shoulder to shoulder at the balustrade. On his way through the house, Sam had laid what had seemed a sure trap to divert his father's attention, setting the television in Tom's study to the Turner Classic Movies Channel, but Booth must have walked by during a commercial break.

"Okay, okay. What if, like, a gigantic hole opens up in the middle of the campus and it swallows all the characters?" Sam asked. "Could there be some fun in that? And suppose if there were mimes, too, a visiting mime troupe, and we put them in the gigantic hole and let them mime for their lives. How about that?"

"This poor young man who becomes a drug addict, for instance, and a little later, abracadabra, he turns into a little puddle of clothes. It is so harsh. And I do understand that college isn't all fucking and giggles, but it's certainly more fucking and giggles than you make it seem. I also think that young people are more self-aware than you give them credit for being. In fact, most young people I know, especially the young females, are—"

"Do you listen to anything I say, Booth? Because I have this impression that, to you, my voice is on the same frequency as a dog whistle."

"No, no. Samuel, I listen to everything you say."

"Because I was just being sarcastic. About the clowns. Did you catch that?"

Booth raised an eyebrow at him. Errant gray hairs stuck out from the

15

eyebrow like frayed wires. Several of the wires had dandruff. "I thought they were mimes."

"Yeah." Sam dumped the last of his coffee over the side of the deck. The bluebird alighted.

Sam was aware that he was not an especially relaxed person. He was reactive. Optimism was not among his favored emotions. But Booth brought out the worst in him. Sam just wanted him to butt out. It was 2002, and Sam was twenty-two. He thought he had earned the right to finally have a bit of his own space. "Can you move away an inch or two, Booth? There's a whole deck over that way. We don't have to share this one spot."

His father's shrug seemed to imply that the request was over the top, but he was willing to cooperate for civility's sake. He shifted down the railing a few feet.

"Okay, then," said Sam. "I'll grant you that it's heavy. The story is heavy. So what?"

"So nothing!" Booth's chuckle boomed across the open air. On film, he had utilized this same sonorous chuckle on many occasions, often when playing the role of an insane person. "It is a very grave work of art. There is nothing wrong with that."

"Terrific. We agree. Thanks." It was easier to submit. The sun was warm on Sam's face. He breathed the good scents of dirt and leaves and thought about the drive to come, the privacy of his car, his future, not seeing having to see this man.

"You are perfectly welcome. But you see, this is a story about college students, and you have endowed it with the gravity of the Manhattan Project. And that is what I mean when I say that it could be construed as a bit *portentous*." Booth gave the railing of the deck a sharp knock for emphasis and beamed out at the treetops as if he had conquered them. "Think about letting some light into the thing. You can do that, can't you, think about it?"

Sam nodded. He wasn't changing a fucking thing.

"Good! That is all I wished to say. However it turns out, I am terribly proud of you." Booth spread his arms wide. "You are, and always have been, and always will be, an incomparable delight to me, and—I am sure I don't need to add—to your mother. She could not have loved you more. I could not love you more."

Sam touched his father on the shoulder and slipped inside the house and upstairs to the attic.

Other people found Booth charming. Women generally agreed that he was witty and adorable. Men instinctively took him as an authority. Tom Ritts, as forthright and sterling a character as Sam knew, let Booth sponge off him incessantly. Allie, Sam's mother, had continued to coddle him after their divorce. It could make Sam feel wild if he thought too much about it, as if the whole world were an airtight tank filling with water, but no one else would admit that they were getting wet, let alone help him find some way to escape.

His mother had given up everything for Booth: college, music, her business. Tough, resourceful, a withering teaser, Allie had never been one to suffer nonsense—except when it came to Booth, from whom she had been capable of suffering nearly any amount. Tom at least had the excuse of having grown up with Booth. Allie had essentially raised the man's child on her own and absorbed his absences and adultery for nearly twenty years before divorcing him. Then, after everything, she continued to invite Booth to holiday dinners, where he was allowed to sit in his old chair, and talk his bullshit, and eat way more than his share, and act altogether as though he had never been cast from their home.

Sam could recall a particular Christmas Eve in the early nineties. Booth's arrival had been imminent. His mother had been in the kitchen, cooking for her ex-husband.

"I'm disappointed in you, Mom," Sam blurted. He had been thirteen, a craterous zit aching and glistening in the center of his chin.

Allie looked up from the trellis of piecrust that she was attempting to puzzle out. She frowned, blew her bangs out of her eyes. His mother had been one of those middle-aged women whose faces remained smooth while her brown hair spilled white. "Not too disappointed to help set the table, I hope."

"Why?" Sam asked. "Why does he have to come?"

"Because I love him, kiddo," said Allie. "Because he's your father." She smiled and shrugged, her expression full of sympathy and love for Sam, before adding, "And because it's my damn house."

His ears had grown hot. "Mom." What was he supposed to say to that?

His mother had tipped her head from side to side, the same way she did when she was contemplating a restaurant menu. "Just set the table." Without waiting for a response, she returned her attention to the crust. "Oh," she added, "you know, I was flipping through *TV Guide. Hard Mommies* is on sixty-four tonight. Have you seen that one? That's the one where Booth plays the mumbly mobster."

After Allie's death, Tom offered his attic to absorb the few possessions that weren't liquidated with the house. This was why Sam had come south from Quentinville—the location of Russell College and of his apartment—to Hasbrouck the previous night, to rummage the contents of the attic. He was looking for things to sell.

The attic was a long pine-smelling hallway with canted ceilings and triangular windows on either end. Sam kept to the center of the room so he wouldn't bang his head on the ceiling and sat on the floor, dragging the boxes over to sift one at a time.

There were Sam's baseball cards, his comic books, and a footlocker of red plastic figurines called Nukies that he had collected feverishly for a couple of years in his early adolescence. These one-inch statues were intended—with their humps and bulging eyeballs and claws and dripping flesh—to portray the mutant peoples of the post-apocalyptic world. Sam spared a moment's tender thought to the child who had amassed the little horrors and spent so many solemn, satisfying hours arranging them on surfaces. Then the cards, the comics, and the figurines went into a forty-gallon garbage bag, the Sell Bag.

When their tops were popped, a clutch of cardboard tubes divulged well-preserved posters of *New Roman Empire, Devil of the Acropolis, Buffalo Roam,* and a few other Booth Dolan classics. The posters went into the Sell Bag, although if he didn't get a fair price, Sam planned to create a Burn Bag.

Last was a shoe box containing pieces of costume jewelry that he could not recall ever seeing his mother wear. He ran a few of the necklaces through his fingers and felt bewildered and unhappy. As often as she had frustrated him, Sam missed his mother to such a painful degree, and on such a basic level—wishing for her at that moment the way he remembered wishing for home one summer when he went away to camp, ecclesiastically—that it made him ashamed and scared. The feeling was so powerful that some interior sluice usually prevented him from thinking about her at all. But the unfamiliar jewelry had him blinking at tears. The beads of one necklace felt hollow between his fingertips, but as hard as he squeezed them, they didn't pop. Sam let out a breath, put the jewelry into the Sell Bag, and wiped at his face with the neck of his shirt.

Wadded in the corner of the shoe box was a faded black cloth. Sam pulled it out. The cloth was lacy, scalloped at the edges; it was a pair of panties, twelve years old, he knew.

Booth had offered to help load the car, but when Sam came downstairs, he discovered his father on the couch in Tom's living room. The television must have snared him on the second pass. On the screen, an alien and some children were flying through the sky on their bicycles against the backdrop of the moon.

Sam watched from the doorway. *E.T.* was among his least favorite movies. He thought it was sentimental and disingenuous. In *E.T.* the kids saved the day. His own childhood of divorce had unquestionably had its moments, but what he remembered most was feeling bewildered and ineffectual. Also, E.T. was magic, and magic annoyed Sam. Magic was puppets, lighting, computer animation, and latex.

"You still want to help me carry my stuff out?" he asked, not knowing why he bothered.

"I'll be right there," said Booth, leaning against the arm of the couch, head propped on fist, making no move. He was sitting in exactly the same position when his son stopped by on his way out the door.

"I'm leaving," said Sam.

The older man clicked off the television and, with a grunt of effort, shifted around to look at his son over the arm of the couch. "Already?"

"Yeah." It was about a two-hour drive north to Quentinville.

"Very well, then. Two last pieces of advice. One: have fun! It's supposed to be fun! That is why they call it *entertainment!*"

"Ah," said Sam, "I'd always wondered." The man's philistinism was ceaseless. Like Tom's mansion, it spread ever outward.

Booth flourished the television controller. "And two: get your coverage!"

"Coverage" was the most basic principle of filmmaking, whereby you made sure to "cover," say, the angles of a two-person conversation at a restaurant table. There was a master shot that showed both people, a medium shot of the one on the left, a medium shot of the one on the right, a close-up of the left, and a close-up of the right. Perhaps you also snapped a cutaway or two, the bell ringing above the door as someone enters, maybe, or a geezer on a nearby stool sipping coffee. That was it: you were covered.

Coverage was the director's first responsibility. Coverage was the essence of responsibility. To be reminded of such a thing by Booth Dolan—well, now there was a faultless irony.

Who did the man think he was?

Sam strode into the room, tore the pair of panties from his pocket, and threw it at Booth's face.

The article of clothing missed Booth's face and landed on his shoulder, like a very small net. His father recoiled, snatched the panties off, and studied them with a perplexed grimace. It was bullshit, though. He knew. They both knew exactly to whom the panties belonged, and the singular, unpardonable place that they held in their shared history. Sam waited for the lie, waited for it like waves in the dark, the interval between crashes.

"Jesus Christ, Samuel." Booth blinked at him. "Why did you just throw a pair of underpants at me? What is wrong? I'm sorry I got caught up in the film and didn't help load the car."

"Never mind," said Sam, thinking, miserably, He's actually not such a bad actor when he wants to be. "I need to go."

Booth held the panties, crumpled in his hand. "What do you mean, 'never mind'? You don't throw underwear at people without cause. Look, don't hurry off. Relax. Why don't you stay and watch a movie with me?" His grimace opened into an anxious yellow smile. "There's always something good on cable."

"I can't," said Sam. "Goodbye, Booth."

He left his father's hand hanging in the air, left the room, left the house, climbed in his car, put it in reverse, backed out into the street, and got going.

2.

When it came to making the film, Sam began with two key advantages.

The first of these was that *Who We Are* could be made relatively cheaply. The script included no special effects, no costly Hollywood-style spectacles, no stunts, no explosions. Many other elements of a typical production were irrelevant: set design was unnecessary—the college was exactly what they needed it to be; the actors could provide their own wardrobes; and the conceit of the film was such that lighting continuity was not particularly important—all that mattered was that the "day" of the movie gradually fade into "night."

It wasn't as though Sam didn't care how the movie looked; he didn't want it to look bad, but he didn't want it to look too good, either, and he certainly didn't want it to appear planned or affected or, God help him, fucking "covered." If they couldn't flag a given shot—block the excess light—a little resultant flare on the lens wasn't going to end the world, and it might actually add to the audience's sense of realism. Light did sometimes shine too brightly, after all.

Sam's professor and adviser, Professor Julian Stuart, had greased the wheels of the college's bureaucracy and, in exchange for a relative pittance, arranged for twenty days of full access to the major locations. On top of that, much of the necessary equipment was already available to borrow from the film department. Julian had also proved instrumental in helping Sam assemble a cast and crew. To earn an independent study credit, a small group of juniors and seniors had eagerly signed on at no cost except board.

None of which was to say that the movie could be made for free.

The "relative pittance" that Russell required to allow them to tramp freely about the college grounds was enough to purchase a new car. Because the film department's equipment had been manhandled by thousands of trust-fund fuckwits, there were still a number of pieces that he had to rent, including the camera and several lenses. The 16mm stock that Sam had decided to use was cheap by Hollywood standards, but not by any other standards. Developing fees, video transfer fees, and storage fees were significant and unavoidable. The cast and crew, meanwhile, did have to be fed, and though the summer rates for Russell's dorm rooms were not exorbitant, the cost of a whole hall of them added up.

Sam had also consented to the necessity of hiring one true ringer, a middle-aged makeup artist named Monica Noble who had experience in the theater. When he posted an ad for the position on Craigslist, she initially answered just to mock him for the amount of money he was offering, but ended up signing on because she was attracted by the challenge. It was the makeup artist who had to make the actors' physical transformations—hairstyle changes, beards, scars, etc.—convincing. If she pulled it off, Monica Noble would have quite a calling card for herself. Nonetheless, she had promised Sam, "If you don't hand me eight thousand dollars in new twenties and tens the moment I step off that bus from Philadelphia, I am stepping right back on."

And those were just the things he had to have. Should he strike a financing geyser, high atop Sam's wish list was the rental of the carnival rides and attractions—Ferris wheel, teacups, duck shooting galleries, etc.—that the college brought in every year for the actual Spring Festival. While he was prepared to make the film without them, their inclusion would add a degree of verisimilitude that couldn't be created otherwise.

No matter how you cut it, rides or no rides, the movie needed at least thirty-five thousand dollars (and preferably three times that amount), every penny of which he needed to raise in under a year.

Which led to the matter of his second great advantage: Sam had determined to absolve himself in advance of any and all crimes, moral or otherwise, committed in the service of the film, from the first dollar raised to the locking of the final print. Whatever bullying, manipulation, or duplicity was required, he was duty-bound and preforgiven to do what was best for *Who We Are*. When it was over, he could strive to make whatever amends were possible.

"I don't believe you," Polly said. "You're such a totally nice guy." She was in Florida. Sam was on his couch in New York. It was October then, a couple of weeks after he'd seen Booth in Hasbrouck.

"Not about this. You only get one chance. It can't suck."

"Why not?"

Since their breakup the previous spring, the parameters of their relationship had grown murky. Through the end of the school year, they had continued to sleep together on occasion, and since Polly had returned home to live with her parents at their retirement community and take some time off before joining the workforce, they had been having semi-regular phone sex. Sam was careful not to probe too eagerly into the matter of whom besides her parents she had been spending time with, and he was deliberately vague about his own spare hours, not least because there was mortifyingly little to reveal. Since graduating and moving to the apartment, Sam hadn't done much except work on the script and watch movies checked out from the library. He certainly hadn't been getting laid.

Polly had the supple, amused voice of a sexy disc jockey, and Sam knew that, unlike a disc jockey, she was sexy in real life. This wasn't to say she was beautiful—her tits were a little too big, her mouth was a little too big, and her bottom teeth were uneven. Rather, her allure came from her attitude, which was unapologetic, and her perspective, which yo-yoed between sunny and scandalized. Polly's parents had been in their mid-forties when she was born, too old and tired to put up much of a fight, and their daughter was accustomed to getting her way. At Russell, she had studied to be a preschool teacher. Sam thought she'd be a good one; Polly was smart, not afraid to be silly, but impossible to budge if she didn't want to budge.

It was true that they shared few enthusiasms. Polly was far more likely to want to curl up on the couch with a novel than go to a movie theater. Fat Russian novels were special favorites because, she said, the combination of sex, violence, and cold weather made her feel "safe and cozy, and so freaking lucky not to be a nineteenth-century Russian person." Televised sports were another passion of hers that Sam couldn't match. Pretty much anything besides golf and auto racing, she'd watch and sort of narrate what was happening, a habit that by all rights should have been tremendously annoying but which Sam found endearing. "Oh, look!" she'd exclaim after a football player scored a touchdown and all of his teammates piled on top of him. "They're so happy!"

Although Sam was fairly sure he didn't love Polly, he liked her a lot—and couldn't resist the way she wound him up.

"Why can't it suck? Is this a trick question?" He could never be certain if Polly was being willfully obtuse in a flirtatious way, or just willfully obtuse.

"No," she said. "I really want to know. And if you're going to be crabby about it, maybe I ought to hang up right now."

Sam sensed that his hopes for phone sex were on the verge of slipping away. He dropped his feet off the couch and sat up. "It can't suck because it can't. Because I'm not making it to suck. Who goes into something that they really care about, that's really personal to them, and thinks, Oh well, it'll be okay if it sucks?"

"All I can say to that, my dear, is that you've clearly never been a woman."

Sam was prudent enough to refuse the bait. Polly let him hang for ten or fifteen seconds. When she spoke again, he could hear her smile. "Obviously, you're not making it to suck, but it's not a matter of life or death. It's a movie."

Polly had never been able to comprehend what it was like to have Booth Dolan for a father. Just the opposite, in fact: after years of listening to Sam's grievances, it was clear that she had come to regard his alienation from Booth as being pretty adorable. Sam didn't suppose she'd ever understand—and perhaps this was part of the reason why, despite his attachment to Polly, he couldn't imagine them together in the long term—but after he'd reflected upon his interaction with Booth that morning at Tom's, it now seemed to Sam that the relationship with his father had suffered a final break.

One needed look no further than the old man's quintessential role as the diabolical traveling salesman of cures and elixirs, *New Roman Empire*'s Dr. Archibald "Horsefeathers" Law, to understand that a movie wasn't a matter of life and death. It was life and death.

Early on in the film, Dr. Law—Horsefeathers—holds forth before a crowd of skeptical hippies. He is a grinning fat man in a checkered suit, a neckerchief, and a bowler hat.

"I am not a miracle worker!" he cries, removing his hat with a flourish, letting it tumble end over end along his arm. The charlatan casts around, fixing the eyes of each person in turn. In the background, an off-kilter caper begins, plucked on warbling strings. "I am a physician specializing in the deeper body. There is no magic about this. My medicine is, quite simply, a scientific treatment for the soul!"

Perhaps he was a different person before *New Roman Empire*, but ever since—as long as Sam had known him—Booth had played the part of the magnificent bullshitter ceaselessly. Two busted marriages, two children he saw infrequently, and Booth talked and talked without ever saying anything. Meanwhile, after thirty-plus years in the industry, Sam's father's greatest contribution to cinema was, in all likelihood, two days he had spent in 1975 on the set of *Yorick,* one of the many "lost" films of Orson Welles's cash-strapped late period, as yet and probably forever unreleased. The years had dribbled away for Booth, and despite never being a real director in the first place—real directors did more than get coverage—now he had nothing better to do than criticize his son.

It didn't matter, as Sam's best friend Wesley Latsch pointed out, that everyone's father had cheated on everyone's mother, and that everyone's father was mortifying and insufficient in a thousand ways. "You take your old man far too personally," Wesley said, and Wesley was right. Sam's resentment was achingly common.

But it just didn't matter: because Booth was Booth, and Booth was his father.

And because, goddammit, the old fucking pervert had squirreled away a pair of his mistress's panties for twelve years! And then he had lied about it right to Sam's face!

Who We Are was only a small independent movie. It might never find distribution, might never make it beyond a few minor midwestern film festivals. But it was important to Sam. It was his statement, his vision, his movie. It wasn't supposed to be just a couple of hours of escape, of people running around and splatting each other in the face with pies. To him, it was serious. *Who We Are* was about the costs of growing up—and the costs of not growing up. And that was heavy stuff, and Sam made no apology, not to Booth, not to anyone. Maybe it wasn't fun, and maybe it wasn't entertainment, but he was going to show them something real.

"I mean, it's not even a big movie. It's not like one of these ones with elephants and submarines and everything in it," Polly went on. "You're acting like it's the biggest thing ever."

"What movie has elephants and submarines?"

"Don't be a snot. You know what I mean. Like *Star Wars.*"

"Look, Polly, to me, it is pretty much the biggest thing ever. To me, it's a lot of money and a hell of a lot of work, and I've put a lot of thought into it. And all I'm saying is that if I have to kick some ass to make it what I need it to be, then I'm prepared to do that. I've never cared about anything so much, ever."

"Well, well, well. That's quite a statement, young man. Ever?"

"Ever." Sam decided he'd better throw the track switch before Polly started to prod him about his childhood, or his fears, or some other libido-extinguishing subject. "Let me give you an example: if getting this film made requires me to debase myself over the phone, follow the whims of some depraved sex maniac in Florida, I'm prepared to do that."

"No!" Polly cried. "Absolutely not! I just want to have a nice conversation for once. Besides, you just told me how you were going to squash all us little people to make your opus. I no longer trust your motives."

"I didn't say that. I've never said the word 'opus' in my life." Frustrated, Sam rose from the couch and began to pace across the twenty or so feet of his apartment's living space. It had come prefurnished with a desk, a single bed, a strip of maroon carpet remnant, a dusty plant, and a kitchenette, the cabinets of which so far contained one plastic plate and a mostly empty spray bottle of Febreze, both left by the previous resident. The window by the desk offered a view of the parking lot and the identical neighboring sections of the gray-walled, grayer-roofed development. Sam looked out the window and saw a couple of boys spitting into the medicine ball–sized pothole in the parking lot. The huge pothole was the landmark he used to find which part of the development he lived in.

"Let's just talk about something else. What else is happening?"

Sam asked her if he had mentioned the odd, heady smell of the hallways in the complex, like a drugstore, like Silly Putty, that medicinal-industrial odor. Polly said yes, he'd mentioned it. Had she told him about the dear biddy who lived in the neighboring bungalow and knocked on the door at four in the morning to bring them a fresh-picked gourd? He said she had. They were both so careful to stay clear of each other's social lives, there wasn't much left over.

"I was afraid that we'd become old and uninteresting," Polly said. "I just didn't expect it to happen so soon. What happened to the fascinating boy I went to college with, Sammy?"

"Well, shit, Polly. I don't know. Hey, are you going to invest in my movie or what?"

Polly shrieked. "Now I feel really soiled! First you want me to help you masturbate, then you turn dull, and then you ask me for money. What's next?"

"You give me money?"

"What's the magic word?"

"Please?"

"More."

"Pretty please? Pretty, pretty please?"

"See, polite is sexy," she said, and smacked her lips. "Okay, bitch! Take off your pants, go to the refrigerator, and get out the butter."

Sam didn't have any butter—or margarine—but in addition to the plate and the mostly empty sprayer of Febreze, his predecessor had bequeathed him a huge jug of electric-blue liquid soap called the Blue, whose label bore a cartoon of an impressively coiffed shark. Once Sam had retrieved the jug from the bathroom, he yanked down the window shade and jumped onto the bed. He wriggled out of his pants and boxers and squirted out a big handful of blue soap. "Got it. Now what?"

Polly directed him to rub up his stuff real good. "But don't you dare ejaculate before I tell you! Not so much as a dribble!" Sam was close after four or five hard strokes, so he slowed down, limiting himself to the occasional paddle.

For the first time, Polly mentioned that she was alone in her house. Mr. and Mrs. Dressler had gone to the local clam shack for the early-bird special, and here she was in her panties, and now here she wasn't in her panties. "Oh, look," she said, "the dining room table . . ." There was a creaking sound as she climbed on top of it—or somehow, like a Foley artist, concocted a noise that perfectly replicated the sound of a 110-pound woman climbing onto a Shaker-style dining room table, which struck Sam as fairly unlikely. Polly informed him that she was pulling up her skirt, lying on her back. The wood was nice and cool against her ass, and across from the table, on the wall behind her daddy's chair, there was a mirror. "And I can see all the way into myself, Sammy."

"Jesus," Sam said. He had started to speed up again and had to squeeze himself to hold off.

"Sammy." In a whisper, Polly described how she was fingering herself, sliding her finger up and down, separating the hot, slick folds. He better be buttering himself; she was so incredibly tight, they were going to need all the help they could get. "Sammy, Sammy, Sammy . . ."

The Blue was lathering around his penis and dripping bubbles into his pubic hair, spilling onto the sheets, making a mess. At the same time, he was trying to keep the soap away from the tip of his penis, because who knew what the hell was in the Blue. There was a dangerous tingle along his shaft, which might have been his imagination. But he was huge, digging his heels into the mattress, shaking all over; Sam could see clearly enough that what was exciting was that Polly was telling him what to do, that it was unlike every other aspect of his existence, wherein he struggled to contain and order. He had a suspicion that he was not the only director who, when it came to sex, liked to switch roles.

"Are you filming me? I want you to film this. This is my movie. My movie."

"Okay."

"Whose movie is it?"

"Yours, Polly."

"Good. Are you ready? Are you on your mark?"

"Uh-huh," Sam managed to say, and when Polly said, "Go!" he was gone.

He asked Polly if she came, too. "Eh," she said.

"Do you want to keep going?" Sam sort of hoped she didn't. He wanted to clean up before anything dried. Gobbets of blue soap, bubbles, and semen were mixed and spattered on his genitals, thighs, left hand, and the sheets between his legs. It looked like a member of the Blue Man Group had been shanked to death.

Holding a mingled puddle of soap and genetic material in his cupped hand, he maneuvered himself off the bed and around the kitchen bar to the sink. Sam tucked the phone between his ear and shoulder, turned on the faucet with his clean hand, and stuck his semen-and-soap hand under the water.

"Well . . ." she said.

"What?"

"Would you mind asking me again? For money?"

Now it was Sam's turn to feel soiled, but he had made a promise to himself—he would do what he had to. At least Polly was a friend. So he asked her again, and again, and again, please, pretty please, please with sprinkles.

Three days later, he received his reward in the mail: a two-hundred-and-fifty-dollar check from Ms. Polly Dressler. The subject line read, "For the BIGGEST thing ever!!!"

Polly's contribution got Sam started.

A pawnbroker in Quentinville paid him six oleaginous hundred-dollar bills for the haul from the attic. The posters and the footlocker of Nukies—the toys now a popular subject for retro T-shirts—were the big earners.

To various acquaintances, he pitched hundred-dollar shares for Executive Producer credits and made a few sales: an aunt bought one, and so did a cousin, and a couple of friends from his Hasbrouck High School AV Club. An elderly neighbor, whom he'd been cultivating for years by admiring the shininess of her lawn pinwheels, went in for three shares.

Among other notables, his godfather, Tom, gave the most. He cashed a five-thousand-dollar savings bond and decreed that his godson never speak of it again; Tom didn't want any frigging shares, either, it was a gift. Wesley Latsch invested his life savings: the three thousand dollars his grandmother had given him for graduating from college.

The morning of the first snowfall, Sam awakened at eight, sat at his computer, and by nine-thirty had successfully applied for four credit cards with a combined credit line of six thousand eight hundred dollars.

Nearly halfway to his rock bottom budget, Sam hadn't broken a sweat. He felt lucky, fated, charged—he had asked for money, and people had given it to him.

Several more inches of snow had fallen when, a few days later, his winning streak was confirmed by a twitchy junior film student named Brooks Hartwig, Jr.

3.

A solid crust of snow sealed the Russell grounds. It was months yet before the scheduled start of production. Sam was there to scout the college's remote south meadow, which was the setting for Russell's annual May Festival, where much of the film's action took place.

It was a Sunday morning. If there were any students awake at this hour, Sam assumed they were up only to use the bathroom and would promptly return to bed.

Perched on a bench at the edge of the meadow, he panned around his handheld camera. The diffuse winter light threw a blue cast over everything. Through the eyepiece, he took in the acres of untrammeled snow and tried to imagine the summer scene, the potential arrangements of tents and rides, how to fit them together for sight lines and continuity and whether it would be possible to—

"Hey!" said someone. "Hey, hey, hey! Sam!" A blond tuft flipped into the foreground, creating the illusion that some alien grass had sprouted up through the snow.

Sam lowered the camera.

Cheeks ablaze, bangs covering his eyes in a white-blond shag, a purple scarf knotted around his neck, Brooks Hartwig, Jr., waved his arms as if trying to signal a rescue chopper. "Sam! Sam! Hey! Hey!"

"I see you," said Sam.

"Yeah?" Brooks sounded unconvinced.

"That's what happens when you stand in front of a lens, Brooks. You appear on the other side. That's what makes the magic."

"Magic! Yeah, yeah! That's what it's all about, right? That's crazy." Brooks clapped excitedly.

Sam suspected his only hope of getting rid of Brooks was to agree with him. "Yes. Magic is crazy."

Brooks blinked several times, grinned. "But hey, right. Sam. I heard you were making a movie. I was thinking that I could be your assistant director."

"Ah," said Sam. "I don't know, Brooks."

Brooks continued to grin. "Uh-huh. So what are we doing right now?"

Sam's acquaintance with Brooks was limited: a film history seminar a couple of years earlier, a handful of other encounters in and around the film department. Someone had told him once that Brooks was the heir to a fortune, either pharmaceuticals or paper products, he couldn't remember. Sam was familiar with Brooks's work. The previous spring he had survived a viewing of the sophomore's Intermediate Film short. The film concerned a taxidermist (played by Brooks) who is bullied into committing suicide by his collection of judgmental animal heads. At one point, a massive and intimidating elk's head—marbled horns like lance tips, oily black eyes, gums exposed as if in rage—languidly castigates the taxidermist, "I'm sorry to say it, little man, but the more I see you slopping around formaldehyde like that, the harder I find it to conceive of any reason for your continued existence." Shot in deep-focus black and white, the whole thing had made Sam feel as though he were trapped in some seamy theme park where everything was designed from the nightmares of the puberty-ravaged fourteen-year-old son of Dracula and Jane Goodall.

"Look, I'd love to have the help, but I've got all the crew I can afford, Brooks. I'm producing it myself, and it's just a little movie, you know?"

Brooks brought a finger to his mouth, and as he spoke, he began to gnaw at a hangnail. "Oh, but I was thinking that I could chip in, maybe. Pay my own way. Like, what if I gave you, like, oh, maybe, five thousand bucks? So I could be a sort of partner, you know? Team up, you know?" A tic started above Brooks's right eye, and his white-blond eyebrow began to wiggle.

"Seriously?" Sam asked, and Brooks said, "Uh-huh, uh-huh," and after eight to ten seconds of thought during which time his heartbeat filled his ears and his breath swelled in his chest and he realized that a golden egg had practically rolled up against his shoe, Sam decided to be greedy. "Could you make it ten thousand?"

Finger still in his mouth, Brooks nodded eagerly. "Sure!"

"You know," said Sam, "I did like the puppetry in your movie a lot. No strings. It really looked like the elk was talking. And not just talking but pissed off. That was impressive. The whole mise-en-scène was—I won't soon forget it."

"Thank you. It was a very personal film."

"That's great," said Sam. He told Brooks he was hired. "Now stop that." He pushed Brooks's hand away from his mouth.

Brooks's eyebrow leaped dramatically, as if in celebration. "Yay!" he whooped. He spat out the hangnail and asked, "Oh, so what does the assistant director do?"

"Whatever I tell him to." Sam clapped Brooks on the shoulder and sent him on his first mission. "Go stand in the middle of the meadow. I need some scale."

"I have a little bit of a cold," said Brooks. The meadow lay beneath two and a half feet of crystalline powder.

"That's okay," said Sam.

Brooks set off, with each step dropping crotch-deep in the snow. Once he reached the middle of the field, Sam directed him to move around in a wide circle. After Sam filmed this, he commanded Brooks to head for the woods at the far end of the field. "Don't fucking stop, okay?" he yelled. "Just go and go!"

The little figure waded away, sinking into drifts and bobbing back up, purple scarf occasionally flapping like the tattered standard of a listing ship. About five hundred yards out, at the edge of the woods, Brooks stopped and looked back.

This was far enough. Sam put an arm up and waved for him to turn around. The blond dot of the AD's head nodded, but instead of looping back, he continued in the opposite direction and vanished into the trees.

Sam waited, shuffling back and forth along the bench for a couple of minutes, before retreating to his car. He put the heat on full blast and noted the dashboard thermometer: fifteen degrees.

On a studio-style production, an assistant director performed more of a managerial position, but Sam didn't have a big enough crew to require that kind of help, and in any event, he wouldn't trust Brooks to manage the night shift at a Zoney's Go-Mart. In his mind, he decided to drop the "director" part and just go with "assistant." Brooks was a weird fucker, and his puppet psychodrama was less a work of cinema than it was a plea for analysis; but for ten thousand dollars, he could be allowed to perform a few basic tasks.

Half an hour passed. The light dimmed. From around the perimeter of the field, the shadows of the trees leaked out, forming rows of black dominoes. It was toasty in the car, but the thermometer on the dash said that it had dropped to ten degrees outside. Sam had a vision of his AD walking on and on, carrying out his orders indefinitely, like one of those legendary World War II Japanese soldiers who, in their decaying uniforms and their dotage, supposedly continued to guard remote islands in the Pacific. The possibility occurred to him that Brooks might fall into a snow-disguised culvert, break a leg, and freeze to death. A bear might eat him; Brooks Hartwig, Jr., in his blond twitchiness, looked like a perfect snack for a ravenous bear.

Sam was beginning to grow worried when he realized the potential instructiveness of the situation. His policy of self-forgiveness was being put to the test. The question he needed to ask himself—that every director needed to ask himself, perhaps—was this: if the success of his film depended on it, was he willing to let a bear devour the AD?

There were some movies—*Citizen Kane* and the like—that unquestionably passed the worth-feeding-an-AD-to-a-bear threshold. For that matter, there wasn't an urbane jury in the world that would have held Truffaut responsible if he had let bears eat as many as three or four ADs in order to get every priceless frame of *Jules et Jim* in the can. But as much as he didn't like to admit it—as much as he believed that it could, and believed that he had to believe that it could—Sam knew that it was impossible to say whether *Who We Are* would rise to that level.

"Fuck." Sam would have to go reel him in. He reached for the door handle, swiveled in his seat—and met the gaze of Brooks standing at the driver's-side window.

"Did you get what you needed? I can go back out." The window muffled Brooks's voice. His blond eyebrows were tipped with frost, and his nose was the gory scarlet of a Christmas carnation.

"Yes. I got it. Thank you, Brooks. Now get in."

"Yay," croaked Brooks. He came around and climbed in, accompanied by a shroud of arctic air. Rocking back and forth in his seat, he put a bare hand up for Sam to see, fanned it in front of his face. There were faint blue moons under the fingernails. "I can't feel anything. I could put it in a furnace and, like, whatever—feel nothing."

Sam felt an unwelcome spasm of conscience. His new AD's earnestness was unsettling, as well as nearly palpable, like a dog's pant. "Please don't put your hand in a furnace, Brooks."

"Of course not! I would never!" Brooks rocked and giggled. "I saw a guy get struck by lightning when I was a kid and, like, people are much, much more flammable than you might think. He, like—he really went up, the guy."

"I bet," said Sam.

They drove to the College Center, and Brooks went to fetch coffee, as well as a five-hundred-dollar advance on his investment from the ATM. When he returned, they sat in the toasty cab and Sam explained *Who We Are*—the characters, the time scheme, the changing details, the high-speed shifts in characterization. After he finished, he asked Brooks what he thought.

"Neat," was Brooks's underwhelming reaction.

"Glad you approve."

Brooks blew his nose on his purple scarf. "Hey, you know what's weird?"

"What's that?" The response was out of his mouth before Sam realized what a mistake it was—in the area of weird, his new AD needed no encouragement.

"I sometimes have this sensation, right? That I'm being filmed by a documentary crew." Brooks blinked a few times. Filaments of snot glistened on the scarf's fringe.

"But why?" Sam couldn't seem to help himself. "Why would they want to film you? What's the documentary?"

Brooks slapped his knee and shook his head. "That's what I can't figure out! That's the weird part!"

"No, Brooks. That is not the weird part," said Sam.

"Huh?" The AD grinned.

"Listen." Sam sighed, then extended his open hand. "Don't be any stranger than you have to be, Brooks."

The AD gave an eager nod and placed the packet of money in Sam's palm.

4.

Sam had already made overtures to a fledgling production company called Bummer City, located in Queens and run by two young Russell alums. Now, after considering the script for months and making numerous suggestions that Sam promised he would take—while simultaneously promising himself to never, ever take—the Bummer City boys had signaled their willingness to write a check for forty thousand dollars. Together with the money and credit already on hand, this gave Sam a total of nearly seventy thousand dollars, his dream budget.

Which was why he needed to take Bummer City's last proviso seriously: that he convince An Actor to play the small but pivotal role of Merlin, the only character in the script who never changes at all. A middle-aged drug dealer, Merlin operates out of the far stall of the basement bathroom of the science library, dispensing pharmaceuticals to the other characters. Parked on the john, wearing the same clothes, reading the same issue of *The Economist*, he is immune to time and, in an odd way, the story's sole adult.

Located in a residential section of Astoria, the Bummer City Productions office was a house, and the house was basically a man-size playroom. While Ted Wassel and Patch Brinckerhoff, Bummer City's copresidents, apparently had offices on the second floor and a screening room in the basement, the first floor—their conference area—featured several wall-mounted televisions, an array of video game systems, and a wet bar. Posters for lousy seventies movies lined the walls; among them Sam immediately bird-dogged a framed *Devil of the Acropolis*—Booth cowering before a snarling, toga-wearing werewolf—identical to the one he had pawned.

"You need some cred at the front of the picture," said Wassel. "You need you An Actor."

"Yeah, that's the thing," Patch Brinckerhoff reiterated. "An Actor."

"An Actor," repeated Sam.

"An Actor. A Name. A Name Actor." Wassel put his hands out and pantomimed the weighing of two immense balls. "A Real Actor."

At Russell, Patch and Wassel had been film majors two years ahead of Sam. They had codirected a pair of inexcusably sincere documentaries: one about a majestic and dying elm tree on the quad, the other about the brutality of the campus police. They were computer science majors—geeks—but lacked the social inhibitions that rendered most of their brethren harmless. Their enthusiasm was always on full display, and success only made it worse.

Post-graduation, Wassel and Patch had amassed a small fortune through the development of an image-based search program known as WOUND (We Open Up New Diagnoses). If you were a subscriber and had, say, an anomalous-looking blister on your arm, you could take a digital photograph of it and submit it to WOUND, which then sent you back a series of matching images along with potential diagnoses.

Sam had tested the program by taking a photograph of a smashed pigeon. WOUND had responded by e-mailing several images of hairy men with chest gashes and the advice that he go to the nearest ER. Sort of impressive, he had to admit.

The three men had gathered around one of those enormous wooden spools that Sam recalled from the basements of his youth. These spools had seemed to hint at the secret pleasures of male adulthood. The fathers who had them in the basement were the same fathers who were liable to have dartboards, neon beer signs, and lots of sports-related knowledge. Sam had fantasized about having one himself someday. In reality, they were shitty tables. The spools were too tall to set your elbows on, and you had to be careful not to let anything fall into the hole in the middle, because if it did, you were never getting it back.

The use of the spool as a conference table exemplified why dealing with Bummer City was so disheartening: Patch and Wassel made him feel like a toy. Before long, he imagined they would be dressing him in a San Diego Chicken costume and demanding he moonwalk, but there was no getting around it. Investors were hard to find, and harder still when your project—an indie film—had no realistic financial prospects. Sam had printed an investment contract off the Internet, promising a minuscule rate of interest; and to make them feel like they were legitimate participants in the process—that Bummer City Productions meant something—he had added a clause that put them above the title. When you got right down to it, however, what he was essentially asking for was a donation.

"Well, who are you thinking about, Wassel?"

"Hoffman," said Wassel. "Dusty."

"Rainman," said Patch. "Ratso."

"Guys," said Sam. "That'd be great, but—"

"—John Paul Jones."

"Yes! He could definitely do it. Good one, Wassel."

This suggestion momentarily stumped Sam. He was not aware that the bassist of Led Zeppelin had ever acted. He couldn't even remember which symbol represented the guy. "Really?"

"He's a great actor."

"Great, great actor."

"*Last of the Mohicans*, bro."

"Ah," said Sam, understanding that they meant Daniel Day Lewis. He opted not to correct them. If they wanted to believe that the world's greatest living thespian, whose name they couldn't get right, might be interested in playing a role that took place entirely in a bathroom stall, that was their privilege.

Wassel presented Sam with a list of other possibilities. It was written in magenta crayon on the back of a crinkled flyer for a shoe store. The third name on the list, after John Paul Jones, was Johnny Deep. Toward the bottom he noticed Meryl Strep, and below that, John Belushi.

Both men dressed like little boys but from different periods. In a checked short-sleeve shirt buttoned all the way up, big black-framed glasses, and a buzz cut, Wassel represented the fifties. Patch was the seventies: jeans with a blooming rose appliqué on the butt, cowboy shirt, Yoo-Hoo baseball cap, and flip-flops.

"These are some great names." Sam tucked the shoe store flyer into his pocket. He realized that he truly did not like these men. "I can try."

"You can try," cried Wassel, "and you can fucking succeed, brother!"

Wassel and Patch exchanged high fives. Patch rode an invisible bucking horse around a circle. "A drink for the Abyss!" yelled Patch, and poured the rest of the Woodchuck cider he had been drinking into the hole in the center of the spool.

Sam could feel his self-respect plummeting like a fat kid shoved off a high diving board. He waited until he heard it hit the water with a flab-scalding *splat,* then said, "So. We have a deal?"

"You get us An Actor, then fucking A, we have a deal."

Patch broke into an air-guitar solo, culminating in a violent crank of an air whammy bar. Wassel said they'd better get some coke, ASAP.

As futile as it obviously was, Sam went ahead and blind-mailed the script to the agents of the twenty-nine living members of Patch and Wassel's list (changing Merlin to Guinevere for Ms. Strep's copy), fully expecting to receive zero responses. It was a good-faith effort. He planned to return to Patch and Wassel in a month's time, tell them he'd tried, and plead for them to forget about getting An Actor, and just to fork over their money.

And then, incredibly, three weeks after the mailing, Rick Savini's agents notified Sam of the actor's interest in the part.

Savini had played the barfly in the Tarantino movie about all the different gangs simultaneously attempting to break into Capone's vault; he'd starred in *Clunkers,* the Coen brothers film about the harassed generator salesman with the sick wife and the sociopathic son and the house with a haunted bomb shelter; Savini had fallen in love with a madwoman in a Soderbergh film; and he'd played an alcoholic dentist for Jane Campion. Rick Savini made Sam think of Jack Lemmon—sensitive, funny, small—but more stepped on, somehow. He was good. He was really good.

In *The Dirt Nap*, a somewhat obscure indie Sam particularly liked, Savini played a doomed numbers runner. Right before Savini is executed by his best friend, the best friend attempts to comfort the numbers runner by explaining that they're going to bury him in a nice place, in the concrete of a brand-new public swimming pool. A lot of people remembered Savini's semi-famous response—"Aw, man. Kids are going to be peeing on me for eternity, Lester"—the last words before his friend pulls the trigger. What remained with Sam was the actor's face, the glum hook at the right corner of Savini's mouth as he ponders the ice-crusted mud of the yawning rectangular hole in the ground. That look was so smart, and so hurt, that it made the dialogue redundant. You could tell what he was seeing: a murky, eternal view of sky through green water and kicking legs.

Savini had given remarkable performances as conmen, streetwise losers, and ordinary men harried to the brink. The kind of ragged self-awareness that defined the morose, ageless drug dealer was his specialty. Rick Savini wasn't simply An Actor; he was ideal.

It was a tricky part. Merlin not only spent the entire film in the remote bathroom stall, but he had just one set of lines, which he spoke with slight variations to everyone who knocked on his door.

INT. FERRER MEMORIAL LIBRARY—BASEMENT LEVEL FIVE RESTROOM
Brunson, jonesing, stands outside Merlin's stall. He gives the door a sharp rap.
                                        CUT TO:
INSIDE THE STALL: Merlin sits on the toilet lid, perusing *The Economist*.

                    MERLIN
I'm in here.

BRUNSON

I really have to go.

MERLIN

Well, you'll just have to wait your turn. I'm going to be a while. I ate Peruvian last night. And some Haitian. And some of whatever that stuff is they eat in Seattle. I stuffed my fucking face.

BRUNSON

Peruvian is good.

MERLIN

Indeed it is.

BRUNSON

How long are you going to be? Ten minutes?

MERLIN

Better make it twenty. I got a ten-turd pileup on the intestinal freeway.

Merlin stands. He sets down his *Economist* and removes the cap from the toilet tank. Inside are several rolls of bills, a plastic bag of drugs, and an automatic pistol. From the bag he fishes out a vial of powder.

BACK TO:

OUTSIDE THE STALL: Brunson slips a twenty-dollar bill under the door.

MERLIN (O.S.)

I'm telling you, though, buddy. The Peruvian stuff is good, but it's serious. I'm not slagging on Peru here. I'm just saying you need to consume in moderation. Take it from one who knows. It goes down a hell of a lot easier than it comes out.

The vial comes rolling out from the under the door. Brunson snatches it and dashes from the restroom.

CUT TO:

INSIDE THE STALL: The drug dealer resumes his seat, opens his magazine.

MERLIN

Can't say I didn't warn him.

(It was notable, perhaps, that Merlin was the only specific element in the script that Booth singled out for praise. "The fellow who lives in the restroom stall, the drug dealer, him I did find quite amusing.")

That the agents presented Rick's participation in the context of his usual salary—a fee well in excess of the forty thousand Bummer City had promised—was irrelevant. Sam didn't hesitate to respond that it was no problem. It didn't matter that he had tapped everyone he knew or that it was too risky to press Wassel and Patch for more. (To request additional funding from Brooks was a last, last resort. Dealing with the AD made Sam feel like he was sticking his bare hand in a dark, mossy hole—the guy was just off—and he preferred not to unless there was no other choice.)

He'd figure something out.

5.

Occasionally, Sam allowed himself the release of an evening on campus, where, between sips of frothy beer in plastic cups, he tried to impress girls (usually freshmen, sometimes sophomores) with the details of his endeavor. A (very) few were stirred to invite him back to their vanilla-scented dorm rooms. More often the young women of Russell seemed to find his approach transparent. One comely sophomore, an artfully cracked iron-on of Germaine Greer stretched across her braless and forthrightly nippled chest, told Sam that he made "the art of cinema sound like bomb defusal." He said that was exactly what it was, "but only if you know what you're doing." She smirked and said, "Nope. Nopety-nope-nope-nope." The result was, that night, and most others like it, too drunk or too stoned to make his way home to the apartment, he crashed in Brooks Hartwig, Jr.'s, dorm room/lair.

These drop-ins, no matter how late after midnight Sam knocked on the door, were always welcomed by Brooks, who was nocturnal.

"Sleepover!" he said the first time Sam showed up. "Yay!"

Shitfaced, Sam clung to the doorknob and put his finger to his lips. "Down to a dull roar, please, Brooks."

"You can make a bed out of my laundry, okay?"

"No." Sam lurched to Brooks's mattress and flopped down. "You can make a bed out of your laundry."

"Oh." Brooks gave an appreciative nod, as if some long-puzzled-over concept had finally clicked. "Right."

The AD never complained about Sam's visits—not about the discomfort, or the distraction from his studies, or the intrusion on a potential booty call. Though in Sam's defense, it became clear that he wasn't hindering the other man in any way. Brooks was apparently undeterred in his nightly procedure, which did not in any case include studying, sleeping, or amorous appointments.

If he awakened before morning, Sam would inevitably open his eyes to see Brooks, hunched Indian-style on the floor while something foreign and esoteric and creepy played on his laptop: a Dutch movie where everyone moved backward, talked backward, and the subtitles appeared backward; a dubbed Portuguese movie that was a single seventy-two-minute take of an eerily upbeat chef matter-of-factly guiding the viewer through an old family recipe for making soup out of a lonely person. While he watched, the AD rocked continuously, like some kind of holy man. The behavior disturbed Sam but also intrigued him. Where did Brooks find these things? Did he actually enjoy them? What were the names of the drugs that Brooks consumed, and what quantities?

The semiotics of these films, and of Brooks's own film, struck Sam as baldly psychiatric. He could understand why someone might want to make one—to see if it could be done, as a strange joke, maybe—but he had no earthly idea why someone would want to watch them.

"Brooks," he demanded one night, "what is the point of this shit?"

Sam lay in the bed, his bladder very full, watching Brooks watch the soup movie, which took place entirely in a large, dingy kitchen with checkered tiles.

Off to one side of the kitchen there is a bathtub, and in the bathtub there is the lonely person, a young woman in a one-piece purple bathing suit, persuasively glum with her straight-ahead stare. The chef, though his dubbed patter is as ebullient and seamless as that of any real television chef and his smiles and flourishes are also in keeping with the genre, evinces a criminal dissipation. Half-shaved, he claps around in ragged flip-flops, and wears a dingy unexplained bandage at the side of his neck. After filling a bucket with water, the chef returns to the bathtub and the lonely person, soles snapping against the linoleum, and explains, "I'm using water. But if you would prefer broth, that is fine, too."

It was February, a new year. Predawn light limned the edges of the sheet hung over the window.

Seated on the rug a few feet away from his open laptop, Brooks stopped rocking back and forth. He swiveled around to squint at Sam with bloodshot eyes. "Oh, like. Like . . . What do you mean?"

Intoxication tended to inflame Sam's incredulity. "I mean, if I have to listen to this—whoever—warlock, necromancer—person—explain why the miserable soul should be allowed to soak in a quart of vinegar poured from a chipped pitcher, then you might at least tell me *why*."

"Why? Uh . . . why not?" Brooks blinked.

"No, Brooks. That is not a satisfactory answer."

Brooks blinked some more. He scratched at his forehead. "Well, it's not like anything else, is it?"

"No. Still not satisfactory. Go again."

"It's about soup, making soup. What other movie is about making soup, Sam?" The AD scratched his chin and rubbed his nose. For no real reason, he swept a hand through the empty air. "And the main ingredient is a person!" he blurted, as if Sam might have forgotten.

"Let's add some onion!" The chef dumps a fistful of diced onions into the water at the lonely person's feet, then makes a show of wiping his hands. "Optimally, the onion should be from the garden of a man who has cancer. At the very least—the very, very least—you should rub your onion on a cancer person."

Either Brooks was brainless, or he was hiding something, or he was a complete madman. Sam wanted to poke him with a sharp pole for being so unfathomable. "Let's try this another way, Brooks. Name one normal movie that you like."

"What do you mean by normal?"

"A movie you saw in a goddamn theater. And not a theater where everyone had their hands inside their raincoats."

The younger man dropped his head into his hands and made a noise as if a doctor were sticking a tongue depressor down his throat. A minute or two elapsed. The gagging noise continued. Sam reached his arm out from under the blanket to fish around on the floor near Brooks's bed. He found a balled-up white sock and hurled it at him. The sock sailed over the AD's head to strike the wall with a soft thud. Sam fished again and came up with a box of kitchen matches.

Brooks glanced up. "I'm sorry. I'm blanking. I mean, you know, like— I like pretty much all of them. You know? Because it's just— It takes you away. They take you away. The movies do."

Sam, arm cocked, box of matches in hand, hesitated.

In a film theory class, Sam could sit at a seminar table and highlight the intertextual fatuousness of *E.T.* with the best of them—could chortle at Spielberg's (frankly colonial) infantilizing of his spaceman, who is dressed and bathed and plied with candy and even jammed into a mound of stuffed animals—but what truly bothered Sam about the movie was that it was simply *dishonest*. No living being, in this galaxy or any other, was entirely good. *E.T.* was as fake as Jesus.

His own cinematic predilections began—and nearly ended—with that single negative criterion: dishonesty.

Of course, fraudulence abounded across cinema. Anyone who had ever been privy to a relationship between truly opposite personalities, for instance, had to be aware that most romantic comedies were utter horseshit; and if you'd ever spent more than a layover in Europe, you recognized that behind every "prestige" picture set in the golden French countryside or on the verdant Italian coast was hidden the actuality of rank plumbing, apathetic service, ambient anti-Semitism, and very few nonsmoking oases.

B movies, however, were the worst. These beacons of untruth—not only the stock and trade of Booth Dolan but also the breeding ground for Spielberg, Lucas, and other brokers of the meretricious—were composed of everything that Sam abhorred: characters who are absolutely good; characters who are mindlessly evil; otherwise retiring female characters who turn into unstoppable killing machines whenever children are endangered; black characters whose sole attribute is nobility; characters who say funny things while being held at knifepoint or gunpoint or facing some other existential threat; characters who are wholly defined by their sexual traits—like horny females deserving of death and impotent venal males; brilliant preadolescents; brilliant serial killers; attractive streetwalkers; tanned scientists; God and heaven; the devil and hell; people with magic powers—"superheroes"—who dress up in costumes and fight crime but never use their magic in a sexual context, which would be the first thing that a normal person would do (and definitely the first thing Sam would do); spaceship control panels of unlabeled, colored lights; canted—"dutched"—shots used to suggest the presence of the supernatural; extreme wide-angle lenses—"fisheyes"—to suggest first-person intoxication or disorientation; shots that dive, swoop, tornado, or otherwise behave as though the viewer is a fussy toddler in a high chair who needs distracting, and the camera is a spoonful of mashed peas coming in for a landing; and (excluding a handful of special cases) sequels.

By the opposite token, the movies that Sam considered exceptional were varied, artful, and—centrally—true. There was the icily beautiful and terrible childhood of Bergman's *Fanny and Alexander;* there was Truffaut's *The 400 Blows* and the meticulous hearing it gives to the existence of a resoundingly unspecial boy; there was Lumet's *Dog Day Afternoon,* a tragedy about two hopeless men—the first hopeless in love, the second hopeless in his loyalty to the first—that was disguised as a bank robbery caper.

The single take in all of cinema that Sam loved best was in *Dog Day Afternoon,* when Al Pacino's Sonny asks John Cazale's Sal if there's a country where he wants to escape. Sal replies, "Wyoming." It's a simple two-shot: Sal to the left, Sonny to the right. Lumet doesn't try to highlight the moment with a cutaway to a close-up. The line should be a gut-buster, but the laughter never slips past your lips. Because, as the two men look at each other, as the viewer sees that Sonny sees that Sal doesn't understand, we realize that these criminals threatening murder are basically children, and there's nothing amusing about that, it's heartrending and awful. Sam could remember, at age fourteen, watching a rented DVD of *Dog Day Afternoon,* alone in the house—Allie out,

Booth far away—the pitch black of a northeastern winter night pulled over the living room window, the pulsing, weeping bullet hole of a zit on his neck forgotten in the rapture of the film. When Sal said "Wyoming," Sam—all by himself—cried out to the empty house, "Oh, God! Will you guys please just give up? They're going to kill you!"

And it was just a two-shot. The director hadn't intruded, the actors hadn't seemed like actors, and it was so authentic, so recognizable; the exchange was the sum of every dismayed realization ever shared between two men throughout history. It wasn't too much to say that until he saw that moment in that film, Sam had never come close to comprehending how agonizingly difficult it was to explain yourself to another person, to make him see you as you really were. It was like trying to explain Wyoming.

The few films Sam loved were the antithesis of dishonest. There was often humor in them, and sometimes romance and adventure, but in each case the directors steered them to a conclusion that was resonant—undeniable—and spared no one, certainly not the audience.

"You can help yourself," said Brooks. "I've got, you know, a whole box of boxes under the bed."

Sam was still holding the box of matches, pulled back to his ear, ready to throw at the AD. "You really can't think of a movie you dislike?" It was a genuinely mystifying notion. Even Booth proclaimed some perverse standards.

The AD seemed to sense what Sam was thinking. "Sorry," Brooks said. He scratched his cheek, wrinkled his nose, scratched his nose, and rubbed the top of his head. He made another swipe at the air again, as if to ward off a fly, but there was no fly.

"Whatever, Brooks. It doesn't matter. Forget I asked." If the AD wasn't on something, he should get on something. Sam dropped the matchbox on the floor and pulled the blankets tight to his chin.

On the laptop, the half-shaved chef drags a hot plate the size of a truck tire over to the bathtub and slides it underneath. The lonely person, the young woman in the purple bathing suit, does nothing, just lies in the tub. "And now," says the chef, the dubbed voice becoming slightly wistful, "there is nothing left but to wait until you have brought the mixture to a great boil. There will be a stink. Sorry about that. And do not be surprised when the pitiful creature commences to beg. That is the most regular thing of all, essential to the flavoring of my dear grandmother's soup. Okay. I've had a nice time cooking with you."

Brooks rocked back and forth.

The coils of the giant hot plate begin to glow brighter and brighter, and the credits begin to roll. The chef sits on the edge of the tub, crosses his legs, and digs at his neck bandage. The lonely person stares ahead.

Sam dragged the blanket higher, over his head.

Other nights, from the apartment, Sam called Polly at her parents' condo in Florida. Once he thought he heard her shush someone in the background. He didn't say anything about it, but after that he called her less.

For months he relentlessly revised the script, paring away dialogue, simplifying transitions, doing everything he could to make the film operate like a flip-book moving forward on smooth dual tracks of narrative and time. Sam's personal shooting script was spliced with hand-drawn diagrams of the camera angles and movements that he wanted. He knew precisely how it would go—each day, each setup, each scene.

In the winter months, he saw his movie a hundred times. Seated at the desk in his apartment, at the window overlooking the parking lot, he watched it scroll across the frosted panes and thought it was beautiful and perfect. *Who We Are* was going to give shape to something that had been nipping at him and his friends for their entire lives. It was the story of the generational burden they carried, their shared realization that nothing made sense until it was too late to be changed, that they were never given anything like a real chance.

His first movie, *The Unhappy Future of Mankind,* filmed on a VHS camcorder when he was twelve, had starred his Nukies, those bright red plastic children of the radiological apocalypse born with flippers for hands and melted faces like stretched bubble gum. The film was shot entirely in his bedroom, where Sam directed the Nukies on a doomed stop-motion wagon train from the door to the dresser. The quicksand rug swallowed some. A Stonehenge-like monument of textbooks quaked and fell, crushing half a dozen mutants. During one extended sequence, empty sneakers gave eerie pursuit after a few terrified stragglers and finally ground them out. But the remaining refugees strove on, though they never seemed to get farther than the open space in the middle of the bedroom floor where everything was staged. Sam could still feel the deep ache from the hard rubber eyepiece of the camcorder digging into the bones of his eye socket as he reached around to shift a figure forward a quarter of an inch so he could press the red button, capture the twitch of movement, press pause, and repeat.

It struck Sam that *Who We Are* was essentially the same story, except with people instead of nuclear deformities.

Each time *Who We Are* played over the window, rolling from black to black, he loved it more. When it was finished and he came to himself, a groove cut across his elbows from where he'd leaned against his desk. He yawned.

The window was streaked with melt. Outside, the grass was greening and buds were popping on the dogwoods. The boys were back at the pothole, dropping pebbles into the darkness. Someone was on the phone. Rick's deposit, said the voice at the other end. They hadn't received it.

"Oh," said Sam. "That's strange. I'll check with my bank right away."

6.

On a morning in May, Sam arrived at Rick Savini's home in Westchester County with his tools and supplies. They were scheduled for a script meeting that afternoon, and he was several hours early.

The house was part of an upscale development, tucked away behind a stand of elm and pine. The main road described a lengthy oval linking all of the ten or so homes of the development, and exited onto a bustling suburban route. While studying the actor's home on Google Earth a few days earlier, Sam had determined that Rick Savini's driveway had no fewer than a dozen potholes. He planned to fill them all—and following that, to take a look at Rick Savini's roof. In the Google Earth photos, Sam thought he discerned some discoloration at the eaves, a telltale sign of weathering.

Once he had unloaded the necessaries—bags of hot patch, bucket, shovel—Sam removed his shirt and set to work. First he used the shovel to round off the potholes, made them nice and clean. When that was done, he mixed his patch in the bucket and went from hole to hole, pouring up to the brim.

By ten o'clock, the sun was high and hot, and the work was done. Although the job had not been difficult, Sam was out of the habit of manual labor. He took a seat on Rick Savini's steps to rest.

A sort of minified English manor, the house was planted in the center of an acre or so of greensward. The structure sat on a base of checkered brickwork, and the main body of the building was painted white with gray counterpoints. From one corner of the gabled roof poked a stubby turret. On his first pass through the development, Sam hadn't been sure which house belonged to the actor. The other houses were similar, pulled from the same broad-shouldered mold. Only the accents varied—nickel plate on the front door instead of brass, trim in light blue or beige instead of white, a bell roof on the turret rather than a conical top, or sans turret completely.

While he leaned on his elbows, Sam observed a yellow butterfly as it drew a jagged line graph in the shadows of the front door overhang. When the butterfly passed into the light, it disappeared, swallowed by glare.

The scene dissatisfied him: the great, glossy house and same-y neighborhood, hacked out of a forest and screened from the hoi polloi driving past on the main road, the middlebrow affluence it broadcast. Compared to Tom's ever growing LEGO castle, say, it was painfully bourgeois. He had expected better from Rick Savini. What made someone want to be like everyone else? He supposed there was a comfort in similarity, but wasn't that like deciding that you didn't want to be *anyone* anymore? It was like deciding to be less alive. He couldn't figure that.

Wesley Latsch, Sam's best friend, didn't seek anonymity, but he did greatly prefer to connect via e-mail as opposed to face-to-face. Wesley estimated that at least 75 percent of the time the person you were talking to was simultaneously thinking about pleasuring him/herself. "E-mail is an antiseptic mode of communication, and that's a good thing."

("Are you thinking about pleasuring yourself right now?" Sam asked, and Wesley said, "Oh, sure.")

A thrush gargled. Marigolds bunched from a pair of trough-like flower boxes on either side of the porch. Flies circled and settled and crawled in the creases between petals. Drops of sweat slid down Sam's spine like small, light fingers.

Or maybe the house was a kind of disguise; a McMansion was the last place you'd expect to find an independent film star. Sam imagined his actor—and even as he thought of him as *his,* he could feel Polly lifting a satisfied eyebrow, pleased to see him conforming to her fantasy of him as a young DeMille, dressed in those dorky lion tamer's pants and terrorizing a crew of dozens with a bullhorn—sitting on this very step, communing with the part that he had written. Savini would let the serenity of the morning lure him out of himself while the character came in, like a possessing spirit. Sam smiled to himself. Somewhere in the surrounding woods, a stream was flowing, hushing its way over rocks.

Behind him, the door—a prodigious oak piece cut to fit a Tudor arch—banged wide.

Sam lurched up, spun around, slipped on the gravel footpath, and fell on his back.

"Who are you?" Rick Savini crouched forward, holding a long knife with his wrist turned out to present the blade at a deadly, tilted angle. He wore a Brooklyn Dodgers home jersey and a pair of cutoff jean shorts. Sunlight spun along the knife's edge. "And what the hell are you doing?"

"I'm Sam." A hundred tiny shards of rock pressed themselves into the bare flesh of his back. "The director." He scuttled backward on his palms. "We're meeting today?"

"Sam. What have you done to my driveway?" Savini stopped at the foot of the porch but didn't lower the blade.

"I patched it." Sam got to his feet. "You had a bunch of holes."

"Kid. Man." Savini straightened. He gazed up at the overhang and took a deep breath. Without looking down, he sheathed his weapon in a belt loop. "I'm sure your heart was in the right place, it's a sweet gesture and everything, but those holes. That was how I remembered which house was mine."

In person, the actor appeared even more harassed than he did on the screen. His eyes were not so much sunken as withdrawn, dug deep into the sockets for protection, like soldiers in trenches. He looked as if he had spent the night crammed inside a glove compartment.

What a face!

Even as the blood was finding its way back to the tips of his fingers and toes, Sam found himself reflecting on how perfect Savini was going to be in the movie. And they had something in common: Sam used a pothole to remember where he lived, too!

"I'm really sorry about the potholes. I completely understand. Do you want me to dig one out?"

"Yeah, maybe. If it's not too much trouble." The actor thumped down on the step where Sam had been sitting before. "Ah, Jesus, it's bright." Puddles of reflected light oozed on the surface of the driveway, and Savini raised a hand to shield his eyes. "Fuck you, sun."

"Not a summer person?" asked Sam.

"Not so much. You may have noticed, I have a delicate complexion. And allergies. I get headaches. Some of my ancestors were sewer rats. I don't like how damn long the days get. It's stressful."

"Stressful?"

"The push and pull of it. You know, it can go either way: 'Is this day gonna hang on for me a little longer?' or 'Is this day ever gonna fucking end?' People go nuts in the summer. Serial killers? Most active in the summer. Look it up."

Sam couldn't help offering that he didn't see the difference from the rest of the year. "There are always days that go on too long and days that you don't want to be over."

"Yeah, but the brightness of the summer makes the feeling more acute. And you're young. I don't expect you to understand. I'm pale and old. Summer and I have history." Savini squinted from under his hand. "I thought you weren't coming until the afternoon."

"I wasn't supposed to—but Rick, listen. You're going to have to do the movie for scale." Sam was standing in the direct light, the sun burning his already inflamed shoulders.

The squint tightened. "Pardon?"

"Scale. I can only pay you scale."

"So, what, you thought you could, like, work off the difference in trade?"

"Sort of. I was also going to take a look at your roof. It's pretty beat up."

"You couldn't just ask me?" Rick Savini flung out his hand as if to knock back Sam. He flopped on the porch and landed with a thump, arms thrown out. "What the fuck. Sam. Look, I liked your script okay. I thought it would be funny to play a part entirely in a bathroom stall. But this is just very fucking unprofessional."

"I'm sorry," said Sam.

"No, you're not," said Rick Savini. "It's not even ten, is it?"

"Rick, I don't want to be a prick about this, but you have to be in the movie."

"No, I don't. And you are being a prick." The actor raised his head slightly, dropped it against the porch. He did it again and then a third time. It made the sound of melons being dropped on a counter.

"Please." Sam realized in that instant how wobbly the ground had become. He took a deep shaking breath. The tears in his throat were, to his own astonishment, real.

But they weren't enough. What Sam was feeling was want. What the part called for was need.

So he did what he had to. He thought of the worst, saddest, most horribly mundane moment of his entire life and broke his own heart all over again.

Playing on the single screen of the Memory Theater was *If You See a Vegetable, Kill It and Eat It.* It was a short film, set at a bus stop, costarring Sam as himself and, in her final performance, Allie as his mother.

"I am such an old lady," she says, and yawns, tucking a loose tendril of gray hair behind her ear. "Pooped at one in the afternoon."

He hops out, grabs his duffel from the pickup bed, and goes around to her window. Allie starts to roll the window down, but he tells her not to. "If we kiss, you might get your old on me," he says.

She laughs, tells him he's a little shit, to call when he's there, to wear a coat. "And if you see a vegetable, kill it and eat it, okay? Now I'm going home to take a nap and dream old-lady stuff."

"Okay, cool. I'll have my people call your people." He gives the window a knock and turns. The bus is already at the station.

"Please, please, please—" Sam sobbed.

"Don't do that!" said Rick Savini. "Do not fucking do that! You're taking advantage. You're overstepping your bounds. You woke me up scraping your damn shovel. It's not right." The actor pointed a finger at him. "You know, I didn't say anything about it when I agreed to the deal, but I knew your . . . Ah, shit. I want to give you the benefit of the doubt, kid. But this is not right. You were raised better than this, I'm sure of that."

Sam broke the gaze. He wept. His flaming shoulders shook.

"Goddammit. Do what you want." The actor lurched to his feet and went inside. The door slammed.

51

■ ■ ■

Sometime after noon, Sam happened to glance down from the roof and see Savini walking around. The actor, wearing a wide-brimmed straw sun hat, inspected the series of fills in the driveway, which were seamless except for the darker color. A minute or two later, he went back inside. A little while after that, he hollered for Sam to get his ass down if he wanted lunch.

More weary than nervous, Sam descended. He had told himself that he was absolved of shame, but this time, the verdict hadn't stuck. He felt wrung out; he felt like he'd walked into something face-first.

They ate at a dinette in the kitchen, which had steel appointments and the hypersterility of an operating room. Central air snored faintly from the bowels of the house and made Sam's damp shirt turn icy.

Rick Savini planted a cold whole chicken on a tinfoil server in the middle of the table, flipped Sam a paper plate and a packet of plastic utensils.

"I'm going to play the part straight. I'm in and out in a day." Savini, standing at a counter, dismembered the bird as he talked, using his long silver knife to hack off the drumsticks and separate the body. "And you're cutting out the part where Merlin takes a dump."

"Why?" asked Sam. He could concede that it was obvious, but it was a funny part.

"Why?" The other man paused. "One, because it's his office. Who drops a deuce in their office? And two, there's a few things I don't want to do on film, and pretending to shit is at the top of the list."

"Okay," said Sam, The logic of the former point was hard to refute; as to the latter, he guessed he could see where the actor was coming from.

"Super." Savini stabbed three hunks of chicken and, with a finger, shoved them off onto Sam's plate. "Leave the potholes filled. I'll find a different way to remember my house."

"Okay." Sam picked at his cold wet shirt.

Savini knifed himself a piece of chicken and sat down. They ate for a while without talking. The meat was salty and gluey. Sam considered requesting pepper, but didn't dare. Instead, he said, "I like your knife."

"It's a *Lord of the Rings* replica." Savini sawed off another piece of chicken. "It's Bilbo's sword, Sting. I got it from *Flight Emporium*."

"The airplane catalog?"

"Yeah. They have some tempting shit in those things."

"Are you into those—swords?"

"No. I'm just a sucker for airplane catalogs. I fly so much for work. The stuff they sell, you don't exactly want it, but you want to know if it works or what it looks like up close, you know? So I got this. And it is a real sword. I actually use it around the house quite a bit. The edge glows in the dark, so it doubles as a half-assed flashlight." The actor cupped his hands around the tip of the blade to show Sam the flare of fuzzy blue light at the tip where some kind of glow-in-the-dark finish had been applied.

"So are those, like, elvish runes on the handle?"

Savini grimaced at the hilt. "I don't know. Probably."

Sam nodded. His teeth were nearly chattering, but his stomach had loosened. It was working out. Savini's loquaciousness had encouraged him; the actor couldn't hold a grudge. What Sam had done, it had been worth it, and the actor understood.

"You know, seriously, this isn't how you're supposed to behave." Rick Savini took a deep, huffing breath. "Kid. I know you're a kid, but—it isn't."

The half-eaten bird lay between them on the table, grisly flaps of skin peeled back, white meat hanging in ribbons. The unmarked steel surfaces gleamed, but only dully. They hadn't bothered to turn on the lights.

"I know," said Sam, and maybe he did, but not as well as he would learn.

Who We Are filmed from mid-July to mid-August on the Russell campus.

7.

On the first day of production, they did a table reading of the script with Sam subbing for Rick Savini—that was it for rehearsals. Rehearsals had never worked well in his career as a student director. Rehearsals seemed to solidify performances, to turn everything into dance steps, and to sap the tension. Worse, rehearsals gave the actors openings to suggest script changes. Sam supposed that he might have needed to be more negotiable if the actors were experienced, but luckily, that was not the case here.

He liked to walk through the blocking as briskly as possible, make sure the actor knew his marks, and get right into it. For the first couple of days of shooting, though, the performances were just so-so. There was too much tension, an atmosphere of fearful competition. Everyone seemed to be clenched, piling on the business, barking their lines, becoming weepy-eyed during brief, ironically intentioned exchanges about things like whether or not Captain Morgan was a real guy, or if vampires could contract herpes, and if vampires could contract herpes, were they totally up the creek, because how do you medicate a dead person, etc. Sam pulled an actor aside. "A little less," he told her, and when that didn't work, he said very softly, "Pretend you don't give a shit." Though this did seem to help somewhat, the actress cried off and on for the rest of the day. Then, in the scene where Brunson smokes meth for the first time, the actor who played the role, a hulking drama major named Wyatt Smithson, improvised a line; exhaling, he added in a stoned drawl, "Bite my bag, Republican America." Without yelling "cut," Sam shoved past the tech holding the boom, strode into the middle of the shot, and swatted the actor across the back of the ear with the rolled-up cone of pages that constituted that day's shooting script. The impact produced a rubbery snap. The thirteen-odd people on-set went silent. (The composition of this group was typical for the shoot as a whole: three actors, nine crew members, and one stranger; there was Sam, the director; Brooks, the assistant director; the director of photography, Anthony Delucci; Professor Stuart in his official capacity as the script supervisor and his unofficial capacity as the jack-of-all-trades; Wyatt; Linc, the obstreperous and annoying actor who played Hugh; George, whom Sam was somewhat defensive about casting as Roger, Sam's alter ego, because he was the handsomest of the actors, with a jaw that could have deflected bazooka shells; Quinn, universally known as "the Eskimo," today in charge of a flag that was actually a sheet of black poster board; Elia, nicknamed "Toughie," too petite (i.e., too anorexic) to lift anything or assist in the moving of anything weightier than a ream of paper, leaving her to handle the clapper and carry Sam's Production Office, a three-ring binder of notes, receipts, and contracts, which she lugged by holding it tight against her chest with both arms and groaning a lot; Big Alex (also sometimes referred to as "Straight Alex"), who on most days performed as the gaffer; and Regular Alex (also sometimes referred to as "Bisexual Alex" or "Al-experiment"), who usually handled the boom; the middle-aged makeup artist, Monica Noble; and a white-bearded maintenance man from the college who had wandered by and taken a seat on his toolbox to observe the proceedings.) Perched on the edge of a dorm room bed, clutching the smoking pipe, Wyatt stared at Sam. The director held his breath. The attack had been entirely instinctual; he had reacted not out of anger but out of alarm, as if Wyatt had touched a live electrical current and needed to be knocked loose. Sam was appalled by what he had done. He assumed that everyone would leave now, quit. But no one moved or spoke. Wyatt tentatively reached up to rub his red ear. Sam tucked the cone of pages into his back pocket. "Well, do you want to do it again?" The actor nodded his assent, and the director clapped his hands, said keep rolling, and hurried back behind the camera. Everything was better from then on; the actors' fear seemed to be focused not on each other but on him. The performances became more restrained. They hit their marks and did what he wanted them to do with a minimum of fucking around. Sam didn't care if the crew thought he was an asshole. The director was responsible. And if he was going to be responsible, then he needed to be responsible, no one else. It was an undeniable fact that no person alone could create a movie. Only the actors could perform what had been written; Monica had to make sure they looked right; the DP had to film it; the gaffer had to light it; and everybody else had to do everything else. As small a production as *Who We Are* was, there were dozens of moving parts. For the movie to come together, each individual needed to fulfill his or her special role. Sam couldn't be everywhere, and he couldn't do everything. Which was why he needed to convince them that he would hurt them badly if he caught them doing anything except what they were supposed to be doing. He made a mental note to assault someone on the first day of his next film, to prevent any time from being squandered. One morning they were setting up for a close-up of Linc, and Brooks suggested Sam apply a catch light, a soft light that was situated to catch a glimmer in the eyes of an actor. It was an effect that a seasoned ham hock such as Booth Dolan liked for the suggestion of vigor it produced. Sam considered it cheesy. Maybe it made sense for movies about Santa Claus or talking animals, but not *Who We Are*. "Because Hugh is really in his element, right? He's got that shine, right, and he's feeling it? That catch light, okay, it emphasizes that," Brooks said, scratching his head, nodding and grinning and leaning from foot to foot. His proximity made Sam itch. "Brooks: No. No catch light," said Sam. "No?" said Brooks. "No," said Sam. "Please?" said Brooks. Sam shook his head. "I'm sorry, Brooks, but I can't. It would be corny and bad. Have you shopped?" First among Brooks's daily chores was the shipping of the previous day's reels to the film processor in the city; second was the purchasing and arranging of the crew's daily repast. To this end, the AD was strictly mandated to buy only discounted sandwiches, discounted cookies, powdered lemonade, and those snack items that could be purchased in bulk, such as plastic kegs of stale cheddar puffs and infant-sized chip bags. Brooks said that he had done the shopping. "Good," said Sam. "Now you need to go far away from me. Come back when you can be not irritating." The AD scratched his nose and bit his lip and frowned, grinned, nodded, and dug some more at his scalp. He swung around on his heel and went weaving away, into the nearby woods, and disappeared into the shadows. A bill for $587.34 appeared in Sam's apartment's mailbox. A man named John Jacob Bregman, a special effects artist located in La Honda, California, had discovered his address on the Internet and insisted that Sam make reparations on behalf of his father. It seemed that Booth had contracted Bregman to make a high-quality latex nose for him—a very puffy nose with a hairy mole on the left nostril—but, following delivery of the organ, had failed to make payment. Sam's father's cell phone had been cut off, and Bregman's attempts to contact Booth through regular mail had been returned to sender. "Do you know what painstaking work it is, Sam, to make a nose with a realistic mole?" wrote the artist. "I am sorry, my friend, but when the father does not pay, his debts must fall to the son. This is the oldest of civilization's codes." The accusation had the ring of truth: Booth was among acting's foremost enthusiasts of prosthetic noses and rarely performed without one, and he was also among mankind's least reliable beings. Nonetheless, Sam thought John Jacob Bregman was being a tad medieval with the father's-debt-falling-upon-the-son stuff, not to mention presumptuous. He threw the letter away. When they were setting up the next morning, Brooks emerged from the woods. Sam did not ask if the AD had spent the night alone in the animal kingdom; it seemed better not to know. As they filmed the scene in which Rachel quietly slips away from Roger, passed out on a blanket in the field behind the festival grounds, a family of squirrels trooped into the frame. They moved in a line, one by one, splitting a trail in the long grass. Sam whispered in the ear of his DP, Anthony Delucci, "Stay on the squirrels." Anthony raised his head to frown at the director. It was not a pleasant sight, Anthony's frown. The DP, though only twenty, was stout and balding, and had, likely due to the innumerable hours already spent behind a camera in his two decades, a bulging right eye that gave him the mien of a mad scientist's halfwit assistant. Sam had toyed with the idea of performing as his own DP, but since he was already acting as his own producer and editor, he had decided to give the job to the very competent sophomore from Vinalhaven, Maine. The basics—the line of force and so on—were second nature to Anthony, and he was brisk in his business. In fact, he was probably better than Sam needed him to be. (For Intro to Film, the DP had made a short film from the perspective of a lobster gazing out at the restaurant doors across from its tank, seeing the people going in and out. Anthony had used plastic bags to create his own gels, dimming and coloring the lighting to a murky green tint; in order to give the lobster's eye a subtle, irregular drift, he mounted the camera on a water bed. The camera's weight caused it to sink and rise on the mattress. Though the short was totally static, it had been unnerving, to float there in the gloom and witness your killers passing by.) If there was a problem between them, it was primarily a matter of language. Anthony's Maine accent was a babyish drawl. What he called a "two-shat" was actually a "two-shot." When he asked "Befoh or aftah?" he meant "Before or after?" Sam was with him that far. What Anthony was saying when he referred to Brooks as "That cun-ed," Sam felt in his heart couldn't be complimentary but truly had no clue. However, the DP was, at least as far as Sam could understand, amenable to the director's aesthetic strictures: that they use only a short range of medium lenses (28 mm, 35 mm, and 50 mm), and that as much as possible, everything be shot handheld—employing a tripod only in a couple of particular instances, and definitely no steadicams or dollies at any point. (Although his reasons for these limits were partly financial, Sam harbored a powerful distrust for lenses that explicitly warped spatial relationships, and he viewed wide-angle lenses as being especially wicked. Welles had used wide-angle lenses to revolutionary effect, but always for a specific purpose—in *Citizen Kane,* for instance, wide-angle lenses had added depth to the images, which continually gestured at the depth of the mystery of Kane. Several directors had shot dramatic close-ups of Booth with wide-angle lenses for no appreciable reason except that it was striking, and on a big screen, this resulted in bringing him so close that you could count his nostril hairs. Besides being unpleasant, it was so jarringly unrealistic, it reminded a viewer in bold: **YOU ARE WATCHING A MOVIE.** That was why Sam was dedicated to shooting handheld and midrange, a position that Brooks fecklessly tried to argue him out of. Why, the AD wanted to know, was a movie somehow more plausible when the camerawork was shakier, because wasn't the audience therefore more mindful of the actual filming than they were when a movie was made in a "movie-movie" style? "Like, it doesn't make sense, right? If you don't want to make it seem not like a movie, shouldn't the camera be, like, not so present?" Sam explained that he was forgetting something crucial. "What was that?" Brooks asked. "I am the director," said Sam.) "Moh?" asked Anthony as the squirrels moved along. "Yes!" hissed Sam. Anthony shrugged and dropped his head back to the eyepiece. The DP tracked the squirrels until they came to the base of an elm tree and set to work raiding a discarded bag of Cracker Jacks. When they played it back, this all seemed intentional, an echo of how Rachel's attention is shifting from Roger. Better yet, on second viewing, it was apparent that they weren't squirrels at all—they were gigantic fucking rats! These monster black rats had up and decided to take a broad-daylight foraging expedition. They were marvelous, these rats! Inquiries, requests, and pleas inundated the director. Sam didn't have all the answers. He had most of them, though, and was good at faking the rest: "Yes, when she hits her mark"; "No, not yet"; "I think you already answered it yourself, don't you?"; "That should work"; "If it means you'll go away, Brooks, okay, you have my permission." They were right on schedule. Julian Stuart, his vandyke so curled with pride that it threatened to double back on itself, had taken to wandering around crying, "It is happening! By God, it is happening!" at random moments of the day. Sam himself was so excited about what they were getting that he couldn't sleep. On the first day of the second week of the shoot, he received the initial video transfers (the celluloid having been developed and burned to disc), and after they wrapped that night, he hustled to the film department's editing suite to get started immediately. He edited until his hands started to shake. Too restless to hold back, Sam maintained this routine, shooting all day and editing all night. When he was too jittery to continue editing, if he still couldn't sleep, he watched television in his apartment. Booth was always on two or three channels, and Sam Dopplered between them. Of a particular night: on Channel 98 his father in his toga in *Devil of the Acropolis*, and on Channel 186, wearing a hawkish prosthetic nose as the "famed satanologist" Dr. Graham Hawking Gould in *Hellhole*. He issues warnings in both: about Spartan werewolves in the former and hellholes in the latter. Back and forth Sam went, sucked into them simultaneously, not sure why, and for once not willing to examine it or to search for an excuse. "It seems damned odd, does it not, Timon, to speak of 'ethics' while this foul beast roams the city, staining the agora with the viscera of the innocent," ponders Plato, playing the peacock feather at the end of his fountain pen against his cheek. "By God, it's the devil's hole!" exclaims Dr. Gould, shutting a leather tome so savagely it belches a cloud of dust. Civilization was beset by threats! Sam frequently found himself chuckling. When the credits began to roll—Athens saved, hellhole plugged—he felt soothed, and could drift off into a couple of hours of sleep. But Sam's check for the cable must have bounced; toward the middle of the second week of production, he lost all his channels except for the one with the Christian puppets. He largely abandoned sleep. He edited until he couldn't anymore, and afterward, he walked around the campus until dawn. Out walking one night, Sam recalled how Polly had asked years earlier whether it was "some sort of Oedipal-type deal" that drove him to make films. The comment had pissed Sam off so much that he abruptly stood from where they were sitting and left her calling after him. It was about three in the morning when he remembered the instance. He found an unlocked Russell College security kiosk and called Polly. "It's kind of late, dude," she said. Sam told her to never mind that, did she remember what she said to him that time about the Oedipal-type deal? "I honestly have no memory of that," she said. Sam told her to just listen: "This thing happened, with these rats . . ." It had been one of those moments; people were going to yell at the screen; they were going to cry out, "Those aren't squirrels—they're rats! Uh-oh! This is not a good sign!" Sam was aware that he was almost raving, yet unable to restrain himself. He wanted her to know that he was finally what he had always wanted to be, doing what he had always wanted to do. "I don't want to rehash the same stories, Polly. I could give a shit about mythology or theatrics. I want to put something on the screen that's original the way real life is original, and surprising the way that real life is surprising." Polly yawned and said she wasn't sure what that meant now, "Oedipal-type deal." She went on, "When was that, sophomore year? And you've been brooding on it all this time? You know, I think that means that I'm your muse, Sammy. Am I? Am I your muse? Refresh my memory about Oedipus?" He told her that Oedipus was the mother-fucker. "Oh, right! Duh!" Polly laughed. Sam told her she ought to come visit the set. She could be an extra. "Hey, you know what's hilarious? That you'll let the rats improvise but not the actual actors," said Polly. He conceded that was somewhat amusing. "Listen: are you seeing some-one?" Polly said not to be ridiculous. She asked him what he was wear-ing, told him to take it off, pronto. He locked the door of the kiosk and drew the window shade. There was grumbling about the food, Brooks reported. Big Alex had found some green-tinged turkey in one of the discounted sandwiches; Wyatt had pelted Brooks with a handful of cheddar puffs, and they had stung like rocks. "Just act like they're kid-ding," advised Sam. The day before they filmed a particularly emotional scene—when Brunson tears apart his room looking for a misplaced vial of dope only for the room to abruptly heal itself and Brunson to sud-denly develop needle tracks along his arms—Wyatt asked the director how he should prepare. Sam told him to practice his lines. "Is there something I should listen to or something I should watch for inspira-tion?" asked Wyatt. Sam replied that the script was full of inspiration. "Practice your lines, Wyatt." The actor wondered if he should post an ad on Craigslist, for a drug addict to hang out with and to help keep him awake all night. Wyatt pointed out that Daniel Day Lewis had learned to scalp people when he was acting in *The Last of the Mohicans*. Sam pointed out that was untrue. Wyatt said it was, he'd read it somewhere, Daniel Day Lewis could scalp a man as well as any Indian brave. Sam yelled for Toughie to bring him an extra-thick roll of script pages. Another $587.34 bill arrived from John Jacob Bregman. It came with a picture of Booth's puffy nose with the hairy mole. The mole was impres-sive; it had a single pendulous hair on the tip and a cancerous luster. "I put my heart into this nose," wrote Bregman. He persisted that it was Sam's duty to right his father's wrong. The man was so anodyne in his entreaty—earnest bordering on holy—that Sam was troubled enough to try calling Booth himself, but of course, his father's cell phone was still disconnected for nonpayment. Rick Savini arrived for his day of filming at the end of July. "You want to put an obie on me?" The actor had spent a few minutes sitting in his stall, touching the walls, contemplating the space, sitting on the lid of the toilet in different ways, and then announced he was ready to go. An obie was what he called a catch light. Sam made a noncommittal noise. "Good," said Savini, "me, neither. I hate that Santa Claus crap." They were on the same page throughout. Savini hit every mark, spoke each line of drug code with the casual assurance of a veteran dealer. The entire bathroom setup was wrapped before four in the afternoon. Sam drove him to the Days Inn, and Savini spent the trip with his hand on the sun visor, tweaking it continuously to keep the glare off his face. "Sorry about the sun," said Sam, and the actor said, "Ah, never mind my bullshit. It's all uphill after the solstice. Soon enough it'll be fall and I can relax." Rick registered under the alias Steven Pink; they went upstairs together to establish that his room's air-conditioning unit was functioning (it was), shook hands, and said goodbye without embracing. The next morning Rick Savini was gone. Monica Noble, the tetchy middle-aged makeup artist responsible for maintaining the film's motif—the actors' changing appearances—began to weep intermittently. Sam asked what was wrong. She wailed that she was only one single individual person and it was too much. Sam embraced her. "I know you're not going to let us down, Monica," he said. "I won't," she said. "I know you're not going to fall to pieces and ruin this experience for these other people who are working so hard for no money at all, and who believe in you and trust you," he said. "I won't," she said. "You can't," he said. "Gosh," she said, "thanks, asshole." Rain started falling, kept falling. The budget instantly grew precarious; the shoot was on its second-to-last weekend; their rental contract for the Ferris wheel and the carnival games had to be extended. They'd only been able to use them for a day. Everything that remained to be filmed, even the stuff that had nothing to do with the Spring Festival location, was supposed to happen outside. Sam was determined to use the rides, but he didn't want to film everyone walking around and blinking at each other in a downpour. It would be distracting, and he hadn't planned on it. They waited; they couldn't do anything; they couldn't do shit. On the third straight day of rain, Sam extended the rental contract yet again, even though it was destroying the budget; he didn't know what else to do. Water sheeted down the transparent walls of the rented pavilion. The rotten-sweet smell of mud and soaked grass coated everything. Sam prayed for a stranger to burst in and attack him so he could kill someone in self-defense. Why had he not thought of a cover set, the director asked himself, an alternate way to shoot the remaining scenes? The answer instantly materialized: because he was a dipshit. In his willingness to pardon himself for any and all crimes committed in the name of his film, he had failed to recognize that nature was the one player who could not be cajoled, enticed, tricked, guilt-tripped, or smacked across the ear with a cone of script. Nature was an ice-cold son of a bitch. The actors huddled on folding chairs, as removed from the director as possible, and whispered. Anthony lay on his back on a table with the Black Bag—the bag used to cover the magazine when changing film—pulled over his head, as though he had been executed. Julian paced around, thumbing "The Blue Danube" on a light meter at double time. The relative quiet was broken only by the occasional sharp rip of peeling gaffer's tape as Regular Alex added another length to the mummy-like tape sculpture that he was creating; it was about the size of a toddler, and atop its segmented silver body was a single cheddar puff. The tape sculpture's working title was "Alien w/ Tiny Yellow Skull." Brooks sat by himself and burned kitchen matches. "Are you getting this?" he asked the question under his breath, apparently to himself. "Hmmm? And what about this?" One after another from a box he carried in his pea coat, the AD picked out a match, struck, and stared into the flame, shivering. "What the hell is wrong with you?" Sam snatched the box of matches away. Brooks stared at the ground. "Well?" Sam demanded. "A lot, I think," admitted Brooks, and laughed and frowned and laughed. The last laugh was wistful. "A lot." Sam commanded him to go outside and stand in the rain. "I need you to report to me the moment it stops." The assistant director exited between the flaps of the tent, out into the downpour. There was a round of applause from the rest of the crew. "That guy is creeping everybody out so bad," said Olivia Das, the actress who played Florence-Diana-Aurora-Divinity-Florence. Everyone gathered around to discuss Brooks: the matches, the twitching, the staring, the invisible documentary crew that he sometimes mentioned was following him around. "I hate everyone here," said Monica Noble, dabbing at her eyes with a napkin, "but I hate Brooks most of all. I hate Brooks even more than I hate you, Sam." Wyatt Smithson piped up to suggest that it was Brooks who had stolen Rick Savini's sword: "It'd be just like the freak." Someone had stolen Rick's Sting? Sam was dismayed, angered; that sword was how Rick Savini protected himself! "Othah day I begged for that cun-ed to get something othah than old sanditches, and he just laughed at me," said Anthony. Through the plastic walls of the tent, Brooks could be seen out in the field, sneakers buried in a rushing brown stream, hands pocketed, blond bangs plastered over his eyes. "Listen," said Sam, as it dawned on him that a scapegoat might be just what the production needed to pull itself out of its doldrums, "we aren't going to let the bastard ruin our movie are we?" The crew yelled, "No!" Their united front in the face of rampant idiosyncrasy was stirring, and Sam was finally able to bring himself to grapple with the circumstances. "Okay," he said, "let's improvise." The company worked through the night to create a rave inside the Russell gymnasium. Sam asked Julian if he had keys to the theater department, and although the professor didn't, he proposed that they try the window of the first-floor women's bathroom, which was in the back of the building, obscured by a hedge, and usually unlocked. "How do you know that?" asked Sam. Julian said he didn't. "It was just an idea I had. Intuition. A wild guess. I mean, how could I know something like that? I don't eavesdrop on women. I don't listen to their secret talk about their mothers and their lovers," said Julian. "Okay," said Sam. "I don't listen to their demure tinkles," continued the professor, looking off now, talking to himself. "Stop," said Sam. "Please stop." The professor snapped back, his expression offended, but said no more. They boosted Toughie through the unlocked window, and she let them in the door. From the costume closet, they dressed up the extras as pirates and flappers and Bedouins and cardinals. Strobe lights were requisitioned and tapestries were draped. New shots were blocked, the dialogue rewritten, and to catch up with the schedule, Sam rode the crew through fifty-four setups in a single day. When the rush was finished, he had slept one hour out of seventy-two, lowering his average to under three per night since the start of production. The next morning he fell asleep in the lobby of the Days Inn; he was there to meet Wassel and Patch, come north from Astoria to visit the production for the day.

(Sunk into the crinkling embrace of a plastic-covered armchair, beneath a gilt-framed picture of guests enjoying the complimentary breakfast, the director dreamed that he was screening a blank reel for a theater of human-size Nukies.) The weather cleared. Brooks left the field and came to Sam. Black mud caked the AD from shoes to hair; he looked like a swamp monster. "The rain has stopped," said Brooks. "Thank you," said Sam, and was about to apologize for not calling the AD in sooner—before appreciating that he might need to utilize the crew's hatred of him again. "Begone," he said, and the AD squished off. Wassel and Patch bought all the doughnuts at the local Dunkin' Donuts. "We have the doughnuts, bitches," said Wassel. "Dough-nuts!" sang Patch. Patch, who was collecting the state quarters and was, additionally, tremendously high, went around demanding that people let him sift their pocket change. "You ate the doughnuts, now it's time to pay the piper." Everyone cooperated. "Look at you, Patch," said Wassel. "Just look at you, you're a damned bloodhound for commemorative coinage!" While she was applying some touch-ups to an actor, Monica Noble appeared to Sam to be unusually resolved; she was not, for the first time in days, teary. Sam asked if she was feeling better. Monica chinned toward the producers, who had instigated an impromptu game of leapfrog nearby. "And I thought you and Brooks were hemorrhoids," she said. They exchanged a high five. That night Sam called Polly again in hopes of a replay but got her machine. There was a call-waiting beep. Rick Savini wanted to talk about his roof. "Can I get another year out of it?" Sam wasn't a roofer, but he thought it'd be okay for another five years. "All right. Another thing: you owe me a Sting," said Rick. "Some reprobate lifted it, and I'm pissed." The director assured him that it would be taken care of. Then Rick surprised him by saying, "You know, I knew your mom." Sam was aware that Booth and Rick had crossed paths in the eighties. (This was on the time travel–themed anthology picture, *A Thousand Deaths*—the one in which Booth's deranged caveman chieftain had munched the pigeon. In another segment of the film, Rick had a nonspeaking role as a spaceman.) So it wasn't totally confounding, but it was out of nowhere. "Yeah?" replied Sam. "Yeah. I liked her," said Rick. "She was a strong person. I hated it when she died." Sam thanked him, and Rick said, "Look, Sam, I'm just telling you," and that was essentially the end of the conversation. Later, strolling the lanes of the campus, Sam found himself beside the security kiosk. He tried the handle and it was locked. Through the window at the top of the door, Sam saw that the trash can into which he had ejaculated was overturned. A cluster of huge black rats was squirming over the spilled garbage, nibbling on things—probably snacking on his semen, he thought. It was awful, and yet he stood there and minutes passed while he observed the rodents' banquet. At the apartment complex, his mailbox contained yet another $587.34 bill from John Jacob Bregman. Bregman had included a wallet photograph of his own son, a moppet in a Dodgers cap and overalls, holding out an empty bowl. "My son is begging you," wrote Bregman. "Be the man your father refuses to be." The nose Booth had stolen was the void in his son's belly. Was the frown on the moppet's face a wince of hunger or of chagrin at being forced to pose as the Tiny Tim of La Honda, California? It was so unnecessary! You bought a nose, you paid for it! What was so hard about that? It was the middle of the night. Sam folded up the letter and the photograph and tucked them into his back pocket. There was nothing to do except watch the Christian puppets until daylight. The episode's theme was sharing. "Jesus loved to share," explained a large flocculent yellow bulb with nine wobbly eyes and black lady legs. "He thought sharing was pretty darn cool, Jesus did." Scenes were filmed and often filmed again, with the actors making the same movements but in slightly different costumes, as well as the changes to their hair and makeup. This provided for the splicing that would create the impression that the characters were growing older in the course of minutes and seconds. The long days became longer. They were well overbudget. Although the video he'd seen wasn't amazing, there were enough authentically peculiar moments—not peculiar in a forced way, as if he'd cast dwarves as campus cops or something, but peculiar in a true way, like a sneeze in the middle of a screaming argument—that the director believed he could stitch together a fairly compelling whole. It wasn't exactly what he had imagined, but it was promising. He already felt like he'd pulled it off. By then, the third week of filming, Sam was happy, saner than he'd been in months, and cold all the time. His over-riding sense was one of relief, of near-escape, of leaping from a speeding cattle car into the dark, hitting the ground hard, rolling, and coming to his feet to find that, thank God, nothing was broken. No one—not even Sam—seemed to doubt that he was in control. On the eighteenth day of filming, he felt a lump on the side of his neck, roughly the size of an almond. As cold as the rest of his body was, there was a burning sensation at the back of his eyes, and his knees seemed too loose in the sockets. "You kay dare?" Anthony asked when he saw Sam shudder and hug himself even though it was hot and humid. Sam said he thought it was a virus. The next morning he couldn't swallow. The inside of his throat felt as though it had been scoured in his sleep. He was freezing. Bonfires were crackling behind his eyeballs. He managed to dress but collapsed outside the door. When the director didn't show up at call time, Brooks went searching and found him lying in the hall of the apartment complex. The AD called an ambulance. While a nurse drew Sam's blood, the director clutched Brooks's hand. He whispered that he was afraid. Brooks reassured him that because of his art, Sam would be immortal. The AD's hands jerked from his sides, as if trying to shake off an invisible grasp. ("I worry about you, Brooks," Sam croaked, but Brooks said not to, that he would be immortal, too. It was all being filmed for posterity.) A doctor informed Sam that he had mononucleosis. The director slept. Brooks picked up three more days of dorm rooms for the crew, gave each person a hundred-dollar per diem to keep them busy, and shut the production down. Seventy-two hours elapsed in a trembling, bleach-speckled strip, as if Sam were watching events recorded on a VHS tape that had been left to cook in the sun.

Then his fever broke, and he checked himself out to finish the movie.

They had shot chronologically as much as possible, and *Who We Are*'s last scene was the last thing they filmed. It was shot at sunrise, leaving them time for only two takes.

The scene finds Roger as he slouches, hungover, back out to the meadow. All around him, the revelers lie in the grass, passed out. From another part of the field, a figure walks to meet him. It's Florence-Diana-Aurora-Divinity-Florence.

"Hey," calls Roger.

"Is that you?" She raises a hand to her eyes.

"Yeah," he says. "Who are you today, anyway?"

Florence-Diana-Aurora-Divinity-Florence shrugs. "It doesn't matter." She steps over a mound in a sleeping bag, and they stand face-to-face. They stopped being friends back in the midafternoon, forty minutes and two years ago.

Breaking the stare first, Florence-Diana-Aurora-Divinity-Florence casts a gaze around the field. The sleepers are motionless. They're sprawled here and there at all angles, as if shaken out on the ground from high above. In the moments before full dawn, everything—the pine trees crowding the field, the discarded wrappers and crushed cups, the sneakers pointed at the sky—is coated in a hard glaze.

"Everyone looks like they're dead, don't they?" she says.

Roger yawns. "Maybe they are."

The shot reverses, and the two characters are aflame in the first light, as they were in the beginning, dressed in their freshman clothes and with their freshman haircuts and soft freshman faces.

8.

The wrap party was held at the local Hoe Bowl. In Sam's one game, he rolled an ignominious 72. A couple of times, the director dozed off at his lane's scorer's table, and he spent the entire night nursing a ginger ale. He remained unwell, though not unhappy.

Olivia Das sat with him for a while. Her best aspect was a narrow, half-flirty, half-threatening gaze that suggested she was sizing you for filets. "I had such a lovely experience doing this," she said. "I just wish that Brooks had blown off when you stuck him out in that hurricane."

"That's a mean thing to say," said Sam.

"He's a firebug, Sam! He's the most horrible, dangerous geek I've ever met, and you're very lucky he didn't kill a bunch of us for his collection."

"Brooks is not a serial murderer. He's an eccentric. He took me to the hospital when I was sick."

"Did you know he filmed a porn when you were in the hospital? One of the tech guys saw. He said it was bestial." Olivia regarded Sam with her predatory look. "Barf, barf, barf."

"I don't care. And if you offer me a single detail"—he made a snipping gesture—"I'll edit you right out of the movie."

The actress called him a prude, smacked him in the side of the face with a peppermint-scented kiss, rose, and twisted off in a drunken drama-girl pirouette, bob flipping.

Eighties music blasted from the alley's overhead speakers. A group of blitzed crew members slid Julian down a lane clattering into the pins, where he lay for some time, like a discarded doll—a passed-out old professor doll, accessorized with urine-stained corduroys. Shards of green and pink light dripped off the mirrored ball, smearing colors over the walls, floors, and faces. Although he was seated, Sam felt wobbly. Dozens of people embraced him, kissed him, clapped him on the back. To the director's sore ears, the voices of these well-wishers sounded distant, as though they were coming from one end of a long hall, and he was at the opposite end. He felt like he could fall asleep any time he wanted.

Anthony was in a quizzical mood. The DP kept coming over and sitting down beside Sam, gazing at him soulfully. This was off-putting, not only because Anthony was a man but because of his protruding eyeball.

"What's up?"

Anthony yawned. "Tie-id."

Sam said he could relate.

"You know something?" The DP scrunched his bugeye nearly closed. It made him look ancient and wise, like a sea captain. "You don't have to be such a cun-ed all the time."

"Anthony, I don't understand what that means."

Anthony gave him a friendly pat in the chest. "I think you do dare. I think you do."

A while later Brooks passed through, dressed as if he had just wandered away from a community theater production of *Guys and Dolls* in a pinstriped vest and a porkpie hat. He pulled on the seven or eight gruesome long hairs sprouting from his chin, saying, "Yay, man, yay! We did it, right?" to anyone he could corner. When he made his way around to Sam, he inquired if the director needed anything.

"Just a couple hundred bucks," said Sam.

Brooks reached to get his wallet.

Sam put out a hand. "Kidding."

"Oh," said Brooks.

"Thank you," said Sam, "for everything. All your help." He wanted to be more specific, to give the AD his due, express what an essential contribution he truly had made. Gratitude was not an easy thing to articulate, though, not if you didn't want to be honest. And if Sam were honest, he'd have to say, "The shared unease we felt toward you saved the movie, Brooks. If you were not such a rich weirdo, I couldn't have pulled it off."

Instead, he said, knowing it was inadequate but wanting to be kind, "It would have been really hard to do this without you."

The little blond man laughed, nodded several times. He said, "Likewise," and shuffled away.

A few others visited the table. The Eskimo offered Sam pot. "I want to ease your suffering," the grip said. Sam declined. Another person asked, "Wasn't your father in some movies back in the seventies? Why didn't you cast him?"

"It never even occurred to me," Sam said, not lying.

A flash came: had Anthony called him a cunt-head? Was that it? Sam couldn't deny it, and in his weakness, he momentarily forgot his immunity to such charges. For those few seconds he allowed himself to ponder absently whether it had all been necessary, if maybe he could have relaxed a bit, loosened his hold, enjoyed himself more . . . but the idea drifted off like a chunk of flotsam. He was too sick, and anyway, it was too late.

Wyatt Smithson dropped into the booth beside him. "A question."

Of all the actors, Wyatt had been most difficult. Confused by the script, frustrated by basic blocking, he was the only actor to whom Sam occasionally resorted to giving line readings. His guilelessness was why Sam had cast him in the role of Brunson, a character who spends the entire story trying and failing to keep pace with his own evolving emotions. He had done a damned fine job with the part, too.

But now that the production was complete, Wyatt was simply himself, in no way a bad guy but definitely something of a knob. The actor exhaled breath of beer and popcorn into Sam's face. "A question. For you, my man."

Sam slid down the padded bench to stand. "I'm leaving, Wyatt. I'm exhausted, and you're wasted. What's your question?"

Wyatt scanned around, searching for something. His eyes were shiny, and his nose was drippy. "I think I have the clap," he said.

"That's not a question," said Sam. "But I wouldn't be surprised if you do."

Wyatt had settled on a bowling scorecard. The stiff square of paper crinkled around his nose, and he honked. "Yeah?"

"Good night, Wyatt." The director turned.

"Wait! My question!"

He waved over his shoulder and pushed open the doors of the bowling alley.

"One thing I always wanted to know. Who are we? You know? I never got—"

The doors closed on Wyatt's question, and Sam stepped out into the buzzing late-summer night.

The bed at his apartment beckoned to him like the promise of every good thing—Christmas and blow jobs and Starbucks—rolled up in a single package. Sam couldn't recall ever wanting anything more, not even to make the movie.

A few yards into the parking lot, he stopped to pop the top off his bottle of antibiotics and dry-swallowed a couple of pills. The black shades of campus, the gabled roofs and the church bell tower, rose above a distant tree line. Off to his right, an engine turned over.

Sam looked and saw Brooks's car, a yellow Porsche, the interior lit a glowing neon blue. He could see the AD in the passenger seat, and he raised a hand. Brooks didn't respond. The AD's attention was fixed on the lit match he was holding up in front of his face; from Sam's position, the flame was a tiny, wavering hook.

The man in the Porsche's driver's seat leaned forward. This stranger, his face largely obscured by an explosion of cottony beard, gave the director a two-fingered salute. He might have been vaguely familiar. Sam didn't feel compelled to chase the connection.

He pocketed his pills and went to his car. He drove to the apartment, the pair in the sports car forgotten long before he pulled into a space beside the big pothole. It was late, and he needed to rest.

There was a crackle as he lay down on the bed. Sam rolled on his side, dug a hand in his back pocket, and found the $587.34 bill from John Jacob Bregman of La Honda, California. The photograph of the boy holding out the empty bowl fell from the folds of the paper.

He studied the picture, the boy's frown and his half-shut eyes. Sam asked himself if he was falling for such crude extortion. Maybe the kid was frowning at the realization that someday, someone might come rattling his mailbox, insisting that he remit a blood debt. Maybe he just had sun in his eyes. Maybe he was about to laugh. Or maybe his little stomach was legitimately hungry. Sam clenched his teeth and stared upward. About a foot above his head on the wall, there was a nickel-sized spot of blue gunk.

Yes, he was falling for it—had fallen for it.

Sam groaned. He heaved himself to his feet. He went to find his checkbook and, while he was at it, a wet paper towel.

To create an assembly of *Who We Are,* Sam hunkered down in the film department's clammy cell of an editing suite for two weeks before the start of Russell's new school year.

The room was in the basement of a building that the film department shared with the theater and dance departments. Audible through the ceiling was the clangor of the teenage ballerinas attending summer camp. Their rapid footsteps and delighted screams trembled the mold-peppered ceiling panels and reverberated off the pipes, an echoing, giggling stampede.

Surrounded by a collage of wrinkled and tape-patched posters and flyers tacked up for either inspiration or ironic amusement by decades of film students (*The Godfather* was sandwiched between *Leprechaun*—"Your luck just ran out!"—and *Mary Poppins,* for example; regrettably, *New Roman Empire* was up there, too), Sam sat before the large desktop computer that ran the department's video editing software. Here, he continued the process of sorting the hours of footage that he had begun work on during the shoot.

What he was searching for was the film that he had watched so many times in his apartment window. But the mono pulled at Sam, and he was drowsy always; he felt slow and rubbery, as if he were trying to run without knees. He truly did not feel his best.

From the poster on the wall, Booth, a black pinwheel inside each eye, stood astride the boards of Dr. Archibald "Horsefeathers" Law's bunting-festooned wagon and dangled an oversize gold pocket watch before a crowd of hypnotized onlookers.

The film couldn't wait, though. Wassel and Patch were pushing for a screening, and Sam wanted to keep them happy, because he needed more money for post-production—needed it for ADR (additional dialogue recording) where the source sound was no good, for music, for festival entry fees, and for a dozen other things.

Sam applied a narrow strip of black electrical tape to his father's unsettling eyes, but it wasn't much of an improvement—the black visor just made Booth creepy in a slightly different way. Sam waved the poster off, refused to be distracted by it or goaded into tearing it down, and did his best to push through.

Several times a day he nodded off in the middle of work and awakened to find a crazed EEG reading jerked across his notepad and, on the computer screen, the film ahead of where he remembered, playing new scenes.

"How's it coming, boss?"

And just when Sam was at his lowest ebb, Brooks usually appeared.

The AD was working on a project of his own, cutting actual celluloid on the antique flatbed that lived inside the walk-in closet at the rear of the editing suite. As to what he was hacking away on into the small hours of the night, Brooks offered no hints, but typically, when Sam came on in the morning, he was still at it. A rattling, snickering sound of turning reels could be heard coming from under the door, punctuated by the occasional squeak of what must have been a razor slicing off frames.

On an academic level, Sam would have been curious to observe Brooks using the flatbed, whereon an editor cut the actual celluloid. While this had been the mechanism for film editing across the vast majority of the medium's history, with the advent of digital, it was suddenly fascinatingly barbaric. Brooks, however, kept the closet locked.

Though the rumors that Olivia had relayed about Brooks's activities during the shutdown—aka *Brooks Hartwig, Jr.'s, Day Off*—did temper his interest. Sam surmised that it was something along the lines of a snuff movie starring marshmallow Peeps. With his iffy health, he didn't need the nightmares.

"It's coming along, I guess. It's a movie, anyhow," said Sam. He yawned. It was an evening a few days after the wrap.

"Yeah. Yay, right? You're happy, right?"

"Uh-huh. I've got a big yay in my pants all day long, Brooks. I'm just trying to get over this mono."

"Right, right." The AD wet his chapped lips, grinned. Both of his eyelids were twitching slightly.

The situation with Brooks nibbled around the fringes of Sam's conscience. Recently, as different expenses had come home to roost—rental bills, developing fees, transfer fees, and storage fees—Brooks had, with nary a word of complaint, stepped in to pay. The four days of torrential rain had sent the production plowing into the red, and there had been no other choice. This last-minute outlay, added to what the AD had already invested, came to a number that made Sam tense.

Not for the first time, he found himself wishing that he liked the AD more. Then again, if he had, he would not have been able to make the movie he wanted. If Brooks had been his friend, or hadn't been so awkward or so uniquely irritating, Sam couldn't have made such good use of him. Maybe what Anthony had said was true: maybe Sam had gone over the top. But he had needed what he had needed. Given a chance to do it again, Sam thought he would do it the same way.

Except that Brooks wasn't right. Sam didn't want to think about that, but sometimes it sneaked up on him. He saw things that other people didn't see. To be driven and tough was one thing; to continually leverage a person like Brooks Hartwig, Jr., was perhaps another.

The AD began to rub his hands together furiously. His right eyelid abruptly jerked upward, sharply enough to appear painful, as if an invisible fishhook had caught it on a line and an invisible fisherman was reeling him in.

"Brooks," said Sam. "Come on, man."

"I can't help it."

"I really am going to pay you back," Sam said.

The AD's mouth curled down, and he shook his head in a childish, overemphatic way that caused his bangs to flop. "No, no."

"Yes," said Sam. "Yes, yes."

"But you've already paid me. In education, right? I've learned so much. We're square. We're completely square. Right?" Brooks put his hand on the doorknob of the flatbed closet, took it off, put it on, took it off, giggled.

"Okay, Brooks." He didn't give a shit what Brooks said; Sam was paying him back. "Don't kill yourself staying up all night."

Upstairs, outside, in the gloaming, prepubescent dancers loitered on the stone steps. They were drinking viridescent energy drinks from tall, unlabeled plastic bottles. One of the girls wrinkled her nose at Sam. "Who are you, anyway?" she asked. The other little ballerinas broke into wild peals of laughter.

"Sam," he said.

"Oh," she said. "The Famous Sam. That explains everything."

Twice, Sam watched the assembly. Both viewings took place in the editing room, at the computer station, on the last day of August. On the following afternoon, he was scheduled to screen *Who We Are* for Bummer City.

The first time he was alone. The experience left him nauseated.

He found himself mouthing the lines, and it made him feel like everyone who watched it would do the same thing, because it was all so obvious. In one scene, Linc had a huge, glistening booger in his left nostril, and Sam couldn't conceive of how they could ever be able to afford to digitally remove the huge, glistening booger, and they had to keep the scene, because the scene was essential, and Linc had a huge, glistening booger in every take. Lots of people wouldn't have noticed, but to Sam, Linc's huge, glistening booger was a booger eclipse that blotted out everything else on the screen. More generally, the visual conceit of the film—the high-speed changes to the characters' appearances, their hair and their clothes—was not always as successful as he had anticipated. Some of the wigs were fine. Some of the other wigs resembled, well, wigs. Some of the hair extensions were fine. Some of the hair extensions looked like they were attacking the rest of the person's hair. Every male in the cast had, at some point in the story, developed bizarre facial hair, a neck beard or a Confederate mustache or whatever. Why had he acquiesced to that? Was the movie supposed to be set at Russell College or Sasquatch College? The temporary sound track—which Sam had harvested from an award-winning foreign film about a man who is paralyzed in a freak accident, becomes evil and insane, and tortures his sweet wife by demanding that she fuck strangers—suddenly seemed, like the award-winning movie itself, grotesquely unambiguous. Sam didn't know what he'd been thinking. Up until that morning, he had esteemed the award-winning foreign film far above the rest of contemporary cinema, and considered himself to be in total accord with its damned representations of love and faith. Now, because of the sound track, the award-winning foreign film seemed superimposed over *Who We Are,* and it threw a pall over what was already palled, so you had two palls, and it was a tremendous downer. *Who We Are* was intended to be downbeat, but it wasn't supposed to be paraplegic-madman-torments-his-saintly-wife-to-death downbeat.

These issues were piled onto the types of failings expected of an early cut: the occasional yellowish tint where the color-correction guy at the lab had fucked off, which gave scenes a jaundiced complexion; the imperfections in the location sound that muddied dialogue in some places, and in others, because the crummy mikes had picked up nothing from the background—no wind, no footsteps, etc.—created the impression that the actors were performing inside an invisible bubble; and several viscous passages, places where Sam's efforts to clarify the narrative needed refining.

There was a pervasive stiltedness that he had never noticed. The actors played everything on edge, as Sam had written and directed them to do. They roamed around, constantly testing the edges of the frame; they kicked furniture; the female actors all cried at least once; and the male actors, in their quieter moments, with their abrupt, wiry beards, speaking about their broken families and their no-future hometowns, came off more like rambling drunks than conflicted college students. The unrelenting force was numbing.

It left Sam to contemplate the unnerving prospect that Booth's initial concern might have been valid. Did the lives of those young, comparatively blessed people warrant such a grave attitude? In a way, didn't the fact that he himself—whose greatest ongoing problem was that his father was a buffoon—managed to make the movie at all, to pour thousands of dollars of other people's money into a fantasy, invalidate the story's concerns? The ozone layer was disintegrating. Animals were wandering out of the last woods to be flattened by Mack trucks. People blew themselves up to kill other people. Israel, Palestine, genital cutting, missing nuclear arsenals, HIV, the World Trade Center, secret wars.

Sam realized that he was a despicable person.

By the time the computer screen faded to black, he was doubled over in the office chair with a trash can wedged between his shoes. His cell phone rang.

His godfather, Tom Ritts, and his nine-year-old half sister, Mina

Whipple-Dolan, were at the train station. Tom had traveled south from Hasbrouck to Penn Station to meet Mina, then accompanied her north to the college so she could visit her big brother, and so Tom could view the rough cut of *Who We Are*.

9.

On a cold but eye-wateringly sunny Saturday morning in the winter of 1989, Sam Dolan was alert for trouble. As the F train shuddered along the elevated tracks into the borough of Brooklyn, he sat on a vibrating plastic bench and squeezed his hands together. His father loomed above him, gripping a crossbar, grinning around at all the other passengers. Booth's excitement put the boy on edge. They were on their way to visit Orson Welles's nose.

The boy, aged ten, had long ago come to regard his father as a cause of some concern, and that day's journey south from Hasbrouck to Brooklyn's Museum of Cinema Arts seemed tailor-made for mortification. Booth was at his worst in public.

When Booth spoke, his voice had a way of expanding to fill every inch of available space, even if that space was a parking lot; it wasn't a voice, it was a Voice, like the everywhere-at-once voice that aliens broadcast from their spaceships in movies when they threaten to vaporize the United States. Any person within cannon range could hear it when his father said, "Samuel, will you stand by here, or would you prefer to accompany me to the pissoir?"

At six feet six and approximately two hundred and fifty pounds, Booth didn't blend in anyway. Sam's father didn't walk; he waded, upper body tilted five degrees south of perpendicular, shoulders leading to split through gales no one else could feel.

But to Sam, an unassuming boy genuinely comfortable only in the company of his mother, his plastic figurines, or the dead—there happened to be a very pleasant graveyard up the street from his house—the noise and size of his father were not the worst of it. They were, if anything, merely aggravating factors to the real problem, which was that Booth was so weird.

■ ■ ■

The train swept into a curve, and everyone shuffled two steps to the left. A dollish, steel-haired man in a neat brown suit and two-tone shoes lost his balance and stumbled into Booth's gut and bounced off. Booth embraced him in a one-armed hug before he could fall. "Steady, young fellow. I've got you."

"Oh, thanks you," said the dollish man, regaining his feet. "Thanks you, mister."

"You are perfectly welcome!" Booth reached out and straightened the man's lapel. "I'm accompanying my son to see Orson Welles's nose!" He swung a massive bearded smile onto Sam a moment before the boy could make a point of peering intently to the right, down the subway car, where a lady sat slumped against the wall, asleep inside a tall fur hat.

"Oh, that's interesting," said the dollish man.

"They got the man's nose?" This question came from a disbelieving woman in a silver jacket, holding on to the crossbar a few steps down the car. "How's that?"

Booth's chuckle pealed off the steel walls of the car. "It is not Orson Welles's actual nose, I assure you, madam. It's just a mold. Welles would have filled it with latex in order to create a theatrical nose, like this—" Booth plowed a hand into his trouser pocket and came out with a yellowish blob. He quickly massaged the prosthetic back into shape and held it for the woman to see—bridge, tip, nostrils.

"You always carry a nose in your pocket?" she asked.

"Yes." Booth drew back slightly. "Don't you?"

A dozen or more of the train's riders were laughing as they went rollicking into another curve.

Sam thought he could feel his soul clenching up, like toes in a pair of cold, wet socks.

Although his parents were married, the arrangement was mysterious. The reasons were twofold: first, Booth was almost never around, kept away in California by his work as an actor for weeks and sometimes months at a spell; and second, Allie was an adult, a normal person who ran a normal business, who could cook things besides pancakes and fried baloney sandwiches, who did not keep fake noses on her person or use the term "pissoir." That is to say, she was nothing like Booth, and Booth was nothing like her, but they claimed to love each other, and Sam was the proof.

The boy regarded Allie as his parent, and Booth as his . . . something he couldn't put his finger on. It bothered Sam, the lack of a word that could explain Booth.

Unlike most fathers, who maintained entire, cranky rule books about chores and grades and not touching the tools in the garage, Booth had only one unbreakable commandment: *Thou shalt not speak during the movies.* ("You cannot watch the movie if you are talking, Samuel. I cannot watch the movie if you are talking. Let your voice be heard only if you are definitively ill. Not if you are feeling a bit peaked. I mean, if you are pervasively ill, on the precipice of vomiting or pants shitting. If this is the case, you may speak.") What Booth lacked in rules, he made up for in preferences, preferences that he supported with on-the-spot fictions that were frequently bizarre and yet, to a person of Sam's overcast nature, often painfully compelling.

When Sam was five, Booth encouraged him to stop slamming the car door by explaining that cars had feelings, and the oil stains on the driveway were car tears. Mess demons gained entry to the human world through portals made of dirty laundry, Booth informed Sam at age six. Later, his father explained to him that while the sugar in Mountain Dew was bad for eight-year-old Sam's teeth, a far greater danger lay in the drink's main chemical compound, P-S 7—Penis-Shrink Number Seven.

"But you drink it," Sam protested. The lecture had been precipitated by a request for a sip from Booth's can of said beverage.

"That's because it's too late for me, Samuel. The damage has been done." Booth popped the tab and swigged. He coughed a few times. "Long before the deleterious effects of P-S 7 were made public, my penis had already dwindled to the size of a pencil eraser. Let it never be said, my boy, that deliciousness is not without its costs."

It didn't matter that Sam's relationship to his own penis was at that time strictly utilitarian; he sensed the organ's long-range significance and immediately went Mountain Dew–cold turkey. Years after determining that P-S 7 was a figment of Booth's imagination, he still had not recovered his taste for Mountain Dew. He continued to endure prickles of empathy toward cars on oily patches of asphalt. The sight of scattered laundry inflicted him with a sense of foreboding.

His mother was not weird. She made herself clear. There were certain basics that she required from him: do well in school, be presentable, eat his vegetables, help around the house, and most of all, be happy. Allie came right out and said it. "My big thing, kiddo, is I want you to be happy, you know?"

By contrast, Booth once told him, "Samuel, I want you to grow up to be the sort of man whom other men want to punch, and to be punched by, and to laugh with, and to consume great volumes of Mexican beer with. I want you to be the sort of man whom beautiful women want to slap and then to apply tender kisses to the spot that they slapped."

The kissing part made Sam flush. On top of that, it sounded like what his father wanted was for him to get his ass kicked. "Huh?" he replied.

Booth sniffed abruptly, flaring the mustache of his spiky beard. "I am afraid that I do not see how I can be any clearer than that." He made a "come here" gesture and enveloped Sam in a smoky, scratchy embrace that was both comforting and discombobulating.

There was a story Booth liked to tell about his son's birth, how, as a newborn, Sam resembled an angry little leper and it had been a sign of things to come. To get Allie's attention, Booth sometimes dropped to all fours and prowled around her legs, making realistic growling noises and snapping at the tails of her shirt. During movies, though he never uttered a word, Sam's father did sometimes moan quietly at the sad parts, at the deaths and the farewells.

Because they were rated R, the boy had never been permitted to see any of his father's movies. (The movies Sam was allowed to see either were rated G, PG, PG-13 or dated from the black-and-white period. The irony was that, as far as the boy could tell, all black-and-white movies included murder.) Booth's movies were, his mother said hauntingly, not the sort of movies that were intended for children. No less impenetrable was Booth's own sketch of his film career: "I make the sorts of pictures that legitimate people legitimately enjoy, if you understand my meaning."

What Sam had discerned about Booth's movies derived primarily from some posters that he'd turned up at the back of a closet. There was one for a movie called *Black Soul Riders* that showed a black man punching George Washington in the face. The *Hard Mommies* poster had a woman in a yellow bikini washing a red sports car. On the *Devil of the Acropolis* poster, his father, dressed in a toga, was being menaced by a werewolf. *Rat Fiend!* had a big, scary rat, and *Hellhole* had a big, scary hole. Sam's father wore a straw boater, and his eyes were pinwheels, and he dangled a pocket watch before a mesmerized crowd on the poster for *New Roman Empire*.

The implausibility of the scenes was vivid: there had been no black men in diamond-studded leather jackets when George Washington lived; the breasts of the woman in the yellow bikini were bigger than her head; monsters weren't real. What Sam saw in the posters seemed dangerous, and the boy felt guilty about returning to the closet repeatedly to study them.

The oblique references that his parents made to Booth's films did not lessen Sam's apprehension. Once, as his father was preparing to leave the house, Allie had wagged a finger at her husband in a mock-scolding way and said, "You be careful out there now, Plato. There are a lot of werewolves running around."

"What?" Sam asked, piqued by the mention of werewolves, immediately perceiving an adult subtext. "Plato? Werewolves?"

Booth slowly lowered himself to a knee and placed his big hands on Sam's shoulders. "Samuel," he intoned, "my son. Your mother is being hilarious. She is referring sarcastically to a picture I made, wherein my character, the immortal philosopher Plato, was slain by a werewolf."

Sam asked his mother if that was true.

"Yes," Allie said. "I am being hilarious."

Sam's best and most relaxed times with Booth were those mute hours spent shoulder to shoulder in front of the television watching old-time movie marathons, or sitting in dark movie theaters. Even there, it seemed they liked them for divergent reasons.

Although Sam had been to a church precisely once—for the baptism of a classmate's infant sibling—the exalted possibilities of film had beguiled him as far back as he could recall. Each movie was formed and populated from air, set inside the frame by a person known as the director—a human being who would, along with the actors, someday be less alive than what he had managed to place on film. The implication was immense. At night Sam lay in bed picturing the events of his plain day on immaculate celluloid: a close-up of his mother, hair in her face, exhaling as she scoured a blackened pan; a wide shot of everyone in math class bent over their tests, and Sam looking up, and pretty Gloria Wang-Petty looking up at the same time, and their gazes finding each other for a second, and then the two of them ricocheting back to their papers; a long static view of his street: the leaves sifting in the wind, the low rock wall of the graveyard bending away left, a squirrel crouched on the yellow line.

For Booth, a movie was all a movie was—it was an entertainment, it was a goof, it was people in costumes. A movie was "diverting," "amusing," "a wonderful yarn." A movie was just what happened.

"My favorite part will always be when they sing down the Nazis," Booth said of *Casablanca*. About *Citizen Kane,* he barked, "The old man loved that fucking sled more than anything else in the world, didn't he, Samuel?" As soon as the credits rolled on *The Empire Strikes Back,* Booth declared, "Wasn't that dreadful when he had to cut open his space camel and climb inside its guts!"

His father had shifted away down the couch, twisting to meet his son's eye. In a pantomime of horror, he rubbed his beard and blinked at Sam. "My God, can you even imagine, Samuel? To be forced to dig out the steaming viscera of a dead space camel to gain shelter!"

Was his father serious, or was he joking? Who was the child, and who was the adult? It didn't elude Sam that their perspectives seemed to be reversed from what might be expected: his own musings on eternity versus Booth's exclamations about space camel guts. Or was it that when his father said these things, he was subtly mocking Sam? Mocking him for being so enraptured, for traveling so deeply inside the screen for those one hundred–odd minutes? Teasing him for his unspoken belief that film had bestowed upon Rick's Place, and *Rosebud,* and Luke and Han and Leia, something infinite, something better than regular life? Did Booth think he was stupid? The notion frightened Sam. He didn't want to be stupid, and he didn't want to be embarrassed for being stupid. As much as he wished for Booth not to behave confusingly, Sam yearned to be enlightened, to be smart enough to understand, no matter what, to be a source of pride. The man was his father; he wanted Booth to like him.

"Yeah," tried the boy, who was too old to admit aloud that the swathing of his father's smoky, scratchy hugs felt good. "Space camel guts are pretty gross."

Booth ruffled his hair. "Know this, Samuel: if we ever found ourselves in a similar pickle, stranded on an icy planet, exposed to the elements, I would eagerly cut myself open, stem to stern, and dump out my own guts to make you a sanctuary. It would be an honor to be your sacrificial space camel." His father looked at him expectantly.

"Okay," said Sam. "Thanks."

The mold was enclosed within a glass box, and the glass box rested on a wooden plinth. Situated in the center of the museum's long white-walled gallery, the plinth stood only a few steps from the stairs. A clip at the base of the box held the plate-shaped mold upright, so if you went around to one side, you saw into the vessel of the nose where the latex was poured, and if you went around to the other side, you saw the nose as a nose from without, where it had the broadly jutting aspect of a truck fender. It was the nose of a hard man. An angled spotlight burnished the organ from bridge to tip.

Sam thought about what a big face Orson Welles must have had. A yellowed letter requesting the mold, written by Welles to his makeup artist, was framed and set into the plinth. Welles wrote that he required "A nose fit for a real working class bull of a fellow." Sam thought the artist had done a good job.

There were other exhibits lining the hall, which extended at least the length of a basketball court. He saw a row of old-fashioned wooden camera boxes on tripods, mannequins wearing costumes, televisions on the walls showing films. Sneaky music—lots of plinking keys and rattles—played from hidden speakers. A few other museumgoers were scattered around, studying with their arms crossed, but it wasn't crowded.

Booth circled the Welles display, tilting his head one way and another, expressing clucks and grunts of assessment.

Keen not to say something disappointing, Sam waited. For support he had brought a favorite Nukie figure and squeezed it in his fist.

If his mother had been there, he could have been more relaxed. Allie had canceled on the long-scheduled trip at the last minute; because someone was sick, she needed to work at the café. "Oh, God. Mom. Please come," Sam said, and Allie widened her eyes at him and put her hands on either side of his skull. "Kiddo," she said, gently rocking his head around. "Son of mine. Short person. It's just a museum. It's not an earthquake. It's just a train trip with your old man. You might even enjoy yourself."

"All right. Here is the question: should we steal it?" Booth gave a sly glance down the hall and then the other way, toward the stairs, sliding his eyes to look without turning his head. "Make replicas for ourselves, form a father-son bank-robbing team?"

Sam laughed. He was usually able to maintain his circumspection, but Booth's side-to-side play was irresistible. "Definitely."

"What shall we call ourselves? The Nose Gang? The Noseys? The Nose Boys? The Snout Men?"

"The Snout Men!" For some reason, the word "snout" was funny, too.

"Yes! Snout Men is just right." Booth mimicked the patter of a reedy newsreel: "*The infamous Snout Men struck the Kansas City Depository yesterday morning, terrifying customers and bank executives and escaping with a hundred thousand dollars in gold bonds and Missouri's entire reserve of Kleenex.*"

The boy grinned at his father. The image that came to mind was of dogs in pin-striped suits, holding submachine guns and leaning from running boards, pink tongues lolling. "Snout Men," he repeated, liking it so much. Maybe this was the day when whatever it was that was missing—not in his father but in him—resolved; maybe Allie was right; maybe he would enjoy himself.

"So. Do you like it?" Booth had bent to be closer to Sam's level, but now he straightened.

Sam took a deep breath. "Yeah. It's really neat."

"Yes, Samuel. It is neat. Beyond neat, in fact. It is gorgeous." His father swept a hand over the top of the case, and his thick platinum wedding band scraped lightly against the glass. "They say that the eyes are the gateway to the soul, but it's nonsense. Eyes, ears, mouth, hair, chin, jowls, all secondary. The nose is what gathers all the pieces together. It's in the middle. The nose leads. It is the face of the face. Change the nose, and you instantaneously change everything else about a countenance.

That's how simple it is to make a new mug, Samuel. If only it were so simple to transform the other parts of ourselves, yes?"

Sam found that, as Booth was speaking, his fingers had floated up to touch his own nose. He quickly dropped them. "Yeah."

Booth tapped his wedding ring against the case. He eyed Sam steadily, his beard fully closing over the faint smile that had accompanied his disquisition. "You know, son, I am so glad that you are here with me, that we can look on this beautiful disguise together. It is terribly special to me."

The boy blushed. To try and cover it, he blurted, "It's fun to think about it, you know, on his face and stuff."

"That is fun, isn't it?"

"Yeah."

"I knew him, you know, Welles. We made a picture together."

"You did?" Per his father's insistence, Sam had seen a number of Orson Welles movies: *The Third Man, The Lady from Shanghai, The Stranger, Citizen Kane.* They were excellent, with lots of shadows. Welles had a commanding voice and bright eyes that seemed to find their way beyond the screen to pick at you where you sat. No other black-and-white actor was as alive. "What was he like?"

Booth rubbed a hand along his jaw, forcing his fingers up through the curls until they found his temple, where the hair was speckled gray. The sound-track music that played from hidden speakers in the ceiling dipped, the entire orchestra dropping away except for a lone string instrument, keening. Booth breathed. He shuddered. "I can only tell you—that he had—"

It occurred to Sam—horribly—that his father was about to cry.

"—he had quite a large face," Booth finished, and shot a wink that made the boy giggle again.

His father told Sam to go ahead and look around if he wanted. "I need to commune with this marvelous sniffer for a few moments longer."

The boy strolled down the museum's main hall. He felt released, carefree, as if he had passed a test.

At the railing of the wooden camera exhibit, Sam took out the Nukie. The bright red nuclear man had legs where his arms should have gone and arms where his legs should have gone, so he stood on his hands, and his legs shot out at antenna angles, the feet hanging limp, like underdeveloped wings. The slight twist of the lips on the figure's face transmitted something along the lines of *I knew this would happen.* He was one of Sam's favorite guys.

Sam placed the Nukie on the railing and cast around, considering which camera had the best position on him.

"Hey, there."

A few feet off, beside a tall glass case containing an array of prop swords, stood a woman in a tall fur hat. Below the hat, she wore oval sunglasses with tinted blue lenses, a yellow raincoat, a dark blue dress over stonewashed jeans, and high, velvety black boots.

"Oh. Hi." It was the sleeping lady from the train, he realized.

"I'm Sandra. You must be Sammy, huh?" Sandra removed her sunglasses. She had prominent cheekbones, deep-set eyes. Something about her aspect recalled a tintype photograph he once saw in an antique shop. The picture had shown a pioneer woman in a wilted hat, posed holding a shovel; the woman's hard, angular features and her expression, simultaneously stoic and dazed, had unnerved Sam. Sandra's hair was a shade darker than the amber of the tintype, a muddy blond.

"Do I know you?" He wasn't nervous; it was a public place, and she was a woman. She was also, he decided, pretty, sort of. All put together, her crazy clothes made a crazy kind of sense.

"I'm a friend of your daddy's."

Sam nodded. "Okay." He gestured down the hall. "He's over there at the nose."

"I have a present for him. It's a surprise. So happens I followed you boys all the way from Grand Central just to make it. Tricky me, huh? You mind if I give it to you to give to him, Sammy?"

"Ah, sure, I guess."

From a pocket of her raincoat, she withdrew a crumpled pink gift bag. Sam walked to her, and Sandra handed it to him. Whatever was inside the bag was soft, probably fabric.

"Thanks a bunch. Hm. You know, from listening to Booth—I thought you'd be, I don't know. *More,* somehow." She opened her mouth wide and produced an odd croak. "I guess other people's kids are always disappointing, though, huh?"

It took Sam a moment to identify Sandra's croak as a laugh. To have a peculiarly layered stranger in a fur hat judge him as lacking was an entirely new experience, so he did the easiest thing and concurred. "Uh-huh."

"Sammy, Sammy." She said his name as if he were a gooey-eyed kitten in a shoe box. "Your father's really quite a man, isn't he? You must be proud. Big movie star and everything that he is."

"I've never seen any of his movies."

"Probably best. They're awful. Booth is the Zeus of awful. That's why I like them, you know?"

"Uh-huh," said Sam. Again he was just being polite, letting himself be borne along by the current of adult inquiry.

"What's that? Some kind of toy?"

"It's a Nukie. They're guys, they survived a nuclear blast. This one's got his arms and his legs switched around, see—" He held up the figure for her to see.

"Ugly." Sandra slipped her sunglasses back on. "I suppose I was never much of a toys and games person. Chernobyl was a CIA operation, did you know that?"

"What?" He had never heard the word "Chernobyl" before.

But Sandra wasn't interested in illuminating it for him. "So. What's your mother like?"

"My mother?" His mother took care of him. He relied on her, and he admired her, and he trusted her. They went for walks together. He knew she listened to what he said because the questions she asked made sense. If there were other people around and Sam had forgotten to button up his fly, Allie would very casually say, "Oh, hey, kiddo, did you happen to remember to lock the door before we left home?" and he could fix himself without anyone noticing. Thin white streaks shot through her brown hair on either side, but her face was young. She was his mother. Without her, he'd be lost.

"Like anyone's mom, I guess."

"I bet you really love her, huh?" Before Sam could answer, Sandra continued brusquely, "Of course you do. Of course you do." She grabbed the tongues of her raincoat's belt and sharply knotted them.

Sam reconsidered his original observation: in her blue sunglasses and yellow raincoat, what Sandra actually resembled wasn't a clown but some outlandish Saturday-morning cartoon spy. On the subject of spies, how had she known that they would be passing through Grand Central Station?

He was about to ask when she said, "Don't look at me like that. It's rude."

"What?" asked Sam.

The way her mouth twisted was like she was fighting it. Sandra inhaled. "Oh, you know. Like you're trying to peek inside my head." She turned and cut around a platform bearing a prop sled and disappeared, though once she was out of sight, Sam could still discern the clopping of her heels against the wood floor.

"What have you there, Snout Man? Loot?" A couple of minutes had elapsed, and Booth had finished and come over to the picket of cameras.

Sam had been concentrating on sliding his Nukie along the exhibit rail. The wadded pink gift bag was tucked in against his elbow, an afterthought.

"It's not mine." He extracted Sandra's gift, a finger catching the single fastening of Scotch tape, ripping the pink gift bag, and a black swatch of cloth spilled onto the floor. Sam bent and picked up the lacy panties. He held them out to Booth. "It's supposed to be for you."

On the subway back to Grand Central, Sam recounted the meeting—Sandra's "surprise," her questions, how she had made a face at him before she turned and left.

"Damned odd," said his father. This time, instead of standing up and holding a strap, he hunched on the plastic bench beside his son. "Lunatic woman. Pointless gesture. Makes no sense at all." Booth stared fixedly at the spattered, rubbery surface of the train floor. He shook his head and patted the boy's knee. He told Sam to push the whole thing from his mind. "Must have been a lunatic, handing out rags like that."

"Okay." Though it had been unusual, and he hadn't liked the way she had sneered at him, Sam's primary feeling was one of sleepy satisfaction. The trip he had dreaded had turned out okay. His father had behaved. Orson Welles's nose had been pretty good. On the Metro-North, Sam fell asleep and dreamed about cameras that crept around on their tripods like spiders but were harmless as dodos. Booth shook him awake.

The Hudson was white, shining. Sam shut his eyes and shifted away.

"Perhaps you'd better not say anything to your mother about that lunatic woman, Samuel. I would hate to worry her."

"Okay," said Sam. "I won't."

"Excellent. Loose lips sink ships," said Booth. "And we won't mention anything to her about you trying to steal the nose mold, either."

Sam opened his eyes. "Huh?"

Booth leaned forward to gaze past Sam, out the window at the shimmering water. "Already erased it from my mind, Samuel."

His protest emerged in a dry-mouthed squeak. "But I never said that! I didn't want to steal anything!"

"Yes, you did." Booth's gaze remained focused on the water. His beard was tinted auburn by the reflected light. "But now it's gone. Forgotten. The record has been scrubbed. It's not even secret because it never was."

"Oh, Booth. You awful fat man." Sandra whooped. "He says he loves me. He says he wants to make a film with me. He promises to give me orgasms. So many lies. Lies stacked on top of lies."

Three years later, at New York Presbyterian Hospital on the morning after Mina's birth, an older Sam Dolan found himself in the presence of his father and his father's new wife. Allie had chauffeured him to the city to meet his new sister. Although by then he was well enough acquainted with his stepmother—wannabe actress, professional dogwalker, perhaps not a full-fledged madwoman but, without a doubt, some genus of cuckoo—Sam was nonetheless barely thirteen, no less a virgin than he had been at ten, and mortified by the sexual reference. When it came to Sandra, he sometimes almost felt sorry for his father.

As the two went back and forth, he cradled his newborn sibling against his chest.

"Your stepmother is a dreadfully unhappy woman, Samuel." Booth, a mountain of tweed wedged into the cup of a plastic chair, sat beside his wife's hospital bed. A crumpled procedure mask bloomed from the breast pocket of his shirt. They held hands.

"Your father is right. I am dreadfully unhappy. And," she said, "it's his fault."

Booth smiled warmly from his wooly, iron-patched beard. "But by this angry womb we have been granted a beautiful daughter, and for that I am thankful."

Sam proposed to take Mina for a walk.

"Darling, I will ask you please to never characterize my womb again," he heard Sandra say before he shut the heavy hospital door.

Sam moved down the hallway with Mina. He'd never held a baby before and was surprised by how little there was to it. She was about the size of a loaf of bread. Her eyes were that unearthly newborn blue, and shiny, like rock candy. She gaped at him.

"I've been where you are now," Sam told the baby. "My experience may be of some benefit to you. I'm very sympathetic. But I'll be honest: it's going to bc frustrating."

As if in acknowledgment, Mina blinked.

Allie poked her head around the corner at the end of the hall. "All clear?"

He delivered the baby to his mother's arms. "Oh, goodness," said Allie. "Look at you, sweetie. Does your dad do good work or what?"

Allie and Booth had, after everything, remained friends. It made Sam want to hurl bricks through windows.

His mother dipped her nose to Mina's face and made kissing sounds. "And what is this we have here? What is this?"

"A baby. I'm pretty sure it's a baby," said Sam.

"You've met your big brother, Sam? Your big brother who is always going to be there for you? How great is that?" Allie made more kissy noises at Mina. "And don't you be fooled by all the silliness. He can be serious if the need arises."

10.

"I feel left out." For the course of the screening, Mina had been directed to wear noise-blocking headphones and sit facing away from the screen. She had arranged herself Indian-style on the editing room floor and begun to sort through a folder of head shots that Sam had taken of the actors wearing their different looks.

"Sorry, pumpkin," said Tom.

Sam pulled lightly on her ponytail. "It's for your own good, hon. This movie could definitely stunt your growth. Also your sense of drama, characterization, and pacing."

She began to arrange the head shots into various piles. Messily blond, dressed in an ensemble of various pinks, his sister also wore a domino mask, à la Zorro. "I don't know what you're saying. With the headphones, everything you say is 'Meh-meh-meh' in here. 'Meh-meh-meh.' That's all I get. "

The head shots seemed to keep her occupied. Except for the squeak of her markers against the gloss of the photographs, once the movie started, Mina fell absolutely silent and, Sam predicted to himself, would stay that way for the ninety-three-minute running time. Such a display of calm might have been unnerving in other children her age, but his sister possessed a preternatural focus. Though only recently turned nine, Mina often evinced the grim determination of someone who faces a daily traffic jam on the way to work. Her character and her obvious intelligence intrigued him, and intimidated him a bit, too. Why was she wearing a Zorro mask? Little girls didn't care about Zorro, did they? He was never quite sure how to handle Mina.

Sam shifted his attention to Tom. For the first fifteen or so minutes of the film, he observed the older man closely—until his godfather gave him a sidelong glance, accompanied by a throat clearing.

Sam kept his eyes forward after that but had a sense that Tom was enjoying himself. He laughed frequently—a kind of hiccupping grumble that originated deep in his throat—and during Roger's transaction with Merlin, Tom was even moved to cry out, "Don't do that!"

INT. FERRER MEMORIAL LIBRARY—BASEMENT LEVEL
FIVE RESTROOM
Roger crouches to push a bottle of antibacterial hand cleanser under the stall door.

CUT TO:

INSIDE THE STALL: Merlin, seated on the lid of the toilet, glances up from his copy of *The Economist*. He sees the bottle of hand cleanser.

MERLIN

What's this?

ROGER

Hand cleanser. I thought you might like some.

MERLIN

You did, huh? Well, I'm in here. It's occupied.

ROGER

I really have to go.

MERLIN

You'll just have wait your turn. I'm going to be a while. I ate Peruvian last night. And some Haitian. And some of whatever that stuff is they eat in Seattle. It was a buffet-type situation. Anything you want, pretty much.

ROGER

I like Jamaican.

MERLIN

Yeah, I ate some of that, too.

ROGER

How long are you going to be? Ten minutes?

MERLIN

Better make it fifteen. I got a major case of the turds.

ROGER

Great. But don't forget to scrub your hands.

MERLIN

Oh.
(beat)
Yeah.

Merlin picks up the hand cleanser. He removes the lid from the toilet tank, drops the bottle inside. He rifles around, finds a bag of joints, picks out two. Then he puts them down the back of his pants, inside his underwear, and appears to clench them between his buttocks.

He unclenches his buttocks, removes the joints, smells them, makes a face at the stink, and rolls the drugs under the stall door.

ROGER (O.S.)
Come on. Put 'em in a Baggie or something.

A couple of crumpled bills bounce under the door.

MERLIN
Leave me alone. I'm in here.

Tom's laughter was contagious. Sam had watched the scene at least three dozen times, but he found himself laughing, too.

He knew better than to put too much stock into his godfather's reaction. It could never be overlooked that Tom's favorite film was the execrable *Forrest Gump,* that story of a mentally handicapped man who continually finds himself at the fulcrum of history and, due to dumb luck and the goodness of his heart, inevitably influences these moments and the people he encounters for the better. Even Booth, usually among popular entertainment's stoutest defenders, had voiced his horror at the film's intimation that simplemindedness was a virtue, and its catchphrase, "life is like a box of chocolates."

"I have known a few mentally challenged people in my day," Sam had heard his father explain to Tom, "and I would be the last one to seek to cast aspersion on their characters. But their lives are very, very hard. Good luck does not rain down on them. It is not just one splendid adventure after another for the mentally challenged. Most people don't want to look at them, let alone assist them or befriend them. Robin Wright doesn't fuck them. Life is rarely a box of chocolates for them—it is far more often a box of turds."

"That's not the thing." Tom was altogether undeterred. "The thing is that Forrest had a great life and did a lot despite his limitations. He's not every retard, Booth. Forrest's just himself."

While there was no question of Tom's decency, he was no critic. If his enthusiasm for *Forrest Gump* didn't offer proof enough, his unshakable loyalty to Booth did.

The men's relationship was of the kind that would be inconceivable except they had grown up together. If they had met each other after the age of, say, nine or ten, there was no way they could have been friends. They had absolutely nothing in common, as far as Sam could tell, except that they both liked movies, and they both were impressed by Booth. Tom's attachment to Booth would have made him unbearable if he didn't seem so helpless to it.

Sam had tried—more than once—to convince Tom that he shouldn't let Booth sponge off him. The last time, the tall, balding contractor had run a hand over his freckled, sun-damaged head, and squinted at Sam as though they were sharing a private joke. "Well, buddy, what can I say? I love old Booth. He's just bigger than everyone else, you know?"

"You like him because he's fat?"

"No, no. I like him because he's a good time, buddy. When Booth is around, he makes things happy."

This explanation stymied Sam. His godfather was so unaffectedly genial that to argue with him felt petty.

What traditional paternal support and guidance he received as a young man had come primarily from his godfather. At Sam's few misbegotten ventures into competitive sports, Tom was a lanky, arms-crossed fixture on the sidelines; and it was his godfather who had helped him glue together the thousand dementedly tiny pieces of a model of a P-51 Mustang. In high school Tom gave Sam his first job, helping out with his crew off the books. Once, the summer house they were renovating burned down overnight—a lightning strike. "Oh, sugar," his godfather said when they pulled up the drive into sight of the charred pit that only yesterday had been a two-story cottage. He was no more taken aback than he would have been if his shoelace had snapped. "Looks like we're back to Go."

On Sam's seventeenth birthday, it was Tom who handed him a packet of condoms.

The two had studied the small black rectangular box with the glitter-speckled neon script for several agonizing seconds. Tom cleared his throat. "There're instructions, I think."

Sam nodded.

"You're basically going to want to just stretch it on over your dick," his godfather had felt the need to clarify, and thank God, that was where they had left it.

It bore repeating: Tom was a good person, but he was no critic. Perhaps in light of his profession, even if he did grasp how broken the movie was, he might nonetheless have labored under the assumption that it could somehow be repaired, or that, like his ever spreading Sears kit house, might be improved by a few additions.

But he was a real audience, and he did seem to like it.

In the rave scene, right when Brunson screams at Roger, "Look at me!"—the addict's eye is swollen from where the fraternity brother hit him, and he is wobbling on his feet—Sam risked a peek at his godfather. Tom's eyes were shiny, and he was blinking rapidly.

Roger turns away from Brunson.

ROGER
I can't talk to him when he's like this.

Brunson blearily stumbles out of the frame, past Claire.

ROGER
(TO CLAIRE:)
Tell him I can't talk to him when he's like this.

She takes Roger's hand and he gives her a spin. They dance in the direction of the departed Brunson, and go kicking through a pile of the clothes that is all that remains of their friend.

CLAIRE
Do you ever think it might have helped? If you'd talked to him?

Roger shakes his head. He doesn't want to talk about Brunson.

They dance on.

Bald but for a half-halo of gray hair, face pecked and chiseled by forty years of outdoor labor, Tom sniffed. He smoothed his hands over the tails of his pilled flannel shirt. Sam patted him on the back.

"It's good." Tom gripped Sam's wrist. His eyes were red-rimmed. "It's really good. I liked it an awful lot, buddy. Growing up is a bitch no matter how you slice the thing, isn't it?"

Sam shrugged and thanked him.

"Your mother would have been pleased. I hope you know that—"

"Lunch, lunch, lunch!" Sam swept his half sister off the floor, holding her up in the air, swinging her so she giggled.

At the campus cafeteria, they took a table that faced onto the quad. It was the week of freshman orientation: a few guys were throwing a yellow Frisbee around; a couple of girls were stringing paper cranes from the branches of a yellow willow.

"Was it a masterpiece, Tom?"

Mina was pushing around roasted carrots on a plate.

"Yeah," said Tom. "Pretty much. Buddy here knocked it out of the park." He spoke through a mouthful of hamburger.

"There must have been something you didn't like," said Sam.

"No, I told you, it's good," said Tom.

Mina selected a carrot and raised it to the light, as if to assess its purity. "Tom wouldn't lie, Sam. Tom's not like that."

"I know, hon."

"If I was to criticize anything," said Tom, "it'd be that I wished there'd been more of the guy that lives in the john. He cracked me up."

"Poop. It's the funniest." Mina sighed languidly and stared out at the quad, wrist cocked so the carrot touched her chin. The girls decorating the willow, having exhausted their supply of cranes, had commenced hanging empty cigarette packs from the branches.

"Can I see?" Sam pulled over the folder of head shots that Mina had worked on during the film.

Across the forehead of the first actor, the sophomore brunette who had played Kira, Mina had written in red marker, *Crushed in a accident.* Sam flipped to the next head shot. *Shot in the brains over and over* was written on this one in green. The next actor, a smiling Olivia Das, was labeled simply *Drowned*. He went through some more: *Ate to much and exploded. Real dragons burnt him to ashes. Strangers got her.*

"This is terrific, Mina," said Sam. "Can I keep these?"

"Okay. Whatever. I'm going to rest my eyes for a second." She put her head on the table. She smiled at him. Her blue eyes fluttered shut inside the holes of her Zorro mask.

Sam slid the folder over to Tom. His sister's breathing regulated as she fell into an abrupt sleep. He studied her—lips parted, cheeks flushed, mask slid crooked up her sweet, pale temple—and the floor behind her seemed to gape. Sam envisioned the chair tipping back, her rag-doll body tumbling into darkness, into drugs and madness and the hands of evil men. It was melodrama, he knew, but Mina was the only kid sister he had.

There was also the distinct possibility that Sandra was an even worse parent than Booth. North of forty now, her ambitions for a career in the arts long since lapsed, she was still walking dogs for a living, and her never especially sparkling attitude had become so assiduously bleak that a person who didn't know her would probably assume that she was making a weird woe-is-me stab at humor. Sandra's days of wrecking other people's marriages were past. Now it was her time to roost, gargoylelike, paranoid and snappy, on the rubble of her union with Booth. Sam might have liked to take some petty satisfaction from his stepmother's downturn, except that she was also his sister's mother.

The last time Sam had spoken to her—he'd called to talk with his sister—Sandra had gleefully informed him that she had a growth on her forearm, and she figured that with her luck, it was pretty much a slam dunk it was cancer. "So tell Booth to get his party hat ready! I'm sure he'll want to throw a big shindig and give everyone free money once the witch is dead."

Among Sandra's craziest notions was that Sam's father was secretly rich. If this were true, it was a secret to Booth as well. Sam hadn't seen the man in an unstained pair of trousers since the mid-nineties. "What the hell, Sandra. What if Mina's listening on the other phone?"

Sandra puffed on whatever it was she was smoking, then smacked something—a fly, or perhaps some cheerful thought that had made the mistake of becoming corporeal in her presence—with what sounded like a magazine. "She's gotta learn sometime."

"Huh." Tom straightened the photos into a neat pile. *Family curst,* said the one on top. "I'm not sure it's any big deal. Kids like to press buttons."

"You really think that's all?"

"Yeah. Probably. But, if you're really worried, maybe you should talk to your pop."

"My pop."

Tom ignored his godson's tone and continued on cheerfully. "Old Booth's going to get a kick out of the guy in the john. When are you going to show it to him?"

The younger man made an openhanded gesture—*someday.*

"You still on the outs with Booth?"

"The way you say it makes it sound like I'm mad because he didn't say hi to me when we walked by each other at the mall."

"I don't mean for it to sound any way, buddy. I'm just asking."

"Look. Booth was never around. He never kept his promises, and he screwed off with anything that moved, and his career is—it's just the worst joke, you know. And he married Sandra, who you know very well is fucked up, and where's that supposed to leave Mina, Tom?"

Tom smiled; his godfather's front teeth were the color of weathered teak. "Your mom forgave him, buddy. Old Booth's the only dad you've got. He's not perfect, but he's got his merits."

In her sleep, Mina hiccupped.

"You know, Allie would have loved that movie. Loved it. You know that, don't you? Your mom was tough, but she'd have cried her eyes out."

Sam had no response to that. He'd never been able to predict his mother's reactions to films—and that was as far as he was willing to let his thoughts go on the subject.

For a few minutes, they didn't talk. Tom ate. Sam sipped his drink. The girls outside were hanging condoms on the tree. The wrinkled latex glistened in the sun. One of the girls rushed at the other and tried to wipe her spermicide-coated fingers on her friend's face. They laughed and grappled.

His godfather wiped his mouth with a paper napkin. "You need some cash for all this?"

Sam told him not to worry. He would put their lunch on Brooks's meal card. Too many drugs or not enough, Sam couldn't say, but lately, the AD never seemed to stop moving. He jittered from place to place, picking things up, putting them down, opening drawers, closing drawers, all the while enveloped in a reeking sulfurous bubble, the result of who knew how many struck match tips. Maybe it was the toll of all the hours he spent bowed over the editing machine, slashing at film. But Brooks had told Sam that he might as well have the meal card; he was too busy to eat, the AD said, and anyway, it ruined his appetite, the cameras watching him chew.

When Tom deposited Mina in the backseat of the taxi to take them to the train station, she woke up and stared at Sam from behind the eyeholes of her mask. "I'll call you," he said. "In the meantime, try not to fixate so much on death and tragedy. You're a kid, you've got nothing to worry about."

His sister yawned. "I had a dream about you."

"Yeah?" He picked a lock of sweaty blond hair from her forehead, tucked it behind her ear.

"You put a dynamite stick in your ear, and all of your hair caught on fire." To help him visualize this, Mina wiggled her fingers over the surface of her scalp. "But you were, like, 'I'm okay, I'm okay! Everyone relax, I'm okay.' I could tell you were just lying to make us feel better."

"Dreams are funny," said Sam. "Hey, don't ever put dynamite in your ear."

The cabdriver cleared his throat.

Mina didn't pay him any mind. "Oh! Oh! Dad's going to take me to Paris. We're going to raise hell. You should come with us, Sam."

"Maybe I will," he said, and felt sad, and thought, That son of a bitch.

Her look was disappointed. "I bet you won't."

Sam gave the roof of the car a slap. "I love you." He kissed his sister and stepped back. "Safe trip." He nodded to his godfather. "Tom."

As the car pulled away, Tom leaned over Mina to yell, "It was a damn decent movie, buddy! Makes you think, you know?"

The taxi turned onto the college's main drive and continued out the gate.

"My first review," said Sam.

■　■　■

The cafeteria had closed—it was late in the afternoon, past four—and Sam had to bang on the door until a line cook appeared to let him inside.

Brooks's meal card was on the table where he'd forgotten it. Sam pocketed the card. Out the window he saw the two girls seated on the grass beneath the tree. The paper cranes twisted lightly on their strings, and the plastic wrap of the cigarette packs shimmered. The condoms hung like dead withered things but glowed from within, a hearth orange. It was a magic tree. Sam wished he had a camera; he'd have liked to capture it on film.

A couple of raps on the glass caught the girls' attention.

One was a pudgy brunette with her temples sheared to the skin, and the other was a tall redhead with bangs in her eyes. They both wore the expressions of the deeply baked, blissful and staggered. They grinned at Sam from the opposite side of the Plexiglas. *I like your tree,* he mouthed.

The brunette threw her arms around her friend and giggled into the redhead's neck. Meanwhile, the redhead pursed her lips and placed a greasy finger to the window glass to draw a simple question in spermicide: WHY?

He held up his finger, *Wait,* and went outside to explain.

11.

In truth, it wasn't that much fun. For normal people—that is, for the vast majority who are not possessed with balletic flexibility—sex works better and makes far more sense in even numbers. Odd-numbered sex is a math problem. Everyone is calculating where to be, measuring distances, dividing resources, and inevitably, ending up with fractions. The effort to keep all the parties involved is likely to go well beyond pleasant frustration to end in discomfort and/or confusion. At some stage in the evening's exercises, for example, Sam bit a thigh only to realize that he was actually biting his own arm, gone numb beneath the weight of one of the girls.

It was, however, the last night when he felt about himself how he always had—like a person on the way—and because of that, he regarded it more wistfully than he would have otherwise. Afterward, Sam was who he would always be, complete, finished, wrapped.

■ ■ ■

Roughly eight years later, his best friend, Wesley Latsch, proposed a theory: the threesome had exhausted Sam's personal reservoir of good luck. "Why do you think that people win the lottery and then their lives fall apart?" asked his best friend.

Wesley shook his head, not at Sam but at the scrolling computer screen on the desk in front of him. Following a few aimless years in the advertising industry, Wesley had found a niche as a professional blogger. The genesis of his career realignment had been the penning of a list entitled "Seventy-Four Things That Cause Unnecessary Fatigue." The list—which included everything from #7, "Dating," followed by #8, "Laundry that must be air-dried," to "Jazz" at #28, and "Criticizing people face-to-face and being criticized face-to-face" at #30, to #53, "Waiting in lines," and #73, "British-style crosswords"—had led Wesley to appreciate that if he were ever to find happiness, it would be in a job that, at the very least, allowed him to work from home, at hours of his own choosing, and liberated from the hygienic regulations of the office world.

"Everything goes wrong because they have no luck reserves. The lottery uses it all up. Then they have no luck to fall back on, and all the negative forces in the world zap them."

"You make luck sound like sunscreen," said Sam.

"You had sex with two attractive women to whom you owed no attachment. For free. You ran your luck reserves down to nothing."

They were roommates then, on a Thursday in the fall of 2011, and shared an incommodious fourth-floor walk-up in Red Hook. The living room window held a view of a solvent-colored notch of the Gowanus Canal. Sam sat on the couch, surrounded by boxes of shit that people sent to Wesley.

Once he had concluded what he could no longer brook—i.e., unnecessary fatigue—Wesley determined that what he was ideally suited for was "cultural criticism." Besides his exacting nature, his term of service in the warrens of advertising had gained him a lifetime's worth of experience with unsatisfactory products. Thus was born his blog, *The Swag Hag Chronicles*. The Hag offered his thoughts on movies, music, books, electronics, toys, doodads, tools, household items, fair-trade coffee beans, hot sauce, whatever, so long as it was free. In this capacity, it was only under the most extraordinary circumstances that Wesley was forced to expose himself to the enervations of his list.

His legions of readers regarded the Swag Hag as a kind of one-man no-bullshit consumer-advocacy strike force. He offered only two grades: *NOT EVEN FOR FREE*, and *YEAH, I'LL TAKE IT*. About the latest Madonna album, Wesley had decreed, *Listening to this album made me feel like I was trapped inside a Tetris game while strangers slapped my fat rolls. NOT EVEN FOR FREE.* More favorably, about the Gourmet Artisan three-speed food processor, he wrote, *The average human heart weighs ten ounces. On high speed this processor turned ten ounces of raw chicken into a frappé in thirty seconds. Therefore, this processor can render your archenemy's heart drinkable in under thirty seconds. YEAH, I'LL TAKE IT.*

"What about people in, you know, the poorest, most war-torn countries? Places where there's guerrilla fighting and no clean water and asshole corporations are sucking up all the oil and precious metals?" Sam tore open a box from a company that made joke items. "Why are the people in those places so unlucky?"

To this, Wesley responded with a murmur of consideration. On his computer screen, there was a looping video of a German shepherd on its hind legs, punching a man in the face. Over and over, the dog's forepaw shot out, and the man stumbled backward, his comb-over flipped up into a tragic Mohawk.

Here was the nut of modern life, of Sam's life. Embarrassment was entertainment; people devoured humiliation like fucking bonbons. Every stupid thing you ever did was forever. Because of the camera on the bureau, the guy you most regretted fucking fucked you for all eternity. Because it was on film, your slip, your car crash, your drunken confession never ended; you kept slipping, crashing, slurring, continuously. When did it become such a crime, Sam wondered, to be careless? He felt very sorry for the dog, and sorrier for the man with the comb-over, and sorriest for himself.

In the box from the joke company, there was a selection of fake noses: bulbous noses, needle noses, flat noses, and crooked noses of various sizes and colors. They had nothing on Orson Welles's fabulous nose at the Museum of Cinema Arts, but they would be fine for a kid's Halloween getup. As he turned the shapes over in his hands, the rubber tacky against his skin, Sam was, naturally, reminded of his father.

The year his parents began their divorce proceedings, when Sam was eleven, Allie marked on a school form that his parents were separated. The elementary school guidance counselor, Mr. Alford, had called Sam in for a session.

"Tough times at home, huh? I'm awfully sorry to hear that. Not uncommon, though. Well, do you think you'll live?" the counselor asked Sam. Mr. Alford was widely considered to be a dork. On Halloween, for instance, he was one of the teachers who really went for it in the costume department. That year he had been the Scarecrow from *The Wizard of Oz*. Sam, hunched on a couch against the wall, noticed bits of shed straw mashed into the gray rug of the guidance office floor.

"I'll be okay," said Sam, and Mr. Alford said, "All right!" and suggested they play checkers for the rest of the period.

For a few minutes they pushed around the pieces. Alford asked if he could ask a question. Sam shrugged.

"Okay: your dad. I've seen a bunch of his movies at the drive-in—over in Hyde Park, you know? And he always looks so different from movie to movie. What do you think his big secret is?"

"False noses." Sam hopped a couple of the guidance counselor's red pieces. "He has these two big cases of false noses."

"No way!" Mr. Alford slapped his knee. "That's all? Prosthetic noses? Really? It's like his whole face changes!" He shook his head, grinning.

"Your turn," Sam said, and Mr. Alford said, "Oh! Right! Sorry!"

The descendant of that boy carefully replaced the lid on the box of noses. Sam twisted around to where a much bigger box sat on the floor, opened its flaps, and dropped the nose box inside. Then he gave the bigger box a shove with his foot. It fell over with a thump and vomited a gush of packing poppers.

On the computer screen, the German shepherd continued to strike. Wesley tapped his computer's space bar. "You've stumped me with this poor-places issue, Sam. I don't know why some countries and peoples are so unlucky. It could be I'm completely wrong. Maybe there's no such thing as luck at all. Maybe fucking and winning the lottery are just things that happen. I hope it goes without saying, I would much rather I'm wrong. I don't want to believe that your epic bone session with those two stoned girls created some karmic liability. Who would want to believe that?"

It was late afternoon. The low sun deepened the color of their sliver of the canal from glassy pink to impenetrable vermilion. A slab of Styrofoam sailed by on the current. Two small flags, U.S. and Puerto Rican, poked up from the Styrofoam. It was a brave and fragile picture, Sam thought.

"But let's not get too lost in these philosophical questions," Wesley went on. "Let's keep our eye on what's important: two girls at once. Whatever else, that goes in the win column."

12.

The next morning Sam did, without a doubt, as he extracted himself from the arms and legs of the two women, and the large mound of quilts that had served as their makeshift bed, feel like a terrific success. (The two actual beds in the room, both singles, were too small to accommodate the group. There it was again: the issue of engineering. "This is like an operation!" the redhead had complained sometime in the middle of the episode. "A *love* operation," the brunette had added in a sultry bass, and that cracked them up so much, a break was required to smoke more pot. Thoroughly stoned, Sam was emboldened to confess that he was feeling a tad inadequate. "You *are* inadequate," the brunette had said, "but that's what girls are into.")

While the sex itself hadn't been all that pleasurable, he found himself viewing it in experiential terms: just as he was sure that, with this first movie under his belt, his next would be even better, it seemed likely that, with practice, his group-sex skills could only improve. Wait, he had made a movie, hadn't he?

A new sensation of boundless possibility made every detail of that morning stand in relief. It felt as if he were home for the first time in a long time; it felt really, really good.

Dressed only in his boxer shorts, Sam carried the rest of his clothes in a bundle down the hall to the coed bathroom. When he urinated, he noticed that one of the girls had lightly written *CUTE!* in tiny letters in green ink on the head of his penis. Sam sighed happily at the sight. The letters were so ornate and feminine, furling at the tips. He had an urge to photograph it, except he didn't want any pictures of his penis floating around in the world. In the shower, the word faded to faint shadow.

The day's plan was: pack his gear, drive to Queens for a late-afternoon screening with Wassel and Patch. The producers had been making eager noises. "Two words," Wassel had told him when they spoke on the phone. "Rick, and Savini." Patch, who had also been on the line, chimed in, "No, no. Just one beautiful word, sluts: Ricksavini."

Sam put on the rest of his clothes, left the dorm, and started to walk across campus in the direction of the film department.

The magic tree, the yellow willow decorated in cranes and condoms, was a few steps from the dorm. Shrunken by their exposure to the air, the condoms had the appearance of discarded husks. Ah, he mused, how sorrowful is the short prime of the prophylactic bloom!

He continued along the sidewalk, which ran the campus's single long, looping one-way street. A Tibetan flag, hung from a dorm room window, waved majestically in the breeze. Someone's old-fashioned alarm clock went off in a pinging fire-alarm burst and was quickly silenced. The potpourri scent of the grounds, the late-blooming flowers and the fresh mulch, the dewy grass and the cut straw on the spring beds, mingled and made his eyes feel huge. On the stoop of one brownstone dorm, a bird-watcher sat peering through binoculars, focused on the top of a pine tree. A bicyclist in yellow and green spandex shot past with a thrum. Everything seemed auspicious, young, well intentioned. The chapped feeling at his groin made Sam feel strong, toughened. Even the thin, oily ribbon of smoke rising above the trees initially seemed to forecast good tidings, an all-clear signal lit by allied forces.

But—wasn't there familiarity in the sight? His nose itched, and Sam scratched it. He stopped, thought; there was something there, and it was unpleasant, like the rotten black underside of a felled tree, another smoke signal, another time, one that had broadcast not the all-clear but distress. The memory was too deep, though, and it slipped back into the murk.

He resumed walking.

As Sam turned onto the swoop in the path that drew away from the cluster of brownstone dorms to the brick complexes of the various academic buildings, he was compelled by an unprecedented urge to whistle. (Sam was not a whistler.) The tune that came to him was jaunty, a series of quick trills interspersed every few notes with a slippery-sounding bend. It took a few runs to place:

"The Huckster's Lament," the main theme in *New Roman Empire*, composed by Booth himself on the oue.

"The Huckster's Lament" was the song that played each time Booth's character, Dr. Archibald "Horsefeathers" Law, began to make his pitch. "I am not a miracle worker!" professes Dr. Law, and pauses sharply, drinking up the attention of his audience. This is when the theme begins—the pluck of the oue's strings is warped and drunken. "I am," he continues in a hushed voice, "a physician specializing in the deeper body. There is no magic about this. My medicine is, quite simply, a scientific treatment for the soul!"

It had been years since Sam had heard the riff or seen *New Roman Empire*. On a level of craft, his father's sole directorial credit had none; from a visual standpoint, the movie was static, as repetitive as a metronome: medium two-shot, close-up of speaker, close-up of reacting actor, again and again. Except for two or three brief dolly shots, that was it. A play on a stage was more dynamic. A comic strip was more dynamic.

New Roman Empire was so hokey, too, so unconcealed, such a "yarn." The con man tricks everyone into trusting him, and it's left to a few fearless young idealists—i.e., hippies—to stop him from razing the whole town. That was it. You could fit the entire thing on one side of an index card. It was a fairy tale.

Finally, there was the movie's lead character, a fun-house reflection of Sam's actual father—excessively theatrical, lying about everything, inexplicably beloved. When Dr. Law talked about his "scientific treatment for the soul," Sam could hear Booth—Sam was ten or eleven at the time—wondering why he was so insistent on bland truths. "Don't you want me to enliven your childhood?"

So it was peculiar that Sam should have found himself, on that marvelous first day of the rest of his life, whistling the sound track of a movie—and a man—that he objected to so completely.

In the middle of the lawn that fronted the building, a man outfitted in the gray jumpsuit of a Russell College maintenance worker stood spraying foam onto a smoldering pile of junk. A few ballerinas watched from a safe distance. As Sam approached, he could see that the junk was computer equipment. He stopped whistling. "What happened?"

"Vandals," said the maintenance worker. "What a disgrace. What a disgrace." He had a light accent—*de*-sgrace—and a full white beard.

"A complete and total *de*-sgrace," echoed one of the ballerinas, and her peers giggled.

Whatever the maintenance man said in reply, Sam didn't hear, because he was running up the steps, pushing through the oak doors and inside, jumping down two stairs at a time to reach the basement.

Set against the back wall of the editing suite was a long gray worktable. On the worktable was a series of pale shapes: squares, rectangles, machine-cut ovals. These shapes marked the places where, the previous day, the film department's various monitors and CPUs and keyboards and other pieces of equipment had been. One unremarkable pale oblong on the desk, bookended by two larger squares, had been left by an external hard drive containing Sam's work in progress, his film.

The panic lasted under a minute. Sam paced a few circles in the room, hyperventilating the damp air, trying to understand what it meant, how what had happened related to him.

The obvious answer clicked into place: it didn't mean anything, and it had nothing to do with him.

Someone had an ax to grind with the film department. Someone had received a C on a final project and had stewed about it all summer long and had decided to take revenge by flambéing the editing gear. It was a baroque and stupid scenario, exactly the sort of thing that some overdramatic, overmedicated little shit would come up with.

Jesus, Sam thought, what a waste.

Under the gray worktable stood a row of filing cabinets. He slid open a drawer in the middle. The drawer contained over a hundred DVD cases, lined up in neat rows of black plastic. Among these cases were two copies of the assembly of *Who We Are*—even before screening it for himself, he had made these—as well as the video transfers from the film lab. There were, as well, copies of several extended sequences that he had stitched together in the process of assembling the assembly. Everything was backed up.

He pulled the two DVD cases at the front of the drawer, the complete cuts that he had burned onto blank discs the previous morning. Sam popped open the first case. It was empty. He looked in the next case—

also empty. Slowly at first, he began to go through the rest of the cases in the drawer—empty, empty, empty—until finally, in his fever to open them, he ripped the covers off of some of the cases, snapping them at their plastic hinges and tossing them aside.

They were all empty. There was not a single disc on a single spindle.

Sam climbed the basement stairs and went back outside. He strode to the thigh-high pile of burnt, foamy computer pieces. The maintenance man hadn't moved.

"It almost looks like some kind of art, doesn't it?" The maintenance man stroked his jolly bush of a snow-white beard.

Sam put the heel of his sneaker against the torched, hollowed husk of the computer monitor and pushed. The monitor toppled with a dull crunch. On the blackened grass beneath it was a large puddle of silver plastic, embedded with the finlike protuberances of a few DVDs that hadn't melted completely.

"Oh," said a ballerina. "Cool."

The maintenance man agreed. "Yes. Kind of neat."

The full horror of the situation was evident: all of the digital material was gone; Sam would have to order new transfers and re-edit the entire movie from scratch. He would need to placate Wassel and Patch for at least a week while he built a new assembly. Even doing that—because fall classes were about to open—was predicated on his finding a new editing suite, which would likely require tapping Brooks for more money. As distasteful as that might be, it was the least of his concerns at that moment.

Sam returned to the basement. He took out his cell phone and dialed the film lab in Astoria.

"Fuck," said Sam. "Motherfucker."

"Pardon?" The receptionist at the film lab, Celluloid Services, had picked up.

"Sorry," said Sam. "I'm having a bad morning. Someone just tried to destroy me." He asked how quickly they could make new transfers, how much it would cost, whether it would help if he drove in to pick them up himself.

While the receptionist left him on hold, Sam permitted himself to fantasize about capturing the vandal who had committed this atrocity. Optimally, he'd get the bastard on-camera and film his confession. He wondered if Brooks would consent to hiring a private detective, preferably an unscrupulous one who wasn't averse to beating a few people to get to the truth.

Sam could feel his mind gleefully skipping away, like some demented man-child escaped from a remote sanitarium. His outrage was scrabbling through the dense hedges walling the facility off from society, and now it was heading for the picturesque village in the valley below, where there were people to gnaw.

It was so stupid and pointless. He felt ambushed, picked on, and very, very angry.

To alleviate some tension, he went to the poster of *New Roman Empire* and ripped the blindfold of electrical tape off Booth's face, tearing away a strip of poster.

The receptionist was on the line again. "Your partner checked everything out."

"Uh-uh. I don't have a partner." This display of ineptitude momentarily buoyed Sam. There was not a single other competent person in the entire world; for the benefit of society, he had to persevere. "You looked up the wrong account."

The receptionist asked if an individual named Brooks Hartwig, Jr., had signed for the account with a Visa ending in the digits 1512. Sam acknowledged that this was so; Brooks was his assistant. "Call him whatever you want," said the receptionist, "but he cosigned, and he paid, and he already checked it all out."

"Checked out what already? I'm not following you."

"The negative. The film. Everything."

Sam told her she wasn't making sense.

The receptionist spoke with exaggerated slowness. "The man. Who paid. For this account. Closed it out. He took the negatives. Of the film. *The* film. He carried it away. He carried it out the door. Beyond the walls of this place. He could do that. Because he paid. Does. That. Make. Sense?"

The white-bearded maintenance man was still pondering the foamy wreckage of the editing suite. The ballerinas were gone. The sun, appropriately, had slid behind a bank of metallic clouds, and the bright morning was now a dim afternoon.

"You are really upset?" The maintenance man was quizzical.

Sam didn't stop or respond, only threw a brief, irritated glance over his shoulder at the man as he walked away. The connection between them from that night in the parking lot of the Hoe Bowl when they had exchanged salutes—the man in the driver's seat of Brooks's Porsche—had not yet resolved itself in Sam's mind. It wasn't until later, in the dark of the basement theater, when the maintenance man was projected across the screen in all his glory, that Sam finally knew him.

The ramifications of something having happened to the film, the actual celluloid, were too vast to contemplate unless there was absolutely no other choice. He focused on finding Brooks.

First he tried the AD's dorm room. The door was, as was customary for Brooks, unlocked. Sam threw it open without knocking: no one.

The squalor inside—unmade bed, scattered clothes, massive punch bowl on the desk filled with black water and the stubs of several hundred dead kitchen matches—did suggest that the AD had been present recently.

Sam checked the computer lab, the student parking lot, the cafeteria, the health center, and the auditorium. He peered through the windows of the gymnasium—a place he could not conceive of Brooks visiting voluntarily—and observed nothing but dust phantoms hovering above the basketball court. There was no sign of Brooks around any of these places.

While he hurried from location to location, he repeatedly called the AD's cell phone. It went to voice mail without a ring. He kept leaving messages: "I'm trying to find you, Brooks," "I'm still trying to find you, Brooks," "You're not here, either, Brooks," and so on.

At the science library, Sam descended all the way to the bathroom in the deep stacks where they had filmed Rick Savini's scenes in the toilet stall.

Here, he rested on the toilet lid to catch his breath. Sweat made his shirt tight on his chest, and his calves tingled with pinpricks. The walls of the stall were covered in the signatures of the cast and crew. The basement air had a thick submarine texture. Sam held his head.

An exchange from Brooks's short film about the haunted animal heads occurred to him:

The elk, on its plaque above the fireplace, watches as the taxidermist (Brooks) stuffs a squirrel at a rough wooden table. Its jet eyeballs slide back and forth. "You know that there are—things," it says. "Around you in the air. Floating. All kinds of things, little man. But you can't see them."

"What are they doing?" asks the taxidermist. He sets aside the squirrel with trembling hands.

"Passing judgment," says the elk. It chuckles dryly. "You never even knew you were on trial, did you?"

Brooks had mentioned to Sam that he received a C on the film. It was one of those winter nights in the AD's dorm room. Brooks was watching the backward movie on his laptop. Sam was in the bed. The actress on the computer screen jerked and staggered as she traveled in reverse along a sidewalk, a movement that suggested, troublingly, the pull of giant invisible wires, of a giant invisible fishing rod, reeling in a catch.

"They said it was 'grotesque' and 'tacky.' But, like, if they can't accept the world that's right there in front of them . . ." Brooks twisted around and extended himself across the rug on his stomach, to reach under the bed where Sam lay.

Brooks emerged after a moment with a box of kitchen matches. He fished out a match and attempted to strike it off his belt buckle—nothing. "Anyhow," he said, "'yay' for passing, right?" On his second attempt, the match ignited.

A message buzzed Sam's cell when he emerged from the library. It was Wassel. "Hey, man, your assistant delivered the DVD this morning. He seemed super crazy, by the way. Extremely impressed that you have your own personal Renfield. Anyway, should we watch this without you or what? I thought you were going to give us the live and in-concert director's commentary."

The sweat on Sam's body turned cool as he listened, and his legs went wobbly. The relief knocked the wind out of him. He dropped onto a bench. Hard pellets of rain started to fall, and it took him two tries to dial the producer's number with slippery fingers.

"I'm on my way," Sam told him. "And for God's sake, keep that DVD safe."

■ ■ ■

In Ossining, Sam stopped for coffee and a fill-up. While he was inside the gas station, his phone buzzed again. The cell's display read BROOKS.

Sam stepped outside and huddled under a rusted overhang to keep from getting wet. The dirt parking lot was a brown pool shivering with raindrops.

"Brooks," he answered. What he ought to say next—the right question—eluded him. He didn't understand what had happened, what was happening, how exactly his AD was involved. All he dared say was, again, "Brooks."

From the other end of the phone, there was quick, shallow breathing, and behind that, the hollow thud of wood battering against wood. "Brooks! Brooks!" someone cried.

"I can't talk long." The AD was breathless.

"Why can't you talk long? What's going on, Brooks?"

"Everyone's upset with me here. I burned down Mom's cupola. Are you upset with me, Sam?"

"I'm not upset with you," said Sam. "I'm confused. I'm really, really—confused. Brooks, what did you do with the film?"

The AD sobbed, laughed, hiccupped. The thudding noises continued. "Are you getting this? I bet you love this. Great material, huh?"

"What?" asked Sam. "Getting what?"

"Not you," said Brooks. "Someone else."

Sam thought of the countless times he had seen Brooks push at the air, how often the AD had chuckled about the ghostly documentary crew he claimed to see.

"We called the fire department!" cried the distant voice.

"Uh-huh! I'm sure!" Brooks yelled back.

"Brooks," said Sam. "You went to the lab, and you took out the film—"

"I didn't realize it was already so flammable, right? Like, I knew it was flammable, but I didn't know it was, like, nuclear. So the lighter fluid was superfluous and . . . And Mom is not happy."

Words came out of Sam's mouth: "You didn't realize what was so flammable?"

"The short ends," said Brooks. "Our film's short ends."

"My film didn't have any short ends."

Heavy objects were shaking loose, falling to the ground in an avalanche of bangs and crashes. "I'm not sure how long my fortifications are going to hold, Sam."

Across the boiling lot, at the gas pumps, a fluttering plastic banner advertising a two-for-one wiper-fluid deal broke one of its plastic ties. The banner unfurled from its remaining tie and crackled loudly in the wind.

Sam pictured the flatbed in the closet of the editing suite and listened in his head to the rustling, whirring sounds that came from under the door—the slicing sounds. He saw a razor squeaking back and forth, and the excess celluloid wafting to the ground.

There was more knocking and cracking and bumping.

"Go away!" Brooks screamed. "You're invading my privacy! This is my room!"

"Brooks." Sam pressed against the cold cement wall and sank to a crouch. "What were you cutting at the flatbed?"

"I told you. I was trimming off the short ends from our movie." Sam could hear him dragging something to brace the door that was under assault. "Whatever, right?"

"No—no. Whatever, wrong. What did you do to my movie?"

"But listen, I called because I don't want you to worry. Because, yay! Yay, they're going to love it! Everyone is going to love it!"

In front of Sam, the parking lot was a lake. "You burned my film? The actual film?"

"Yes, but we don't need it now. The movie's all done. It's all short ends once you've locked down the final cut, right? And I'm telling you, they're going to love it." Wood splintered on Brooks's end of the phone. "Oh. Wow . . . I think they actually did call the fire department."

A rush of air filled Sam's lungs, and a wild giggle swirled up his throat. Everything was going to be okay. "I don't believe you. This is a practical joke. Amazing, Brooks. You totally had me." The director blurted a laugh. "I mean, incredible. And I definitely deserved it. I've been an asshole. You got me."

"*Sam.*" Brooks teased the name out, speaking it the way people in bad movies said, "*See? Food,*" when they were trying to befriend a non–English speaker or a feral child. "*Sam.*"

The ax struck the door again. Furniture legs groaned.

Tears were rolling down Sam's cheeks. God, what a prank! "But seriously, what did you do with all the film, the DVDs, the transfers? And the editing equipment and the hard drive?" The sheer involvement of the ruse was breathtaking! Brooks must have gone to the trouble of finding junk computer equipment to destroy. "I mean, Julian's going to want his stuff back. School starts on Monday."

"Sam, all that matters," said Brooks, "is our movie. Forget about that stuff. It's all gone, right? So what's the point, right? Nothing matters except the final cut, right?"

There was a last crash—the door coming down—and something made of glass shattered. Brooks wailed, "I told you I was sorry, Mom!" and the connection cut.

Sam went back inside to pay. When he stepped out again, he walked across the lot in no hurry.

The hard drive was crisped. The DVDs were melted plastic. The reels were gone. Brooks had put a match to them—a kitchen match, undoubtedly. The exact parameters of the devastation were not yet clear to Sam—there was the DVD at Bummer City—but he could perceive the shape. Soon it would be entirely visible. So what was the rush? The rain soaked his shoulders, and the muddy water covered his sneaker tops.

The loose two-for-one banner snapped outward from its remaining tie, flopping and waving spastically. The sight bothered Sam. It made him think of hair-metal rockers, of some guy in spandex and heavy makeup wagging his tongue around a microphone. Something about the banner's flapping seemed ambiguously dangerous, too. Sam decided to fix it. He set his coffee on the hood of his car and went over.

The plastic length was like a section of tarp, heavy and less flexible than it appeared. Sam pulled the loose side of it straight, toward the island of gas pumps and the stanchion from which it had broken free. The plastic rectangle captured the wind like a sail and bowed. Sam's wet sneaker soles slid on the wet surface of the cement island, then slipped, and he sat down. The gusting banner towed him, ass bouncing along the cement as he kicked his sneakers for purchase, carrying him over the lip of the island and, with a splash, into the deep water of the parking lot.

13.

"Hey, Wassel." Sam had parked his car, badly, and lurched through the rain to the door.

Wassel took in the director's appearance. "Hey, Aquaman."

"Oh, boy, look at you." A pretty young woman had joined them in the entryway of the house in Astoria. She wore tight black jeans and a man's dress shirt. "I'm Greta," she said, and stuck out her hand. "I'm the boys' assistant."

Sam said he was pleased and held up his muddy hands in a *don't shoot* gesture. It had crossed his mind that he might just as well turn the car around and retreat to the apartment, go to bed—whatever Brooks put on the DVD, whether it was the short about the taxidermist or some hodgepodge of scenes from *Who We Are* or something else, it was an apocalypse, and Sam didn't believe he needed to know anything more than that. He didn't turn around, though. He followed the signs, crossed the bridge, and resigned himself to the baseline comfort of knowing that once this was done—once they'd seen whatever Brooks wanted them to see, viewed the corpse on the steel table—there was nothing else to do.

"I fell down," Sam explained.

"Yeah, you did," said Wassel. "You fell right down in the mud." His Esso work shirt identified him as MERLE, ASST. MECHANIC.

Greta went to find Sam something to wear.

The two men waited in the entryway. On the wall was a lobby card for a movie titled *Cannibals of the Yukon*. The artwork showed a grizzled 49er's head, elaborately mustached and sucking on a cheroot, cut off from the body and served up in a bed of parsley atop a gold salver.

"Say. You okay there, brother?" asked Wassel.

"I'm uneasy about the condition of the film," said Sam. The details were exhausting and irrelevant. Once the DVD was playing, he was confident that the situation would swiftly become clear enough.

Wassel chucked him on the shoulder. "No worries! We know it's just a rough cut."

Patch appeared. He had been upstairs working on his state quarter collection. "Finally got a Delaware from the Denver mint."

Wassel gave him a high five.

"There's a Philadelphia mint, and there's a Denver mint, and around these parts, it's mostly Philadelphia." Patch registered Sam's immobile expression and mistook his not giving a shit for lack of comprehension. "So a Delaware quarter from the Denver mint is a crucial score."

"I don't care about state quarters. I don't even think about them." Sam didn't mean to say it aloud, but now that it was out, he felt no regret.

The producers exchanged glances. Water plinked from the tails of Sam's shirt. Patch cleared his throat. Wassel said, "Hey, no kidding, we are psyched to see this film of yours. Psyched to the utmost."

Patch seconded. "One fucking word. *Ricksavini.*"

Greta reappeared with a black garbage bag. "It was all I could find."

They cut a neckhole in the bottom of the garbage bag, and Sam drew it over his head and wore it like a tunic. The four of them trooped down to the screening room, the director last in line, rustling.

A dozen plush red seats faced a wall-sized screen. In the rear, on a raised platform, a DVD projector was mounted. On one side of the room was a concession stand appointed with a popcorn maker, a variety of candy, and in a row between the Milk Duds and the M&M's, several neat packets of cocaine.

Greta started a batch of popcorn. Patch chopped some coke on the glass counter of the concession stand. Wassel slipped the DVD from its sleeve and inserted it in the projector. While the popcorn began to rattle and ricochet in the pan, they took turns snorting up lines with a rolled buck.

"You want to introduce the fucker?" Wassel lifted his head, squeezed the bridge of his nose. He passed the rolled bill to the director.

Sam took it, dropped his head, did a couple of bumps. Ice crackled along the ridges and valleys of his brain. He felt the ecstasy of unnecessary cells breaking away, of fresh, sleek contours emerging and emerging and emerging. He suddenly comprehended what it was to be a crystal, and then he was a crystal.

"The real butter," said Patch to Greta.

"Yup," she replied, first sweeping the leftover coke dust off the counter and onto the fresh bucket of popcorn.

"Sure," said Sam. "I'll introduce the fucker."

■ ■ ■

Standing before the screen, damp-legged, draped in a trash bag, Sam addressed his audience of three. Wassel, Patch, and Greta sat smiling, shiny-lipped, powder ringing their nostrils.

"I honestly doubt that words can do justice to what you are about to see. All I know is that I wrote a script and we filmed it. It was a story about how we start off trying to make something new, but by the time we figure out what that means, we've lost the spark. We're already locked on some track, the same as our parents.

"I really started working on this film when I was a kid, when I saw a whole bunch of my toys die crossing my rug. That changed me, I think.

"Then my parents divorced. My dad wasn't around much, and when he was, he lied and he let me down. So what, right? Your dad was a prick. Join the club, right? But a while ago, my mom took me to the bus station, and then she died, and maybe that doesn't matter to you, but it's kind of a big deal to me.

"So I made a film.

"Probably not this film. What we're going to watch now, I don't know. Something upsetting, I bet, but I don't know. As far as my film goes, I want to dedicate it to my mother, who sometimes frustrated me but deserved a lot more than she got."

Sam thumped down into his front-row seat. The other three clapped. "*Ricksavini*," said Patch. Wassel pronounced that it was time to fire the bitch up. "Rock and roll," Greta exclaimed through a mouthful of popcorn.

For the first five minutes, everything was—normal.

The camera, positioned in the center of the quad, swings rightward. We take in the dark dorms, the great trees shrouded and blue in the predawn, and above the archway of the library, the illuminated clockface, arms arranged at four o'clock. At the next cut, the camera is in the center of the quad again, but it is morning. When we swing right this time, dawn is coloring in the panes of the dorm windows, and the library clock reads six o'clock.

Cut to Roger asleep in a tangle of sheets. Cut to Kira, slapping her snooze button. We shuffle through the rest of the characters, all in bed: Florence, awake, smilingly immersed in a copy of *The Da Vinci Code*; Claire, sleeping, hugging her pillow tight; Hugh, crashed out in his clothes, holding an empty Heineken bottle; Brunson yawning as he does curls in his boxer shorts. Cut back to Roger, no longer alone in bed, Claire asleep against his chest, hugging him tight. Cut back to Kira, slapping the snooze button again, and where before her wrist was bare, now it's tattooed with a bleeding heart. We find Florence again, now reading Wittgenstein, a grim set to her mouth; Hugh continues to sleep but in a different position, buck-naked and facedown amid a scattering of Pabst cans; and Brunson is performing pull-ups in his doorway, hair damp with sweat.

Under Sam's ribs, something shifted and he remembered to exhale.

The split second of false relief: it was the stock trick of every shlock-meister who ever snapped a magazine into a camera. It was the hunted woman at the foot of the dock, her back to the glassy lake; it was the good man catching the rail of the caboose, pulling himself up with an *oh ye of little faith* wink to his faithful sidekick; it was the war-torn lovers ten years after the Blitz, jostling shoulders in the flower market, gazing at each other as if they'd each been shaken awake from the same nightmare.

A title card announced:

In Association with Bummer City Productions
A Dolan & Hartwig Film

The murderer's gray hand rips the water and grabs her ankle; a puff of smoke rises from the embankment, the good man keeps grinning even as the hole opens in his throat and black blood leaks out and the sniper's rifle reports; his wife appears, her husband appears, and not a word passes between them before they move apart forever.

And Sam fell for it.

In this one context, at least, he knew that his father had raised him better.

There is a stationary shot of a forest, a shot Sam didn't film. It is of an elm grove that lies beyond the field where the festival is held. A faraway figure bounds between trees.

Back to Brunson as he skips down the steps of his dorm, carrying a six-pack. "Getting an early start?" asks Kira. She lies on a blanket in the grass with her boyfriend and plays with his fingers as she speaks. "Who says I ever stopped?" Brunson replies. "Today's the day we find out who's who, separate the bros from the chaff. Know what I'm saying?"

At that, the film cuts back to the elm grove. The focus slams forward—a seamless programmed zoom, the kind of technological flash that Sam would never sanction—and the viewer rushes over the deadfall, moving at bullet speed toward the figure.

"I already know all about you, Brunson." We're in the quad again. Kira calls after the receding figure. "I know who you are." He flips her the bird without turning or stopping.

A creature dances in the clearing between the trees, white hair and white beard blown out in masses of curls and corkscrews; eyes sunken in charcoal-colored eye shadow; a pair of goatish horns are somehow attached to its head. The animal's hooves clump across the Acadian stage. It plays a pan flute as it gambols—"The Huckster's Lament," naturally, the short flats teasing the long sharps, the musical equivalent of a cat chasing its tail— and its furry brown shanks bounce and shake like Chinese dragons on parade. It is a satyr, and the only thing that it wears is the furry leggings.

Sam recognized him then—the maintenance man, the man from Brooks's car.

The jig brings the satyr around in a circle to face the camera head-on. The satyr's penis swings, actually swings, like a bell clapper against the insides of his knees; the penis is as gnarly as a tree root, as long as a hatchet handle, an instrument so appalling that it cannot really be described, only compared to other things.

For everything that he couldn't understand about what Brooks had done, the director in Sam could grasp at least this: the desire to put a wonder to print.

The satyr ceases to play and stops with one hoof hanging in the air; the hoof must be some kind of shoe covering designed to look like a hoof, and to make hoof beat–like noises. He lowers his panpipe. His white-haired ball sack dangles gruesomely. His penis—exists. It is there. "Who are we?" asks the satyr.

Behind Sam, Patch made a wordless noise, expressive of discomfort. "This, like, troubles me. So, so much," he managed. Popcorn crunched between someone's teeth.

The animal of pleasure and darkness and myth closes his deep-set eyes. "We are all Jezebels." His regret is heartfelt. He isn't a bad actor.

There is a crinkly noise as the satyr begins to urinate on the forest floor. This, too, somehow suggests ruefulness.

For another seventy-one minutes, it goes on. During this time the satyr discovers an issue of *Hustler* beneath a rock and masturbates to a photograph of a nude woman wearing a bear's head, sits in the crook of a tree to pop the zits on his thighs, weeps and whispers and moans and dances, rolls around in the dirt and leaves, plays his pan flute some more, engages in intercourse with a log, and otherwise surrenders his every human inhibition. His convulsions are intercut with the anxious lives of Sam's college students, as if he is their dream, or vice versa.

Besides Sam, Greta was the only one to make it all the way through.

In the middle of the film, during a series of quick cuts between the satyr—boner-laden—stalking a woodchuck along the banks of a stream and Hugh fecklessly searching the stacks of the science library for Merlin's bathroom, Patch became convinced the cocaine was poisoned. The producer had dropped to the floor, crawled out of the room on his forearms, and locked himself in a closet. Wassel had called Sam a son of a bitch and rushed out to obtain quaaludes.

Greta ejected the DVD from the player, returned it to the blank case, and handed it to Sam. He shrugged out of the garbage bag and gave it back to her. They went upstairs.

"I liked it," said Greta. Her eyes were bloodshot, one slightly wider than the other. Several times he had heard her gasping, on the verge of hyperventilating. "I really liked it. Did he really have sex with the tree, or was that a special effect?"

It had certainly appeared unsimulated to Sam. "Yes," he said. "I think he really had sex with a tree."

He felt like he was standing next to himself, like his spirit—soul, whatever—had been knocked loose from his being in some kind of amazing collision. If he stayed calm, perhaps that other phantasmal piece of him fluttering nearby might regain its bearings and decide to slip back inside his body.

Sam opened the front door. Wet, humid air washed in. The rain was as heavy as before. A parking ticket was plastered to his windshield. "Goodbye. Please tell everyone that I'm sorry."

"But what does it mean? The movie?"

"What do you think it means?"

"I asked you first." Greta waved a finger at him.

Sam wondered if this was what it felt like to have a concussion. "It means that everything's a joke," he said.

"Everything?" she asked.

"Everything."

She put a hand on her hip. Her expression said she thought he was being facetious. "But it was so sad."

14.

Sam drove four hours north with the DVD case on the passenger seat beside him, and when he parked outside his unit of the development, he left the case sitting there. Though the disc contained all that remained of his work, the fragments meant nothing. Sam had, as he piloted the car along the rain-swept straights of I-87, halfheartedly considered the idea of extracting what was left from Brooks's satyr stuff and, after a bit of calculation, came to the conclusion that it would be pointless. The movie had been gutted of at least forty minutes of irreplaceable material, then refilled with insanity. The film Sam had made was gone. The DVD was merely an artifact. He supposed he'd throw it out.

Inside, Sam sat at the desk, watching the raindrops pepper the parking lot and the pothole bubble. He pressed his forehead to the glass and let the cool of it spread from temple to temple. Thoughts of Brooks, of Brooks's superendowed maintenance man, of whatever it was the two had intended, of how badly he had let everyone down—Tom and Wesley and Polly and his mother and Mina and Rick Savini and Julian and the crew—entered and exited his mind as swiftly and meaninglessly as a solid block of technical credits scrolling off the edge of a screen.

An impulse that he could not justify made his hand reach for the telephone. As illogical as it was for him to want to contact Booth at such a baneful moment—to seek consideration from the least considerate person—the compulsion was powerful, nearly reflexive. It was like in those diners that still had tableside jukeboxes, whose pages of hit songs generally dated from the mid-nineties. Sam couldn't recall the last time he'd encountered one that worked (not since childhood), yet he could never resist plugging in a quarter and pressing the buttons.

Sam picked up the phone and dialed. It rang three times before his father answered. "Yes? Who is this?"

He cleared his throat. "It's me, Dad. Sam."

"Samuel! How lovely to hear from you! Let me ring you right back, all right? A Gypsy caravan rolled up a few moments ago, and I just need to send them on their way." A woman laughed in the background; music was playing, other voices. "Five minutes, ten at the most."

"Oh, sure," said Sam, realizing that he had no idea where in the world his father was at that moment. Booth had already hung up.

He climbed into bed, waited for a half hour or so before accepting that this jukebox was as broken as all the others, and gave himself over to sleep.

In the morning, before thoughts of anything else—before the movie, even—Sam awakened to remember what Mina had told him about how their father had promised to take her to Paris. Booth, compulsive prevaricator that he was, was at it again, showering disenchantment on someone else's childhood. Sam wasn't going to let him get away with it. The time had come to inform his father that if he made Mina any more promises he couldn't keep, Sam was going to punch him in the face.

Aside from that, there was the matter of a certain prosthetic nose—puffy, with a very realistic mole—that Sam had only just recalled. While he was at it, he planned to insist that the money his father owed be handed over immediately. The damned nose had cost him $587.34.

He thumbed in his father's number. There was a single ring, followed by a recording explaining that the customer he had dialed was currently unavailable. In other words, Booth's payment was, as of the morning, officially overdue again.

Sam packed his few things. He was decamping for Brooklyn; he could stay in Red Hook with Wesley until he figured out what came next.

Outside, after the deluge, it was sunny and chilly, and everything at ground level had an icing of mud.

Sam got in the car. He started to reverse, checked in the rearview mirror, and stamped on the brake. He put the car back in drive and went forward into his space. Sam got out.

Perhaps ten feet behind his vehicle's rear bumper was a yawning black pit.

The night's torrent had caused the parking lot's big pothole to expand into a sinkhole. The pavement had fractured in a webbed pattern, and huge chunks of macadam had spilled into the hole. The resulting cavity was about the shape and size of a luxury hot tub.

Sam carefully approached an edge and peered into the well. The sides gave way in a jagged slide of ocher-colored mud. At the deepest visible point was a slick of pearly water streaked with oil, but where the absolute bottom lay was impossible to tell.

He returned to his car.

Instead of reversing, he drove forward, bounced over the curb, and crushed a low hedge. Sam executed a wide, spraying arc across the muddy lawn of the apartment complex before thumping down over another section of curb and back onto the drive that led out and away.

At the bottom of the housing development's driveway stood a large corrugated trash can. Sam braked, buttoned down the passenger-side window. He plucked the DVD case from the passenger seat and flicked it in the direction of the trash can. The case struck the lip and clattered onto the pavement of the entryway median. Close enough, Sam thought, if he thought anything.

COMING ATTRACTIONS

(1969)

1.

To the unenlightened, the derelict Western New York Limited switching yard was an all-purpose dump, a place for the local populace to deposit junked cars and other pieces of large-scale detritus free of charge. It wasn't a proper scrap yard, per se, but no one seemed to mind; it was convenient, and the railroad sure as hell wasn't coming back.

To the disaffected sorts who squatted there—dropouts, dodgers, runaways, the homeless—it was known as Tomorrowland. Allie could see two opposing ways to interpret the title: either the designation was intended as predictive of an apocalyptic future, littered with stinking and rusting garbage, where there were scant reserves of clean water; or, less bleakly, it was meant as a comment on the residents' cooperative use of very limited resources—makeshift shelter, scarce food and water, a dearth of hygiene products—the label for a rough model of the way forward, a stepping stone in the direction of a more sensible world.

That morning Allie, who was depressed for a number of reasons but most of all because she had not taken a shower, had a cup of coffee, or slept in a bed for three days, leaned toward the former.

From behind the wheel of the lifeless Pontiac Parisienne where she currently dwelled, Allie watched a tall, heavyset man hop from the tracks and surf down the gravel embankment to the flat ground of the yard. His enormous grin was visible at fifty yards. If the car still worked, she would have seriously considered running him over.

The heavyset man stopped at a spot in the center of the yard. He picked up a hubcap, swished it around, nodded to himself, and then whacked it viciously three times against the bent front fender of a sepulchral DeSoto. The clangs resonated around the embankments, redirecting off the ten thousand metal surfaces, thrumming on the air and through the ground. Allie felt the reports through the driver's seat of the Parisienne and instinctively clenched the wheel.

"Good morning, men and women of the future!" the stranger cried. "My name is Booth Dolan, and I am a filmmaker. I am most keen to begin photographing my maiden production, entitled *New Roman Empire*, but I lack one vital element: a cast.

"That is where I hope you good people will come in."

In the wake of this racket, the residents of Tomorrowland emerged, somewhat shakily, from their various berths: Mayor Paul parted the moldy red curtains at the rear of the front end–less hearse that was his residence. Marty and Anissa crawled from their bed in the doorless green boxcar. Adam and Brittany shuffled onto the porch of the depot to blink out from beneath the lichen-crusted eave. Allie shouldered open the door of the Parisienne and climbed out.

The only one who didn't show a face was Randall, the paranoiac inhabiting the engine-less hollow beneath the hood of the DeSoto that Booth Dolan had gonged. "Fuck you, man!" Randall's voice came through the airholes punctured in the rusted metal. Allie had never seen the man, but it was said that at night he sometimes felt safe enough to leave his nest to forage.

"Oops! My friend, I did not realize you were in there. I am very sorry." Booth flipped aside the hubcap and gave the hood of the car a gentle pat.

The stranger wore a black suit. His jacket was wrinkled and dusty-looking, and his thick, hairy wrists protruded from the cuffs of his white shirt. The hair at his temples was buzzed military-short. The morning sun threw his shadow hugely against a segment of discarded train siding propped against a heap of tires. It was easy to imagine him playing football, a position on one of the lines, or manning first base. Whoever this Booth person was, he clearly wasn't one of them.

"You drunk?" asked Marty.

"No. I'm inspired," said Booth.

Marty yawned. "Oh. That's okay, then."

"Hold on, mister. This is private property." Allie had come up beside the DeSoto.

Booth tipped his head to her. "Pardon my intrusion. And you are?"

"Allie. What's it matter?"

"It could not matter more." His mouth pulled into a solemn frown.

"Oh, please." Three days earlier Allie had been a shy, whispery freshman on a music scholarship in good standing at SUNY-Hasbrouck. Today she was petulant, distrustful, and near to washing out. Her transformation had occurred as the result of an introductory meeting with her adviser, Professor Murton. They had been alone in the second-floor studio, and at his request, she had sat down to play a piece by Bach.

A few measures in, the professor clapped his hands to stop her. "No, no. That won't do, my dear." Professor Murton rose from his seat and paced around on the hardwood floor, tapping an index finger against his philtrum. A bald man in gray suspenders, he had a quick, purposeful walk that conveyed an intense, searching intellect.

Allie had to concentrate to keep from squirming on the bench. She wasn't used to being critiqued, let alone by someone so experienced and important.

"You have talent, but . . . there is a tightness. A snarl in you, in your playing," he announced after a few seconds. He made a scissoring gesture with his fingers. "It needs cutting loose."

"Oh." Come to think of it, Allie thought, her stomach did feel a little tight. "Okay."

"Good. Good, good. Then what I'd like you to do," he said, approaching to lay a hand on the chest of the piano, "unless you have any objections, of course, is this: play the 'Etude' again and— Actually, no, not that, something much simpler. 'Für Elise'? Yes, that's it. You play 'Für Elise,' but *standing up*. No bench. *Standing up*. Are you with me?"

"Yes, I understand." She smiled to show how eager she was to please him and to liberate her technique.

"Right, then," said Professor Murton. "So you stand up to play. And then, as you begin, I shall come around behind you, raise your skirt, slip down your panties, and with the most exquisite gentleness, gain you from the rear."

"Uh," said Allie.

"I think you'll find the experience tremendously freeing." Professor Murton closed his eyes and nodded as if savoring something delectable. Light lay on his naked scalp like grease.

"I should go," she might have said, although in her hurry to put space between herself and the professor, Allie wasn't sure if the words came out. She bolted from the studio, the heavy door slamming shut on Professor Murton's calls for her to wait. She hadn't been back to campus since, staying instead at Tomorrowland, trying to figure out what to do.

"I want to give all of you eternal life," Booth said. "I want to put you in my movie."

Allie scoffed. She couldn't remember ever being in a nastier temper. But the others were listening intently.

"What kind of a movie?" Lanky and beaky, Mayor Paul had walked over from the hearse. He was in long johns, and his feet were bare. Mayor Paul's sweet, stoned character made him well liked by everyone. Although he wasn't an actual elected official, he had naturally assumed a leadership role: divvying up supplies, defusing arguments, negotiating with the police when they made one of their occasional raids on the camp; also, his hearse was the most impressive wreck.

"An important movie," said Booth. "A true movie." The large man in the black suit extended a hand to the golden-bearded dropout.

The Mayor's hands remained at his sides. "Yeah? What's so true about it?"

"Everything, every second of it, though especially the part where we show that this war, and everything to do with it, is a dirty damned farce. A farce played by a few evil men who jerk us all around for their personal amusement, like puppets." Booth kept the hand in place.

"Pleased," said the Mayor, finally raising his hand. They shook.

Adam lit a spliff and walked over with a milk crate, set it down, sat on it. Brittany came over, too. She hopped up on a discarded radiator. Randall's voice leaked from the holes in the trunk in an agonized whisper: "Don't trust him! He sounds like a weirdo!" Mayor Paul told Randall to be cool; his objections had been entered into the public record. The disembodied voice fell silent. A few others approached. Someone said, "Tell us more."

The stranger removed his wrinkled jacket, draping it over his forearm. He propped a foot atop a battered icebox, leaned forward, knee on elbow, and without saying anything, cast an unhurried look from one member of the audience to the next, all the way around.

When Booth's gaze lit on Allie, she found herself abruptly transported to an illustration in a storybook that she had spent many hours contemplating as a child. The illustration depicted a man in a coat with tails, holding a long orange cat by the head and legs as if the animal were an accordion, and playing it as if it were an accordion; musical notes swirled from the cat's ears. Listening nearby, a beautiful woman in a bright red dress swooned. The musician and the cat stared off the page with eyes like Booth's eyes, wide and bright, eyes of absolute conviction. It was, she would have been embarrassed to admit, the most romantic image she knew, an image Allie had kept in her heart for years, calling it ridiculous to herself but loving it anyway.

She scoffed again and looked away. But she did not leave.

The morning was mild for October. A bird called, less a song than a cackle, rippling through the air above their heads.

"It begins," said Booth, "with a medicine show."

The story is set in the town of Nix-on-Avon, where a group of young men and women have taken to helping the elderly and infirm for no money at all. These peace lovers, inspired by the example of Jesus Christ, help in the fields, paint houses, and even serenade sleepless children with windowside folk songs, steadfastly refusing any attempts at financial remuneration. If there's plenty of food, they accept a bite to eat or, if it's a cold or rainy evening, the shelter of a shed or hayloft, but not money. They are called "the Young Americans."

For the magnates of Nix-on-Avon, the movement is catastrophic: commerce has ground to a halt because of the sudden fad for bartering and trade; the banks are desolate; the now unnecessary police force spends the day playing cards and napping in the empty jail cells.

"But what can we do?" asks Mr. Jones, the owner of a rifle factory, worrying his emerald ring. The burg's titans have convened a meeting. Mr. Jones's beautiful daughter, Daughter, is one of the Young Americans.

"What we need is a war!" one man barks. A few of the men chuckle mirthlessly. War is the best business in the world! They should be so lucky!

From outside comes the tinkling of a bell and clopping hooves, alerting them to the arrival in the street of a novelty—an old-fashioned horse-drawn cart.

"There it is: the medicine show. Dr. Archibald 'Horsefeathers' Law's Mobile Hospital! Horsefeathers Law, Purveyor of Rejuvenating Liniments, Healthful Syrups, Wake-up Powders, and General Remedies! I will play Dr. Law! I am the villain." Booth winked conspiratorially at the gathering. A few people giggled.

Booth raised a finger to signal that there was more. "And did I mention that you, all of you here, you're the Young Americans? You see, all I want is for you to be yourselves."

Dr. Law offers his services to the businessman. It will be no great difficulty, he claims, to "cure" the Young Americans. His fees are very reasonable, he adds, especially for this kind of work. He invites them to please call him "Horsefeathers."

Mr. Jones asks if he's cracked. "How could such a thing even be possible, Dr. Law—er, Horsefeathers? How can you 'cure' do-gooding?"

"Pshaw! There's a cure for everything!" Dr. Law climbs on a chair and looks down on the rich men. "Why, it so happens that I have, after a great deal of study—and a long sojourn in the deepest jungles of South America, where monkeys speak and the wisest of men walk on their hands—*concocted an antidote for peace!*"

That night, when Dr. Law arrives at their encampment, he addresses the Young Americans with an altogether different pitch. "I am not a miracle worker!" he warns. "I am a physician specializing in the deeper body. There is no magic about this. My medicine is, quite simply, a scientific treatment for the soul!"

After a clanking search among the many pockets of his topcoat, Dr. Law produces a pickle jar filled with inky liquid. Here, he says, is his special Curative of the Inner Aura Juice—CIA Juice, for short—guaranteed to cleanse the spirit of all physical weakness.

"I will offer a free sample to anyone who would like one"—he grins to reveal his several gold teeth, and angles the jar so they can see how prettily the black liquid oozes—"so long as you call me Horsefeathers!"

The Young Americans are weary; the work they've been doing for their neighbors is hard on the back, on the knees and the feet. A cure for physical weakness sounds good. It's probably just grape juice, but since it's free, what's the harm?

Except for those six or seven who are away helping to plow a widow's turnip patch, all of the Young Americans accept the free samples of CIA

Juice. They take turns sipping from the inky jar. "Sure is bitter," notes the rifle magnate's lovely daughter, Daughter Jones. "Say, what's in it, anyhow?"

"Oh, a great, great many things!" says Dr. Law.

"Like what kind of things, Horsefeathers?" she asks.

"Well, for one thing, dreams!" The doctor explains that he grinds them up into a fine powder using a special mortar and pestle.

The next morning the Young Americans awaken in hypnotized states.

One girl goes to a train track and sprawls on the rails. Another youth picks his way carefully down a steep riverbank, pries a large stone free from the mud, and wades out into the middle of the river until his head disappears beneath the surface. Daughter Jones digs a neat grave and climbs down inside.

She is pulling the loose dirt in on herself when Horsefeathers rushes to stop her. "My dear, my dear!" he cries, dragging her from the hole. "What kind of a gentleman allows his wife to bury herself? I consider it a matter of principle that I should bury all my wives personally!"

The rest of the Young Americans return home to their parents. They proceed directly to the nearest mirror. The boys hack off their long hair and shave their beards; the girls hastily apply fresh makeup. They open their parents' closets and take out suits and ties, ankle-length dresses and Sunday shoes.

In the middle of Main Street, the Young Americans make a pile of their old rags—torn jeans and sleeveless blouses and sandals—and light a bonfire.

The bankers and business owners look on, delighted—except for Mr. Jones. After refusing to accede to the very reasonable price for Dr. Law's services—Daughter's hand in marriage—his fellows locked him inside a basement.

Finally, Mr. Jones manages to break the lock and dashes into the street. "He took her! You've got to help me! Law took my daughter!" Mr. Jones grabs the arm of a newly sheared Young American. The boy shakes him off, straightens his tie. Mr. Jones turns to a girl in a high-collared black dress. "Please, I'm begging you!"

This Young American grimaces. She reaches out and touches Mr. Jones's lapels. His face opens in relief. Her fingers tighten. A hard push sends him stumbling backward into the bonfire. The narrative climaxes in a brief civil war between the "New" Young Americans and the out-numbered "Original" Young Americans.

"The forces of community and fellowship seek refuge in a church, bar-ricade the doors and the windows against assault! There are so many attackers, though, so many of the hateful armed with their shiny new rifles! They are about to beat down the walls!" Booth threw up his arms. "Except—!"

His listeners twitched as if he had thrown grit in their faces. The Mayor was clutching his scraggly-haired chin. Adam, seated on the egg crate, had nibbled his spliff down to a blackened quarter inch. Brittany was chewing her nails. From the trunk of the DeSoto came a moan of despair.

"Except . . ." Booth fussed over the word this time, cocking his head to the side, lowering his voice. He let his hand sift slowly through the air, orchestrating in slow motion.

"Don't be obnoxious," said Allie. "Just tell us what happens." He had sucked her in, too, the bastard.

She supposed that her room back home in Buffalo was the same as always. She pictured the robin's-egg-blue wallpaper and the upright piano, the snapshots of her friends from the high school band on the corkboard, and the vaguely poignant glossy photograph of an unsmil-ing Van Cliburn with his otherworldly hair, seated at a baby grand. It would be so easy to go home. Allie's parents had been uneasy about her going so far in the first place. "Are you sure you're ready for *this*?" asked her tiny, cement-skinned, wheelchair-bound grandmother, an eighty-seven-year-old woman who had sent eight sons off to conflicts in foreign lands and who at this late date was suffering from not one or two but a whole grab bag of terminal ailments, and yet whose hushed voice betrayed that the notion of her seventeen-year-old granddaugh-ter attending college, living in a dorm on her own, opened the door to depths of existential dread so grave that even to speak of it aloud was frightening. "Yes," Allie had said, "I'm ready," but she was having doubts now. At home, her bed was a bed, not a Pontiac. At home, no one wanted to "gain" her while she played Beethoven. In Buffalo, pecu-liar men didn't just wander up and inflict upsetting stories on her. If she went home, her parents would take care of her.

"Except that just before the final moment, just before they break in"—though he spoke to them all, Booth had fixed his eyes on Allie and was giving her his magician-with-an-accordion-cat look—"the CIA serum wears off. The Young Americans wake up. They put down their weapons and gaze at the wreckage that surrounds them." He made a show of wiping his hands. "The end."

There was shifting inside the DeSoto's trunk, followed by a belch and a sigh. Adam picked the nub off his lip, flicked it into an engine block sprouting brambles. Mayor Paul said, "Yeah, yeah." Marty patted Booth on the shoulder. Anissa said it was a neat story. Brittany said she could see the whole thing. A consensus had formed: the big guy in the suit was all right.

"Good, good. It's settled." Booth bowed. "I'll be in touch." He stepped off the icebox and departed the way he had come.

Allie stalked back to the Pontiac. "What am I going to do?" she asked the interior of the car. The urge to weep was strong, but she managed to beat it back. She sniffed, and the smell of leaves and burn filled her nose. An odd thought surfaced.

Allie returned to the group; they had stayed around the icebox to fire up a fresh joint. "But what about the girl and the creep with the medicine show?" she asked.

There were murmurs of assent. Oh yeah, what about that part?

Randall spoke up from the hood of the DeSoto. "You should go ask him. I'm pretty sure that guy works at the Nickelodeon in town. I'd recognize his fat voice anywhere. "

2.

Allie stood on the opposite side of the street to stake out the movie theater.

A narrow brick-faced two-story structure, the theater building was belted by a lit marquee of yellow and white lights, which on this night promised COMING ATTRACTIONS: but no titles. The ticket booth was empty, and the poster frames that bracketed the double doors were blank. But around five o'clock, people began to show up and go inside.

The sun was descending, the moon pinned to a jagged reef of maroon in the left quadrant of the sky, the air turning from cool to frosty. Allie paced. She wasn't sure what she hoped to achieve by confronting Booth about the story's loose end. You didn't have a wicked charlatan kidnap some poor girl and not explain what had happened to her—but it was only a story, right? Maybe chasing after this Booth Dolan person was just an excuse to avoid the real issue, which was that she was avoiding the real issue. Allie had fled. Professor Murton had spoken to her the way he had spoken to her, and she'd run. Was that how it was going to be? But if it was—if that was who Allie was; if she wasn't, as her grandmother had feared, ready for *this*—why was she bothering with Booth? Wouldn't it be simpler to find an old DeSoto and hide in the trunk?

Allie jerked her army jacket tight and swiveled, strode the other way. It was damned thoughtless, leaving a story unfinished like that!

The people entering the movie theater appeared older—stiff-gaited men, women wrapped in shawls. She didn't see Booth. A few minutes passed and the arrivals ceased. Allie crossed over.

A handwritten flyer was tucked into the corner of one of the poster frames: REPUBLICAN PARTY OF ULSTER COUNTY, BINGO FUND-RAISER, 5:30 PM. In the side window of the ticket booth was another sign, professionally printed: THIS SPACE AVAILABLE FOR RENT, 555-3237.

Allie loitered indecisively under the marquee. From a distance, she must have looked like a girl who had been stood up. A chill tickled her nose, and she turned her head to sneeze.

At the corner where South Acorn intersected Main, there was a light. A blue VW Bug idled before a red. While he waited, Professor Murton, who was tapping his fingers against the wheel and had his pipe dangling from his mouth, happened to stretch his neck so that his gaze shifted to the parallel side of the street. That was when he saw Allie, and she saw him jump in his seat, like someone had pinched him.

From behind the glass concession case in the corner of the lobby, a hunched man in a VFW garrison cap informed her that it was a dollar for two cards and two dollars for five cards. Although there was no popcorn machine in evidence, the entire area smelled of butter and salt. Her stomach reacted with a gurgle. Marshmallows were the primary foodstuff in Tomorrowland.

Allie told the man behind the case that she was there to see Dr. Law. VFW, without glancing from the book-size chunk of scrap wood he was whittling on the counter, said there was to his knowledge no such physician on the premises.

"Booth Dolan, I mean." Allie was in a hurry. The professor had gestured from his car for her to stay where she was; he wanted to talk. She was making fists, digging fingernails into palms; her own cowardice appalled her. The countless high school harassments boiled up: catcalls that she'd pretended not to hear, exams that she had studied hard for and let cow-eyed football players copy, the smirking biology teacher who had referred to her and the other two female students who dared to breach the sanctity of his lab as "the little mommies," and so on. The memories were as vivid as bruises and hurt like bruises. She had loathed herself for running then, and she loathed herself for running now.

"Hello? Did you hear me? Booth?" She could have slapped the man in the VFW hat.

"Oh yeah," VFW said. He set down his project—the words KEEP OUT had been neatly etched into the wood—as well his pocketknife, and made her wait while he carefully swept his filings off the counter and into a bin. "The guy."

The lights were on in the theater, and the older people Allie had seen outside were seated in the rows, holding their markers and bingo cards at the ready. Booth and an assistant, a long-faced young man in gray flannel and brown boots, commanded the runway of stage in front of the screen, which had been closed off by heavy purple drapes. While Booth drew the numbered balls from a bunting-draped cauldron, his assistant recorded the calls on a chalkboard.

"B-nine!" Booth's bass voice echoed in the small auditorium, ringing off the vaulted ceiling, and crashing against the back wall. Allie touched her hair, half expecting it to be blown back. She thought of going with her family to see Charlton Heston in *The Ten Commandments*.

"B-nine!" he repeated.

There was also a boyish quality to him, perhaps due to his clothes; Booth wore the same too-short, rumpled suit as that morning. Allie concocted an image of his mother, a normal-size woman in a tapered suit like Harriet Nelson wore, standing on the top step of a ladder to help her adult son get dressed, grunting and straining to yank the sleeves of the coat down on his upraised arms and get him inside it. In the dimness at the back of the theater, Allie couldn't help smiling to herself at the sweet idea—before reminding herself that there was no time for mooning. Professor Murton was in pursuit. She rushed along the right-hand aisle.

Booth's partner drew a large **B-9** on the chalkboard.

"Nine?" asked a voice situated below a sunhat festooned with dusty cloth zinnias.

"Yes, Sarah," said Booth. "'B-nine' is the new call. Have you been so blessed, my dear?"

Sarah hissed and shook her head sharply, causing a zinnia to plunge from her hat down into the darkness between the rows. "No."

Booth spared a glance for the ceiling. (An angel with Mary Pickford's face—eyes raccooned with kohl, one wing larger than the other—played a harp as she soared across the small golden dome at the center of the ceiling.)

Allie reached the stage. "Hey," she whispered, waving him over.

He approached, beaming. "Allie, is it?" He had recovered his smile in an instant. "Tom, would you please take the bridge for a few moments while I speak to my friend?"

The long-faced young man said, "Okay, buddy," and nodded to Allie. "Ma'am."

Booth hooked her elbow with his and began to lead her up the aisle.

"Did he just call me 'ma'am'?" asked Allie.

"Tom's very courtly," said Booth. "I think it's terrific."

Allie slipped free of his arm. "Stop. Is there another exit out of here? There's a creep following me, and I need to—"

"Wait. You're being followed?" asked Booth. His bulb of a chin, which was the only small thing about him, was furrowed in concern. "I'm not going to stand idly by and let you be hounded from pillar to post. Let me speak to this person. What is the problem?"

Allie blushed unhappily.

"Please," he said. "You can tell me."

For a few endless seconds, she sought to unearth the politest, least embarrassing way to explain Professor Murton's idea for improving her playing—and then she gave up: "It's my adviser. The creep? He wants to 'gain' me while I play piano. While I play Beethoven, he wants to."

Booth was aghast. "Is that how he actually put it? He used the verb 'gain'?"

She breathed out. "Yes. That was how he said it."

He groaned. "I can see why you're upset." He gently touched her arm again. "Allow me the satisfaction of snuffing this tiny fart, will you?"

Uncertain, Allie did not immediately respond.

"How will I know this man?" asked Booth.

"He's got a pipe?" Perhaps because she couldn't figure out if he was serious, or if he was joking, or if he hadn't tossed aside his magic cat and climbed right out of her old storybook, this statement of fact came out as a question.

"A pipe," said Booth, and snorted, and went shoulder-first through the door to defend her honor.

She peered through the crack between the door and the frame to see Professor Murton standing near the concession stand. Besides being bald, the professor was somewhat walleyed, which endowed him with an expression of permanent incredulity. He was like some perverted mole-person. Allie used to love to play the piano. Now, whenever she played, she'd probably be half distracted, worrying about Professor Murton sneaking up from behind. A part of her hoped that Booth would walk up and punch him in the face. Yet from another angle, she viewed herself shrinking behind the doors and thought she was the one who deserved punching. Who had she thought she was, going off on her own, imagining a career of clapping auditoriums and grand pianos shimmering under stage lights, fooling herself and everyone else into believing that she was ready? Allie's palms ached, and she was glad of the pain.

"Wait a minute." Booth stepped across the red carpet with its motif of golden fans. "You there: ugly man. I want you to stop harassing the young woman you followed in here, immediately."

"Pardon?" Professor Murton removed his pipe. "I just came in to speak to a friend of mine. Her name is Allie. She is a young woman, but I can assure you that I'm not harassing her. You're mistaken." He frowned and craned his neck as if having a hard time making Booth out. "Did you just call me ugly?"

"I did," said Booth, "and now I'm calling you a menace. And now I'm calling you an asshole. Get out."

"You can't talk to me like that!" Professor Murton's tone was one of such earnest grievance that Allie could barely believe this was the same man who only a few days before had suggested he "gain" her.

OWEN KING

There was a creak as the man at the concession stand sat up on his stool. He was gray-haired, in his fifties at least, but of imposing mass; the sleeves of his polo shirt stretched tight around muscled biceps webbed with faded indigo tattoos.

"What's this, then?" the older man asked.

"Nothing, Irving. Just ejecting an undesirable," said Booth.

Allie, watching, had for the moment forgotten her own relationship to the situation. Booth's display astounded her; she thought she might be witnessing an act of chivalry.

In the theater, down the rows behind her, Booth's assistant, Tom, announced, "It's A-four, folks. A-four."

Booth clenched his fists and stepped toward Professor Murton.

The professor edged back and bumped against the counter. He blinked rapidly, underscoring his molelike aspect; it was as if he had just emerged from his hole and into the light.

"I don't know what the problem is," spoke up Irving. "But this is an official Republican Party event. Good people are playing bingo here."

"Oh! Oh! It all makes sense now!" cried Professor Murton to Booth, his voice screechy and triumphant. "I should have guessed from your bullying that you were a Republican!"

"You bastard," said Booth. "That was a hell of a nasty thing to say."

There was a soft *pop* as Irving yanked his pocketknife loose from the chunk of wood where he had planted it upright. "Take it outside. Or I'll take the both of you outside."

"Now, Irving." Booth had spotted the pocketknife. "Let's not lose our heads. I can handle this—"

At that moment, Professor Murton feinted left, then darted right again. Nimbly for such a large man, Booth jumped in front of him, all at once eager, Allie saw, to maneuver the other man away from the counter. The professor, for his part, was unaware that Irving was armed.

"Move from my way!" Professor Murton jabbed his pipe, stem first, in the air between them.

"Never!" Booth heaved up his right fist and slapped his right bicep with his left hand.

Allie had no idea what this last meant, though she thought it translated to a violent—possibly sexual—threat, and it was very shocking. She realized that she should be looking for another way out, but there

138

was no way she could leave during such an exciting part. Allie squeezed her sore hands together and bounced on her heels.

"Are you mocking me or threatening me?" asked Professor Murton.

"Rest assured, you will know if I am mocking you," said Booth.

"You want to know something? You're a fat jerk! Enough of this! Where's Allie?"

Booth ignored the slur. Instead, he said, "Let me tell you something," and with no further warning, he began a discourse on Professor Murton's unsightliness. He calmly explained that the port and starboard set of the professor's eyes was highly aberrant among human beings. This feature was, conversely, "quite common among the minor prey of the animal kingdom, those low creatures of the swamp and jungle that must guard from attack on all sides." Booth clasped his hands at the base of his spine and paced to the old-fashioned ticket chopper that stood in the center of the lobby. The gold-painted chopper was shaped like an obelisk and stood about waist-high. On the verge of his conclusion, Booth placed a hand on the pointed top.

It dawned on Allie that he was imitating a lawyer—a movie lawyer. Booth wasn't putting his hand on a ticket chopper; he was putting it on the newel at the corner of the jury box and preparing to tell the assembled that this individual, the accused, was guilty of the capital charge of murder in the first degree. What a wonderful big ham was this Booth Dolan with his wrists sticking out of his suit! He was actually kind of fun.

"But the advantages of flanking eyeballs are limited to those primitive creatures who face threats from many, many predators. Human beings have evolved. Therefore, such a trait is, in a human male, an obvious backward step. You must understand: no woman could ever feel attracted to such a bizarre-looking person.

"Now," Booth finished, "if you would be so good as to fuck off."

"Criminy," said Irving. Booth's speech seemed to have deflated his anger. He retook his stool and laid down the pocketknife. A goofy grin was playing on Irving's mouth.

Professor Murton repeated that Booth was fat. "You'll just get fatter, too! You're sucking in your fat gut right now!"

"I told you not call me names, you wretched man. Leave. Go. Depart. Ooze away on your belly back to your hovel. She doesn't want to see you," said Booth.

"Oh, shit on you, pal. You've got no right to come between me and my girlfriend."

At that, Allie found that she had charged through the doors and into the lobby. "I am not your girlfriend!"

The men turned to stare at the woman in the army jacket. The doors flapped behind her in great whooshes. She pointed at the bald man. "You're a pig, you know that? You're my adviser. You're supposed to be someone I can trust."

Professor Murton licked his lips. "Allie. Let's talk. I want to talk."

"But she does not wish to talk to you," said Booth.

"It's all right." Allie didn't need to be protected or rescued; she never had. Her grandmother needn't have feared: she was ready. "I can speak for myself."

Booth nodded and retreated a half step, ceding the floor.

She pointed at the professor and said firmly, "Please leave me alone. I have nothing to say to you. "

"Allie." Professor Murton's cheeks were sweaty, his eyes watery. He held his pipe with both hands. "Oh, Allie."

He was so sad and bald. His pretense, his confidence, they were totally gone; Booth had peeled him like a dead trout. Allie pitied him. Had she actually let this awful little man upset her?

"Look, I just want to talk, okay? Can't you just hear me out and not be such a—such a cunt?"

Allie inhaled.

"Now you've done it," observed Booth.

Professor Murton's smile twitched. "I could have said that better."

Allie turned to Irving, who was already on his feet again. "Hey, mister. Could you help us out?"

With the assistance of several able-bodied Ulster County Republicans, Irving O'Dell was pried off the professor and his knife wrested away before he managed to inflict any major injuries. The sheriff, a Republican and a bingo enthusiast himself, was on the scene to ensure that neither party filed charges.

However, this authority did administer a stern dose of morality to both men. He demanded that Professor Murton stop "trying to dick college girls," or else there'd be hell to pay; and then he put it to Irving in no uncertain terms that in Hasbrouck, NY, no one was allowed to disembowel a son of a bitch just because the son of a bitch was a son of a bitch.

(Softening somewhat, the sheriff added, "If we did things that way, Irving, why, I'd be a mass murderer myself.")

3.

Afterward, they walked to the Hasbrouck Diner, and Booth watched Allie devour a plate of turkey and mashed potatoes. "Marvelous," he said. "I could watch you eat all day, Allie."

"Please don't," she said, and Booth laughed, and Allie let her mouth hang so he could see the half-masticated food on her tongue.

When the waitress returned, Booth informed her that he had been stirred—stirred to order a turkey dinner for himself, as well as a strawberry frappé, rolls, and a bowl of gravy to dip them in.

Allie thanked him for standing up for her.

Booth said it was his pleasure; she'd been on his mind all day. "You'll make a fine Daughter Jones."

There were a couple of problems, Allie said. "The first is that I've never acted. The second is that I've never wanted to act."

Booth raised an eyebrow. It occurred to Allie that each of his shoulders was just about broad enough to sit on, like a pair of matching porch gliders. He said he didn't know what she was playing at, but it was a waste of time. She was an actress. She did want to act. "You can't talk around me," said Booth. "You can't bewitch me with that mysterious smile of yours. I've read your file. I know all about you."

"Don't you ever get worn out, being so full of it all the time?" she asked.

She insulted him with such talk, Booth proclaimed. She insulted herself. She insulted them both. They were both very insulted.

"You don't, do you?"

"No," he said. "Never."

The Nickelodeon, an independent theater—and not a particularly fancy one—had belonged to Booth's uncle. It featured a single screen, a hundred seats on the floor, and another twenty in the balcony. It had closed that summer. Television kept the older folks at home, and the teenagers could go across the river to the cineplex in Hyde Park, smoke pot in the parking lot across from FDR's house, and spend the whole day sneaking from one picture to another.

They had returned to the theater to sit in the balcony and neck. Booth's mouth tasted like all the things that he'd eaten. To her surprise, it turned her on, made her feel as though he were starving for her.

She asked Booth what they were going to do with the place.

He shrugged. "I don't know. Maybe you could do something with it?"

"Oh yeah?" Allie was mostly playing along, but already the memory of her weeks-long college career was beginning to take on a hazy quality. If the point of college was to prepare you for life, then in a sense, telling Professor Murton to leave her alone made it redundant—if she could defend herself, she was prepared for anything. "What should I do with your movie theater?"

"I'll have to think." Booth produced a flask and a box of dusty-tasting Milk Duds.

Who was her favorite actor, he wanted to know. She said Montgomery Clift. Booth thought that was superb. He asked her who her favorite director was, and she admitted that she couldn't name one and, for that matter, had never been clear on what they did. Allie said, "You remind me of a book I had when I was a little girl. It was about a magician and a tomcat and all the trouble they started and how they got out of it. The cat could be an accordion when he wanted. You don't happen to have a cat that can be an accordion, do you?"

"Not yet," said Booth. "But I have had my eye on one for some time."

The director, he explained, was the person who provided the vision for a film. He was the one who arranged all the elements—the story, the actors, the settings, etc.—into a pleasing shape. The greatest director was Orson Welles. His movies looked the best, and they were the strangest, and moreover, with apologies to Montgomery Clift, Welles was also the best actor. Booth said that Orson Welles was like a dinosaur. That was how much presence he had. It would take a whole village worth of huntsmen, armed with spears and rocks and fire, to knock him down.

"Have you always wanted to be one?" Allie asked.

"A dinosaur?" said Booth. "Yes. From my earliest memory."

"No, a director."

"Heavens, no. It sounds like an awful lot of work, don't you think?"

"But you're directing this movie, aren't you?"

Booth grumbled lowly. "Not willingly. No one else would hire me, Allie. I've been forced to employ myself."

"Oh, don't try and make me feel sorry for you," said Allie. "You'll get through it somehow. Do you know how to direct a movie? The mechanics of it?"

"How hard can it be? I've seen plenty of movies. Point and shoot. Make sure you get a medium one and a couple of close ones. Nothing fancy. I don't pretend to be Orson Welles. All I need is to tell the story. Point and shoot. I suppose I can manage that." He aimed an invisible elephant gun and took a few potshots from the balcony.

Allie told him to be careful with that thing.

They kissed some more.

He was twenty-nine, this gravy-breathed, bookshelf-shouldered boy in the wrinkled and dusty suit.

Booth recounted to Allie how he had tried to make it as an actor in the theater, living in a basement apartment in Brooklyn and taking classes at the school of a famous acting teacher. She had not been encouraging. "Booth," the teacher said, "dear heart. I love you. You're very funny. When you are up there, I want to watch you. The problem is that no matter what you are doing, as soon as you speak in that basso profundo of yours, I come apart at the seams. You make me giggly even when you are dying of gangrene."

While he was living in New York City, the only part Booth managed to land was as the fifth banana in a production of *Waiting for Lefty* that was so far Off-Broadway it was performed in a garage and most of the actors were actual taxi drivers. The revival ran for a single show. A portion of the audience, drivers of Eastern European and Russian extraction with limited English, had become confused. The verisimilitude of the play was such—the play being a play set in a garage, and some of the actors being drivers acting as drivers—that they came to believe the fictional assembly to decide whether or not to strike was actually happening. When the actors began to chant, "Strike! Strike! Strike!," several of these men in the audience, anti-Communist refugees from the USSR, became incensed and stormed the stage, yelling, "No! No! No!" Punches were thrown. Booth escaped being clobbered only by proclaiming to an agitated Muscovite wielding a chair leg that, if given the chance, he would punish the corpse of Stalin. "Friend," said Booth, palms up, to the man, "I swear it to you. I would not hesitate to abuse that fascist's dead body. I would be glad to do it. I would throw his pelvic bone for a dog to fetch."

His New York City sojourn was an ignominious experience, and Booth resolved that he had no choice but to write and raise a production of his own. He had returned to Hasbrouck, quickly sketched out the script of *New Roman Empire,* engaged his friend Thomas as set designer, and that very morning contracted most of his youthful cast, Allie included.

"Now let me serenade you," he said.

From the projection booth, Booth retrieved a peculiar guitar. It held eleven strings and a body shaped like a bisected watermelon. On the neck there was a stamp of a silver crescent moon. He had salvaged it from a garbage mound in the Bowery.

"Listen." He played her a song of his own composition called "The Huckster's Lament."

The progression of his plucking, the notes warped and slippery and somehow tuneless and melodic at once, put Allie in mind of a time when she had lain at the top of a high, grassy hill and rolled all the way down. At the bottom, she had tried to stand, and the world had swung away like a gate banging wide, a thousand colors streaking across the surface of her right eye, and it felt like her head was about to come apart, but it wasn't bad, it was good, and her legs folded beneath her, and she was back on the ground, smelling grass and blood up her nose—and so high, and so glad. She remembered the feeling, and it was even better to feel it a second time.

He swayed back and forth as he played, a shadow against the silver sheet of the blank screen behind him. "Well? What do you think?" asked Booth.

Allie stood and padded down the balcony steps to where he stood in front of the railing. She put her hands on his shoulders and smoothed the bunched fabric. "I think," she said, "that if I had a ladder, I could climb right up on one of these great big shoulders of yours, take a seat, and have myself a nice look around."

They made love—not without some difficulty—on the steps of the aisle.

"So how come you're such a movie fan?"

"Well, as you know, my uncle owned this theater. So I watched a great number of films as a boy. When they went to work, my parents often deposited me here for the day. If I was lucky, I got to see whatever was playing three or four times before they came back to pick me up."

"That's sad, Booth."

"Oh, no! This screen was the most pacific babysitter I ever had. It took me all around the world and introduced me to the most extraordinary people. It rewarded me with the education of a lifetime."

"If you say so. My babysitter used to take me to the park and let me ride the swings and stuff. I thought that was pretty nice. Fresh air, you know?"

"Poor child!"

Since they had the place to themselves, she suggested that they screen a picture. Booth's face fell. The reels were always returned to the distributors, and no more had been ordered since the theater's closing. But then he remembered the intro reel, the forty-second lead-in stitched to the front of every film. It asked the audience not to talk during the feature, to use the ashtrays and not to put out their cigarettes on the rug, and advertised the delicious concessions available in the lobby.

Three times they watched the animated yellow and blue butterfly that was the central figure of the intro reel twinkle across the screen, spilling in its wake the Hasbrouck Nickelodeon's rules and advertisements.

After the third, Booth asked her what she thought.

Allie leveled with him. "That was the lousiest movie I've ever seen."

"Dreadful!"

They made love again, this time at the top of the balcony stairs, on the landing, where it made more sense.

"Do you see yourself as an activist?"

"What an awful thing to say!'

"But the story, it's kind of political-seeming. CIA Juice. Nix-on-Avon. The kids and the riot and stuff. Right?"

"No, no. It is all for entertainment, I assure you. Don't get me wrong: I hate fascists of all stripes. I hate the big fascists who try to destroy our world. I hate the little fascists who talk, talk, talk through the whole movie. Can't stand them. If, to you, the film is a parable of fascist threat, I don't have the least problem with that."

"What's fascist about talking during a movie? Isn't that just rude?"

"It's fascist. It's terribly fascist. It spoils the communal experience of the theater. Go to a movie with a dictator sometime. I bet he'll never shut up."

"I have a hard time telling when you're being serious."

"At the moment I am being almost entirely serious. It ought to be a felony to speak during the showing of a movie."

"So your movie is only, what, a lark or whatever? All pretending for fun?"

"Yes! It is entirely for fun. We dress up and we tell a story." Booth smiled faintly. "Can't that be enough, Allie darling?"

Allie wept. She was drunk and happy. She thought that sounded wonderful. She thought that was plenty.

It was morning. "Breakfast?" asked Booth. "We could go back to the diner. Someone might remember us and be scandalized."

"I wish we could just stay here." Allie was curled up naked in a seat, huddled under Booth's jacket. "I don't feel like getting dressed. I wish that there was a movie showing, and it was called *Coffee,* and it starred coffee and maybe, in a supporting role, cranberry scones."

Booth chuckled. "It's not a bad idea, you know," he said.

"Yeah." Not really paying attention, she yawned, pulled the coat tighter. It would take over a year for Booth to convince her that her off-hand comment was a potentially creditable enterprise, that the way to hang on to the property was to convert it into a café and serve coffee to college students and sell baked goods from the glass candy case. Before that, Allie had to officially drop out of college; she had to sell her music books and her metronome and live in sin with her boyfriend; and Booth had to direct a movie, and Allie had to act in it.

"Now be quiet, Booth Dolan. You're not the only person in the theater, you know." She fell asleep thinking that there was something she meant to ask him about.

4.

After a year of intermittent shooting—through mechanical breakdowns, lack of funds, lack of film, snowstorms, rainstorms, and a hundred other minor disasters—*New Roman Empire* was completed. The residents of Tomorrowland, Allie and Mayor Paul and Marty and Anissa and Adam and Brittany and all the others, including Randall (who eventually mellowed to such a degree that he moved out of the DeSoto trunk and into a truck cab), gave their performances according to readings from Booth before each shot. His friend Tom Ritts, the bingo assistant, was handy, and he built Dr. Law's medicine wagon, as well as many of the other props; he even improvised a short dolly track. A few of Hasbrouck's theatrically inclined residents chipped in to fill different roles; no less a personage than Irving O'Dell, the Vice President of the Ulster County Chapter of the Republican Party, took a turn. (He played the ill-fated Mr. Jones.)

Booth cajoled, and made promises, and hugged, and kissed. No one was paid. Infrequently was anyone fed. Everyone accepted these realities. It amazed Allie, the way Booth managed so many people and always knew what to do, what to say, and what not to say.

It took Tom a couple of weeks to build the wagon from scratch, using a combination of discarded railroad ties, wood scraps, and the wheels from a Studebaker. When Booth saw the finished construction, he told Tom that he loved him.

"Gosh, Booth." Color ran high up Tom's forehead where his light blond hair was already receding. "It's just a lot of rubbish no one was making any use of."

"It's not rubbish now," said Booth. "It's beautiful, and you damn well know it. You've made an astonishing vehicle with nothing but a few simple tools and your bare hands. Your ingenuity, Thomas, is matchless, and if you can't say it, then I must."

Booth's friend excused himself; he was pretty sure there was something somewhere that needed hammering. "Best of luck," Tom told Allie. "He's like this full-time, you know."

Contingencies never appeared to cross Booth's mind. Whatever needed to work, he assumed would work, and if it didn't, he found another way to make it work. "Coverage!" was his mantra. As far as Allie could make out, coverage meant that he filmed three different angles for every scene if there were two actors, four if there were three actors, and if there were more than that, he shot the crowd and did close-ups for the important ones.

Embarrassment was an emotion Booth seemed constitutionally incapable of suffering. Impatience and anger were strangers to the production. He went around in costume, right eye tucked behind a pince-nez, boater on his head, wearing a fake nose webbed with gin blossoms, while advising the women that they were stunning and yanking down the pants of men who weren't paying attention. Booth made what must have been complex and taxing—organizing large numbers of people, keeping track of what was going on, being kind on short rest—seem natural and carefree.

In one scene, Allie, as Daughter, was supposed to cry but couldn't. Her face felt rigid, like a too-tight mask. She was desperate not to disappoint him.

They left the setup in front of the depot to talk in the tall winter wheat that grew along the south embankment overlooking the yard. Below, Tom was tinkering with his track in preparation for sliding the monster of an Arriflex camera alongside Dr. Law's slow-rolling wagon.

"Maybe I should try and think of something sad?" A fluttering commenced in Allie's chest, every sort of loss on butterfly wings: her grandfather whom she had adored so much, and the family dog, run over by—

"No!" The huge purplish blob of a fake nose that Booth was wearing to play Dr. Law made him look like an entirely different person, so it was like hearing his voice come from the mouth of a stranger. "We are putting on a show, my love, not plumbing your psychological depths! We are not sadists! Just think about how sad Daughter must feel to be leaving her friends behind, and do your best. That is all I could possibly ask of you."

"Really?" She peered past the awful nose to his hazel eyes.

"Really," promised Booth.

Here was the beginning of their problems, Allie later thought, because it established between them an equilibrium based on desire rather than on need. Booth asked from her only what she felt comfortable giving; there was more there if he demanded it. The gesture of benevolence was planted, like a single post in the middle of a field and knotted with a rag, to show roughly where one property ended and another began. What could really happen if you took a step or two beyond the invisible barrier? Allie never knew, except that it was against the rules. You didn't go over there. To require something of the person you loved was trespassing.

What wasn't evident to her then is what every adult comes to understand as the selflessness of infatuation wears away to reveal the bald and homely creature that is our absolute self: dreams are collateral for life, and you must be willing to forfeit them, every last one, for the people you love.

In the background was Buffalo, her blue wallpaper, her cheap little upright piano, the corkboard of her friends and poor beautiful Van Cliburn, and every day of childhood. In front of Allie lay marriage and motherhood and a cottage by a graveyard and a series of fateful allowances.

But in that moment Allie said, "Thank God! I love you, you know." She tore off his nose and kissed him.

Tom's hammer clanged against a railroad tie, a warped bell toll. The winter wheat caught a spring breeze—it was spring now—and quivered in mute applause around the lovers on the rise.

5.

Roughly two years later, in the early summer of 1971, the Continental Cinema Association (CCA) ran *New Roman Empire* as the second picture in a double bill (following a horror movie called *Cannibals of the Yukon*) on a hundred screens in the Midwest and Texas. The initial proceeds were better than anticipated and the movie gained a bit of unexpected steam, perhaps in part due to a bemused review by a critic for *The New Yorker*. When the critic's flight to Los Angeles had engine trouble and she was stranded in Des Moines for the night, she visited a local drive-in. "The obviousness of the parable, the woodenness of the acting, the feeble visual design, near-far-near-far—sensationally terrible! . . . I actually laughed out loud when one poor, brainwashed do-gooder shoved a simpering Republican patriarch into a bonfire . . . All that tempers my enthusiasm for this comedy is the suspicion that some people might miss the joke . . . The Young Americans are brainwashed, for instance, by CIA Juice! . . . This is funny-dumb, not funny-smart, let alone funny-deep, and if we can't tell the difference (director-writer Dolan can, I believe), maybe Nixon is the president we deserve."

The movie continued on to brief runs in Los Angeles, New York, a dozen cities in the Rust Belt, and eventually, a handful of stops in Europe. While it played in mostly downmarket theaters—the ones with the floors tacky enough to rip the soles right off your sneakers if you stayed flat-footed for too long—that didn't change the fact that it was now in the black.

There was a trickle of additional reviews: the *Voice* heartily approved; it was "a clown-stumble insult to the bloated transparent spasmodics that pass for 'important' cinema these days." The third-string critic at the *Times* thought it was abominable. "Dolan is absurd, his lead actress appears to have been lobotomized, and the supporting players are either diseased or strung-out or both . . . The sideshow has a place, one reluctantly concedes, but must it be this sideshow, and must it be this place?" A Catholic priest in Pittsburgh read about the movie in the newspaper, then demanded that his congregation boycott it. A notoriously liberal pastor in Cincinnati recommended it to his parishioners. In *Cahiers du Cinema*, a renowned critic-director mentioned *New Roman Empire* in passing, as part of a letter in defense of popular entertainment: *"Le film est primitif, soit; mais M. Dolan offre en même temps une vision singulièrement américaine. Les gentlemen sont des traitres lâches; les idéalistes sont des enfants bêtes, et le criminel est un gros élégant."*

Among the letters of the legendary Irish theater impresario and wit Micheál MacLiammóir was the opinion of Orson Welles, who caught a showing of *New Roman Empire* that fall:

"I watched a movie today that I suspect I may have filmed during some extended blackout period while I was inebriated or in a fugue state. It is called *New Roman Empire*. I perform under the alias Booth Dolan and declaim ad nauseum, like a horrible fat Punch doll. Most of the filming appears to have taken place in a junkyard. Delightful. Sent me off like a belt of nitrous oxide." (From Los Angeles, dated 9/27/71.)

MacLiammóir's response to the picture fell along similar lines:

"As fate would have it, the picture you mentioned in your letter showed up at the local. It was the most pitiable thing I've ever witnessed. You were right: a delight." (From Dublin, dated 12/28/71.)

The wagon shakes along a dusty road. Daughter leans her head against Dr. Law's shoulder. There are chapped patches on her cheeks and gruesome moons under her eyes. Her hair is the color of old newspaper; she is ancient. Dr. Law appears unchanged. He whistles a familiar tune.

"Where are we going?" Daughter asks.

"The next place," he says.

"What's happening to me?" she asks.

"You're growing up," he says.

"Why are you doing this to me, Horsefeathers?" asks Daughter.

"You know, that's only a nickname." Horsefeathers chuckles. "Seeing as how we're such good friends now, you might as well know, my real name is—"

The image of the smiling con man freezes and flips away, end over end, like a playing card on a spring. The first credit appears: *Directed by Booth Dolan.*

QUINLAN

Have you forgotten your old friend—hmmm?

TANYA

I told you we were closed.

QUINLAN

I'm Hank Quinlan.

TANYA

I didn't recognize you.
(beat)
You should lay off those candy bars.

QUINLAN

Ah—it's either the candy or the hooch. I must say I wish it was your chili I was getting fat on. Anyway, you're sure looking good.

TANYA

You're a mess, honey.

> —Orson Welles, *Touch of Evil* (dialogue between
> Welles and Marlene Dietrich)

PART 2
THE LONG WEEKEND

(2011)

Thursday Night and Friday Morning

1.

The wedding was officiated by, of all things, a poet. It was a marriage between two university professors, held at a DUMBO restaurant and event space called the Stables, a designation that referred to the building's original incarnation as a residence for the horses of Brooklyn. From the mullioned windows on the second floor, the Brooklyn Bridge could be seen arching toward Manhattan in the September dusk. The steel beams were gargantuan and gray, the traffic a jerking ticker tape of headlights.

It was a view Sam Dolan knew well. He had filmed several weddingographies at the Stables. The bridge was a perfect punctuation mark for a weddingography, a metaphor that made sense to everyone and never failed to please the clientele. That the metaphor's obviousness made it worthless in his own eyes—a Pavlovian trick of the heart—didn't matter. It wasn't for him.

Sam shot the ceremony from the center of the half-moon balcony that overlooked the hall. By sitting on the balcony floor and slipping the camera between two newels, he could capture a slightly tilted view of the troika at the altar. This placement kept bobbing heads out of the frame while maintaining an angle gentle enough to suggest the notion of loving relatives passed on, observing unseen, hovering mere inches above the heads of the living like phantasmagoric mistletoe.

He did his best to think these things through, to approach the endeavor with care, and to treat weddingography as an art form—a predictable, maudlin, shitty art form, perhaps (okay, definitely)—but an art form still.

As the weddingographer, he recorded the ceremony and the reception, then molded the raw materials into a preordained narrative: harried preparation, holy union, raucous party, romantic escape along a bridge to the shining city of the future. The last things to disappear from the video would be the stars twinkling in the suspension cables. That was what they wanted, and that was what he gave them. If Sam did it right, performed like a pro, the story should always come out the same, happily ever after.

You had to do something. He did this. He went through the motions; he got the coverage.

What taxed was the ritual of the event itself.

The weddings gave Sam a sense of déjà vu, like a low-grade fever. Toasts would be raised. People would cry. There would be food smothered in brown sauce. "Brick House" would be played. People who shouldn't dance would dance. A child would mess in its tiny trousers. Nearly everyone would enjoy themselves, and whoever didn't could be edited out. The faces changed, the religions changed, and once in a while the bride didn't wear white, but it always came out the same way. Once you saw it enough, a union of perfectly matched hearts started to seem like a recurring nightmare.

"So," announced the poet. "This is it. Welcome to the show. Welcome to the show."

"Well, what do you expect?" Polly had asked him. "Weddings are happy. They don't usually have weddings for people who hate each other."

Polly had been the one who started him in weddingography. Three years before, she had insisted that he film her marriage. At the time Sam was employed at an independent video store in Park Slope, renting Cassavetes films, and sometimes dreaming about murdering the kind of people who rented Cassavetes films. The wedding gig, he had to concede, seemed a thrilling departure by comparison. One job led to another, and so on. He had retired his position at the video store—liberating their copy of *Opening Night* on his way out the door—and taken up weddingography full-time.

In a way, his career was all Polly's fault, and when he was feeling particularly repressed, he gave himself license to bitch to her about it. Down from Westchester on this gritty, blustery afternoon in late August, a few weeks prior to the wedding at the Stables, they had met off Union Square at the City Bakery for hot chocolate. "I'm just saying that it gets to be a drag. Anyway, the busy season is almost over. The wedding factory only operates at half capacity during the winter."

"I'd go to a wedding every weekend if I could," said Polly.

"You think you would, but you wouldn't," said Sam.

"Sammy, please. What's so awful about people being happy?"

He refused to dignify this question with a response.

"I think the reason is that you've forgotten what it's like to be happy," she went on. "Whatever, though. You can sit there and say that true love sucks, but that won't stop it. You'll find out one of these days." Polly reached over the table to pat one of his unshaven cheeks.

The occasion of her trip was an appointment to see her therapist, and she had brought along her son, Rainer. He was an infant, staring out from the nest of his carrier with wide, shifty brown eyes. The carrier rested on a chair between them, and as they talked, Rainer's eyes darted back and forth between them, like a tennis judge's. The baby's watchful presence felt accusatory; although Polly had married and given birth, she and Sam had never stopped sleeping together.

"I'm curious. What exactly would you like to happen? What would raise a wedding to your aesthetic standards?"

Sam asked if she was teasing. He distrusted her use of the word "aesthetic."

"No, I'm not teasing," she promised. It was Polly, though, and she was trying to conceal a smile behind her mug of hot chocolate, so that hardly constituted a definitive answer. With her large green eyes and crinkled chin, amusement was programmed into Polly's countenance. Even after so many years, he found it hard to resist, the implication in her face that she knew a funny—and very possibly filthy—secret. But it could be tedious, too.

She swiveled to the child and put on her baby-talk voice. "I would never tease that man! Would I yank Uncle Sam's dick, Mr. Rainer?"

Rainer goggled at her, then at Sam, before producing an infuriated squawk.

"Don't say that in front of him." Polly's choice of words was a purposeful tweak. Rainer's mother had undertaken the task of yanking Uncle Sam's dick on more than one occasion, skillfully, and with Uncle Sam's encouragement.

She leaned forward, and Sam didn't fail to notice the parentheses of her pale cleavage, which had always been enticing and, with the galvanizing arrival of young Rainer, only more so. "Answer my question, then."

What sort of intrusions might make a wedding worthy of real celluloid, as opposed to the digital that he ran off in endless megabytes? Sam pictured an eruption of red ants spilling from the beak of an ice-sculpture goose. Every wedding had at least one senile granny; there could be a moment of opera, Grandma tearing out her nose tubes, clawing upright from her wheelchair, and letting loose with a keening minor note that exploded a hundred glasses. What would they do, all the guests in their formal wear, if a massive claw plunged from the sky and scooped the entire five-tiered vanilla cake with the trowel of a single talon? Sam knew what he would do: keep rolling.

"Catastrophe."

"Catastrophe? Like an earthquake?"

"No, like a real catastrophe. Like Pompeii."

"You want everyone to die horribly? At a beautiful wedding, Sammy? Those poor people all choked on ash and got turned into fossils." Polly stuck a finger and thumb into her hot chocolate, picked up the planetary hunk of marshmallow floating there, raised it to her mouth, and gasped. "You would die, too, Sam!" She let the marshmallow plop back into the chocolate. "You do know that I don't want you to die? You do know that no one wants you to die?"

"Yes, I fucking know that. Look, obviously, I would only shoot a Pompeii wedding if I had some sort of lava-proof position."

"Rainer certainly doesn't want you to die, does he?" She tickled one of the baby's pudgy brown cheeks and shook her head at him and smiled and crossed her eyes. Rainer drooled. "He *loves* you," said Polly, still goggling at the baby. "Yes, he *does*."

Sam sipped his hot chocolate. It was delicious, August be damned. At the surrounding tables, other young women were enjoying hot chocolate with their adorable moppets, their girl friends, or their gay pals. Everyone appeared amused, flummoxed by the impossible marshmallows. On the exterior of one of the City Bakery's large street-side windows, a diminutive vagrant dressed in an oily overcoat, blond beard tangled and matted, talked and gestured sharply with his hands, though there was no one near him. As Sam observed the unfortunate's conversation with the air, he concluded that the affair with Polly was another sort of pantomime. It wasn't helping her or him; it was just what they were accustomed to doing. The vagrant's overcoat billowed in a gust of wind, and he spun, flailing at the garment, as if he didn't realize he was wearing it and thought it was chasing him. Sam sipped again. Maybe the chocolate was a tad acrid.

"You do realize that some person is going to want to marry you some-day?"

"Maybe we'll elope."

"I can promise you that no woman, unless she's an orphan or a prostitute, honestly wants to elope. And if the woman's an orphan, it's only because she doesn't know any better."

Sam said he hadn't known that.

Polly said he could ask anyone. "Boy, you are going to make your wife tear her hair out. Your attitude is going to make her want to hang herself with her own garter. Thank God for Jo-Jo."

Jo-Jo was Polly's husband. An ex-ballplayer fifteen years her senior, Johannes "Jo-Jo" Knecht, born overseas to a German mother and an American serviceman, had been a light-hitting backup catcher for the late-nineties Yankees championship teams. The tabloids had nicknamed him "the Good German," and New York fans had esteemed him for his ability to block home plate against stampeding baserunners.

In the third game of the 1998 World Series, Jo-Jo had earned a measure of national fame when he checked the homeward sprint of a San Diego Padres shortstop named Esteban Herrera. The highlight of the collision shows Herrera breaking for the plate on a squeeze play, bracing for the impact by locking his forearms over his chest, until at the final moment he appears not to connect with the Yankees catcher so much as ricochet off a forcefield, flying backward several feet, all the way to the batting circle, where he lands on a twelve-year-old batboy. Herrera was lost for the Series with a concussion, the batboy ended up in traction, and the Padres were swept in four.

In retirement, Jo-Jo had taken a position providing studio commentary for Yankee broadcasts. His speech retained a faint Anglo-German accent that lent his insights a canny ring that people apparently liked; Sam thought he sounded like the Artful Dodger blended with a smidgen of Terminator. In the receiving line at his wedding to Polly, he had hauled Sam into a crushing embrace and tearfully proclaimed, "Nothing but love today, dude, yah?" The retired catcher also held an interest in a chain of used-car lots for which he was featured in an annoying series of television commercials.

None of that impressed Sam, however, who wasn't a sports fan. (Though he knew enough to consider the Yankees objectionable on principle. Talk of the so-called Yankee Way had, to Sam's ear, a fundamentalist ring—like maybe it wasn't the Yankee Way to perform oral sex, or to wear the color yellow during the month of January, or something like that.)

What did garner his respect were Jo-Jo's thighs. They were immense; they had the hard cylindrical shape of watermelons, the freakish kind that won prizes at fairs. It was these living pylons that had given him the power to repel other steroidal men from home plate. Jo-Jo's thighs looked constructed, coopered, like casks.

Although the man had never treated Sam with anything less than cheerful goodwill, Sam feared—quite reasonably, considering the sordid acts he had engaged in, and continued to engage in, with Jo-Jo's wife—that Jo-Jo would find out what was going on and kill him, boa constrictor–style, with his terrible thighs. There could be no ghastlier fate than to be scissored to death between those ham hocks.

Polly had met Jo-Jo when he came to visit the first-grade class that she had been teaching at a charter school in Fort Greene. She told Sam that it was seeing Jo-Jo squished down at the tiny art table, and hearing him interact with a five-year-old named Cricket, that had won her heart. "We're gonna need some of that blue paper there and a white crayon, yah?" Jo-Jo had informed Cricket, and spent a half hour painstakingly instructing the child in the art of drawing the interlocking N and Y of the Yankees' symbol. It didn't seem to matter that Jo-Jo displayed zero interest in the things that Polly liked aside from sports—novels, music, fashion, or gossip. Nor did it seem to make any difference that she continued to like sleeping with Sam.

She claimed they were in love, she and Jo-Jo, and maybe they were. Love could be fraught and bizarre, and there were always secrets, arrangements of which no one else was aware. All you had to do was think about anyone's parents. The affair Polly was conducting didn't, Sam had to concede, rule out some kind of successful, loving marriage.

Who knew how it was behind closed doors, what actually went on between Polly and her husband and her husband's thighs.

"Why are you so concerned with a wife I don't have?" asked Sam.

"Because you're intent on spoiling her wedding by being a jaded poop about everything." Polly moaned. He heard her stomp her feet under the table. "You are so frustrating. I don't understand how you can hate weddings."

"Because they're my job," he said. "And I never said that. I said they were dull and tiresome, and if something awful happened, it would be more interesting to film."

"But you need to have one, Sam. Don't you see? Your wedding is like the birthday party for the rest of your life." Polly's voice had grown small. She sounded the way people sound when they have at last accepted that a beloved and irreplaceable possession—a photo, an earring, the cat—is not going to turn up after all.

What Polly failed to comprehend was that weddings were just one of the many, many things that bored and irritated him these days. He had suffered a great loss, and he could be sour, but with the exception of thoughts about Booth, Sam rarely engaged in conscious negativity. He didn't have the energy.

Sam tried to switch subjects; he asked if Jo-Jo really liked him. Polly said yes, but who cared, Sam was *her* friend. There followed a silence then, which Polly didn't usually permit. It meant she was actually mad.

Rainer released a sudden burble of outrage and kicked his baby shoes. "I understand exactly how you feel, sweetheart," Polly said. "Uncle Sam can be an unbelievable pisser."

The bearded vagrant was gazing in their direction. He gave an exaggerated blink, squeezing his eyes shut tight, then opening them wide. It was the action of a child calling on all his reserves of courage before throwing open a closet door. The man raised a pale, shaking hand. His curly hair and long beard streamed left in another burst of wind.

It was a greeting to some ghost, Sam inferred, and in its tentativeness there was also a feeble plea. For what, Sam couldn't guess. He had to count himself lucky there.

"What are we doing?" Sam asked abruptly. What he meant was: let's stop meeting in secret, having sex, messing with your marriage, messing with your kid's life; it's not fun anymore.

"Don't start." Polly rose and began snatching up her things and stuffing them in her bag. It was time to go to see her shrink, she announced; her tits ached, summer had crapped out on them without so much as a fare-thee-well and, she finished, thanks to him, for days to come she would be ruminating on Pompeii, thinking about people being boiled alive in lava and turned into statues, because that was just how her mind worked.

He stood and put out his arms. Polly hugged him hard, as if she wanted to crack something, then let go, hoisted Rainer's seat, and departed without a backward glance. Sam sat and watched her go.

Polly turned right, lugging Rainer's seat, her free hand lifted to hail a taxi, and passed beyond Sam's sight.

The vagrant staggered off in the other direction, waving his arms around as if trying to ward off a cloud of midges. Then the vagrant was gone, too. Sam wondered what it was like to live like that, pestered by phantoms, at mortal odds with your own head.

Sam took a sip of cooling, clotting chocolate and somehow managed to swallow it.

Only here, now, on this random Thursday night in September, at the nuptials of two middle-aged academics, as the weddingographer filmed from his spot between the balcony newels, an elderly man in academic robes shuffled up the aisle to take a place between the spouses-to-be. This elderly man was the officiant. The program bestowed upon him the title Poet. That was different.

For the occasion, the poet had donned academic robes, silvery at the seams from decades of use. He stooped, craning his neck to gaze at the audience from the pit between his shoulders. The tight white curls of his hair appeared yellowed at the tips, a detail that suggested a life gone marvelously beyond ripe. His voice was piping.

The poet began by telling the assembled, the family and friends of these two middle-aged professors, "So, here we are on the last night of summer. The last night of summer. I thought it would never end. Never end. Well, I guess we'll just have to see what this new season has to offer. This new season." Before continuing, the poet glanced meaningfully at the husband-to-be, then at the wife-to-be. "The woman I loved has been dead for six years now. I think of her each day. Each day. She was a beauty and a wit and a friend. To have known her was, and remains, my greatest blessing. She is here still. Still . . .

"She is. Literally. Literally. I still find her detritus around the apartment. Lena was a woman of innumerable qualities, but few if any of them were better developed than her general scabrousness. Only the other day I discovered that she had left me a used Band-Aid on page 121 of our *Collected Larkin*." The elderly gentleman rolled his eyes and wagged his head. "Thank you very much, Lena."

The crowd laughed.

Sam narrowed the aperture of the lens, carving off the bride and groom, and it was as though the man were speaking to him alone, the eye in the balcony.

"But look at this here—" The poet lifted a finger. There was a Band-Aid on the ring finger. "Look at this here . . . Love is not easy. You carry it around with you forever." He placed his hands on the shoulders of the bride and groom. "It is the most glorious encumbrance a human being can shoulder. But it is not light. No, it is not light . . ."

The poet winked at the groom. He turned to the bride and leaned in to whisper something private in her ear. She giggled.

With that, the elderly gentleman once again addressed the audience, to ask forebearance for a few lines of verse. Not his own, he said, he was letting them off for good behavior. It was a poem by Jack Gilbert called "A Brief for the Defense":

"Sorrow everywhere," it began. There followed a series of juxtapositions between hunger and beauty, sickness and laughter. This gave the basis for an argument about joy, about the necessity for it, the duty of each person to accept it. To refuse joy was an immoral act and an insult to humanity. The elderly gentleman recited with his eyes closed. At the end of each line, his withered voice rose, as plangent as wind through a crack in the wall:

> . . . *We must have*
> *the stubbornness to accept our gladness in the ruthless*
> *furnace of this world. To make injustice the only*
> *measure of our attention is to praise the Devil.*

An involuntary tension locked Sam's hand on the lens hood. At the neck of the camera, the plastic coupling mewled.

The poem concluded with the sound of oars pulling through still water.

The old man coughed. "Okay, that's it. We love you guys. It's going to be a great fall. Get up here, Reverend. Take us home. Take us home. The fondue's getting cold."

As the new husband and wife retraced the aisle, the ovation that followed them seemed too loud to Sam's ears, as though it were coming from somewhere inside himself instead of out. The figures in his lens started to bob and slide, but he managed to film through the blessing and the vows.

The cocktail hour commenced.

Sam dragged himself up by the railing. His legs wobbled, and he bumped into someone. His chest felt swollen. Gray specks drizzled across his vision. Liquid splashed his shoulder, and something hit his shoe.

"Hey." A young woman in a purple halter dress was beside him, holding a now empty cocktail glass. She was short and wore her dark hair pulled into a pair of stubby hornlike ponytails. A tiny pink diamond clung to her right nostril; scratches of light bent and smeared from the stone and across her face; he was tipping, about to fall.

Fingers lightly touched his elbow. "You're forgetting to breathe," said the woman.

Sam exhaled. He tightened his grip on the railing and focused on the floor. The rain on the surface of his vision faded away. There was a green olive on the toe of his right shoe, resting at the tip of a wave in the stitching.

"Are you okay?"

"I'm sorry about"—he meant to say her drink, he was sorry about her drink, but he was looking at his shoe—"your olive," Sam finished.

The young woman told him to forget it. "Really, are you sure you're okay?"

He bent gingerly, picked the olive off his shoe, handed it to her—"Uh, thanks," she said—he apologized again, and strode across the balcony, descended one set of stairs to the ground floor, another set to the basement, and finally made it to the men's lavatory.

On the marble sink counter, Sam put down his camera. The violin strains of the first song of the cocktail hour leaked under the door. One of the faucets was dripping. He leaned against the marble and breathed. *The ruthless furnace of this world.* The words were fluttering in his head, held there in some mental updraft. Sam repeated the line quietly, letting the words slip off his dry lips.

Poetry had never meant much to him. He didn't read it, hadn't known anyone since college who did. (At Russell, there had been three or four gloomy, bilious girls who huddled in the Shakespeare garden in their hairy black pea coats, ostentatiously taking turns reading aloud from *The Norton Anthology of Poetry.* He remembered how furiously they had smoked and the stink eye they'd shoot at anyone who came too close.) Nevertheless, the meaning of the line was clear enough: the world caught you, the world caught everyone in the end, and the world was a fire. Sam felt that he knew that as well as anyone.

The bathroom door creaked open. A man entered and went to a urinal. He finished pissing, he zipped his fly, and he left without washing his hands. In the mirror, Sam saw the man shoot him a suspicious glance before he pushed out the door, and that was when the wedding-ographer realized he was visibly shuddering all over, his hands opening and closing at his sides, his legs shivering inside his trousers, his teeth chattering, the clacking in his skull like someone stabbing a single typewriter key over and over again.

2.

After a few minutes Sam was able to gather himself and return to the reception. Over the next hour, he worked the room, recording the guests as unobtrusively as possible while they mingled and chatted and helped themselves to the hors d'oeuvres and the open bar.

Toward the end of the cocktail hour, one attendee, a burly man in a glaring maroon suit, toasted the good fortune of the newlyweds by beginning to bellow "La Marseillaise." Several others soon joined in. Someone helped the poet up onto a banquet table, where he danced, rigidly, and flapped his skinny elbows like a taunting child. Another part of the room began to sing "Do You Really Want to Hurt Me." An old woman removed her flats and clapped the soles together in an aggressive way.

The bride, who was singing with the "Do You Really Want to Hurt Me" people, lifted the hem of her gown and flashed some thigh at the people singing "La Marseillaise." The groom climbed atop the table where the poet was dancing. He fed the poet a shrimp, and the poet pretended to be a seal. A waiter, a bona fide Frenchman, cast down his platter of stuffed mushrooms, tore off his tie, and threw his arm around the bearded man, joining in with "La Marseillaise." A child had obtained an ice bucket; a miniature flapper of a girl wearing a sequined headband and pink shoes, she began to wander around, swinging the bucket, carefully seeding the floor with ice cubes.

Sam rushed around, weaving between tables and chairs, tracking singing faces, focusing on the banging soles, capturing the deliberate, tottering walk of the girl with the bucket as she moved through the tumult, cubes falling in her wake.

The poet started to choke on a shrimp. The groom performed the Heimlich maneuver, and the old man coughed up the bit of shellfish onto a woman's perm. There was a shriek as someone's aunt stepped on an ice cube and went down with a kick and a thump on the hardwood. The singing petered out, to scattered applause. Dinner was served.

Sam stowed his camera behind the bar for a fifteen-minute break and hunkered in a corner near the open bar to eat a dinner roll and sip a Maker's Mark. His phone vibrated—a text message from Mina:

> Salutations, ex-friend. I'm coming over for the night. Her needs space from her mother.

Recently, his relationship with his sister had become fraught. There had been an inappropriate boyfriend situation, Sam had intervened, and the last they'd spoken, about a week ago, she'd told him to die. Mina was the one person who, over the last few years, had maintained the power to sometimes make Sam do things he didn't want to. In this area, though, her effort to make him feel guilty had failed utterly—she was seventeen, and he was right.

Sam typed back,

> **What is the magic word?**

"Girlfriend?" The young woman in the purple dress with the pony-tails and the nose ring was leaning over Sam, reading his cell screen.

"Kid sister."

Mina's reply popped on the screen:

> **Rosebud, you fucking asshole.**

"Oh, I like her," said the woman.

"Yeah," said Sam, "she's great." He wrote to Mina that he'd be home around eleven or so, set his phone aside.

"So I guess you must go to a lot of weddings," she said.

"Yeah. Most every weekend."

"Wow. How miserable are you?"

"I've considered climbing a clock tower a few times." He reached up to shake her hand. "Sam."

"Tess," said the young woman. "We met when you were about to pass out."

He took a bite of his roll. "I think I had a panic attack."

"Seriously?" Tess's fists were planted on her hips, and she spoke with a flat, slightly nasal affect. It was easy to imagine her demanding his lunch money, easy to imagine handing it over. Sam found this attractive.

"Yeah," he said. "I'm not sure why." He wasn't about to get into it with a stranger. The litany of his life's incinerations was, at the very least, second-date material.

"Well, you seem okay now. Maybe it was that grim fucking poem. 'Congratulations on your marriage, and no pressure, but if you don't enjoy it, you're letting down the rest of the world, which, by the way, is a cesspool.' Hold on a sec."

She stepped away to the bar, and he heard her order a vodka tonic. When she returned, he was finished with his roll and put up his hand for a lift. She obliged and he stood. Tess had a small, cold hand, no rings.

Sam brushed a few crumbs from his trousers. He wore a black suit, a white shirt, and a black tie—dull but all-purpose.

"Are you always so sensitive, Sam? For instance, do you cry often?"

"Would there be something wrong with that? If I cried often?"

"Yes."

"No, I don't cry often. Outside of, you know, people I know dying, or extreme pain. I've always thought of myself as being fairly stoic. I didn't cry when the Towers fell. I just sat there and watched and ate crackers all day. Froze me."

"I didn't cry, either, not that day, anyway. I cried when I saw Dan Rather crying on *Letterman*. That broke my heart."

"I saw that. I don't know if it made me cry, but it was definitely disconcerting. Why do you suppose that is?"

"Because Dan Rather's so old and earnest and wacky. You don't want to see someone like that crying. It made him so real and normal." She drank from her tumbler, sucked on an ice cube, let it clink back in the glass. "How about movies? Do you cry at movies?"

"Not a lot. *The 400 Blows. Bambi.*" Sam pondered for a few seconds—little else came to mind. "I suspect I teared up when they shot Sal in *Dog Day Afternoon*. And maybe when they killed Fredo in the second *Godfather*. Movies with John Cazale tend to get to me."

"Cazale . . . He was in *The Deerhunter*, too, wasn't he? Which brother was Fredo in *The Godfather*?"

Though he appeared in only five films, John Cazale had been the finest character actor of the seventies. His hollowed, haunted face induced all his portrayals with a note of suffering. Each of his five films was nominated for Best Picture.

"Fredo was the pitiful one," said Sam.

Tess snapped her fingers. "Cazale! Now I can see him. Love that guy. Oh, but what about *E.T.*? Everyone cried at *E.T.*"

Sam quickly shook his head. "Nah," he lied, and Tess scowled. "I don't believe you," she said. "It's true," he lied again, casually, instinctively.

It so happened that Sam had recently rewatched the story of the boy Elliott and his magical friend from outer space—sort of rewatched it, anyway. The Brooklyn Academy of Music had run a print of the film for a week a few months earlier. Sam had attended a show with Wesley. The reason Sam had only sort of rewatched the movie was because the screening that he went to was at midnight, which was because Wesley was a sloth, incapable of rising earlier than one or two in the afternoon.

(After waking, Wesley needed to tend to the Internet for several hours, the effect of which was that he was not often prepared to emerge from the apartment before ten P.M. Not for nothing was "Rushing" #1 on his list of "Seventy-four Things That Cause Unnecessary Fatigue." "Crowded environments," #39 on the list, also applied in this case, since the film's run was so short and so popular, and it was even more important because Wesley planned to reassess the film as Swag Hag— someone from BAM had given him free passes—and he claimed that overlarge groups sapped his "critical acumen." Sam, for his part, thought that the Swag Hag's critical acumen was in good shape, considering his recent denunciation of the Ulster County Microbrewery's Rip Van Winkle white ale: *A ratsbane concocted of rubbing alcohol, pus milk squeezed from the blackened udders of dying cows, and a zest of sorrow scraped from the lice-ridden scalps of unloved children. NOT EVEN FOR FREE.*

E.T., meanwhile, proved more to the Hag's taste: *Maybe intergalactic friendship doesn't mean anything to you, you cynical prick, but it still means something to me! If you don't want to be friends with a wonderful little space guy, if you don't dream of flying above the treetops and across the moon on your bicycle with your crazy buddies, what do you dream of? To paraphrase E.T., "I'll be right here—just waiting to hear what the hell it is that* you *think is more awesome than that." I make no apologies. YEAH, I'LL TAKE IT.*)

Due to the late hour, Sam had fallen asleep right after the opening credits, coming around only toward the end, at the part where the pasty-skinned E.T. rises, not unlike Our Savior, from the dead. It was true, the scene made him cry when he was younger. The noxious clouds of stuff it brought up, like disturbed silt—thoughts about Allie and Booth, memories about being a kid, his adult awareness of how much he hadn't seen that was right in front of him—made him nauseated. Sam had shut his eyes and pretended to sleep until the movie was finished.

He didn't want to get into that with Tess or anyone else.

"You must be a robot then. Everyone cries during that movie. Even Republicans," said Tess.

Sam immediately selected the off-ramp away from *E.T.* "Maybe I'm a Republican."

In fact, the few strong political convictions Sam did subscribe to related to sexuality—he was friends with a number of gay people and felt that birth control was the bedrock of civilization—and these were sufficient to make him a solid Democrat. Not that he didn't tend leftward in other ways: he didn't go to church, have any children, or invest; none of his friends worked in heavy industry, coal mining, oil drilling, livestock farming, agricultural farming, or served in the armed forces; the extinction of animals bothered him if he thought about it, though he rarely did; the Confederate flag, he'd gladly use to wipe his ass; various brown people, black people, Asian people, and people with extremely difficult-to-pronounce names had inhabited neighboring apartments during the time Sam had lived in New York City, and never once had any of his neighbors possessed worse manners than Wesley. By the opposite token, his only faintly right-leaning instinct was an abiding suspicion of adults who rode skateboards. But it was the sex issues that he most actively cared about, although "actively" might have been putting it a bit too strongly.

Tess told him not to joke about that bullshit. "This is a bad time. These Tea Bagger people freak me out. I'm sick of hearing that, because I don't believe in God, and I don't want gay people thrown in dungeons, I'm out of the mainstream. I mean, I'm as eager as anybody to stab a terrorist in the eye. I eat hamburgers. I'm as American as anyone."

"The president seems cool." Obama struck Sam as the kind of person who—if there was a dinner party and one of the invitees got dumped the day before and had to come stag—could be counted on to make an effort. He'd tease the newly single buddy about his shirt, demand that he defend the new Radiohead album with a straight face, make an insinuation about the guy's sexual prowess, just basically talk him up so the dumped guy couldn't brood. Whether he was a good leader or not, Sam not only had no opinion, he couldn't even imagine having an opinion.

"Obama's okay. I've been a little disappointed," said Tess. "But it's, like, I've had it up to my ears with old white people who wear cell phones on belt clips. Like they're so damn important, they have to be able to quick-draw their cell phone like freaking Wyatt Earp. Tea Baggers, you watch a report on one of their protests sometime, you'll see, the most homogenous thing about them isn't even that they're old and white, it's that they all have cell-phone belt clips."

Sam groaned. Here was something he did have an opinion on. "Oh, those fucking cell-phone belt clips! I hate those, too."

They exchanged a fist pound.

"I do think the president has turned out to be kind of like the Segway, though. Remember before the Segway came out, all the rumors about what it was?" She raised an eyebrow. Her eyebrows were very black, very thin, and very sharp. "Like it was going to be a space car or a teleportation machine, some amazing leap forward? And it was just this scooter thing. When I voted for Obama, I thought he was going to be a space car, and he's turned out to be a Segway."

"Wait a sec. I don't know if you're being fair to the Segway." Sam didn't usually notice eyebrows, but he liked hers. Tess's eyebrows weren't messing around. "It's incredibly responsive, right? With special gyroscopes and everything?"

"Special gyroscopes are meaningless if they don't come in a space car." She sipped her drink, again sucking on an ice cube before letting it drop back in the tumbler. It could have seemed like some kind of cheesy come-on, but he sensed that it was involuntary, which made it sexy. "John Cazale, though. They don't make them like that anymore, do they? What's the closest thing? Rick Savini?"

Sam shrugged in a way that was meant to indicate he was noncommittal. The parallel was there—the two actors had a great deal in common—but a discussion of Rick Savini was something that Sam very definitely wanted no part of. He was enjoying talking to her, and that was a sure way to spoil it. "I wouldn't want to compare Cazale to anyone else. There's that part in *Dog Day Afternoon* where Pacino asks him what country he wants to escape to, and Cazale, he says, 'Wyoming.' I can't imagine anyone else carrying that line off. It kills me every time."

Tess closed her eyes for a moment, then opened them. "Oh, I remember that! I know what you mean. It's sort of funny, but it's also like—you know, this guy has some serious problems. He doesn't have any idea what he's doing. 'Wyoming.'"

" 'Wyoming.' Yeah. Exactly." Sam was impressed. That was how he saw it, too, and it was exciting to agree.

"You'd never know that the scene was improvised," she said.

"I'm sure it wasn't improvised." He was being polite; it couldn't have been improvised. The scene was too good, too precise. Lumet had directed it.

"I'm pretty sure I read that it was."

"Nah," said Sam. "I'm positive Lumet had the scene nailed down when he shot it."

"I'm really pretty sure I read that it was."

He shook his head. "No."

Tess scrutinized him. The keenness of her look made Sam feel, not unappealingly, like a shabby piece of quartz under a gemcutter's microscope—like he was about to get sawed up. "I guess shooting weddings is sort of like directing, isn't it? You're like, what, a wedding auteur?"

Despite the youthful plating—the dress, the ponytails, the nose ring—Sam put Tess in her thirties, a few years older than he. A few frayed threads around the eyes gave her away. From these features, he extrapolated that she was someone experienced enough with disappointment to appreciate the underrated pleasure of settling for a man who was useless but friendly and not crazy—someone like him, for instance.

Except under circumstances of extreme horniness, he preferred not to tangle with optimistic people. Optimistic people required enthusiasm. To Sam, this was anathema. If you thought of sex as poker, then fervor was what the high rollers bet. He was strictly a low-stakes player, and he knew it; Sam's markers were agreeability and low-key bravado, both as worthless as Monopoly money. They just looked like big bucks when you threw them up in the air.

The band members, a jazz quintet, were plugging their instruments back in. The dancing portion of the evening would begin soon.

Sam told her he had to go back to work, but he'd like to talk to her later.

"Okay." Tess picked up his iPhone from where he'd set it on top of his camera bag. "Are you sure Mina is your sister?" She started to enter her own contact information.

"Caught me. She's a prostitute. But not the one who gave me gonorrhea."

"Okay." Tess handed him his phone.

"Thanks. No, Mina really is my sister. What are you doing tonight, after? Why don't we get a drink?"

Tess reached out and brushed a crumb from his jacket. "I can do that. No more panic attacks, though, right?"

"Sure thing."

"Good, because honestly, Sam, I'm not great at the shoulder-to-lean-on thing. I'm not that nice a person."

He was bent, hoisting his camera, which was why she didn't see his face fall.

Only nice people said they weren't nice, and it was hard to be nice unless you harbored some expectations, still kept a secret to-do list, still imagined what it might feel like to check all the boxes. The subject of politics should have been a warning: she gave a shit. Tess may have looked the part, and she knew her lines, but it was acting, and Sam was not—now, later, evermore—about to suspend his disbelief. No good came of that.

"Uh-huh. I'll see you later." The weddingographer was already moving away, camera poised to document the clothes and the pomp, the laughter and the hugs, the entire joyous celebration.

Tess proved difficult to shake.

During the first slow dance, she was there in the far corner of the floor, gaze plainly fixed on him while everyone else was watching the newlyweds turn in circles. Sam tightened on the bride and groom to make Tess disappear.

At the cake cutting, everyone in the band took up a horn and, as the bride and groom lowered the knife into the bottom tier, let blast a heraldic charge.

A hand touched Sam's left elbow, the side of his free eye. "You want something to drink, Cazale?" asked Tess. He told her he was fine, and she said, "Righto. Carry on."

While he filmed the chair dance, Sam glimpsed her face among the pitching hands and the flipping hem of the bride's gown. This time he surrendered to an impulse to go close on her, pushing the focus past the chair, past hands and shoulders, until her face was near, captured at a three-quarter angle. With her bare neck and the tendril of black hair dangling past her ear, she was pretty, yet also sad, despite a small smile. It might have been the tilt of her head, or the way the lens separated her from the cheering crowd, but as Sam studied her, he thought of the little portraits in big museums: how you saw a fabulous painting of a beautiful sixteenth-century countess in a monograph, and then it turned out to be the size of a birthday card, tucked into a corner of a quiet vaulted room. The exacting miniaturization of those real people—dust now—caused him to feel a pang. You knew that they had been so much bigger.

Sam thought, it's too bad I don't make movies anymore. The shot asked interesting questions. Why this girl? What about her is turned, ever so slightly, away from the audience's view?

Then he thought, What in the hell are you doing? And jerked the camera to the left.

The weddingographer spent the next hour shooting good-luck messages from various guests, got a few atmospheric clips—the band, the waiters, the open bar, the tiny lights strung along the balcony—and at last, the bride and groom dashing to their limousine in a hail of rice. The party would continue for an indefinite period, but Sam's work was nearly done.

On the balcony again, he sat in a chair and filmed the Brooklyn Bridge for five continuous minutes. While as a metaphor, it sucked, it was relaxing, watching the cars pour over the bridge.

"Thought experiment: what do you do if you see someone getting ready to jump off?" Tess had come up behind him.

"Keep rolling," said Sam. He didn't shift from the viewfinder.

"Huh," she said. A few seconds passed, and he heard her heels click away.

If a bride and groom granted a little space for self-promotion, Sam liked to leave his laptop out on a banquet table in the vicinity of the coat/bag check. He programmed it to run an infinite loop of the different wedding videos that he'd filmed. When Sam came down from the balcony, Tess was waiting at the table, transfixed by his wedding reel, an amber-colored drink in her hand.

A dark-haired bride swings in the arms of her groom, laughing and whirling in slow motion as mariachi music fills the sound track, completely out of time. In the next moment, there's a jump cut flashing back to the bride's dressing room. She's in her underwear and freaking out: "I'm so fat!" The mariachi sound track shifts to the next gear; voices whoop over a spray of guitar figures. An older woman reaches for the bride's forearm in an attempt to calm her. The bride belts the older woman with a dainty white teddy bear: "Don't touch me!" Then she's dancing again, swinging in slow motion. This is followed by another jump cut, and now the little white teddy bear is floating snout-down in a crystal bowl of cherry-red punch. An hors d'oeuvre spear protrudes from his back. A title card emerges in blinking, buzzing green neon:

MARRIAGE IS A GRINDHOUSE

The image froze, faded, and another section of the video loop began.

"These are impressive. I mean, I'm not saying I'd want one. But they're impressive."

"Thanks." Sam reached over her shoulder to close the lid of the laptop, picked up the computer, and stowed it in his shoulder bag.

Besides providing the de rigueur weddingography service, which promised a chronicle of all the highlights of the ceremony and reception, Sam offered a deluxe Director's Cut package. At the cost of an extra seven hundred dollars—plus a few minor expenses—he produced a short alternate wedding video designed according to the principles of one of three different styles. The choices were: Grindhouse Wedding, Nouvelle Vague Wedding, and Citizen Wedding.

The Director's Cut videos were primarily exercises in editing and sound-tracking and, in the case of the Citizen Wedding, the use of extra light to create a simulacrum of deep-focus photography. In each case, it was necessary to shoot a certain amount of staged material, although less than people expected.

The Grindhouse Wedding clip was typical. The bride actually had gone berserk on her mother-in-law with the little teddy bear. It was the sort of occurrence that took place all the time at weddings. A minute afterward, of course, everyone in the bride's dressing room was laughing, but Sam instantly recognized the dramatic caché.

For the Grindhouse cut, he trimmed out the laughter, spliced it with some of the dancing footage, slowed the latter way down for maximum strangeness, added a clashing mariachi sound track, and as a topper, filmed the murdered teddy in the punch bowl on a separate day. Patched together, the different parts supplied the hallmarks of the genre: violence adjacent to happiness, slow-motion interludes, and an ironic sound track.

The other cuts were conceived according to similar formulas. With the Nouvelle Vague Wedding, Sam took time out to follow the different principals, stalking them from area to area as opposed to filming from static locations or using a tripod. This provided a rough facsimile of that style's characteristic tracking shots. When he edited the footage, he spliced in clips from a library that he had built over the years by surreptitiously filming episodes in public places that he deemed Gallic: cool-looking women in trench coats, unshaved men unabashedly staring at asses and tits, people drinking from tiny cups at sidewalk tables, face-to-face meetings between small dogs and large dogs, etc. Tack on a Charles Aznavour tune, and voilà.

The Citizen Wedding was probably the simplest. Sam rented a shitload of stationary lighting, planted it around, and hired an extra cameraperson to come and shoot additional footage upward from the floor. In the editing, he flipped the heavily shadowed floor footage to black and white to achieve Wellesian deep focus, stripped the sound, and replaced it with a scratchy vinyl recording of Boris Karloff reading "Kubla Khan."

Tess was impressed. Well, that made one of them.

The Director's Cuts were exercises in the cheesiest sort of mimesis. People liked them the way they liked the Caesar salad at chain restaurants, without anchovies, and without being aware that anything was missing. The cuts were no less clichéd than the fade-out of the Brooklyn Bridge. Sam didn't begrudge people for enjoying them—he hated anchovies, too—but he knew what they were: bullshit.

Tess followed him out to his car, a red compact that he had rented for the job, and stood by while he stowed his gear in the trunk. It was a warm, clammy evening. Pieces of wet trash plastered the pavement. Two steps outside, beyond the envelope of the air-conditioning, Sam was sweating.

"Seriously, those are pretty good," she said.

"Thanks." He slammed the trunk shut. Okay, maybe he begrudged them a little.

"Not just the music and the slo-mo and all that showy stuff. You had a lot of different perspectives mixed in, and it's so steady, you'd think you had multiple cameras all over the place. You ever thought about going pro?"

They walked back toward the restaurant. "What do you mean?"

Tess held open the door, and Sam stepped through. "Pro. Make real movies. Television, whatever."

"Why do you ask?" He noticed the small stack of his business cards on the lobby banquet table and scooped them up, dropped them in his jacket pocket.

"I'm in the business."

Sam nodded. She was in the Business.

He gave her his widest, fakest smile. If the smile had been an e-mail, the subject line would have read, *Hey man, ever thought about trying pheromones?* That he had been considering having sex with this woman suddenly seemed like a skid on black ice. He had plowed into a snowbank and come to with nothing worse than a bump on his head, but he might as easily have been killed. She worked in the Business. Sam wanted nothing to do with the Business. He had his health to consider.

"I produce," said Tess. "Television, mostly. Have you ever seen *Secrets Only Dead Men Know*? The true-crime show? That's where I am right now."

"Wow," he said. In his chest, his heart became a rubber ball, skipping back and forth, gathering speed.

"Are you okay? You looked peaked. Have you been thinking about poetry again?" As she spoke, Tess casually rearranged the bust of her purple strapless dress.

Sam was momentarily distracted. Her breasts were not large, but they had a pleasing definition, the pale tops, and below, neat and purple-bundled, like a pair of bindles. "Wow," he repeated.

Tess followed his eyes to her cleavage. When she looked up, her cheeks were reddening, and she smiled at him, albeit a tad nervously. "So, are we going to get that drink?" she asked.

"Uh-huh," Sam said. The rubber ball hit funny—caught a rib, maybe—and ricocheted under his armpit. The resulting cramp felt like a hand pinching him from the inside. He exhaled tightly. "Can you wait here a sec? I'm just going to run into the bathroom."

"Great," Tess said, and her smile widened. There was a chip missing from her right canine. Sam thought it was lovely, mischievous and sweet, the kind of detail that made a face worth remembering. He hoped it didn't embarrass her.

He returned Tess's smile. "Don't move an inch."

"Hold on." She reached out and pressed the back of her hand to his cheek.

The movement should have startled him, but it didn't. He watched the hand rise up to his face and didn't move, didn't flinch, as her cool skin touched his warm skin, and the bones of her hand pressed lightly against the bones of his face. The intimacy of the moment was as comfortable as it was uncanny; although he didn't know her, he felt like he did. Here was someone he could talk to. Here was someone he could watch *Dog Day Afternoon* with. Sam closed his eyes.

His chest opened, and he could breathe, and he knew he was being craven and that he should stay with her, that he should move closer, not away. She wasn't on a wall in a corner of some museum; she was right here. Tess was right in front of him, touching him, telling him to stay with her, wanting him to stay with her—which was exactly why he needed to go.

"Are you sure you're okay?" she asked.

He opened his eyes. She was frowning. There was a hook of hair stuck to her forehead that he wanted to brush away. Jesus, did he really, really need to go, because it wasn't just Tess wanting him to stay with her; he wanted it, too. He could have reached out and fixed her hair, no problem.

"Yeah," Sam said. "I'm okay."

"Can I ask you something?" She didn't take away her hand. It stayed there against his cheek, cool and butterfly-light. "You won't tease me?"

"No." Her earnestness made him want to cry and laugh and kiss. "I won't."

"You really weren't disappointed by the Segway?"

"No. I mean, I haven't driven one, but I read somewhere that 'you just have to think the direction you want to go in.' That sounded pretty great to me."

Tess nodded. "You're not okay, are you?"

"I told you. I'm fine. Truly. I'll be right back." Sam lifted his hand to hers, gently drew it aside.

3.

Sam descended to the restrooms in the basement. He pushed into the men's, walked past the marble counter, the three urinals, and the three stalls to the far end. Set high in the wall was a broad, deep-welled, frosted casement window.

He pondered the window from underneath. Sam had his father's height but only a fraction of the old man's bulk—just a soft tire around the middle—and he thought he'd squeeze through fairly easily. The problem was that the bottom of the window ledge started at the top of his head. There was no way he could pull himself up.

The obvious solution was a chair that he could step up onto, but to get one, he would have to return to the lobby, where Tess was waiting for him, which would defeat the purpose.

And what was the purpose? To escape from the pretty, passive-aggressive, sad-eyed girl with the sweet chipped tooth and the lovely bindle-like breasts, because he didn't want to say to her face, "I'm sorry. I really like you, I really feel a connection with you, but the thing is, I can't be with someone I like. It's too stressful for me. Expectations frighten me. And you work in television, which is right next to movies, which is another thing that is upsetting to my tender condition"—was that what it came down to?

Yes, that was pretty much what it came down to. He didn't want to make up an excuse and lie to Tess, and he didn't want to tell her the truth. That left a back exit.

In a nearby stall, someone coughed, gave a pained sigh. *"Gas, gas, quick, boys!"*

Sam rapped on the stall door. "Little help, here." He heard the man inside fumbling with his pants, a belt buckle clinking. The toilet flushed once and then a second time. A moment or two after the first flush, there was a noise like a snorkel being cleared.

The stall door swung open, and the old poet who had officiated the wedding staggered out. The stench that followed him was pure rot, the smell of hot compost.

The weddingographer took an involuntary step back.

With his eyes half closed, the poet studied Sam. He pursed his lips.

He swayed. His academic gown was stuffed partially into his trousers. The elderly gentleman cleared his throat and recited, " 'As under a green sea, I saw him drowning.' " He reached for the handle of the stall door and gently drew it shut behind him. "I am dying," he said. "I am dying."

"I know," said Sam.

"The wife, the dog, and finally—me." The poet examined his fly.

"You got it," said Sam, meaning the fly.

The poet regarded him with a deep frown. "Look, what do you"—he made an incantatory wiggle with his fingers—"need?"

Sam put a hand over his mouth and nose as he pointed to the window. "A boost."

"Very well." The elderly gentleman took a few mincing steps to the wall beneath the frosted window. He squatted a little, making a cup with his hands for Sam to step into.

Up close, the frailty of the man was evident: hands knotty and liver-spotted, blue veins thick at the temples, a vibration at the knees.

"That isn't going to work."

The poet straightened, shrugged. He turned to face the door.

"No, no." Sam put his hand on the poet's shoulder. "If you could, you know, get down on your knees." He indicated the floor, which was tiled, and not visibly unsanitary. "I could step up on your back."

The poet took a whistling breath. "I am seventy-eight. Seventy-eight." He shook his head and contemplated the spot Sam had indicated on the floor. He put his index finger to his mouth and ran his late wife's Band-Aid over his lips. The silence between them was underlined by the hush of flowing water.

"Please?" Sam patted the man's shoulder, which felt like bare bone through the cloth of the gown.

With a small wheeze, the poet bent his knees, lowering himself into a true squat. His legs wobbled in his tuxedo pants. Once again, he cupped his hands for Sam to step into.

"I told you, that's not going to work." Sam pushed down lightly on the old man's shoulder.

"Fucking come on!" The poet swatted ineffectually at his supplicant. "I don't want to get on the floor. People defecate here. It's awful. It's awful. Don't make me."

"Please," said Sam.

The poet flapped his hand some more before it gradually settled at his hip. "You're in trouble?"

"Yes," said Sam.

"God. Good God." The old man grunted and pitched forward onto his hands.

"Thank you," said Sam, and planted his right shoe on the base of the elderly man's spine, pushed off—hard—and caught the bottom of the window well with his elbows.

Beneath him, there was a squeaking inhalation, a gasp, and a thud of body against tile. "Ah!" cried the poet.

Sam pulled himself forward, flicked the lock tab, and shoved up the window. He dragged himself through, out into the humid air and onto the wet cobbles of the alley that ran the rear of the Stables.

Once he had gained his feet, Sam crouched to look down through the open window. The poet was lying facedown, limbs splayed. He looked like a corpse waiting for its chalk outline. A slight rise and fall at the back of his gown at least indicated that he was alive. The problem: the sound of flowing water was matched by visual proof that the old man had inflicted significant damage on the toilet; a dark tide spilled from beneath the stall door, brackish tributaries forming in the caulking between the tiles.

There was something hypnotic in the movement of the sewage filling the caulking, reminiscent of a Tetris game. The water moved closer and closer to the poet's body. A few soupçons of excrement were visible on the surface of the dark water.

"Thank you," Sam said. "Look, are you going to be okay? Because I have to go. You should get up. Goodbye. I'm sorry."

There was a groan from the body on the floor, which the wedding-ographer chose to interpret as permission to leave.

Tess had jolted Sam, put him to flight, frightened him badly with her blatant empathy, and there was nothing he needed more than to be else-where immediately. He made it only halfway up the alley before he piv-oted back. As much as he wanted to get away, he couldn't abandon an old man to drown in dank water.

That was the difficulty of commitments, promises, favors, and their like. Only the most basic transactional relations, such as casual sex or purchased sex or watching things on screens in the company of male friends, could be considered truly safe. The result of Sam's brief dalliance with Tess was typical. She had wanted more from him than he could provide, so in order to dodge her inevitable disappointment, he had fled. To make good his escape had required the poet's help—Sam was the one wanting something then—and for that, a remittance was demanded. If he did not go to the man's rescue, the poet's fate would belong to him.

It was fucked up, and it made Sam resent Tess for her interest, and the poet for his assistance, and himself for being so careless as to fall into a position where he didn't have a choice.

This was the essential point that Sam had wanted to make one afternoon not so long ago, when he had appeared uninvited at the door of the apartment of Mina's boyfriend, an eighteen-year-old named Peter Jenks. It was not a happy thing to find yourself locked into a situation at any age, but this was especially true in one's formative years; fatherhood, for example, was the locked room of locked rooms.

That Sam had discovered the presence of a boyfriend in Mina's life through somewhat scurrilous means—he had tossed the contents of her iPhone while she was not present—was secondary to the seriousness of the matter. Once you were a father (or a mother) well, you were completely on the hook, forever and ever.

Young Peter Jenks's parents were doctors, and the family resided in an expensive West Side building in sight of Central Park. A few days subsequent to his meeting Polly for hot chocolate at the City Bakery, Sam made a visit to Peter Jenks that coincided with the pre-parents, post-school hours between three and six. He told the epauleted doorman to call up and say that Peter's future brother-in-law had arrived.

When Peter answered the door, Sam grabbed him in a bear hug. "Peter!" Next, Sam invited Peter to show him to the television; there was something the young man needed to see.

In the living room, side by side on the Jenks family's extraordinarily comfortable gray suede couch, the two of them had viewed the award-winning movie about the demented paralyzed man who badgers his saintly wife to fuck strangers until she is sacrificed to a gang of depraved sailors.

As the final credits rolled, Sam asked Peter, "What'd you think, champ? Uplifting, right?"

Peter Jenks wore a dress shirt and a narrow blue necktie. Sam inferred that he was seeking to make a hip art-school impression, but what he looked like was a miniature guidance counselor. During the part of the movie where evil children pelt the saintly wife with stones, Sam was gratified to notice how Peter slumped down in his seat, visibly depressed, and stayed in that position until the movie finished.

Young Jenks scratched his head as he weighed Sam's question. "I don't know about that."

"Sure you do. How'd it make you feel?"

"Pretty bad, honestly," Peter said.

"Great," said Sam.

"Why is that great?" asked Peter.

"Because, Peter, having you watch this movie was the nicest way that I could impress upon you not only the importance I place on my sister's well-being, but how wise it might be for you to begin to carefully assess your options. Mina is seventeen. You are eighteen. One year makes a big difference." Sam pointed a finger at him. "Do I have to spell it out for you? Do you understand?"

Young Jenks rolled his eyes and nodded—and shifted a little farther down the couch, away from Sam.

"Lovely," said Sam. "What's with the stupid tie, by the way?"

Peter crossed his arms over the tie. "It's the style. I don't think it's stupid."

Sam shrugged; he wasn't convinced. "I'm going to go now. I'm glad we talked."

Peter asked, "Is this a joke, man? Because—"

Sam cut him off. "Don't have sex with my sister. Not a joke. Do not get her pregnant. Don't do it. The nasty little man who made this movie? I have all his movies on DVD. If I find out that you fucked my sister, I'll make you watch every single one of them. And if you get her pregnant, I'll make you eat every single one of them."

Sam left feeling pretty good. He had made his point and, in the process, enriched Young Jenks's sense of the cinema.

But Peter had tattled.

The next day Sam's sister demanded he meet her at the Union Square dog run. Mina was livid. First she called Sam an asshole. Then she said, "You can't control everything, Sam. You can't control me."

"What am I trying to control? I just wanted to get to know him," said Sam.

Mina was in charge of a pair of corgis from Sandra's dogwalking business. Her hair was dyed silver. In the midmorning sun, the rest of her was as inky as a fingerprint. She wore black tights and a black cloak tied with a red rope, and the mauve slathered beneath her eyes was cracking in the heat. How it was that he scared Peter Jenks and she didn't, Sam wanted to know.

"Whatever you can't control, you kill. At least my mother is mentally ill. You just don't want to deal with anything that's real. If you actually talked to Peter instead of torturing him with foreign films and threatening him, you'd love him. But you don't want to get your hands dirty. Now he hates me."

"I did like him, Mina. Honestly. I mean, I'm not sure about the tie thing, but overall, Peter seems like a smart guy. And he needed to see that movie. It's an important movie. If you want to understand twenty-first-century film, you've got see it. I'm not going to apologize for broadening someone's horizons."

His sister gave him the finger. She kicked some dust at him. "Choke, asshole."

Sam sidestepped, maintaining his cool. "Has it occurred to you that maybe Peter decided on his own that things weren't working out? Maybe he even thought, Hey, she's a little young, and I'm a little old, and it's a little creepy."

"He's eighteen and I'm seventeen! You're as bad as my mother, and you're way, way worse than Dad. If someone isn't exactly what you want them to be, you put them down."

"Mina. Hold up. I am not worse than Booth."

"You went through my phone, Sam. You invaded my privacy. Dad would never do that."

Sam knew for a fact that this was not true. Not so many years ago, after all, Booth had gone fishing in Sam's laptop bag and read his screenplay. (Though, it had to be said, this was a radically different set of circumstances. What Booth had done was a case of artistic meddling; what Sam had done was to rescue his kid sister from a hard-on in a skinny tie.)

"You don't know him like I know him," said Sam.

"Fuck you. Fuck. You."

Implicit was Mina's claim that Booth had become Father of the Year material—just because he had taken something resembling an active interest in her life and managed to make his child-support payments on time for a few years. Semi-retired in Hasbrouck, their father was able to get by on a patchwork of voice-over work and a film class or two at the local community college. What had led him to settle down so abruptly, it was reported, was something Booth referred to as an "Awakening" without being forthcoming about any of the details. That was fine for Mina, Sam supposed. His own eye read a trite euphemism for a pang of mortality-related conscience—a bad cholesterol test, maybe.

These days Sam's relations with his father were actually cordial enough. They talked two or three times a year. They had talked last spring, hadn't they? He thought so. There was a history, though, and it wasn't helpful of his sister to cloud the issue by bringing it in. For instance, it had been a long time since Sam had thought about Booth's stealing the screenplay for *Who We Are* out of his laptop bag, and how incredibly annoying that had been, and how it spoke volumes about his father's high-handedness, his outrageous self-importance.

"Remember when he promised to take you to Paris?" Sam asked.

"Only because you remind me! I would have forgotten by now if you didn't always bring it up." Mina kicked more dirt at him, as well as a small chunk of grass that her boot tip dug up.

"Please stop kicking dirt at me, Mina." The grass chunk had hit the ankle of his jeans. "And how'd that go? Was the Louvre nice?"

"Who's to say that he won't take me eventually?" Mina reached down and grabbed up another small chunk of dislodged grass.

"No one, but you're a high school girl in a cape, and I'm a grown man with credit-card debt, so we're going to give me the edge in life experience here. It's not going to happen. Mina, you really, really don't know him like I know him. Don't throw grass at me, please, I told you."

She threw the grass at him, but it missed.

"At least Dad listens to me," said Mina. "You just haunt me. You act like that stupid movie killed you, and now you're a ghost. If you're going to haunt me, I wish you'd at least kill yourself."

Cape swirling, boot heels cracking on the packed dirt, she stalked over to the corgis. They were sprawled under a bench, tongues lolling, admiring the undercarriage of a nearby Great Dane. She roughly snapped the dual leash to their collars and dragged them, plus-four legs scrabbling, to the gate.

"You're taking this too personally," Sam said, who was thinking how wildly, absolutely dissimilar the two instances were, Booth's sticking his hand in the laptop bag and his own thumbing around in Mina's phone. They couldn't be more unlike, really. A laptop bag had a zipper. To get into it, you had to unzip it. If you left an iPhone out, you were practically begging someone to play with it.

"Die." His sister shoved past him onto the paved path heading north, trailed by the hurrying little dogs. "Don't you even care that I'm not in school?" she asked without turning back.

While Sam thought about that, squinting up at the midmorning sun in the trees and trying to calculate the date, his sister receded. By the time he had it—September 14—Mina was almost gone, yanking the dogs off the path, crossing the street, and heading west. "If I didn't care about you, I wouldn't try so hard to keep you from making the kinds of mistakes I've made," he yelled after her, but if she had heard him, she gave no sign.

To Sam's relief, the poet had rolled onto his back. His sister might have hated him, he might be craven, but he was not a killer.

The sinister toilet water had pooled around the poet, transforming him into a human reef. An ugly red gash marked the old man's chin where he had struck the floor as Sam pushed off. His arms were crossed, and a silver flask rested on his chest.

Sam crouched at the open window. "Sir?"

The old man's eyes were open. "Yes?"

"I just wanted to make sure you were okay. I'll go for real now, if that's all right."

The poet unscrewed the cap of his flask and trickled some liquid into his mouth. His eyes stayed on Sam. The edges of his gown curled in the shitty water. He appeared at ease.

The combination of directness and serenity in the man's gaze felt like an invitation. "Actually, do you mind if I ask you a question? There's something I'd like to ask you."

"Is there," said the poet. He screwed the cap back on the flask and returned it to its place on his chest. "Is there."

Sam wiped sweat from his eyes. The atmosphere in the alley was similar to a locker room, muggy like a shower and fishy-smelling. "'The ruthless furnace of this world.' What does that mean to you?"

This elicited a quavering sigh from the man below.

"I feel like"—Sam thought of his panic earlier; he thought of Mina walking away from him; and he thought of Tess waiting for him to appear—"I feel like I've already burned up. And you know, I'm not sure how much more I can contend with. Or am I the furnace? It's not like I mean anyone any harm. I just want to keep my options open."

"Yes." The poet stared at Sam and petted the brushed steel body of his flask. The selvage of gown, lilting gently around him, gave him a holy appearance. Sprawled on the floor, he resembled a picture on a towering vault. "That is an interesting interpretation. But," the poet said, "for my own part, I feel that I have helped you quite enough. Quite enough."

The glow from the first-floor windows helped Sam pick his way along the rear alley through a litter of shredded cardboard and swollen garbage bags.

At the foot of the passage, he paused to make sure Tess hadn't come outside. He pressed into the shadows of the far wall and watched the street.

Forty or fifty feet away, the rental was parked at the curb on the riverside edge of the restaurant. A short, bearded man in an overcoat was inspecting the car—the vagrant, the one he had seen through the window at the City Bakery that afternoon with Polly.

By the fizzy light of the streetlamps, Sam made note of the discolored whorls on the coat, the mismatched buttons, the flapping sole of the right boot. The man's beard matched his hair, bushy and brushy, and obscured his face save for a bandit's mask of skin. This patch of flesh was the color of cottage cheese, and the eyes within were very small.

The vagrant had appeared harmless enough outside the City Bakery, but Sam discerned an excellent reason for caution: a long knife hung from his belt. As the vagrant passed around the hood of the car, the knife twisted from a piece of twine tied to the man's pants, and the blade tip glinted, reflecting some blue light that Sam couldn't see the source of from his angle. The vagrant's overcoat hung to the pavement and shushed with his movements.

Sam stayed rooted. He wished someone would come along, but the street was clear. His shirt was sweated to his chest. Inside the Stables, the wedding was still going on. Voices, laughter, singing, and drums filtered through the closed windows in an ambient rumble.

The vagrant abruptly spun, tearing the knife free. He slashed at the air, squawking, hacking at some unseen assault, filthy overcoat rippling, streetlights wiping his shadow across the pavement. The vagrant dropped the blade and shoved at the air. He fell to his knees. His hands made a circle above the pavement and strangled nothing and repeatedly slammed nothing against the ground. Sam, growing up, had, like any boy, scrapped with his share of imaginary monsters, and so he recognized the movements. But there was no play in the sounds of the vagrant's grunts and wheezes, or in the stiffness of his arms as he choked the life from the unseen. It was real enough—savage enough—to make Sam feel afraid for the man.

The vagrant abruptly stopped fighting. He crawled over to the discarded knife, slipped it into a pocket of his overcoat, and stood. He walked away. Hunched slightly, he moved in the direction of the Brooklyn Bridge and soon melted into shadow.

Sam hurried to the rental car. He was somewhat concerned by the vagrant—it seemed odd that the man should have entered into Sam's orbit at two different, widely separated places. The knife was also worrying. Once he was home at the apartment, he supposed he ought to at least check in with the police.

Tess was the current priority, though—or rather, avoiding Tess. The knife-wielding vagrant was troubling; Tess was an emergency.

He wanted to talk to her, be with her, see her, hold her, force her to admit that the perfect moment in *Dog Day Afternoon* had not been improvised. He wanted her to lay her hand against his face again. Sam liked how dogged she was. He thought she was lovely. There was something about her that he found powerfully relatable. Tess wore her depressed hope like a bad tattoo, a smeared butterfly or a shitty little rose; wore it even though she knew it was no better than a scar; and it wasn't just because it was too expensive to get lasered off but also because it hadn't seemed bad when she was nineteen, and she couldn't turn her back on nineteen, not quite, not yet. He truly wanted to know more about Tess—but it was dangerous, not only for him but for her.

Sam told himself that he already cared too much about her to expose her to what he was, that it wasn't what he was sparing himself but what he was sparing her. A sudden sense of virtuousness got him into the driver's seat of the rental car, got the key in the ignition, got the air-conditioning going, got the wheels turning. That was as far as false chivalry could carry him, though, and by the time he turned the corner around the front of the Stables, he was rightly ashamed again.

And there was Tess. She stood in front of the steps. With a silver shawl knotted around her shoulders and her clutch tucked under her arm, she was talking on a cell phone. Her purple dress fell to her knees, and her black heels raised her an extra half inch. She was too petite to be glamorous, too arranged to be adorable.

As he drove by, she looked right at him, eyes huge with disbelief. Even her ponytails seemed to loll at him questioningly. He could read her lips: *What the fuck?*

Sam waved goodbye.

4.

Three blocks from his building, he parked in front of a shuttered bodega. Mina was probably already at the apartment, but Wesley would let her in, and another aspect of the same impulse that had sent him fleeing from Tess was now pushing him to stop at a certain bar for a drink. Once his self-loathing began to act up, it was hard to resist.

The street faced the Red Hook shipyards and ran parallel to the BQE, which thundered continuously out of sight. Here, the air was cooler because of the water's proximity, and there was a chemical reek.

A few fronts down from the bodega, Sam arrived at the open door of a nondescript industrial building. The entryway gave onto a nameless bar with a vaguely illegal vibe. There was a stage at the rear of the large main room where they sometimes had burlesque performances, while arrayed in a jumble across the open floor were several thrift-store couches, armchairs, and sticky-topped occasional tables.

The evening's attractions had been chalked on a sandwich board propped against the wall:

$3 Cans of PBR
Plus: The Thursday Night Movie Special!

From where Sam stood outside, the bar's back wall, where the film was showing on a square of whitewashed steel sheeting, was obscured by bobbing heads. The decibel level ebbed and flowed but never dropped beneath a solid rumble. At the bar, he got a beer before continuing deeper, sliding between bodies and ducking under arms.

About halfway to the screen, Sam found a clear view from a spot against a pillar. The film was already well along: Roger, Hugh, and Claire were in the parking lot, approaching Roger's car.

At the exact moment when Roger clicks the unlocking mechanism on his key fob, the camera cuts to Claire as she pulls the passenger-side handle, and the handle just snaps—the door doesn't open.

Roger climbs into the driver's seat and turns to squint at the opposite door. His gaze is explained by a close-up on the black plastic lock button.

Claire raps on the glass. The silver ring she's worn on her right pinkie in the last three cuts has multiplied to seven silver rings spread across all of her fingers. There are also some new colored threads strung through her hair.

"Let me in! I want Slurpee!"

"Slurpee motherfucker!" Hugh makes a megaphone with his hands and belches at the sky. A moment ago his blue button-down was merely wrinkled; now it has several juicy-looking stains.

"No!" To be heard through the closed passenger-side window, Roger, whose jaw has developed a patchy gristle, needs to yell, "It's over! I can't do this anymore, Claire!"

"What?" Claire bends to the window and cups a hand to her ear.

"I can't be with you! You're a handle-puller!"

Claire blinks. "What?" She blinks again, starts to tear up.

There was a united bellow from the crowd in the bar—"Drink!"—as the scene abruptly broke off, cutting to find a creature of myth sprawled on his back on the floor of an Acadian forest. The satyr has a grasp of his hard-on.

Before Sam, the thirty or so viewers packed tight around the screen, tipped back their heads, chugging cans and glasses and shooters. There was laughter, hooting, stamping of feet. A man brayed, "The beast is us!" More people laughed.

Sam sipped.

On the screen, the satyr, naked as ever save for his bushy sheepskin shanks and hoof-shaped footgear, releases his penis and drags handfuls of leaves onto his body. This attempt at modesty—if that is what it is intended to be—actually has the reverse effect of further emphasizing the satyr's singular property. Buried to the scrotum in leaves, his stiff penis looks less like an appendage than a horrible white sapling.

"The beast is us," says the satyr, barely above a whisper. The wire halo holding his goat's horns in place has slipped askew, so one is pointing from the top of his head and one is just above his ear. He gives his impossible penis a gentle bat. It shivers back and forth mesmerizingly.

"We are the beast!" The body that belonged to the braying voice leaped onto a table. "We are the fucking beast, people!" He was a small, wiry man in his twenties, wearing chunky black-framed glasses, a John Deere trucker hat, and furry leggings over his jeans.

There were more cheers and cackles, and the drunk in the furry leggings thrust his hips this way and that, screwing the air. Above the scrum, someone clapped a pair of oversize papier-mâché hoofs. Sam sipped.

They showed it at hipster bars, at art house midnight shows, at college theaters, at 4/20 smoke-outs—wherever the followers of camp had a foothold and a screen, *Who We Are* played to packed, goofy, inebriated houses.

There were numerous rites and protocols.

Whenever the satyr appeared, you drank. (This meant that a proper viewing demanded forty-two swallows, one for each of the forty-two cutaways to the frolicker in the forest.) During those interludes where the satyr played the pan flute or his finger chimes, you danced in place. The appropriate responses to the satyr's prompts had to be made en masse; a more veteran *Who We Are* audience than the one in the nameless bar would have spoken "We are the beast" as one. To protect the dignity of Rick Savini, you turned your back to the screen whenever he appeared.

The wearing of costumes was encouraged. Goat horns were good, furry chaps were better. Goat horns, furry chaps, heavy eye shadow, and hooves were best of all. While sober viewers could obviously enjoy the elementary risibility of such an abundance of male nudity, for the full experience, narcotics were recommended. As with any mind-altering venture, it was recommended that newbies attend showings of *Who We Are* in the company of a clearheaded friend in case they should become anxious or start to feel uncertain of reality's bounds. The synthesis of the satyr's visual presence and his elliptical musings were said to cause upsetting effects for some sensitive viewers. In regard to these dangers, one enthusiast told a reporter from the Style section of *The New York Times*, "It's not a sexy deal. If anything, it's asexual. The satyr is old. He copulates with a tree. The whole thing can actually be very terrifying if, you know, you're easily terrified."

Internet fansites had flourished for the purpose of arguing the film's meaning, creating new games to play while watching it, arranging showings and the sharing of tributes. Numerous auteurs staged and posted satyr videos of their own; a satyr at a farmers' market in San Francisco asking bemused customers, "Who are we?"; a bandit-masked female satyr skulking around the ruins of the Parthenon after hours, stroking the pocked columns and cooing to the broken stones; on a roof across the street from Wrigley Field, a satyr in a Cubs hat seated in a lawn chair, earnestly complaining about his cursed team, while at the lower edge of the frame, his penis casually nestled in a hot dog bun.

There was nary a morning Zoo Crew in the country who didn't have the satyr's most famous declaration—"The beast is us!"—plugged in to their control board and ready at the press of a button. A successful English rock band, the Two-Handers, had shot a music video of themselves being chased, à la the Beatles, through the streets of London by a mob of female satyrs. The accompanying song, "Don't Give Me the Poor-mouth, Sister," had made it to the top of several alternative charts in the United States and the U.K.

The provenance of the film was never definitively established. All that was certain was that one day in the autumn of 2003, Sam errantly flipped the only known copy of the film—a DVD labeled FINAL CUT—off the lip of a trash can at the entrance of a housing development in Quentinville, NY. Supported by the fact that he had made no other copies (and that the chronically institutionalized Brooks Hartwig, Jr., had not been in a position to disseminate any copies he might have possessed), it seemed probable that a stranger had picked the DVD up off the ground. A few months later, the movie appeared on the file-sharing networks, and after that, it was everywhere. Makers of goat horns, furry chaps, and footgear designed to look like hooves confronted an unprecedented uptick in demand.

If Sam Dolan had climbed out of his vehicle and deposited the DVD in the garbage, *Who We Are* likely would have had the good grace to be just another lost film—if anything, a curious footnote on the filmography of Rick Savini. This was hard to think about, so Sam tried not to. He often failed.

Amputees, it was said, never stopped feeling their limbs. The elderly victim of a boyhood tractor accident still woke in the night, the ghost of his right arch cramping.

In '04 the growing cult phenomenon of *Who We Are* went mainstream when Bummer City released an official DVD. Their right to do so was arguable, but from a legal standpoint, Sam was outflanked from the beginning. WOUND had gone public by then, and they had too much money to fight. Through Greta—who had risen to the top of the operation and who, Sam hoped, was bilking Wassel and Patch for every penny they were worth—he had gained one concession: the removal of his name from the film's credits. While a search of the Internet was enough to discover his association, the removal was better than nothing (and as it related to his work as a weddingographer, thankfully, for cost-conscious marrying types, Sam's impeccable reel and reasonable prices nearly always trumped any reservations about his past).

Patch and Wassel had hired someone to clean up the assembly—adjusting and brightening the color, hiring a Foley artist to fill in the aural background, etc. The movie actually looked somewhat okay. As *Who We Are* became a dorm room favorite, special editions had proliferated: the Wood Beast Edition™ came complete with hoof gloves that you could clop together during your favorite parts, as well as a manual of drinking games to play during the film. There was also merchandise: coffee cups, posters, bumper stickers, T-shirts, ski caps, boxer shorts, and a lilac-scented spray sold exclusively at Spencer's, Eau de Satyr, that promised to "turn your man into a horny devil!"

A grizzled *New Yorker* reporter better known for his filings from Chechnya and Afghanistan had set aside his passport long enough to pen an ingenuous book-length essay about the film, setting out to understand what its popularity indicated about the next generation of American adults. "I can understand," began the introduction, "why some critical authorities have been a tad squeamish in their consideration of *Who We Are*. The film's central spectacle is, after all, an elderly man with a colossal penis whose antics include urinating, tree-fucking, and perhaps most disquieting for this author, noodling on the pan flute à la Zamfir. *The Bicycle Thief* it is not. But try and find an adult college-educated male who has not seen it, or an adult college-educated female who has not bowed to her boyfriend or husband's insistence that she bear witness also. It is something—and that something is greater than freshman gawping or sophomoric irony." As far as Sam was able to discern, the gist of what the author came around to say was that an ambient sense of amused disappointment was so commonplace among young post-empire Americans—especially the males of the generation—that, when confronted with an absolutely sincere illustration of sadness (i.e., the satyr, naked, wandering around the forest, speaking to himself in adages), they could not comprehend it, but it cast a spell over them nonetheless. The short book's title was *The Age of Chagrin*. The final line was "Lest we forget, it is a naked man we are looking at here."

At the end of the film, the two segments collided in what was arguably the pinnacle of Brooks's vandalization of Sam's dream.

As Roger and Diana stand on the hill and watch the sunrise blaze across the inert bodies of their classmates, a still of the satyr, crudely superimposed over the original image, arms spread in a pantomime of wings, is made to swoop across and around the frame, like a hideous fly. Sam supposed that Brooks filmed the man stretched out on a stool or something, then glued him right on the film. The creature's penis hung at a slant and actually scraped across the sunlit heads of the somber actors.

What Brooks had conceived of with his additions and edits was open to vast differences in interpretation, but Sam gradually came around to seeing it somewhat like Greta had at the screening in the Bummer City basement. Brooks was mad, and madness was pain, and pain was everywhere, between every character and between every scene, in their laughter and in their sex; the pain was in the woods; it buzzed just above their heads. Brooks had been crazy and unhappy, so he had made Sam's movie crazy and unhappy. *Who We Are* was a joke, but not the happy kind of joke.

And it did not elude the former director that Brooks's aims for the film had not been so, so different from his own. They both had tragedy on their minds.

Why so many people enjoyed something that was so plainly a wreck— well, that was harder to understand, or maybe not to understand but to accept, and anyway, he was working on his second beer, trying to focus on the screen, despite the cacophony.

Outside the bar, a young woman stumbled into him. Her T-shirt said WHO WE ARE and had arrows pointing at breasts. The belly button of the shirt was stamped with the Bummer City Productions trademark that marked official *Who We Are* merchandise: an ovoid picture of the satyr's face, grimacing and big-eyed.

"Oops," said the young woman.

Sam was sent scraping along the brick wall and knocked over the sandwich board. "Jerk," he said.

The young woman put a finger to her lips. "Shhh." Her smile was wide, and her eyes were wet and stupid. In her sweet, glazed expression Sam read an existence starred with banality-defining passions: for those kitchen magnets that showed fifties-era housewives performing domestic tasks while musing archly about cocktails and naps, for beaded thrift store lamps, for karaoke, for her fat orange cat whose litter she never changed and who fantasized about cutting her throat while she slept. In other words, a typical fan of *Who We Are.*

"So this is what you do for fun?" Sam tipped his head in the direction of the bar, the movie, the entire stupid thing.

"Uh. Yeah," said the woman.

The guy behind her, the dope who had jumped on the table and started humping, came forward, a cigarette dangling from between his fingers. Behind the smeared lenses of his glasses, his eyes were hugely dilated. "Chillax, friend."

Sam picked up the sandwich board and restored it against the wall. The combination of the fresh night air and the two beers made him feel uncapped, as if his brain were exposed. "Get fucked," he told the dope.

"What?" The guy flicked a little ash, and it fell into the fur of his leggings. "I don't understand."

"I mean"—with his index finger, Sam drew a circle in the air that was intended to encompass the drunks in the street, the drunks inside, and everyone who had ever watched the movie—"that you're a bunch of jerk-offs, and you ought to try and find something better to do with yourselves."

The bouncer stepped from the dark of the entryway. "Better move along, big guy."

The woman made an unhappy face. "I can have fun." She turned to her defenders. "Can't I have fun?"

Sam put his hands up; he didn't want a fight. He started for the corner. Behind him, someone asked, "Who the hell was that guy?"

There was that: he had not actually appeared in the film. Sam still had his face. No one had ever stopped him in an airport and asked, "You were in that movie, weren't you? The one with the Cock Monster?"

Olivia Das, who played Florence-Diana-Aurora-Divinity-Florence, mentioned this incident in the suicide note she mass-e-mailed to her friends and family on July 2, 2007, under the subject heading, THIS IS NOT MY LIFE!! *This is not what I auditioned for,* she wrote, *this is not my life! I wanted to play Hedda Gabler on Broadway!*

The attempt was thankfully unsuccessful (and maybe not completely serious; Olivia had attempted to extinguish herself via an overdose of Mucinex); however, her distress was well earned.

A *Who We Are* credit was a plague sign above the entryway of a career. If you were an actor, the association could have an unfortunate effect on audiences, especially if the work was intended to be dramatic. In the case of Olivia, when she won a supporting role as a social worker in a Spike Lee picture, the audience at a test screening broke into gales of laughter when her character gave an abused wife a stern talking-to. They weren't seeing Olivia's social worker; they were seeing Florence-Diana-Aurora-Divinity-Florence at the Spring Festival, and the quick cut to the satyr, seated on a downed log, humming "The Huckster's Lament" and dandling his balls. The wrong kind of fame was like inept plastic surgery. It gave your face abstract qualities you never bargained for. Spike had to recast Olivia's part.

Rick Savini alone possessed enough of a track record to be excused for his participation. The rest of the cast essentially disappeared from the field.

For serious people, the kind of people who invested money in films, a professional linked to *Who We Are* bore an unsavory odor. Professionals were careful and attentive. *Who We Are* had become a profitable enterprise due wholly to a lack of care and attention. Though Sam Dolan may have been the captain, this line of thinking ran, the swabs ought to have had the wherewithal to notice the water lapping their boots.

Some of the film's veterans had sought Sam out for special opprobrium, but not as many as one might have expected. Linc, the actor who played Hugh, had been sending Sam poisonous gifts for years—a dead rat, used toilet paper, a CD of acoustic demos entitled "Sam Dolan: Cancer Man," etc.—yet most of those associated with *Who We Are* seemed to view it as a kind of natural disaster and saw Sam as a fellow victim.

The one time Rick Savini consented to offer comment on the film, in an interview with *Rolling Stone,* he said only "I don't feel like it turned out the way the kid intended. Let's leave it at that."

"There's just too many cun-eds ear," said Anthony Delucci. "Time ta make a change." They had stayed in contact until a couple of years before, when the DP gave up his dreams of working in film, left New York, and returned home to Vinalhaven, Maine. Luckily, Anthony's father had saved him a place on the lobster boat.

Flight was a common theme among the traumatized cast and crew of *Who We Are.* George, who played Sam's alter ego in the film, went home to Minnesota to live with his mother and became involved in Amway. Toughie lived somewhere on the west coast of Canada now, where she had a kid she homeschooled. Quinn the Eskimo was a monk, an actual monk in an alpine monastery; in a picture Sam had seen, he'd been unrecognizable, a flowing beard with black holes for eyes. Some others—the two Alexes, Monica Noble—had disappeared altogether.

Sam didn't know what had happened to them. He couldn't even find them on the Internet.

Sam had recently received a cryptic postcard from Wyatt Smithson. The postcard's picture was of a beautiful beach, faultless save for the bleached tombstone of a broken surfboard protruding from the sand. The message on the back had been brief:

Dear Sam,
    I ate a piece of dog last night. Just tasted like regular meat. I ate dog. Why did I do that?
    Still trying to figure out who we are, I guess.

Your friend,
Wyatt

Julian, his old professor who had opened so many doors at Russell, had tumbled to the blackest depths of academia—a community college in El Paso.

Then there was Brooks Hartwig, Jr.

Journalists had tracked him to various mental institutions, but Brooks had never spoken. His wealthy family referred all queries about his contribution to *Who We Are* and his condition to their lawyers. In the last year, a public relations official at Stony Brook Haven, a luxury facility on Long Island, had informed a reporter from the Style section of *The New York Times* that "Mr. Hartwig Jr. was resting comfortably" and did not wish to comment.

Beyond which Sam didn't know any more than anyone else. He didn't know whether he wanted to. It seemed to Sam that Brooks was not the only one entitled to some rest.

The sole participant who might have profited from the enterprise, one Costas Mandell, the satyr himself, chose to shun the spotlight. Perhaps that should not have been a surprise. From what Sam had been able to gather, until the day when Brooks Hartwig, Jr., fixed him in his lens, there had never been any reason to suspect that Mandell—a naturalized citizen, a twenty-year veteran of the Russell College maintenance staff, a decorated member of the local VFD—wanted to perform, let alone to share his grand appendage with the world. *Rolling Stone* reported that the shy Mandell had declined numerous requests to act as Santa Claus at the Russell maintenance staff's annual Christmas party, a role for which his snowy beard seemed designed.

Nonetheless, Mandell seemed, in the wake of *Who We Are*'s multiplying audience, poised for a lucrative lap on the reality-television freakshow circuit. But a transcript of his sole public appearance, on a famed shock jock's satellite radio show, revealed profound discomfort:

Jock: Satyr-guy, what we have here is a mail scale. The kind they have in the post office.

Costas: Call me Costas, please.

Jock: Cockstas, did you say?

Sidekick #1: (Laughter) Oh my goodness! This is outrageous! Is that from the actual post office?

Costas: No, Costas.

Jock: Yeah, it's a real mail scale. And what we want is to weigh Satyr-guy's cock on it. Now I've bet Lou here that it weighs twelve ounces—

Lou (Sidekick #2): Just his cock? Or also the balls? Because the balls are where the real heft is.

Sidekick #1: (Laughter) Oh my goodness! This is insane! You're betting on the weight of his genitals?

Jock: Ah, no, not the balls, because that would completely throw off my calculations. Satyr-guy's balls are like cantaloupes.

Lou: They're like hairy sandbags, those goddamn things.

Costas: I'm sorry. I must leave. I'm sorry.

Jock: Hold on there, Satyr-guy—

Sidekick #1: Oh, no! (Laughter) Way to go! You creeped him out, guys!

When Sam thought about the satyr, about Mandell's rheumy line readings, the real sorrow he conveyed in contradiction of all logic—or illogic, depending on how one's mind dealt with the visual impression—despite all the damage the man had helped to inflict, he felt some sympathy. Sam could relate.

Like Mandell, Sam shied from attention. He never wanted to be in movies, and now he didn't want to make movies. All he wanted, in the words of the saddest soul ever frozen on a slide of silver nitrate, was to be let alone.

5.

"You've been to that movie thing, haven't you?"

Sam had just entered the apartment. In repose on the couch, Wesley looked at him from over his laptop screen. Opposite the couch, the television was tuned, unexpectedly, to the Weather Channel.

"You've got that look you get. That dented look. You look like an old guy who lost his false teeth." Wesley was wearing his favorite pajamas. They'd come to the Swag Hag from a children's boutique and were spotted with different-colored Popsicles. He had installed himself in them sometime in July and worn them pretty much every day since. Because of this, the consumer champion smelled like pee and Febreze.

Sam dropped his keys on the table by the door and stuck his sweaty suit jacket on a hook. "Isn't 'Prying into other people's affairs' on the list?"

"Let me check," said Mina. Nested in the red beanbag catercorner to the couch, Sam's sister had apparently already been perusing the three pages of wrinkled, laminated, lined yellow notebook paper that constituted Wesley's personal manifesto, "Seventy-four Things That Caused Unnecessary Fatigue."

Hidden among the various boxes and shipping crates that had arrived for the Swag Hag in the recent months and years was a two-bedroom apartment with one bathroom, a kitchenette, and brick walls. A warehouse atmosphere hung over the place, a mood of impermanence, of moving out and moving in. Sheets of crumpled packing paper and drifts of foam peanuts had collected around the edges of everything.

From the short entryway passage, Sam began to wriggle his way toward the kitchenette.

"What's the 'movie thing'?" Mina's outfit was her standard: boots, black; ankle-length skirt, black; knit stockings, black with maroon piping; long-sleeve shirt, black, centered with a picture of an armadillo skull; watch cap, purple, the word DOOM, stitched on the band (by Mina) in white thread. Several articles of luggage were arrayed around her: a duffel bag, a knapsack, a duct-taped suitcase, and a sewing machine in a vinyl slipcover.

"It's a cult film program at a shitty hipster bar around the corner," said Wesley.

"Were they showing 'The Movie'?" Mina's disdain was undisguised.

"Planning to stay awhile?" asked Sam. His sister, not looking up from the plastic pages, flew him the bird.

He eased between two columns of boxes—from the labels, he could see that one contained books from a publisher, another compact discs from a record company, another packages of microwave popcorn from a food company, while another appeared to be birdseed from a farm supplier. There were four or five others in the stacks that weren't immediately identifiable, but in any event, it was all crap for the Swag Hag to pass judgment on.

On the television, a weatherman massaged a cold front across the eastern seaboard. Sam couldn't remember Wesley ever having put the Weather Channel on, and it piqued his interest.

A few feet farther and he found himself blocked again: a pyramid of tube socks in plastic sacks—from an athletic supply company—barricaded the way. He considered attempting to ferret his way through a small gap in the sacks, thought better of it, and instead began to wearily pull them down one at a time and reconstruct the pyramid behind him. Experience had taught Sam that it would be far less exhausting to move the bags on his own than it would be to harangue his roommate into cleaning up.

Wesley was not easily compelled. He did not generally go outside between Labor Day and Flag Day except to receive packages or food deliveries at the door of their building. This was why he had the anemic complexion of a prisoner committed to solitary confinement. It was also why his interest in the Weather Channel was so unprecedented. Only on very special occasions, such as to have his list laminated or to attend the free showing of *E.T.* a couple of months earlier, did Wesley venture forth.

In another person, this behavior might have worried Sam. From a hygiene standpoint, it was certainly short of ideal, but it wasn't a manifestation of agoraphobia, at least not as Sam understood the condition.

It wasn't that Wesley was afraid of the outdoors; it was that everything he needed to maintain his happiness was either in his computer, on the television, or available for order.

Wesley's mother, Mrs. Latsch—who drove up from Maryland a couple of times a year to visit, assisting Wesley in his biannual trip to the Laundromat and replenishing his supply of vitamins—once related to Sam that, even as a toddler, Wesley was flabbergasted by all the effort expended around him. "I remember we saw a man running across a street, trying to catch a bus, and Wesley asked me why the man was in such a hurry. I said, 'He needs to get to work, sweetheart.' Wesley, he must have been about five, he just shook his head and said, 'Can you imagine?'" At this, Mrs. Latsch poured out a delighted chuckle. She just knew, she said, that her boy was conserving his resources for something important.

Sam had his doubts. He didn't believe Wesley planned much beyond his next appointment with the bottle of lemon verbena lotion in the bathroom. "What's up with the Weather Channel? Jesus, Wesley, you're not thinking of going outside, are you?"

His roommate said the Weather Channel was Mina's choice. "And don't think I didn't detect that note of condescension in your voice." Wesley sighed. "You can be very hurtful sometimes, Sam Dolan."

"The guide said there was going to be a special on natural disasters, but it was a lie," said Mina. "It's been nothing but regular weather so far."

"Mina has been fretting about climate change. She wants her children, and her children's children, not to be drowned by the rising oceans or cancered by the sun's ultraviolet rays," said Wesley.

"Har-har, Wesley the Hutt. What fat roll did you pull 'cancered' out of, anyway?"

"We're on the same side, Mina." Wesley typed something into his computer. "I'm as eager to watch tornado and earthquake footage as you are."

Sam finally reached the kitchenette, shoving aside a knee-high pallet of eco-themed surface wipes to breach the entryway. He opened the refrigerator and helped himself to a bottle of the Rip Van Winkle white ale that the Swag Hag said tasted like the lice of unloved children. Sam thought it tasted like sour cherries.

Mina had finished searching through the list. "Number thirty-four is 'Never pry into the affairs of strangers.' *Strangers.* You're not a stranger,

Sam. Guess it's safe for Wesley the Hut to dig into your sad, bitter life as much as he wants."

She kicked up her spindly legs and clicked the toes of her shiny boots. His sister was at once gamine and bleak, like a fallen elf. How many teenage boys would Sam have to visit with his trusty DVD before Mina safely reached the age of consent? However many it took, but the signs were ominous.

Sam retraced his journey through the scree until he reached the tube-sock-bag pyramid. Here, he took a sharp left into different territory, scraping through the narrow channel between two massive crates to arrive at the television area. He pushed a box off the seat of the uncomfortable armchair angled to the other side of the couch, and sat.

"So, did you have a good, solid pity party at the movie or what?" asked Wesley.

"No, I had a beer at the movie and observed some mouth-breathers in their natural habitat. That was it. Earlier on, though, I did nearly pass out over a poem."

Mina stopped clicking her toes. "Really?"

"Uh-huh."

Sam wasn't sure why he mentioned it. Sympathy didn't mean a whole lot to him as a rule, and if it did, he wouldn't want any from his younger sister. He supposed the confession didn't matter one way or another. They would do what they wanted and make of it what they wanted. Even the people you knew best, you knew just well enough to doubt, to understand that there were warrens of self that went beyond understanding, yours and theirs both.

The thought occurred to him that if he ever met Tess again and shared these reflections, she would be justified in mocking him. "We could have been having sex," she could have said, "and instead, you scurry off to go and brood weakly about the existential limits of your relationship with your sister and the disgusting person you live with? Sam. Come on."

There was gloom, and there was fucking, and if you could be fucking and gloomy instead, that was greedy and sick and you deserved whatever stomachache you got. He had a stomachache, all right.

Sam wished he'd handled the situation with Tess better. He wished he had kept his cool outside the bar. The poet had not drowned in the turd water—there was that, at least.

"What about it made you almost pass out? About the poem."

" 'The ruthless furnace of this world.' " Sam pulled from the bottle and smacked his lips. "That's all I've got. Just that line."

"I don't get it," said Mina.

His roommate paused in his typing. "It triggered a flashback. Remember that time at Russell when you let that girl light your back hair on fire?"

"That happened to you," said Sam.

Wesley scraped a hand through his hair, which had hardened into Saharan waves from lack of washing. "It was me, wasn't it? I was very high in those days. High in the spiritual sense, I mean. Swept aloft by tides of passionate feeling."

"Uh-huh. You were like a comet, Wesley, a luminous spark against the pitch-black depths of the universe. That was you, my friend. That was you."

"I remember my back hair, after the burning, it grew in richer, thicker, darker. Resulting in the glistening, manly pelt I have today. There's a lesson there, isn't there?"

"You let that same girl tie your back hair up in little red ribbons, so that you had all these jaunty little back-hair ponytails."

"That made me feel like a gift for someone very special when she did that."

"You are a gift, Wesley," said Sam. "A gift fit for—"

"Blah, blah, blah," said Mina. "You guys should just make out and get it over with." She kicked off one of her boots, then grabbed the other one by the heel and freed her foot with a vicious jerk. The second boot thumped to the floor.

Wesley said, "Hey, should I order a pizza?" The other two said no. He ordered one anyway, over the Internet.

After a few minutes of the Weather Channel Sam stood, plucked the controller from his sister's lap, and returned to the uncomfortable armchair. A few clicks through the cable listings found an episode of *Secrets Only Dead Men Know*.

What distinguished *Secrets Only Dead Men Know* from the rest of the fraternity of true-mystery shows was the wrinkle of perspective; each show was narrated in the voice of the deceased. The "ghost" of the dead person spoke over still photographs and reenactment footage, furnishing the audience with a guided tour of his or her life and, centrally, his or her demise.

That Friday evening's episode concerned a wealthy fifty-one-year-old retired day trader named Kenneth Novey, who was inadvertently trapped in the panic room of his Saddlebrook, NJ, mansion on the evening of December 31, 1999.

The show's first segment starts in small-town Minnesota, along the broad sun-dappled avenues of Kenneth Novey's boyhood. There are clips of clattering bicycle wheels, empty tire swings breezily rotating, beautiful green trees, canvas sneakers slapping against sidewalk slabs. "Those were good times," narrates the ghost of Kenneth Novey in the wry, gravelly voice of a man of experience. "Everything was so big and open then, I could never have imagined the way it would turn out . . ."

The segment continues through the major events in Novey's life before the accident: the ground-floor position in the successful hedge fund (an ATM spraying reams of money), his Aspen marriage to a Charlotte debutante (a couple of actors kissing under a shower of rice), the birth of his son, Hannibal (a doughy, leering baby), the golden parachute that cleared his days of purpose (the slamming of tall glass doors), estrangement and divorce (the formerly kissing couple jabbing fingers at each other from opposite sides of a conference room table), an increasingly agoraphobic existence in his mansion in Saddlebrook (the male actor, red-robed, eating hummus with a spoon and peering between curtains), and finally, the installation of a panic room (welders welding), and his fatal entrance on the night of December 31, 1999 (the red-robed actor keying open the vault, stepping inside, and the stainless-steel doors murmuring shut).

"I felt safe in there." Novey's ghost chortles. "Safe as a pharaoh."

The show broke for advertisements. The first two commercials were national spots—one for a fancy duster, another for healthful blue potato chips. The third was local, an ad for a monster-truck rally in Suffolk County.

"By God, these are some angry vehicles!" roars Booth in his voice-over.

Sam clicked the mute button.

"It was a totally cute ad," Mina protested. "You can tell that Dad ad-libbed a lot of it. 'Angry vehicles.' That's pure Dad." She dropped her voice into a credible imitation of their father: " 'The Engines of Doom rev their terrible fury! Listen—and behold! Tickets start at only twelve-ninety-five!' He's so great."

Sam unmuted the television, and then quickly muted it again when a tight shot of Jo-Jo Knecht appeared on the screen. He was at the wheel of a 1970 GTO. It was an ad for the used-car chain that Jo-Jo fronted. The idea of the series was simple: a person tried to leave the used-car lot without buying something, and the retired catcher roared up in the GTO to block the departure, à la the '98 World Series and Esteban Herrera's doomed dash for home. The GTO had been desecrated with a pin-striped paint job.

"Hey," asked Mina, "isn't that the guy your skank ex-girlfriend married?"

The show returned, and Sam unmuted the television without comment.

The actor playing Novey climbs out of his cot on the morning of January 1 and, cupping a yawn, uses his free hand to press the vault door's release button. The door doesn't open. The actor presses the button again. The door still doesn't open. A third time, the actor hits the release button. The door stays shut.

"Uh-oh," says the voice-over ghost. "This is . . . problematic."

The actor in the reenactment soon discovers that his secure phone has no dial tone, his intercom is dead, and the wall of security monitors is blacked out. He begins a frantic circuit of his cell, patting the walls, looking closely at the welded seams. While this is going on, the ghost explains that since his divorce, he's often lost track of time; today is the first day of a brand-new century. "Gee. I seem to have forgotten all about Y2K."

It's a programming glitch in the clock of the vault door's locking mechanism that has trapped Kenneth Novey. At the stroke of midnight, the clock turned over to January 1, 1900, and the system overloaded.

A few weeks of playing Ping-Pong against the wall, reading and rereading an issue of *Newsweek* with a DNA helix on the cover, eating astronaut food, and writing letters to his toddler son gradually pushes the hedge fund millionaire into a state of irreversible despair. Kenneth

Novey kills himself with an overdose of Ativan. It's not until the summer, over four months after his suicide and half a year after he was shut in, that his ex-wife discovers him. "For the first time in years," jokes the voice-over ghost, "I was happy to see her."

The actress playing Novey's wife screams and throws her arms around the mummified body in the control chair. One of the corpse's desiccated arms cracks off and hits the floor, raising a puff of dust.

Sam's own laughter surprised him; it had sort of burped out. The credits began to roll. He reached up and squeezed his jaw. There was a big grin on his face.

"Ick," said Mina. "Can I put 'hugging a mummy' on your list, Wesley?"

"You probably should," said Wesley. There was a knock on the door—the pizza. "Will you get that?" he asked.

When the pizza had been paid for and the box brought close enough to the couch for Wesley to access without discomforting himself, Sam announced that he was retiring for the evening. On top of all of the things that had depressed him that evening—job, poem, girl, movie, bar assholes—the television show had made him feel soiled. Through the entire half hour it was on, despite his seat in the uncomfortable chair, Sam didn't shift. He watched in a state of rapture. More to the point: he was entertained. The true story of an unhappy man imprisoned in his own house, so forsaken that no one noticed his absence for months, who finally offed himself, gave Sam amusement. He wanted to see what would happen next. He had been amazed—thrilled, even—by the growing awfulness.

What was wrong with him that he should enjoy something like that?

And there it was: the ignoble awareness that if someone else had made *Who We Are*, he, too, would laugh.

6.

After Sam brushed his teeth, he found Mina waiting for him in his room. She was sitting on the bed and flipping through the stack of mail on his nightstand. "Are these checks?" she asked.

"Yes." Bummer City sent him a residual every month. It was never a lot of money, a couple hundred dollars or so. If it were added up,

OWEN KING

though, he guessed he could buy a small house. "What's up with you and Sandra?"

"Blech. Let's not." Jagged bits of silver hair stuck out from under the band of her DOOM watch cap and made her look tough and street-smart. "Are you ever going to cash them?"

"No."

"Too bad." Mina dropped the envelopes to the floor. She rose from the bed, and the plastic windows crinkled under her stocking feet.

"Thanks," said Sam. "That's helpful."

His sister went to the window. There was a view of a fire escape and the rear of another apartment building and its fire escape. Down below was an empty gravel lot.

Mina's silhouette in the window shrank her, made her the nine-year-old she had been when Tom brought her to Russell that weekend eight years earlier. Sam remembered her little girl's blond hair.

She turned and sat on the windowsill. Her mouth was the same as his and Booth's, but the small, sharp nose came from Sandra. The blue eyes were hers alone.

"Are you okay? You seem worse than usual."

"I thought you hated me." Sam went to pick up the envelopes.

"No. I was disappointed. I'm over it. Plus, Peter's gay."

Sam took the envelopes to his bedside table. "You'll forgive me if I don't pretend to be too upset. You're seventeen. And look, I remember seventeen, and a girl who had a boyfriend, especially an older one, it was always a bad sign."

"A bad sign how? Like, it meant the harvest wasn't going to be plentiful? What century are you from? Seventeen-year-old virgins are in pretty short supply these days."

"Don't be a smart-ass. You know what I mean. I mean don't be in a hurry to grow up. It's not as awesome as it looks."

"Why do you care so much if I have sex?"

Sam clapped his hands over his ears. "Can't quite make you out. Something wrong with transmission system. Over?"

His sister put up her palms in a gesture of détente, and he uncapped his ears.

"I think we should get an apartment together."

208

She looked serious, but Sam didn't see how she could be. "I don't think Sandra would go in for that."

"Say she would."

"But she wouldn't."

"You wouldn't."

The argumentative side of Mina was another gift from her mother. A grudging measure of admiration had to be paid to Sandra Whipple-Dolan's debate skills. No conspiracy was too implausible (see *Katrina*, the secret coordinated assassination of thousands of blacks by the government during), no political cause too repugnant (see *Chávez, Hugo*), and no theory about Booth Dolan too idiotic (see *Dolan, Booth*, B-movie "star," the hidden stores of wealth of), for Sandra to champion.

"If they couldn't find weapons of mass destruction, how could they manage to hide, like, five thousand dead black guys?" Sam once made the error of asking her in relation to the Katrina plot.

Sandra stared through him with the thin-lipped smile of a righteous sacrifice staked to a mound of smoldering tinder. "We don't know yet. But that doesn't make them any less dead, now does it?"

When Sandra argued, it was like seeing a lab rat not even bother with the maze and just chew right through the particleboard to get to the cheese. Pair this vociferousness with Mina's sanity, and you had a sparring partner with very heavy gloves.

"Fine. Let's get an apartment, then," said Sam. "You get Sandra to give the okay, and we'll do it." He knew it would never happen. Sam's argumentative side drew more from Booth, though he was less of a bullshitter and more of a bluffer.

"Glad we got that settled," said Mina.

"Great, let's call her right now," said Sam. He didn't think it would take long.

"She's not home." Mina's sanguinity raised an alarm.

"Well, where is she?"

"Bellevue."

That summer her mother had begun to lock Mina in her bedroom at night. "For your safety," said Sandra mysteriously, and refused to discuss the issue.

Mina's counteroffensive was to go on Happiness Strike.

Each evening when Mina came home from school, she would do her homework and then curl up on the tile floor of the kitchen to sleep. To Sandra's pleas that Mina sit down in a chair, or watch television, or have a bath, the daughter replied, "My place is to suffer." At mealtime with her mother, Mina stopped eating anything except raw vegetables and would drink only tap water, refusing the Brita. Mina began to donate her possessions—favorite clothes that she had designed and made herself, beloved books and keepsakes, jewelry—to passersby outside their building. "Here is something I adore," she'd say, and press a pair of shoes on a stranger.

Finally, when Sandra observed her daughter giving away the tattered baby blanket that had wrapped Mina on the day of her birth, she crumpled. "Why are you doing this?"

Mina told the little girl to whom she'd awarded the blanket to run along. "Be good to Blankie." Mina turned to her mother. "Because there's no point in even attempting to be happy so long as you insist on treating me like an inmate."

("You are so mean," said Sam. He began to check the beer bottles around his bed, hoping for a partial.

"Happiness Strike is a last resort." Mina shrugged. "But sometimes that's what's needed."

Sam tossed back the last quarter of a two-day-old white ale.)

Sandra surrendered and that night left Mina's door unlocked. The Happiness Strike was unofficially called off. It seemed that their problems were at an end . . .

. . . Until a few days later, when Mina caught her mother lecturing a dead beagle named Horatio. The beagle had been elderly, the property of a client, a professor of poetics who said everything twice and who fed the dog scraps so he was terribly fat. While on a walk, Horatio had paused to sniff a late daisy. Sandra glanced away. She looked back, and the beagle had four legs up in the air. He was already cooling.

"It's a twisted game, Mina. Don't give him the satisfaction. He just wants attention." Sandra was on the couch in their living room. The dog lay in her lap. His tongue dangled out, and his eyes were white. A fly buzzed around his black nose.

(Sam slung a bottle cap at his sister. "Oh, come on. I don't want to hear that. That's enough."

"Sorry, Sam. That's nature," said Mina. "Everybody croaks.")

"Don't you? Don't you, you little devil?" Sandra stroked the beagle's dappled forehead. "Booth, Booth, Booth. What will you think of next?"

Mina briskly found a canvas tote and returned to the living room. She held out the open bag. "Hand over Horatio's corpse. Right now."

Sandra frowned but deposited the dead dog in the bag. At the poetics professor's apartment, Mina set the animal on the rug, arranged him as peacefully as his stiffening body would allow, and slipped out before she was noticed.

Back at home, she explained to her mother that they would have to see a doctor, and though it might seem scary, it was for the best. Sandra pulled a few strands of her hair, a mix of blond and gray, and rolled her eyes up to see them. "That dog was not dead, sweetie."

"And I will always love you," said Mina. "No matter what."

Her mother began to bawl. "Promise?"

Mina sat down and hugged her, murmuring that everything would be okay, that in the long run she would feel better.

A week passed, and Sandra took the lithium the doctor prescribed. Mina stayed home from school and kept a close watch. Her mother was subdued but balanced. One afternoon she made banana bread; another, she cleaned the cabinets above the stove for, as far as her daughter could recall, the first time ever. Mina asked how she felt, and the smile Sandra produced was tentative. "I feel like I'm manning the controls to myself. Does that make any sense?"

"Is that a good feeling?"

"I don't know," said Sandra. "I made banana bread. That's a positive sign, I suppose, isn't it?"

When Mina returned home from school that Thursday, there was a smell of smoke in the hallway outside the apartment. She rushed inside to discover fire licking from the edges of the stove. Sandra had put a pile of old photographs of her and Booth, several child-support check stubs, and a Manhattan area phonebook to bake at 375.

After Mina extinguished the fire with a pot of water, she asked her mother what she'd done with her pills.

"They—*went.*" The rueful manner in which Sandra shook her head suggested that the pills had departed according to their nature, like grown ducklings leaving the nest.

"If you don't take them," said Mina, "I am not staying."

"I am your mother," said Sandra.

"Goodbye," said Mina.

Her mother stuck out her tongue and rolled over on the couch, showing her back.

Mina packed her things, went down to the sidewalk, and called Peter Jenks. "Hi, bastard. Isn't your father a big-shot shrink?"

"What do you want with my father? Does your insane brother want to go threaten him with a DVD? Or are you hoping he can ungay me or something? You can forget about that one, Mina. He's a doctor, not a wizard." Since the visit from Sam and the breakup, Peter was being combative.

("The nerve of this kid, right? Which, naturally, makes me love the bastard more than ever," said Mina.

"Naturally," said Sam. All the other bottles had turned out to be empty.)

Mina told Peter to be quiet. She needed his help, she said, and because his deciding he was gay had annihilated her soul, it was the least he could do.

His spine held. "No. I'm on to you."

"Please?"

"Fine."

Mina gave him the rundown on Sandra's condition, and Peter promised to get his father to at least talk to her mother. "But you might as well know, I'm seeing someone."

"Who?"

"David Lima. You know him? From Pre-Calc?"

She did know David Lima. He had shiny black hair, fuzzy sideburns, and lived inside a Killers T-shirt—a very cute boy, no question.

(Sam lay flat on his bed and spoke through a pillow drawn tight to his face. "He does sound cute.")

"So I congratulated the bastard, because what choice did I have? After that, I texted you and came over here. And now Peter just texted me that his old man has taken Sandra to Bellevue for evaluation. Which brings us to the present."

Sam continued to lie with the pillow over his face. "I'm sorry, Mina. It's not your fault. You know that, right?"

"Which part? The insane mother or the gay ex-boyfriend who hates me?"

"Both. Neither. Any of it."

"Don't worry, Sam. We don't have to get a place."

It was hot and black under the pillow. He loved Mina, he did, but he couldn't imagine not disappointing her, which made him feel depressingly Boothlike. "Mina, look, it's not that. This is just a lot to think about right now, you know?"

"Sure," she said. "I know."

Sam was tempted to bring up their father—new-and-improved, post-Awakening Booth and ask why she didn't give him a call, see if the old man might be interested in being, you know, an actual parent. That would have been petty, though, and he needed to be better than that. If he was going to let her down, he at least ought not kick her.

He flipped off the pillow to tell her that they would figure everything out in the morning, once they'd had some rest, but Mina had left. Down the hall, the bathroom door shut.

7.

Sam's first waking thought was that the police were calling to tell him they'd apprehended the recurring vagrant. His second thought was no, it couldn't be that because he'd never gotten around to calling them about the crazy man with the large knife in the first place. He scrabbled around the bedside table, scattering the stack of envelopes again and tipping a cup of water clattering to the floor, before his hand settled on the rattling cell phone.

It was a sext: a photo of Polly's left nipple, the one with the freckle at two-fifteen. This was followed by a question:

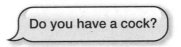

Sam confessed:

Yes. I have a cock.

He pushed himself up into a sitting position against the wall. His answer had already begun to stiffen.

Polly sent another picture of her breast, this time being squeezed by one of her hands.

Sam's next response came more slowly because it was one-handed.

> You are lucky I'm not there. I would fuck you and then some.

Perhaps twenty seconds later, the phone vibrated with an actual call. "'And then some'?" asked Polly in a whisper. "What's that supposed to mean?"

Sam groaned. "It means—"

"Don't you come! I just caught a glimpse into the very bottom of your filthy mind, and I'm curious."

He hissed, his lungs full, the breath at the back of his throat.

"I'm serious! Let go of your penis! I'm not messing around!"

"Dammit." Sam let go of himself. Opposite his bed, a splash of reflected streetlight found the framed photograph on the bureau. The photograph was of his mother, Alison Deidre Byrne Dolan, taken sometime before Sam was born. In it she wore an army helmet, a canary-yellow sundress, and a cool smile.

Sam swung out of bed and went to the bureau. He gently placed the framed picture facedown. By the time he returned to bed, both his hard-on and his desire to humor Polly had waned considerably.

"I'm waiting. 'And then some,' Sam? Be specific, you pervert. I'm starting to get excited here. Are you planning to screw me with, what, a sex toy of some kind? Or are we talking about something truly deviant, like a crutch or an umbrella or something?"

"It didn't mean anything, Polly."

"It meant something. It always means something." She said this in a singsong that reminded Sam of Rainer—it was her lullaby voice. In turn, he thought of Jo-Jo and those fatal thighs.

Even after Polly got engaged to Jo-Jo, she and Sam never ceased having phone sex on a semi-weekly schedule. (They had real sex on a few occasions as well, sometimes in a hotel, sometimes in one of the dressing rooms at an outlet mall off the turnpike north of the city.) She nearly always called him, which was exciting for Sam but only as long as the phone sex lasted. He usually started to suffer pangs of bleakness before the semen on his fingers had cooled. It didn't feel like a game anymore; it didn't feel like a sexy secret anymore; it felt like a bad habit.

"What if Rainer finds out?" asked Sam. This was something he had been doing a lot lately—testing out new lines of argument for why they should stop doing what they were doing—although usually, he got to ejaculate first.

"That's silly. How would Rainer 'find out'? He's a baby. Rainer can barely roll over. Believe me, as long as he gets his share of tit, he's very accepting."

"I mean what if he finds out later. How's he going to look at you?"

"Oh, gee! How will my son look at me if we get caught? Let me think. Do you think he'll look at me—oh no!—*like a whore*?" she asked.

"I didn't say that."

"No, you didn't." Polly inhaled. "I did. Now mind your own business."

"I'm sorry." Part of the fix of the thing was that so long as she was the only one who had anything to lose, any argument he attempted was going to come off as condescending or, worse, fatherly. What was odd was that for once, the awareness that he was not responsible for something was of no comfort to Sam. Polly was his friend. Just because he was hopeless didn't mean he wanted her to suffer.

"It's okay. Forget it." She inhaled again. "Are you going to tell me your dirty fantasy or what?"

"If it meant anything, it meant, like, 'extra-hard.' Like, I'd bone you extra-hard. You know?"

"Really? That's it?" Polly asked, and Sam said, "Yeah, pretty much," and Polly said that was unimaginative and a turn off, and she expected better from him, although she didn't know why. "Don't call fucking 'boning'. It's repugnant."

"Sorry," said Sam.

"Oh, whatever. It's okay. Let's just forget this one." She was putting her jammies back on now. "Well, so what else is going on?"

Sam found his boxers and wearily stepped into them one foot at a time. His adrenaline was ebbing. On top of that, rebuffing Polly always left him feeling as though he'd withstood a siege; the walls had held, but they were shot full of cannonball holes, and there were piles of the mortally wounded all over the courtyard groaning out their last. Her assault took a toll. "It hasn't been the best night."

"Please don't tell me," said Polly.

"I saw Jo-Jo on TV in his Yankee Mobile."

"I hate that stupid car. It turns over like a 747 and wakes up the baby every time. It's a dumb dick on wheels."

"I didn't know he actually owned it."

"There's all kinds of things you don't know about my husband and my marriage, Sam. Because it's private. So quit prying. Find your own husband."

"That's all I've got," he said.

"Not much here, either," Polly said. "Jo-Jo and I watched a funny show. It was about this poor dope who got locked in his panic room on Y2K." She proceeded to recount the narrative of the episode of *Secrets Only Dead Men Know*.

Sam told her he had seen the same show, it had made him feel guilty, and if there was nothing else, he should probably go back to sleep. Polly informed him that if he didn't do something to improve his outlook, one of these days she was going to find someone else with whom to masturbate.

"I met someone tonight," Sam said. It just slipped out. He left out the part about how he had crawled through a bathroom window to escape from that someone.

"Really?" asked Polly after a pause. Then she said, "Oh, sugar. Rainer's crying," and hung up.

By the time Sam returned from taking a leak in the bathroom—an arduous round trip that involved negotiating a hallway blocked by a freestanding hammock from an outdoor furniture company, several family-size tin cans of gumballs from a party supplier, and a scattering of stuffed animals from a toy maker—he had forgotten again about the vagrant with the knife.

Rather, Sam's fading thoughts were occupied with Polly, who, he was bewildered to conclude, had been jealous.

■ ■ ■

His cell phone awakened him a second time. The phone was close, at the edge of the bed where he had set it down. Sam read the vibrating window: Tess Auerbach, 3:45 A.M.

Most of his consciousness remained sunk in a dream about being packed into a large box and shipped to an unknown destination. (The Styrofoam poppers were soft, the box was roomy, and the considerate UPS person kept opening the flaps to gaze down at him and ask how he was holding up. Sam said he was okay. He liked it in there. The face of the UPS person was partially obscured by the chattering zeppelin of an Arriflex camera that he used to film Sam as he lay in the long Sam-shaped box.) A small portion of him was alert enough to be perversely warmed by the sight of her name; Tess had remembered him.

As he grinned blearily at the name in the window the call went to voice mail. When Sam tried to check the message, his hand turned the phone off instead. "Oops," he said, and dropped back into the dream feeling blameless and happy.

There was a scream accompanied by a crash of metal poles. The door to Sam's bedroom banged open, and Mina fell forward onto her knees. She was in her pajamas—a swishing purple running suit—and dawn had flooded the room in pale light.

"What is it?" Sam was awake and out of his bed in an instant, down on the floor beside her, his hand at the top of her spine. "What is it, honey?"

Mina rolled over and clutched her bare foot. She gasped. Sam saw a scrape on her big toe. "I—" The sentence snagged, and she gasped again. "I—"

He embraced her. In his arms, Mina felt like the pieces of something, all the lengths and sections and washers and screws, still in their plastic bag before being assembled. "Please, honey," he said. "Stop. Tell me."

"I stubbed my toe on the frame of that fucking hammock!" she screamed. "Who keeps a hammock in the hall of their fucking apartment?" She sobbed and slapped the floor.

Sam released her and sat back. "You're going to be okay. It's just a flesh wound, Mina. I swear." He was relieved, annoyed, and—mainly—focused on convincing his pulse to slow down.

His sister closed her eyes, inhaled, and stopped crying.

At the same time, the room seemed to exhale, to unlock. The window opened onto the fire escape and a sunny day. Littered across the floor, the piles of laundry appeared soft. Black roots glistened at Mina's hairline, as if the white dye had started to melt. It was barely morning, Sam thought. He didn't have to get up yet.

"Tom called," she said. "It's Dad, Sam. There was a test—and the results— He's dying."

"Dad?" asked Sam.

8.

Sam was dressed, standing in front of the logjam of crates at the entryway. Mina had shoved her sewing machine on him, and now he was holding it in front of him with both hands, like a birthday cake with lit candles. He'd been awake for ten minutes. "Let's go!" he yelled at her.

His sister was by the beanbag chair, fighting the zipper of her duffel. "Fuck you, bag!"

Puffy-eyed, huddled on the couch beneath a calico blanket of recycled carpet fragments—*Green living is our itchy, itchy future. YEAH, I GUESS I'LL HAVE TO TAKE IT*—Wesley moaned.

Mina jumped on the duffel a couple of times, then tried the zipper again. "Come on, come on!"

"Let's lower the volume, guys," said Wesley. "Yelling and hurrying never helps."

"Mina," said Sam. "What the hell am I doing with this sewing machine?"

"I need it!" The duffel closed with a stereo-sound *zip!* "That's right," said Mina. She assessed the duffel a sharp kick for good measure before shouldering the rest of her luggage. In her rush, the straps of the different bags twisted together. "Oh, fuck-snot." Mina dropped everything and started over.

"You need to calm down," said Wesley.

"What?" She had the straps organized and the bags over her shoulders.

"Calm down." Wesley clutched his blanket of recycled carpet fabrics to his chin. "Calm down, deep breath, gather your thoughts."

"Calm down?" Mina asked.

"Never mind him. Let's go," said Sam.

"Calm down," said Wesley. "Hurrying is counterproductive."

Mina looked to her half brother. At the side of her head, her white hair stuck out in a smashed fan, and pebbles of mascara dotted her cheeks, as if a herd of miniature animals had recently stampeded across her face. Her eyes were very wide. Sam wasn't sure what was going through her mind, but he guessed that it was dangerous.

"Wesley," he said, "shut up."

"Calm down?"

Wesley ignored them both. "Deep breaths." To demonstrate, he closed his eyes, inhaled for a two-second count, and then exhaled. Wesley opened his eyes and nodded at her. "See? You feel better now, don't you?"

"That's it. I've had enough of your patronizing, you fat prick." Mina ripped open the side pocket of the duffel bag, tore out a can of pepper spray, and was at the couch in two steps, smashing the fire button.

The spray caught Wesley directly in the right eye. "Ahh! Stop! Stop!" He paddled his hands through the air in front of his face and flopped over the arm of the couch and onto the floor, shrouded in the blanket of recycled carpet fragments.

Sam turned one way and then another, searching for somewhere to set down the sewing machine. There was nowhere.

While Wesley rolled around in the tangle of the blanket, Mina climbed onto the couch and leaned over the armrest, the can still raised to firing position. "Are you okay?"

"I thought we were friends." Wesley had his palms jammed into his eye sockets, rubbing, and his voice came out muffled and teary.

She shot him with another jet. "I almost sprained my ankle on your stupid hammock."

"Mina! Stop!" Sam had given up trying to find a place for the sewing machine. He stood in the entryway, feeling at once impotent and transfixed. "That's enough!"

Wesley howled again, kicked against the floor with his heels, and propelled himself backward into the bottom box of a four-tall stack of boxes. The stack tumbled over onto the incapacitated man's body with a sound like bricks hitting fresh earth. When the quake stopped, the sight of the bare feet sticking out from under the jumble of packaging reminded Sam, inescapably, of another pair of feet, infamous in their ruby slippers, protruding from beneath a crumpled farmhouse.

Mina lowered the pepper spray and glared at her brother. "I just wish that he would clean. This is ridiculous! You know very well I would be a way better roommate." She put the canister in her pocket and glanced back at Wesley—the only part of him that was visible, his feet. "I am your friend," Mina said.

They had reached the front of the building before Sam managed to regain the wherewithal to ask Mina if she thought Wesley was okay. He was still toting her sewing machine.

"Depends on what was in those boxes." She spoke over her shoulder and kicked out the door.

"Jesus Christ, Mina, why did you do that?" He followed her out into the building's open-air courtyard, a small T-shaped area of cracked slate set back from the sidewalk and crowded by a rusted green Dumpster. It was already hot, overcast, the morning light filtered and gray.

The vagrant stepped toward them. What Sam noticed about him immediately was the brightness of his eyes; they were nested in the mass of his copper-colored beard like a pair of shiny green bird's eggs.

"Hi?" The vagrant's voice was throaty. In one hand, he had a long knife, blade pointed up. He blinked at them.

"Hi," said Mina. She went at him, calmly pulling the canister out of her pocket as she moved, and when she was an arm's length away, she blasted him in his bird's-egg eyes.

The man yelped and stumbled backward, tripping over a loose slate. There was a thud as his head struck the paving.

Sprawled on the slates, the vagrant lifted an arm and waved the blade around as if trying to swat flies.

"Drop the knife," said Mina.

The weapon clattered from the man's hand, and Mina hopped aside to avoid its spinning, whisking slide. It clanged against the base of the Dumpster and lay on the slate.

On some level Sam was pondering the knife's action—the vagrant's intention—even as the impulse to defend his sister carried him the short distance from the door to the prone man. The same impulse lifted Sam's foot and dropped it on the man's crotch. As his shoe drove downward, he felt a soft squelching beneath his heel. "That's my sister!" Sam's cry echoed in the morning courtyard, bouncing off the walls, the Dumpster, climbing up the wide shaft between buildings.

The vagrant momentarily sat up, spluttered, vomited orange gruel into his lap, and collapsed back onto his side. He sobbed and made hurt-animal noises.

"Sam?"

He turned to his sister. "I thought he threw it at you."

Mina shook her head. "You're my hero." She dropped the pepper spray back in her pocket and bent to pick up the sword. "Let's go."

Sam took a blind backward step. The vagrant's left hand popped under his sneaker sole. The man expressed a sound like a whoopee cushion.

"Sorry, sorry," Sam said, and jumped off. He looked down at the spitting, weeping little man with grit and vomit in his beard and snot spurting from his nose, lying on the ground in a puddle of filthy overcoat. Rocking on his heels, Sam held his sister's sewing machine and felt insane.

The vagrant's writhing came to an abrupt crescendo: he jerked, gagged, spat, and went still. His chest rose and fell in a shallow rhythm.

Sam gathered himself with a deep breath. "Sorry," he said again, a whisper this time—and he was, too, terribly, wretchedly sorry. But there was no time to think of strangers; his family was calling. Sam turned and chased after his sister.

Brooks Hartwig, Jr., opened his eyes. He rocked his head to look one way, then rocked it to see the other way. They were gone. Except for the crew, he was alone.

He stared into the awful sky. It still wasn't over. It still wasn't dead. He knew because they were filming. "Just do what you do," said the Director. "Ignore us. We're not even here."

"I hate you," Brooks tried to whisper. He wondered if maybe his hand was on fire, but he refused to look.

He was going to have to be very strong and very brave to kill it once and for all, to finally kill the beast. If he was ever going to get these fucking cameras out of his face, someone was going to have to die.

REEL CHANGE

(1991)

1.

Monday's headline was this: Booth, without consulting anyone, had offered to appear at Sam's homeroom for that Friday's Career Day Presentation. Mrs. Quartermain had accepted.

"That should be interesting," Allie said.

Sam didn't care for that—"interesting." He was increasingly attuned to the way adults used vagaries to obscure dangerous truths. His mother, for instance, referred to her marriage to Booth as "liberated," which Sam recognized as a sneaky way of acknowledging his father's long absences. It was as though they were a little less married than other married parents and, by extension, that their family was somehow looser than other families, not as official. He didn't want other people to think that they were different, although he knew they were.

"Interesting how?" asked Sam.

"I don't know—entertaining."

"There's nothing interesting about being entertained."

"Says you," said Allie.

Mother and son were wandering the Huguenot graveyard that sat on the hill a few hundred yards from their house. It was their custom on the afternoons that his mother had off, where they went to discuss the events of the day—what had happened to Sam at school, what had happened to Allie at work, etc.

It was early spring, clear and brisk. The lichen-speckled stones lay scattered and tilted at a dozen different angles. The dead refugees they walked on top of had all ceased to breathe over two hundred years ago.

Sam let his hand trail along the arched top of a stone, scraping the spots of pale green growth with his fingers. Their steps raised milky brown puddles in the grass.

A lean, auburn-haired woman in her late thirties, Allie tended to carry herself very straight and to hold her arms crossed over the chest, like the commander of something. There was a remote quality about his mother that Sam held in great esteem. She listened. She never yelled. She didn't tend to fool around.

Which wasn't to say that his mother was especially severe or grindingly serious in the way that some parents could be—the fathers who barked directions from the bleachers at Little League games; the mothers who, just before the music began at an assembly, couldn't resist running up to pat down an errant hair or smooth a tie. Rather, because of her calmness, she was the polar opposite of those types.

The café had been robbed once. Sam had been there at a café table, drawing. The bell over the door jangled, and he glanced up to see a man in a shiny teal Dolphins jacket run at the counter, snatch the tip jar, tuck it in his elbow, spin, and dash out, rejangling the bell. The thief vanished beyond the windowed doors, never to be seen again. The whole incident was over in less than twenty seconds.

Allie said, "Hey!" but didn't make a move around the counter.

The bell was still tinkling when his mother cast a look at Sam at his table, where he was holding a magenta crayon over the paper, perplexed rather than frightened. Allie crossed her arms and raised an eyebrow. "Kiddo, I don't suppose you'd mind drawing up a label for the new tip jar, would you?" she asked, and Sam giggled and went right to work.

A grown-up didn't perform; a grown-up reacted. His mother was a grown-up. If Allie told him that a thing was, it was; if she told him it wasn't, it wasn't; if she promised that he would feel better tomorrow, he could not doubt her.

Sam had never possessed that kind of conviction in his father, and he certainly didn't now. That winter's episode, the trip to the museum, lingered on the boy's mind. He replayed the events—the odd woman and her questions, how she used baby talk at first and then at the end became so serious and sad-seeming, the panties on the floor, Booth's twisting of Sam's words on the train—and could make no sense of the offense he had committed, and he was baffled and humiliated once more. Allie couldn't have comprehended any of that, and even if the boy felt he could explain it to her, his father had sworn him to secrecy and gave no hint of releasing the oath.

When Booth was about to depart on his latest trip to California, he had swept Sam up in a bear hug and swung him around. "If you're going to look at me as though I've murdered someone, Samuel, the least you could do is reveal the name of my victim!" As it was happening, Sam laughed in self-defense. That night, when his father was gone, he spent a long time in his bedroom with his face buried in a pillow, breathing fabric, and wishing he was tired enough to sleep so he didn't have to go down to dinner and pretend to his mother that everything was normal.

Now all Sam could manage was "Regular people aren't prepared for Booth."

Allie said she didn't believe there were any regular people. "It's going to be fine. Your father understands that this is important. He'll be on his best behavior."

"You don't know him like I know him."

"That may be so." She gave the boy a chuck behind the ear. "I guess you'll just have to tough it out and hope for the best."

They walked some more. Allie said that Tom was coming back that week to finish fixing the ceiling at the café, thank the heavens. Sam asked her if she'd mind adding a few girl touches—curlicues, sparkly glue, whatever came to mind—to a poster he was making for his social studies project on the Trail of Tears. She agreed to take a look.

"You don't think he'll do the leper story, do you?" Booth loved to tell people that Sam, as a newborn, resembled a little leper.

"No. I'm sure he won't." Allie touched Sam's back, and he shrugged her hand off.

A black-and-white cat was crouched out in the middle of the road. Allie yelled at it to move. The cat stared at her the way cats stare at people. "You'll get smushed," she said, and threw a handful of gravel in its direction. The animal hissed and trotted off, disappeared into some bushes. "You're welcome," she called after it, "you stubborn idiot. No one gets smushed on my watch."

At the marker for Henry James Elting, 1833–1845, Beloved Son and Brother, Sam took out two Nukies from his pocket and arrayed them on the stone top side by side. The first of these red creatures had two regular arms, plus a crooked little baby arm that ended in a claw, and droopy antennae. The other had a tail, bulging fists that looked like they could smash rock, a jaw shaped like a shovel blade, and a ragged bucket hat jammed down on its head. Both figures stood hunched and frowning, a not uncommon expression among the jinxed species.

His mother looked on while Sam made a camera with his fingers and zoomed it in and out. "Your men are so depressing, kiddo."

"They've had hard lives," he said.

"Do you know how much I love you?" his mother asked.

"Sure."

He inched to the left, gathering a few jumbled stones into the background of the frame of his finger camera. Sam instinctively sensed that the depth this added to the picture was valuable, that it spoke to how forbidding the landscape was for those few poor descendants of the human race who had lurched up from the toxic sludge of the twenty-second century.

"Do you know how much your father loves you?" Allie asked.

"Yeah."

"Because the thing about your father is that he's not like other fathers. He's not like other husbands, either. And that can be difficult. We've talked about how difficult that can be, haven't we? But what's different about your father is also what's good about him. I mean, you have to ask yourself, you know, what other fathers can order takeout with Animal's voice? Right? I know you love it when Booth does that. Your dad is funny. What other fathers can juggle?

"And lots of men laugh at themselves, but not many like it when women laugh at them. Your father just loves it when people laugh, doesn't he? I hope someday you understand how exceptional that is. What other fathers talk about books or have been to other countries or—" She did this occasionally, started talking to Sam about his father but ended up talking to herself, a goofy grin spreading across her face the way it never did unless the subject was Booth. It was the one time when he thought his mother seemed less than adult.

Sam meticulously tweaked the lens of his imaginary scope, widening and sharpening. When he was satisfied, he cleared his throat. "Quiet on the set!" (This was what Booth said right before he pressed the button on the camera timer and hurried around to stand beside them for family portraits.)

"Oh, sorry," said Allie. She zipped her lips and flung away an invisible key.

Sam operated his invisible camera by turning an invisible crank, adding a faint, helicopter-like whirring noise to make it more realistic.

Allie stood aside in polite silence. A cold wind picked up. The Nukies trembled.

"Cut," Sam said eventually.

"What was the scene about?" she asked.

"Ill tidings," said Sam. He scooped up his toys. "They sense that something bad is about to happen."

"Kiddo," said Allie. "Ill tidings? Wait a sec. Didn't they already live through the apocalypse? How much worse can it get?"

At home, his mother set a pot of water on the stove for tea and asked Sam to watch it while she was in the bathroom. A minute later, the phone rang.

"Hello?" Sam asked through a mouthful of American cheese.

There was a sniff, a small exhalation.

Sam gulped down the cheese. "Hello?" he asked again.

"Sammy? Is your daddy there? I'd like—"

Sam hung up.

Allie came back from the bathroom. "Who was that?"

He shook his head—*no idea*—and took another bite.

2.

Among his fifth-grade peers, Sam believed that he placed squarely in the middle ground; he was not an athlete or a math whiz or a musical prodigy; he was not poor or handicapped or a malcontent; he had no enemies but no close friends, either; except for a Perfect Attendance certificate for the spring semester of third grade, he had avoided any kind of distinction whatsoever, and that was how Sam liked it. He preferred to be outside of things. Attention not only made him anxious, it interrupted his vantage, making him focus on how other people were reacting to him as opposed to letting him focus on how other people interacted. (Girls were of particular interest to Sam. Since at least the beginning of second grade, he had been turning a single multi-faceted question over in his mind: "Girls: what the heck?")

It was evident, too, that the wrong kind of attention—the kind of attention that his father, so large and so different from anyone else, could all too easily draw—could ruin a kid. Sam had seen it.

There was poor Erica Wembley, who had blithely lain out barechested at the public swimming pool. Three years on from the blunder and people still called her Cheese Nips and threw Cheese Nips at her head when the teacher's back was turned.

Ethan Evans had let slip that he had two mothers; Mark Goolsby admitted that his father was in jail for writing bad checks. They were Lesbo Kid and the Convict's Son, respectively. There were others: the one who was caught stealing; the one who cried on the field trip to the apple orchard because he thought he'd lost his Buffalo Bills duffel bag; the new guy who took off his clothes after gym and actually showered in the shower in the locker room for the first time in known history.

It wasn't the cruel nicknames attending these personal catastrophes that scared Sam the most—although the thought of being branded as something like Cheese Nips was lamentable—but the way they transformed someone. You felt sorry for Erica Wembley. You studied her profile, the way she held herself, as if there were a wall pressing against her back. When someone said, "Yo! Cheese Nips!," it was almost possible to see the words hit her and bounce off onto the floor. But the abuse might not even be the worse of it. Sam could imagine bunching up his shoulders and dropping his head, pushing through. What would be truly awful would be the sympathy of bystanders like Sam himself, because no one who witnessed your perseverance would admire you. No matter how tall you walked, you'd only seem more pitiable. To be Booth's son was confusing enough on its own terms. To be revealed as Booth's son in the eyes of everyone else felt like an execution.

"So, your dad's a"—Gloria Wang-Petty grimaced and rubbed her fingers as if trying to get something off them; it was Tuesday, between periods—"like, actor person, and he's coming on Friday?"

"Yeah," said Sam. He had gone to retrieve a juice box from his cubby, and when he turned around, Gloria was in his way, blocking him from the rest of the room. "He's an actor."

"What's that like?" asked Gloria, dark-eyed and intimidatingly tall in her yellow cowboy boots.

Popular and intelligent, Gloria, like all the smart and well-liked girls, radiated not only competence but authority. Sam was afraid of her and also drawn to her. Her black bangs were teased into five spiky arcs. She smelled like banana hair spray.

"I don't know," said Sam. He sensed that she wanted him to say that having Booth for a father was incredibly exciting, like having Christmas morning every day. Although he was willing to lie to escape the treacherous subject, he suspected that such a declaration would only prolong it.

"You don't know? He's your father."

The smell of bananas was making Sam light-headed. He broke eye contact, glancing over the top of the cubbies at the poster of President George H. W. Bush shaking hands with an astronaut. "He has to work a lot."

"What kind of movies is he in? Has he ever been in a musical? I love musicals."

The awful, tantalizing posters in the closet came to mind. In one, Booth had pinwheels for eyes, and the people watching him were plainly in his control, enraptured, faces slack and openmouthed. What would a bunch of kids make of that? Sam himself wasn't sure what to make of it.

"I'm pretty sure he's never been in a musical," said Sam, carefully eliding the first question.

"Does he know famous people?" asked Gloria.

Sam recalled what his father had said at the museum. "He knows Orson Welles."

"Who is Orson Welles?" Her tone was doubtful, as if Orson Welles were a new kid who had just moved to Hasbrouck and made a splash by being talented at basketball or doing skateboard tricks.

"He's a famous director," said Sam. The ground beneath his feet had steadied. "He directed and starred in *Citizen Kane,* the greatest movie ever made."

"I've never even heard of that movie," said Gloria suspiciously.

"Oh," said Sam. "It's about this guy—named Kane." He chuckled for no reason and stabbed the juice box straw ineffectually at the small plastic-sealed aperture.

"So what's your dad going to do with us?"

"I don't know." He tried to change the subject. "These straws never work." In one hand, he raised the bent straw, and in the other, he held up his juice box.

"I just hope your dad's not stupid. I mean, no offense." Gloria rolled her eyes up to inspect her five bangs and brought a hand up to smooth one. "Like, it was cool when Jessie's dad froze stuff with the liquid ice, but it was super-retarded when what's-his-name's nurse mom made us stay late watching that video about shaking babies. And then we had to carry around the flour-sack babies all weekend? Duh, I'm not going to shake a baby, but this is a flour sack. If anything, I'm going to get my mom to turn that sucker into a batch of brownies."

Sam nodded eagerly, although he vividly recalled Gloria and the rest of the girls cooing over their flour-sack infants and bringing them back to school wearing hats. "Yeah. That was super-retarded."

Gloria abruptly reached out and plucked his juice box from his hands. She punched the straw through the hole at the top. "There. Hey, can I have a sip, Sam?" Gloria smiled and squinted at him. "I'm so thirsty."

In the four or five seconds that elapsed before he responded, a realization clicked into place as part of the mystery—Girls: what the heck?—was solved. It was what Sam wanted from them; that is, merely to be permitted to give them what they wanted, to please them, to get them to look at him the way Gloria was looking at him at that moment, like he might be worth something. (Simultaneously, his interest in the other chief aspect of the mystery—what girls might want from him or any male—was abruptly discarded for the next decade.) A bubbly feeling coursed through Sam, a wonderful shakiness that made him squeeze his hands to keep them from flopping around.

"Oh, sure," he said. "Go ahead. Have the whole thing." He hoped she would ask him for something else, for anything.

"Oh, thank you! You're sweet." Gloria took another little drink. "Remember: don't let your dad do anything retarded! Make him be good, okay?"

And things had been going so well.

The bell rang, and she said she'd see him later. Sam stayed where he was. He licked his dry lips.

3.

Allie's café, the Coffee Shop, shared the bottom floor of what had been the Hasbrouck movie theater. You entered under the marquee—

NOW PLAYING
The Coffee Shop
Starring Joe as "Coffee"

—and the Coffee Shop occupied the entire former lobby area of the theater. The counter was arranged along the lines of the old concessions stand, and the bathrooms were vintage examples of mid–twentieth century plumbing, complete with a trough in the men's bathroom. A few horseshoe-shaped plaster moldings clung to the walls, though they were tinted brown with age, their swirls gouged and chipped. Mismatched couches and café tables were arranged around the bare hardwood floor. The stairs to the second floor were cordoned off by yellow caution tape.

As for the theater proper, it had become the offices and meeting hall of the SUNY-Hasbrouck Communist Students' Association. They had their own entrance at the back of the theater, but Sam had peeked inside. Here again, the space's former use was vaguely present. At the foot of the auditorium, there was a narrow, bare stage but no screen or curtain. A random selection of the original seats remained, two or three side by side in one place, a single by itself in another place, and so on. The impression conveyed by the cavernous room was of a mouth with the majority of the teeth pulled.

The visible sediment of the previous institution beneath the newer one struck even a boy Sam's age as telling. The town was like a piece of twice-used drawing paper, smudged and worn thin from repeated erasing.

Hasbrouck had no industry to speak of, just the college with its tides of students, streaming in and streaming out. Hikers and climbers came for the mountains, but departed on Sunday afternoons. Whether a person was renting a couple of days of fresh air, or getting four years of college, ultimately, they were headed elsewhere. Meanwhile, Sam, Allie, and the dead Huguenots stayed on.

It was depressing, honestly, the boy's sense that his town once was a place to be—a place with an operating movie theater—as opposed to a place to leave, probably in favor of somewhere that did have a movie theater.

His father was like all the others: he came and went.

"Did you know that Booth is coming to my school, Tom?"

On the eve of his father's presentation, Sam was at the Coffee Shop, staging Nukies on the steps of Tom Ritts's ladder. Sam liked Tom because, in a way, he was the opposite of Booth; Booth made everything big, whereas Tom made everything small. Allie liked him, too, not least because his tolerant nature was catnip for her love of teasing.

"No, I didn't. But that ought to be pretty decent," said Tom. His upper body was in the lobby ceiling. He was changing the fittings on the ancient pipes above the counter area. These pipes—like the men's room trough and the crumbling moldings, original to the theater—had recently started to drip cold water on people's necks. "Your dad's a real showman, Sam." His voice was a tinny echo.

"Yeah." Sam squared up a Nukie who had her hands lifted, palms outward in the universal gesture for *stop,* with a bloodshot eye bulging from each palm. The boy flicked her with an index finger. The creature plunged to the floor below. "Ahhhhhh!" said Sam under his breath.

"Did you say something?" asked Tom. "I couldn't hear you."

"So why do you like him?" asked Sam. "Booth, I mean."

It felt natural to speak freely with Tom, who was so nonchalant that it was extremely difficult to imagine him possessing the wherewithal to lie about anything or even shade the truth. Maybe it was a matter of supreme self-confidence, or maybe it was simplicity, but Tom was entirely out in front. The threadbare ankles of the older man's blue jeans were at Sam's eye level.

"Why do I like your dad? That's a heck of a question. But let me see," said Tom.

A young man in a tattered army jacket with sunglasses propped in his dreadlocks approached the counter. "Hey, little brother, you got any cinnamon?"

Sam pointed to a short table in front of the roped-off stairs to the balcony. "Over there, Communist."

The young man grunted and shuffled away.

There was the sound of metal tapping on metal in the ceiling. "You know, more than anything, Booth keeps me on my toes. He makes it fun. I bet that's a big part of how come your mom loves him so much, too."

The appeal eluded Sam. "You like that?"

"Sure," said Tom. "What's not to like about feeling happy?"

Sam spotted the fallen Nukie on the floor and stamped on it. He ground his heel around, trying to pulverize the poor freak.

"When my son, your peer, Young Samuel here," said the Booth of Sam's mind, the full classroom arrayed before him, Gloria Wang-Petty in her seat in the left-hand corner of the front row, "was first handed to me by the nurse, he was enrobed in a kind of rough brown cloth, such as an extra will wear in a biblical production. He resembled a tiny leper. And he did not fuss, did not scream or cry. He just glared at me, fiercely glared." There was a wave of laughter, laughter like monkeys screeching, but the Booth of Sam's mind remained stern-faced. At last the laughter ceased. Booth cleared his throat. "It was," he finished, "most disquieting," and this sent them all roaring again. Gloria was in such a state that she was yanking on her bangs, hanging on to them for dear life.

Sam took away his foot. The Nukie was dusty, twisted slightly, but intact.

Allie passed by, carrying a couple of ceramic pitchers. "What's the hold up?" she called to Tom. "You sure you know what you're doing there, Ritts?"

There was a grunt from the ceiling. "Oh, I know what I'm doing up here. It's called 'Not getting paid to fix your plumbing.'"

Allie winked at her son. "Okay, Tom. You keep at it," she said, and swept away with two fresh pitchers.

"Mom?" Sam called after her, and was instantly relieved that she didn't hear him and turn back, because for some reason he knew that if she did, he would break down in tears and beg her to keep Booth from coming, and probably tell her about the woman in the museum, too, about Sandra.

Earlier that day, when Sam had stopped at home to drop off his backpack, the phone was ringing again. "Sammy? Is that you Sammy?"

The contractor leaned out of the ceiling. Grease spotted his face and the blond of his receding crew cut. He wore a gap-toothed smile. "Hey, buddy, what's with the long face? Why don't you grab a wrench and get up here? I could use an extra hand tightening this gasket."

4.

When his alarm rang at seven o'clock, the boy opened his eyes to stare up at the model P-51 Mustang that dangled from the ceiling. He wished it would strafe him where he lay. A couple of minutes passed fruitlessly— the fighter twisted lightly on its wire—and Sam threw his feet over the bed, planting them down on the cold wood.

His father was in the kitchen. Booth, predictably, had arrived under the cover of darkness.

Arrayed in a pair of voluminous black pajamas, he was frying bacon in a skillet and whistling the annoying little ditty he always whistled. Allie was at the table in her blue bathrobe, smiling and tapping her foot. Between them Sam sensed a casual, happy collusion, as if they had just won a game of doubles tennis.

He paused in the entryway, petting the doorframe. His sleep had been unsettled, rattled by dreams of thunderous, indistinct questions. "I can't understand you," he remembered yelling over and over, walking in the house, on the street, in the Huguenot graveyard. The questions kept coming, though—maybe from the sky, maybe from the earth, he couldn't tell, they seemed to be all around. The inflection told him that they were questions, but the words were bottomless and insensible.

"What's going on?" he asked his parents.

"Breakfast," said Allie. She blew him a kiss. "A delicious repast to fortify the young scholar!"

At the stove, his father executed a shovel-and-flip with the skillet; strips of bacon tumbled through the air. Several landed in the pan, and several others on the floor, where they exploded into brown shrapnel on the tile. Allie dropped her forehead to the table with a knock and whooped.

Booth set the skillet back on the burner and performed a mincing dance on the tips of his toes before executing a courtly bow, rolling out his right hand. "Madam. I give you: *bacon.*"

Sam slid away from the doorframe.

"Oh, stay, dear! Samuel, stay! There's more than enough!" cried Booth after him. "The floor bacon can be mine!"

"Never mind," said the boy, retreating. "I'm not hungry."

The phone began to ring. "Oh, Christ," said Allie, "it's probably that breather again."

A few minutes later, on the porch, Sam informed his mother that it was probably time for him to wait at the foot of their driveway for the bus by himself. He said it almost exactly that way: "You know, I think it's probably time I waited by myself, Mom." The gesture wasn't intended petulantly, wasn't intended toward Allie at all. It just seemed, in the face of that afternoon's hopeless appointment, like it was time for him to stand by himself. Sam actually felt brave.

"You're probably right," said Allie, and stuck his lunch money, two dollars rolled in a tube, into the chest pocket of his spring jacket. She hugged him tightly, her long hair brushing over his eyes, and let go. The screen door groaned shut, and the front door followed with a click.

He was immediately sorry, wanting another moment with her. Tears stung his eyes and his nose. He felt stupid for being so upset. The wind blew through his coat. It was gray. The road bent past the Huguenot graveyard. From inside, he heard the muffled sound of his mother's record player coming alive with the light, tumbling intro to a Scott Joplin rag. "There it is, Zelda," came Booth's approving voice carrying clearly outside, "there's the one I like."

Sam closed his eyes and stepped.

Because Career Day Presentations always took place at final period, he had the rest of the day to brood on his fate.

At lunch Sam disconsolately spooned gravy onto a Nukie he had never liked. "Noooo," he whispered, "whywhywhywhy!" The Nukie had the lower body of a worm and the upper body of a nerd.

Mark Goolsby, a sallow, blinking boy, sat across the cafeteria table, eating his cheese sandwich. "That Nukie's really suffering, isn't he?" observed Goolsby.

The two boys were not friends but occasional project partners, both decent, reserved students. A connection based on their fathers—Mark's the check-fraud ex-con, Sam's Booth—had not resolved, but Sam thought there might be something there.

"He had it coming." Sam spooned more gravy onto the figure, which from the worm up happened to bear a likeness to Mark Goolsby—glasses, short-sleeve button-down, tight haircut. Goolsby's mother, a homeopath (whatever that was), was the afternoon's other presenter.

Boot heels clicked on the cafeteria linoleum. An angular shadow fell across the table. Gloria Wang-Petty leaned over to tear a handful of napkins from the dispenser in the middle of the boys' table. "We're all out at my table," she explained.

"Cool," said Mark.

"Mark, did you tell your mother about my nut allergy?" asked Gloria.

"'Course," said Mark.

Mrs. Goolsby was bringing cookies. As far as Sam was concerned, in relation to whatever it was that Booth was planning, this added insult to injury. Cookies were stacking the deck.

"Thanks, Conwict!" Gloria poked Mark in the shoulder. (For involved reasons related to a raucous viewing of a BBC version of *Great Expectations* in the previous year's Advanced English class, and the thick accents employed by some of the actors, Mark's nickname was no longer the Convict's Son, but just Conwict.)

"Anything to be of service," said Goolsby, who (wisely, in Sam's view) had given up actively protesting his nickname and switched to a program of faintly snide remarks.

She turned to Sam. "Hey, Sam."

"Hey, Gloria."

"I'm excited about your dad. I was thinking, and you know, I've never met an actor!"

Sam nodded.

Gloria hesitated. "There's a—" She was looking in the direction of Sam's mashed potatoes. The Nukie's nerd head protruded slightly, like a pink pebble.

"It's a guy," said Sam, who knew he ought to be embarrassed but was too depressed.

"Oh," said Gloria, and shrugged before managing to drum up another smile for him. "Thanks again."

When the bell rang, Sam picked up his Nukie and stuck it in his mouth. He walked to class imagining himself walking to class—being filmed, that is, by a camera on rails, gliding alongside him, because that was how he felt, as though he were being sucked effortlessly forward by gravity, his path preordained—while alternately gnawing and sucking on plastic.

Mark's mother was first. As the cookies circulated, Ms. Goolsby held up a leafing twig. "Would you believe that there's more healing power in this sprig of lilac than in one whole bottle of heart pills?" She waved the twig. "But it makes sense, doesn't it?" She waved the twig some more.

Behind her and to the right, a step or two from the door, Booth Dolan sat beneath the flag and stared at the floor. He had not removed his herringbone overcoat, and by his knees were two oblong steel suitcases. Booth looked like a man waiting for a bus.

Several minutes passed. Mark's mother extolled the powers of native flora. The kids sipped and crunched. At her desk, Mrs. Quartermain uncrossed and recrossed her legs every few seconds.

Sam gazed at his father gazing at the floor and, as he did so, made a mental list of what he felt he absolutely knew about the man who was half responsible for his creation: his father loved Mountain Dew, spicy mustard, Muenster cheese, all-you-can-eat buffets, the novels of Irwin Shaw, the plays of George Bernard Shaw, the stories and poems of Edgar Allan Poe, the music of Mose Allison, hotel freebies, Spanish wine, and German beer; above all other men, Booth admired Orson Welles; he disdained "fascists, bosses, bankers, Teamsters, and critics"; he had "come around, grudgingly," to FM radio; he was large and he was loud; and when he was home, Allie was happier.

These things were, for the most part, alien artifacts to Sam. He could do little more than helplessly bang them together. The last was one of the few he could comprehend, but he couldn't explain it. His father was a knot, and he was knotted to him.

There was also the trip to the museum and the madwoman in the fur hat. Something had happened then, was happening still, and in the meantime, Sam felt that he had failed everyone. He was sorry. He wanted to be better.

The older man glanced up without raising his head, peering from under the flourish of his dark, unkempt eyebrows, and met his son's gaze. Booth winked.

■ ■ ■

"My name is Booth Dolan. I am a storyteller and a thespian. A thespian is an actor. I make believe on a professional basis. I pretend to be people who I am not. You are children. You make believe as a matter of course. I presume that each of you is competent at making believe on at least a semi-professional level. That is as it should be.

"Are any of you familiar with the concept of the double feature? No? A double feature is a showing of two movies back to back. The double feature was the staple of the drive-in movie theater. A single ticket provided you an entire night's entertainment.

"But the second movie of the double feature was always better than the first movie. They saved it for later, when it was good and dark, when the images on the screen could be seen with the greatest clarity. Because that was the one you really wanted to see. The first movie was just the warm-up. The double feature often began while there was still some light, and it could be hard to make out everything happening on the screen—it could be hazy. Everything was perfect for the second movie, though. The second movie had all the exciting stuff: the scares and the surprises and the parts that you'd remember and want to discuss later.

"You are currently living in the first movie of the double feature of your life. It's fine, you're happy enough, but probably some parts are hazy to you. That's the nature of the first feature.

"However, the characters you play in your minds and in your games now are vital preparation for the wild implausibility of adult existence, which is the second feature. As adults, you will experience incredible adventures. Feats of derring-do will be required. You will labor beneath weighty responsibilities. There will be cunning puzzles to solve. Pirates may fire upon you. You should not be surprised to find yourself traveling by night, with scant provisions, along broken roads haunted by wayfarers of unreliable character. Hangers-on of the court may sow intrigue against you. Misfortune will not be a stranger to you; nor will duplicity. Nor will tragedy. There will doubtless be romantic entanglements, as well as many bawdy, humorous episodes.

"So. Make believe. It is important. Your second feature will start soon."

A few seconds elapsed, and Booth's words seemed to remain in the air, thrumming. Sam's eyes darted around the room: Mrs. Quartermain, blinking rapidly, worked her dentures and stroked her gingham collar; Helen Goolsby, having taken Booth's place beneath the flag, had a cookie in her mouth that she was not chewing; in the front row, Gloria Wang-Petty was frozen, pinching one of her bangs; near the windows, in his aquarium, Todd, the class gerbil, huddled inside a paper tube, whiskers flicking.

Booth had ascended precariously to the scooped seat of a molded green chair. His right hand lay against his breastbone. His head was no more than an inch below the classroom's paneled ceiling. He had not yet removed his overcoat.

"Miss—?" His hand shot free of his chest, and he pointed at Gloria Wang-Petty.

She jerked in her seat. "Me? I'm Gloria."

"What is your aspiration, Gloria?" he asked.

"My aspiration?"

"That's right. To what do you aspire? What do you want to be when you grow up?"

"I—I want to be a doctor."

Her interlocutor hopped from the green chair down to the black-and-white-checkered floor with a hard-soled crack that shook the room. Booth swept to the corner, hefted the steel suitcases, and bore them to the worktable in front of the blackboard. The latches were unclipped and the lids were thrown back.

In each case, nestled in gray foam beds, were row upon row of flesh-colored tepees. "Come," Booth said to Gloria.

The girl went to stand beside him. "What . . ." Her voice trailed off.

"Pick a nose, my dear, any nose," said Booth. "I'm sure there's a doctor in here somewhere."

Gloria settled on a discreet little bulb upturned minutely at the tip.

From his overcoat, Booth produced a tube of spirit gum to help secure the nose Gloria had chosen. The effect was arresting. The fake nose seemed to draw the girl's other features—mouth, eyes, eyebrows, ears—closer together, and to render her somehow older and taller, more complete.

Booth selected a nose for himself, a repulsive purplish specimen, squashed and threaded with veins. He raised it for the class to see, and there was a smattering of "ew" and "ugh."

With a couple of quick dabs of gum, he pressed the drunkard's nose into place. Sam's father turned away from the class, twisting his shoulders, stretching his neck, clearing his throat. He drew his spine upward and hunched, as if preparing to enter a low tunnel. At his sides, his hands clenched and then unclenched and stayed there, dangling in gorilla hooks.

Booth shuffled around again.

A wino, likely guided in from the street by a beat cop, presented himself to Dr. Wang-Petty:

"Doc. Doc, I don't feel right. The pain. The pain, all over I got it. There's blood falling down in front of my eyes." Booth had contorted himself so incredibly that he was underneath Gloria's line of vision. The boozer batted his eyelids pleadingly at her and clutched his hooked hands. "It's like . . . like you're on the other side of a red window from me, Doc."

Dr. Wang-Petty, arms folded across her chest, was impassive. "I'm sorry, old man. You have a cancer."

"Cancer?" Booth opened and closed his mouth several times.

"Certain death, I'm afraid. But I promise we will do everything we can to make you comfortable." Gloria maintained her posture.

"Thank you." The wino's voice was full of tears. "Thank you, Doc!"

Booth burst from his crouch. He grasped Gloria's hand, raised it, and threw them both forward into a grand bow.

There was a moment of silence—followed by an ovation.

Sam let out a breath.

They played until the bell rang.

Ronnie Messersmith put on a rightward-tilted nose with a bulge on the bridge and announced that he was the heavyweight champion of the world. Booth approached on his knees to beg in a squeaky child's voice for his autograph. Liz Curbishley utilized a nose that was a perfect isosceles triangle in order to make herself a librarian. "Shhh," she said, and no one said anything. Brian Byrne opted for a pockmarked nose, bristling with sharp white hairs, to become a police officer. "Nobody make a move," he said, and though nobody dared, he cried, "By God, I mean it!"

Sam's turn came right before the end of the period. He chose what he thought of as a wise nose. It was a long and narrow nose whose tiny nostrils seemed to imply a discerning taste in oxygen.

Once it was fixed on his face, he stalked back and forth in front of the classroom, hands locked at the base of his spine. "Raise the lights!" Mrs. Quartermain rushed to comply, flipping the switch for the overheads. "Bring that camera over here!" Mark Goolsby ran to the front of the room, wielding a rolled-up piece of paper for an eyepiece.

"We're ready, Booth," said Sam. "Now get up there and act."

Booth bowed to the director. Then he reascended the green chair and recited the Gettysburg Address.

5.

They drove to Massachusetts, to the Cape, and stayed in a beach house that belonged to someone who owed Booth a favor. Because it was too cold and blustery to go on the beach, they stayed inside, and Booth built huge, spitting fires that made Allie nervous and thrilled Sam. The marsh-mallows charred perfectly in seconds. Before bed, they read Stevenson's *Kidnapped*. Though Booth was the best reader—adopting brogues for the characters, twisting his face into a crazed goggle when he inhab-ited the Jacobite revolutionary Alan Breck—he insisted they each take a turn. Outside, the breakers crashed against the nickel-colored slant of the April beach, all day, every day.

Over a fish-and-chips lunch at a diner a few miles inland, Booth mused aloud that perhaps it was time to take their son on a journey westward, "to the Land of Dangerous Lemons"—his father's enigmatic nickname for California—so the boy could observe his father in action. Sam's heart hiccupped, but he restrained himself to a tight downward nod at his basket of food. Under the table, Allie squeezed his knee.

Home again, one evening Booth took Sam to the multiplex in Kings-ton to see *Journey to Dragon Land: A Gnome Story*, a Claymation movie about a community of gnomes who wake one day to discover that a vul-ture has dropped a dragon egg through the thatched roof of their vil-lage hall.

In the first act of the movie, the baby dragon—a female, named Judy by the exceedingly British gnomes—is born, and they try to dress her like a gnome, but she eats the clothes and accidentally burns down one of their mushroom fields and also eats the carved wooden statue of a famous gnome philosopher that presides over the village green. In the next act, when a diabolical wizard commanding a team of oversize winged white rats tries to kidnap the dragon for black magic, the story shifts from primarily comedic episodes to an adventure. Judy's gnome friends whisk her across several different terrains, chased by the wizard and his flying rats, until they finally return her to her true dragon family and their pursuers are vanquished.

The movie was fabulously loopy, the simultaneously swollen and convulsive quality of the Claymation granting the whole undertaking an unfamiliar, giggly air; the gnomes with their twitchy features were comically apoplectic; Judy the dragon with her wobbly eyes was adorably stupid; and even the evil flying rats were too dense and squashed to be truly terrifying. At the end, when the dragon lord invited the gnomes to stay in Dragon Land, Sam felt so happy that it was almost embarrassing. "You're a right grown-up dragon now, Judy love," said Clive the Elder, patting the giant dragon's forepaw, "but you know, to us lot here, you'll always be the little one, Judy—and there'll always be a biscuit for you." Sam felt better when he noticed that in the seat to his right, his father was smiling broadly, his beard and eyes lit up in the reflection from the screen.

They came out on the curb and stood in the splash of red from the lit THEATER sign on the exterior wall of the cement cube of the theater. The parking lot lay before them, acres of cars and trucks, bodywork shining under the light stanchions. It was night and cold enough to see their breath.

"What do you think?" asked Booth. "Should we go home to your mother, or should we cast responsibility aside and go find a baby dragon to raise?"

"Home, probably," said Sam, and Booth said he was right, certainly he was right, they mustn't get carried away, but wasn't that Judy a doll?

"I think the best part was when they dressed her up as a gnome," Sam found himself confessing fearlessly.

"Me, too," said Booth. "Me, too."

They played rummy with Tom Ritts another night. Allie, losing badly, was aggressive in her attempts to coerce him. "It would set a poor example for my son, Tom, if you were to go out now and leave me, a woman and a mother, holding all these points. I don't know if I'd be able to look at you the same way."

"Do not let Allie manipulate you, Tom," said Booth. "She is a succubus."

"Bicker all you want, you two, but I take my orders from the cards." It was Tom's turn, and he was hunched over in study of his hand.

"What's a succubus?" asked Sam.

Allie reached across the table and gave Sam's hair a tussle. "A succubus is a woman who believes that her very good friend would never go out and make her feel like a weak, terrible failure in front of her young, impressionable son and leave her to cry her eyes out."

"Your mother is behaving badly, Samuel. She is tormenting Tom. She has been possessed by a wicked, greedy, kibitzing spirit. The worst thing we can do is pay attention to her." Booth stretched over to grab the back of Sam's chair and yank it away from his mother's reach.

Tom took a sip from his longneck and continued to contemplate his cards. "You know, people who say they don't care for the taste of beer—I can't understand that."

Sam banged the table with his fist. "Play!"

His godfather discarded a ten of spades.

Sam snatched it up, laid down an 8-9-10 run, a group of three kings, and discarded, victorious.

"Little shit," said Allie.

"The product of my own loins," said Booth.

"Nice play, buddy," said Tom.

Allie had a long-standing appointment to have her deviated septum repaired, requiring an overnight stay at the hospital. Booth called Sam in sick to school, and they filled in for her at the café.

Throughout the morning and afternoon, Booth accepted all challengers in backgammon. To torment the student Communists, he referred to these matches as Show Trials.

In the late afternoon Booth stuck one of his vanquished opponents behind the counter and told Sam he wanted to have an amble around the theater section of the building. He paced the nearly empty floor for a minute or two, picking up bits of trash, before giving up with a sigh and letting the mess spill. The auditorium smelled like a gigantic marker tip; when the student Communists weren't drinking coffee, they were making posters.

Sam asked what it used to be like. His father said, "Oh, nothing special. Typical movie theater. Just a big closet with a screen," but it was obvious that the state of the place disappointed him.

"I'm sorry," Sam said.

"Eh." Booth stuck his hands in his pockets and used a foot to sweep his little pile of garbage toward a wall. "May I make an observation?"

"Sure."

"You have a very severe directing style, Samuel. I've seen the hell you give those plastic people of yours," said Booth.

"They can take it," said Sam.

"Yes, but you see, they're not real. I think you will find that real people don't like to take a lot of shit."

"Maybe," said Sam.

"No. Definitely," said Booth.

His father's probing made Sam self-conscious and vaguely annoyed. He knew how to play with his toys. His memory of the museum day recurred for the first time in several days; Sandra had criticized him about his toys, too, saying he seemed too old for them. Sam didn't like to think about that and quickly shoved it back into its hole. To be here, with his father, in the forsaken little church where so many movies once played, was too special.

"Do you ever use your real nose in the movies?" asked Sam. It had struck him that maybe his father was saving his actual nose for something special.

Booth had come to the middle of the auditorium, where he stood, a hand resting on the back of one of the scattered remaining seats, and gazed up at the darkened balcony. There the rows of seats were all intact but draped in darkness. He didn't seem to have heard.

"Hey, Booth," said Sam. "Dad."

"Never!" His father strode over.

"Why not?"

"Too dangerous—" Booth broke off and sneezed a cigarette butt into his palm. He grimaced and handed it to Sam.

"Oh, dear—" Booth sneezed again, and the cap of a red marker shot from his nostril this time. A third sneeze produced half of a broken Popsicle stick; a fourth brought a gunk-caked dime, and finally, Booth coughed out a crumpled flyer printed with the Soviet hammer and sickle.

After this, Sam's father wheezed a bit and shook his head. "See? Allergies." He chuckled. "Really, though, I must always have a fake nose. It lets me—it lets me not be me. When I use my real nose, I'm merely Booth Dolan, husband, father. And who would pay to see him?"

Sam nodded excitedly, cheeks hot, not really listening, squeezing the dime in one hand. He hadn't known that his father could perform sleight of hand.

They walked up to the balcony.

The aisles were cluttered with boxes, and the air was hot, dusty attic air. They cleared a couple of seats at the rail. Naturally, Sam mimed vomiting over the balcony. Booth gave him a heavy-browed look. Sam slid back in his seat.

"I never wanted to direct a movie in the first place, you know."

"You didn't?"

"No. It's a ghastly task. Everyone expects you to have the answers. You have to constantly deal with people like me, actors. It's a damned zoo, and you're responsible for feeding all the animals and making sure they know their tricks. You have to look after everyone, take care of them, coddle them." Booth shrugged. "Anyway, you might as well know that I'll never direct another one. I hope that's not a disappointment."

"Okay," said Sam. "But wasn't it ever a good time?"

Booth conceded that maybe there were some good times, but not enough. "Shall I tell you about the week I spent in Surprise, Arizona, acting for Orson Welles?"

Sam nodded eagerly: Orson Welles!

"In 1975 I received a phone call," Booth said. "The man on the other end of the line said, 'Booth, there seems to be a gaping hole in my movie where you belong. Are you busy?' And I said, 'Just tell me where to go, Mr. Welles. I'll be right there.' I had no idea how he might have obtained my phone number, and he hadn't even introduced himself, but from his voice I knew immediately who it was." The famed director's new picture had a part that "no one but Booth Dolan" could fill.

The movie, *Yorick,* concerned a community theater company, Booth explained. When the mute, cringing old janitor who has cleaned the little theater for years passes away, he wills his skull to the company to be used as a prop. Although some think this is macabre, the company votes to observe the janitor's wishes, and the skull is put to work as a decoration in a production of "The Masque of the Red Death." Before long the skull begins to enigmatically prophesize to the various members of the theater group, and to wield an unpleasant influence over their lives. Welles wanted Booth to play a supporting role as a town selectman, a consummate bad actor who continually irritates everyone by begging for parts.

Although *Yorick* was never released, Booth treasured the experience. "I never felt so valued, Samuel. Because I really felt that Orson loved me. I really did. And every take was an opportunity to justify that love. 'Just do what you do, Booth,' he'd say to me, 'and if you need me, I will be just over there, relishing your performance.' I can see him now, on his stool, smoking his cigar and grinning at me like a wolf. That grin—he made it seem as though there was something between just us two, something only we understood. And that is what it takes, you know, to be a truly great director. You have to be able to love everyone. Or maybe to be able to make them think you love them."

"Is there a difference?" asked Sam, the question forming before he fully comprehended it.

"Yes, Sam. There is a difference," said Booth. Sam's father was quiet, staring at the empty space above the stage where there once was a screen. The red wall to his left cut his profile out of the darkness, silhouetting the long wiry hairs that protruded from his eyebrows and his beard. "I used to come here when I was your age, you know. Younger, even. By myself. Had the run of the place. I remember for a while I had the stupid idea that the people, the actors, were as big in real life as they appeared on the screen. I was very, very small."

There was another silence, and Sam could see that his father was sneering, as though disgusted. Sam wasn't sure why. A child himself, he knew well that children believed all kinds of foolish things. Sam imagined sitting by himself in a movie theater, seas of empty seats all around him and the massive white screen before him, and the idea just felt wrong, dangerous, like playing in an empty house. "You went to the movies by yourself?"

Booth sneezed. "Excuse me." He ran his hand over his mouth and beard, flicked his fingers sharply into the empty air. "Anyway. Orson. I hope that someday someone loves you that much, Samuel. Loves you so much that you are inspired to transform yourself into whatever they wish you to be."

"Yeah."

Booth gave his son's shoulder a terrific squeeze. "You have a few years yet."

"Hey, you know what'd be a good idea for your next movie? A guy discovers he can make himself into whatever people like. Like not just into other people but also into animals and objects—he's a what's-it. A shape-shifter. He can be anything."

The notion was barely out of his mouth before his father's expression—a grimace—made him regret it. Really, Sam had only been thinking out loud.

"And then what?" asked Booth.

"Maybe he gets stuck as something other than himself. Like, a bear, or—" His mind was suddenly empty of every creature save the bear.

Booth was staring at him with that grimace.

"—a rock," Sam finished, knowing it was stupid, that you couldn't do anything dramatic with a rock. A rock couldn't move or talk.

"A rock."

"Dumb, right?"

"No, no," said Booth. His eyes widened, and he lightly shook his index finger. "We could watch the rock erode. We could film it for, oh, five or ten years, then speed up the film and watch it flake off a few bits. Wouldn't that be thrilling?"

Sam flushed and looked away to hide his shame. "Maybe," he said, speaking into the dark to his right.

The door to the balcony creaked open. "Uh, guys? Is that you?" It was the Communist. "I gotta split in a sec."

"Yes, comrade!" Booth hopped up, and his seat slapped back. "Coming, coming! This young visionary was just regaling me with his notion for a cinematic masterwork!"

His father was already at the top of the stairs, pushing out the door, before the boy had a chance to move from his seat. So Sam stayed there for a while, alone in the balcony, gazing out, envisioning a plain rock that was the size of a movie screen. It was boring, but he guessed he deserved it.

■ ■ ■

Once Allie was discharged from the hospital, they whisked her directly to *Journey to Dragon Land: A Gnome Story.*

Half-stoned, she screamed intermittently with laughter during the early passages of the film, as Judy the baby dragon lays waste to the gnomes' ancestral lands. Once the story turned darker and the winged white rats arrived, Allie clutched Sam's elbow and tucked her face against Booth's shoulder. At the end, when the dragons and gnomes merge groups, she wept openly in her joy.

Outside, Allie threw her arms around their necks, and they held her up.

It was a weekend night, and the multiplex parking lot swung with headlights. Gasoline smells mixed with cigarette smells. Teenagers yelled and laughed. The three of them walked up and down one aisle after another, searching for their car. Allie hung between them as if she was gutshot, tufts of bloody cotton bursting from her nostrils. "I don't even usually like cartoons, but that was so wonderful, all those magical clay people," she said, and cried a little more, and laughed again. Over the top of her head, Sam and Booth exchanged bemused looks. Right then, astray in the parking lot of the multiplex, in recognition of their shared bafflement, the boy enjoyed a newfound sense of good fortune.

When Booth was young, he had gone to movies alone. For Sam, it was different; they were together in the dark, he and his family.

There were even a few dinners at the kitchen table. Sam's parents held hands and sometimes stared at each other so fixedly that it made him nervous and he excused himself.

He fell asleep listening to them listening to records downstairs. The echoing, indecipherable questions in his dreams ceased to bother him. Sam had decided that the reason he lacked the answers to the dream questions was because the questions were not intended for him. A new feeling carried Sam forward, a feeling that his normal life had commenced, with parents who were together more than they were apart. It wasn't that he expected it to be all funny movies from here on out. But he was pleased.

Gloria Wang-Petty gave her nose a sly tap when she passed him in the hall.

Sam responded with a respectful nod. "Doctor."

6.

Booth's agent called on a Sunday afternoon. His father had been home for about three weeks, the longest continuous period that Sam could recollect.

He heard Booth tell the man that he was savoring his time off. When the man replied, he did so at some length, and while he spoke, to demonstrate his boredom, Sam's father made corpse faces at the boy, sticking his tongue out, rolling his eyes up, and so on.

"Here is what you will do, Ivan," said Booth eventually. "Reach down into those pants of yours and give your testicles a wonderful, strong squeeze! Have you got them? Superb! Now I need you to begin counting, and I need you to keep squeezing, and before you know it, it will be Tuesday and I will be there. And Ivan, in the meantime, you just keep squeezing and counting."

When Booth hung up, Allie, who also was listening nearby, made a comical sad face, frowning and using her index fingers to pull down the skin beneath her eyes.

"I'm sorry, darling," said Booth. "It's work."

The job was a voice-over for a commercial advertising a line of pants with wide white decorative zippers on the outsides of the legs. "Future Trousers!" was what Booth called these pants. If everything went according to plan, he estimated that he could be home by Thursday. He told Sam that if he behaved, perhaps they could take young Thomas to see one of the new movies opening in Kingston.

On Tuesday, while Booth waited for his taxi to the train station in Poughkeepsie, Sam stood in the mud room and eavesdropped on his parents, in conference on the other side of the door.

"So you'll be back next Thursday, then?"

"No, madame. This Thursday. Four days hence."

"Really?"

"Really and truly."

"Booth."

"Alison."

"This has been a good thing, hasn't it?"

"A very, very good thing. But listen, if you want a pair of Future Trousers, you don't need to butter me up; you need only ask. I would deny you nothing."

She shushed him. "You know I haven't asked you to change anything? This is all your decision, to come back, to stay. I was okay with how things were."

"I know! Dear me."

"I'm just saying that it would spoil it if you started making promises you didn't keep again."

Booth gargled, and Allie told him not to gargle at her, mister, and he said, "I must ask you a question of the utmost importance," and Sam's mother said, "Uh-uh-uh," in a smiling voice that at last drove the boy from earshot.

The phone rang as Sam was climbing the stairs. He backed down the steps, swung himself around on the newel, and plucked the receiver from the cradle on the small table. "Now, hold on, baby, did you say you were going to be on the four-thirty-three train or the five-thirty-three?"

Allie pushed her way inside, and Sam hung up on Sandra.

"Who was that?" Allie's gaze directed down; in her head, she was likely still with Booth. If she had looked up at Sam, it might not have been possible for him to lie.

"No one," said Sam, and ran up the stairs.

From his bedroom window, he watched his father crossing the driveway to the idling taxi. The first steps were plodding, taken with his chin against his chest. Booth paused to shift his grip on the handles of his two suitcases. His next steps were brisker; the suitcases jumped eagerly in his hands, and his upper body levered forward, as though he were bulling his way through a crowd instead of just crossing empty pavement.

Booth loaded his suitcases himself, went to the passenger-side door. Here, he gave a long, visible sigh. He rolled his neck around. Sam's father dropped into the taxi—the chassis sank—and the car rolled out into the street, turned left.

An abrupt hot flash woke hyacinths in flower beds throughout Hasbrouck, dried out lawns, and forced open windows that had been shut since October.

After school, Allie and Sam climbed the graveyard hill and the embankment to the splintered train tracks of the derelict Western New York Limited. The mossy trestles cut a corridor between oaks and beech and scrub brush. A mile or so along, they stopped beside the fenced-off area of the old depot. Sam slipped his fingers through the chain links and admired the bright mountains of junk in the field beyond. Among the piles of refuse stood a pair of small buildings with caved-in roofs: the depot and the stationmaster's office, Allie said. Several rusting train cars sat here and there, the shadows at their open doors alive with circling insects.

"Spooky," said Sam, but Allie said, "Not really."

They started again and soon emerged from the woods at the side of a road.

Most of the journey had passed in a kind of contrapuntal harmony. Sam talked about the movie he wanted to make: the story of his Nukies' hopeless but dogged flight across the Wasteland. Booth's accusation that Sam treated them too harshly had had an effect, and Sam conceived of the film as a kind of tribute to their perseverance. All he needed at this point—*hint, hint*—was a camera.

Allie made noises in the right places while simultaneously following her own track, speculating about the pros and cons of the various colleges in the area. The idea of Booth's taking a position in a film studies department had caught her imagination, and she had discovered a fair number of openings. It wasn't, she said, as if he were a young man anymore. A routine might do him good, didn't Sam think?

"Sure," he said.

Sam thought constantly of telling her about the phone call and the museum, but he felt excused, dismally, by the certainty that there was no need. The way his father had paused beside the taxi; the great exhalation, the stretching of the neck. Allie believed Booth was returning in another two days. But he wasn't; wasn't coming back, wasn't taking Sam and Tom to the movies, wasn't going to take a position as a professor. The man was a liar.

The boy felt sorry for his mother and embarrassed for the way she loved Booth. That made Sam hate his father, for how he showed that she could be weak.

On the opposite side of the road, several burly men—their blue

T-shirts identified them as members of the Hasbrouck VFD—lugged boxes and furniture from a house with peeling siding. An orange line had been spray-painted across the lawn to mark off a perimeter. The firemen were hauling the contents of the house a couple hundred yards down the road to deposit them at a wide gravel turn-around. A velvety green couch had already arrived at the turnaround, and one fireman was lying on it and smoking a pipe, as if the whole outdoors were his living room.

"What's going on over there?" Sam asked.

"I'm pretty sure they're going to use it for practice. Burn it down." Allie put her hand up to the back of his head, twisted a lock of his hair with her index finger. Sam instinctively sidestepped away from her.

But for some minutes they stayed there watching, lingering at the edge of the trees in the hope that there might be some action. Meanwhile, the firemen went in and out.

Allie eventually pointed out the obvious. "I don't think they're going to do it right now."

They hardly talked on the way home. When Sam did speak up, as they were crunching down the embankment to the graveyard, it was to ask his mother whether she would watch a movie of a rock turning into a diamond.

Allie said, "Maybe if it isn't in real time," and he said, "No duh."

She stopped in her tracks. "Is there something wrong, kiddo?"

Sam shook his head, kept walking.

Back on the street, in sight of home, she put her arm over his shoulders, and he let it stay. "If Booth were here more, you guys could do all kinds of things. Not just the movies, you know? All kinds of things."

Sam said but he liked the movies.

On Wednesday—the day prior to Booth's scheduled return—Mark Goolsby invited Sam to dinner.

His parents, Mark explained, were worried that he didn't have any friends. He didn't mean to presume on Sam's goodwill; he recognized that they were more "study buddies" than friends. "And I know your dad is kind of famous, and my dad is a criminal, but it would mean a lot to my mom." Although Goolsby presented this with a whimsical flail of his hands, Sam wasn't fooled.

"Look, my dad is the biggest asshole," said Sam.

"Sorry," said Goolsby.

"So. What's the menu?" asked Sam.

Dinner was grilled salmon on the Goolsbys' deck. As the sun was setting and the grill was warming, Mark's mom, Helen, showed them around her already blooming herb garden, which was so expansive that it had lanes and little arrow-shaped signs, like a village. She had them pick mint for the lemonade. Mark's dad, Rod, the ex-con, brought out a Frisbee and they flipped it around. The Frisbee was silver, and when it caught the light, it left a shimmering wake across Sam's vision. "Nice snag," said Rod as Sam went skipping up onto a tree trunk to pick the disc out of the air. "Easy," said Sam, and casually flicked the Frisbee back across the lawn, and tripped, and fell down for a laugh. When the food was served, Rod let Sam and Mark split a beer. Mark told a funny story about Mrs. Quartermain pleading to get a student to take care of Todd the gerbil for the summer: "She says, 'He's already got his own toys!' Like this is a huge selling point. And it's like, yeah, he does have his own toys, but they're just toilet-paper tubes and Ping Pong balls, you know? It's not like Todd needs a bicycle or something." Helen apologized to Sam for not having a television. "No, no," said Sam, "this is great," and if that was an exaggeration, it was nonetheless perfect, the four of them, sitting around the table, eating dinner outside in the summer evening.

In the distance, above the trees, a black corkscrew of smoke twisted up and up, like a fissure in the sky. Sam guessed that the firemen were burning down the empty house. He told the others.

Mark's dad said he'd heard of fire departments doing such things. "What I always wonder is, who gets to set the match? They must have to draw straws or something."

"Oh, that'd be awesome," said Mark. "I'd love to burn down a house."

Rod chuckled. "It would be kind of neat, right?"

"Boys," said Helen.

There was a moment of silence, and Sam realized that she—that they—were waiting for him to say something, probably that he'd be eager to light a house on fire, too. But he had been thinking of the sad stream of possessions, the boxes, the couch, the things that once belonged to someone. He wondered how it was that an entire life could end up like that, on the street, and the rest set on fire. Had they died, the people who lived there? If they hadn't died, did it make them feel like they had, to know that their home was being burned?

"I'll be fine, kiddo," Allie had said when he asked whether she'd be okay if he went to dinner at the Goolsbys'. "I've got wine." He could see her at the table by the window, looking out, imagining a taxi pulling up the driveway.

They were still waiting, the little family, looking at Sam, smiling, wanting to hear something good; they weren't waiting for empty houses or mothers drinking wine by windows.

As well as he could remember, he repeated an interesting thing that Booth had told him:

"Do you know what they call this?" Sam used his fork to gesture at the sky, at the smeary haze of orange and amber and raw red that spilled golden traces across the treetops and the lawn. "They call it the magic hour. It's the last light of the day, and it's the best time to shoot a movie. The reason they call it the magic hour is because the light is so warm and so rich, so no one ever looks more beautiful than they do at the magic hour. But the thing is, you have to work fast, because it doesn't last long."

7.

The appointed Thursday passed, and Friday, and the weekend, and when Booth finally did call two weeks later, it was from a movie set in Vancouver. After that, he called every day for a week. Although Sam could not always make out what was being said from behind closed doors, he was able to absorb Allie's tenor, and it was strikingly, almost eerily, modulated. His mother sounded like she was ordering a pizza, striving to be clear about the toppings.

One day Booth called, and her voice ticked briefly upward, became soothing, and her distinct words drifted out to where Sam lurked in the hall. "Shh," said Allie. "I told you, Booth, I told you what would happen. I never asked for a promise, but you made it—shh, darling, shh. Please. It's pointless crying over it now."

Self-preservation, and Sam's own vibrating sense of guilt, carried him outside, down the street, to the graveyard. He insisted to himself that he was excused, that Allie knew enough. The dead Huguenots never argued otherwise, but their silence was suggestive, and he was aware of their bones and skulls beneath his shoes.

They were silent still when he was thirteen, when he sent his father a tape of *The Unhappy Future of Mankind,* the stop-motion movie he had spent months making, and Booth made no response; when he was fourteen, after the divorce was completed, the graves did not stir; not long after his fifteenth birthday, after he'd read an interview wherein his father casually mentioned the many love affairs he had enjoyed during his career, Sam went to the graveyard and laid flat on his face, lips to the dirt, and asked, "Why do I care? Why?" He found an affirmation in the silence of the dead. He did care about Booth and Booth's betrayals, but the hard ground and the unreadable stones and the mournerless burial ground encouraged him to keep trying not to.

One night when Sam was sixteen, ashamed to have wept—even alone—over a television screening of a ridiculous movie about a saintly turnip-shaped animatronic alien and the children who help him escape home, ran to the graveyard and kicked over a stone. The release felt like a cold drink.

He regaled the Huguenots about his newborn sister, and he confessed to them, in the twilight of his high school graduation day, how his feelings of bitterness—as expected, Booth had missed his plane—had given way to relief.

Where there had been a house, a charred square of concrete foundation and a yard of trampled grass were all that remained.

"Yup," said Allie, "they burned it."

Booth was ten days late then. Sam didn't have to say anything; Allie knew he wasn't coming back.

Sam poked around in the ash with a stick. Allie wandered down to the gravel turnaround where the firemen had dumped the house's contents: the chairs and table, the green couch, an upright piano, all of the pieces junky and broken-looking. The boxes had been torn open and looted by trash pickers.

There was nothing in the debris, and Sam pitched his stick.

At the turnaround, his mother had drawn a milk crate up to the piano and begun to run a few scales. Hands in his pockets, Sam shuffled over.

"Hey," he said, "I didn't know you played the piano."

"I don't, really," Allie said. "Not well, anyway." The notes were thin and out of tune, but the rising and falling sequences were lovely. The wind of a passing car whipped his mother's hair and pulled at Sam's clothes.

Allie stopped playing. She closed her eyes and let her hands rest on the keyboard. "I think I'm getting a headache," she said.

"I think you're great." Sam touched his fingers to her cheek. "Keep going, Mom."

Tom Ritts gave him a VHS camcorder for his twelfth birthday. "From your dad," Tom said, the sole instance that Sam could recall of his godfather having told him a lie.

PART 3
THE LONG WEEKEND

(2011)

Later Friday

The Park Slope independent video store where Sam had toiled in the years after *Who We Are* and before making the move to weddingography, was called, with intentional irony, Video Store. The rarified perspective of the concern was exemplified by the way it was divided into two sections: Commercial Fare and Auteurs. The long aisle of Commercial Fare contained a vaguely alphabetical selection of blockbusters, lowbrow comedies, lame horror stuff, and Barney-type crap. In the Auteurs aisle, the films were carefully categorized into subsections by the last names of famed directors (Cassavetes, Fassbinder, Hawks, Mizoguchi, etc.), and beneath each director's section was a tag listing major accomplishments, awards, and what were, by the lights of the Video Store employees, their virtues. (Listed among Scorcese's finest qualities, for instance, were "revolutionized the use of pop music in film," "directed the only Jerry Lewis movie that doesn't suck shit," and "made eyebrows funny again.")

Video Store's staff was equally composed of adrift young BOA-holding cinephiles and middle-aged, burnt-out, quasi-intellectual fat guys. There was a pervasive mood of despondency among this all-male cohort, which made Sam, at this time in his life, an apparent fit. Because of this, and despite the foreboding categorization and the aggressive labels, the vibe was quite different from that of its late cousin, the infamously bitchy independent record store of *High Fidelity* and the pre-MP3 era. The stuck-up record store employees of yore had been, first and foremost, fans, transformed by overexposure to their passion—i.e., music—into red-assed critics. Still, they were enthusiastic, and their pursuit was, early on at least, one they had gravitated toward willingly.

The adrift young BOA-holding cinephiles, meanwhile, were of the type that had not only dabbled in filmmaking classes but also served on the board for their college's film program and, in carrying a print of *Umberto D.* across campus in a gleaming, hexagonal steel case, caught a whiff of the same imperative air as the Secret Service agent who totes the president's red phone; they had brushed up against the industry only to discover, post-graduation, that they lacked either the connections or the extroversion to score the sort of internship that led to a career in production. Video Store was, for them, a stunning reverse. The middle-aged, burnt-out, quasi-intellectual fat guys, meanwhile, were the very despots who had ruled the independent record stores and been downgraded by the obliteration of the retail music industry to the movie rental arena. For these aging tastemakers, Video Store was exile, not just from their chosen field but also from their youth.

The result was that the commerce of the Video Store was transacted drearily. Although the opinions of the staff ran as thick and oppressive as those at an Ivy League faculty meeting, the discriminating borrowers of the latest Wong Kar-wai film received the same grunting service and treatment as the rank and file who took out Hollywood romcoms and action movies. Only the appearance of a young art school female in an ass-length skirt could reliably rouse the members of the staff from their usual semi-conscious condition.

And yet there also ran beneath the thin brown carpet of Video Store, an underground river of the most acid petulance that Sam had ever encountered. One of his coworkers, Denny, a puffy fiftyish former owner of a long-shuttered East Village record store called Opiates, was constantly mumbling something under his breath. After listening closely for a time, Sam deduced that Denny was repeating, "Fuck you, fuck you, fuck you," the way another person might reflexively whistle a favorite melody. Another coworker, a recent Wesleyan grad who never took off his sunglasses and was always sniffling, was fired when it was discovered that he had been meticulously scratching random DVDs in order to render the last five minutes unwatchable. The prematurely bald Zach, who back in his salad days at Brown had conducted a lively Q&A with Francis Ford Coppola before an audience of two hundred, disposed of hours by dribbling spit onto dollar bills from the cash register, then using a pen to trace the spit flecks and, when they were dry, restoring the currency to the till. With no affect or preamble whatsoever, and while nonchalantly filling in every answer in the Friday *New York Times* cross-word puzzle from left to right without stopping, Zach once remarked to Sam, "I think George Romero is a fucking philistine, but I like the idea of a zombie virus, because then I'd have absolute impunity to waste all the kumquats who come into this place." Having dispatched the puzzle, the Brown alum rolled up the paper and dropped it in the trash. "And then go and comfort their witless girlfriends with my cock." It was, Sam decided with a little reflection, perhaps the most frightening thing he had ever heard someone say.

As something of a tweener—a young cinephile but in complete retreat from any desire to involve himself in the making of film; and inarguably burnt out, but nothing like as fat as the middle-aged quasi-intellectual fat guys who used to work at record stores—Sam eschewed convention completely. For the three-plus years he worked at Video Store, he smiled as much as his face could bear, politely rented people their movies, and to avoid fraternizing with the other inmates, grabbed as many solo shifts as possible.

He was present, though, when an indistinctly damaged kid, seventeen or eighteen years old, a regular by the name of Aldo, inadvertently disturbed the dragon that brooded inside the heart of Video Store.

Aldo had glasses like goggles, a big tapered head like Frankenstein, and a foot-dragging walk that suggested a history of wearing leg irons. He came into the store at irregular times and betrayed no hint that he attended school or held a job. Sam surmised maybe Aldo had suffered a stroke or fallen off a roof or otherwise experienced a serious but not physically debilitating brain trauma, although he was totally animated and spoke clearly enough.

Aldo's mistake was to profess one fateful afternoon that he, Aldo, "liked all of those silent movies without the talking." His error was compounded when, in reply to Zach's shallow sigh, Aldo laughed like a drunken hillbilly, cupped his hands around his mouth, and shouted, "Hey, man, you awake?"

The question echoed around the store. A woman looked up, disapproving, from the remote end of the Commercial Fare section. Zach blinked at Aldo.

Sam, who had been filling out an invoice, stepped forward. "Are you looking for something in particular?" he asked Aldo.

Zach snapped straight up on his stool. "I'm awake. I got this guy." He gestured for Sam to back away.

"He's awake!" Aldo shook a triumphant fist.

"Silent movies, huh?" Zach's thin, pale eyebrows arched slightly. "Without the talking."

"Yeah!" Aldo was oblivious. "What should I get?"

"The uncut *Greed*," said Zach. "You haven't lived until you've seen the uncut *Greed*."

And that casually, poor Aldo was hooked by the most pointlessly mean-spirited long con of all time. Zach went on to regale the kid with the story of Erich von Stroheim's legendary original ten-hour cut of *Greed*. In this cut the director had attempted to realize the full power of cinema by adapting Frank Norris's *McTeague,* a novel of dentistry, the West, insanity, and yes, greed, down to the minutest detail.

Wouldn't Aldo like to rent it?

"Oh, man! Yeah, yeah! I gotta see that!"

Oops! Oh, sugar, Aldo. Wouldn't you know. It's out.

By dastardly coincidence, the ten-hour uncut version of *Greed* invariably happened to have "just gone out" mere moments before Aldo arrived. While a quick search of the Internet could have revealed that the *Greed* reels had long ago been destroyed, the kid's interest in silent film was apparently unattached to any kind of research or education. Aldo simply liked the silent movies without the talking, and wanted to see what was the best.

Except for Sam, who refused to take any part, the rest of the Video Store gang happily played along with Zach's scenario.

Von Stroheim's uncut *Greed* was the object of Aldo's unrelenting desire. "Is *Greed* in? Is *Greed* in?" he'd ask.

If Zach was the one on duty, he would become uncharacteristically excited and slap his head in a show of transparently over-the-top frustration. "Gosh darn it, Aldo! Wouldn't you know, a fat-ass in a red suit and a red hat just came in and rented it. You must have passed him on the sidewalk. He was carrying a big sack over his shoulder? I'm so sorry. I can't believe you haven't seen it yet. It's the most bestest, most superest movie ever made."

About this uncanny run of bad luck, Aldo was heartbreakingly good-natured. "Oh, shoot!" he'd say, and the next day he'd be back to see if the fat-ass in the red suit had returned the non-existent movie.

Meanwhile, Zach and the others insisted that Aldo not rent anything else. *You have to be patient for* Greed! they said. *It's such a special movie that we only rent it to people on the special list, and if you want to be on the special list, you can't take out anything else. You just have to wait for* Greed.

This went on for over a year. Flowers grew and flowers died. Snow fell and snow melted. Denny, the fuck you mumbling former owner of Opiates, suffered a fatal brain aneurysm on the 7 train and was replaced by nearly interchangeable sadsack named Danny, who in the pre-digital era had been the proprietor of an Upper Eastside record store called Musee de Grouvre. Through the months and the seasons, Aldo came in—every day. *Greed* was not in.

"Man," said Aldo frequently, shaking his block head, "I just wish I could rent something, you know? I'm, like, bored."

Zach would shrug. "By all means, Aldo. Rent whatever you like. But remember, if you do, you lose your place on the special list, and it might be quite a while before we can squeeze you back on." Zach might pause here, clicking his tongue or petting one of his pale eyebrows, before pressing home the final point. "If that happened, who knows—you might never get to see the uncut *Greed*."

Though Sam did not collaborate, he passively abided this cruelty. Was it possible that some coincidental elements relating to the matter—such as the famed loss of the reels and the not-quite-right-in-the-head film enthusiast—made him instinctively shy away? It was possible.

Sam did once summon the nerve to say to Zach, "This Aldo thing . . ." He winced to show his discomfort.

"I know, I know. I feel the same way," said Zach. "I keep thinking how laughable it would be if shithead died without ever finding out how stupid he was."

One February day, Sam was the only employee able to make it through a snowstorm for the midday shift. Video Store was empty the entire afternoon; the phone didn't ring a single time; the only thing visible through the frosted surface of the plate-glass front window was, faintly, the rotating emergency lights of passing snowplows.

And then Aldo burst inside, glasses steamed and speckled with flakes, and cried, "*Greed! Greed!* Is it finally in?"

Sam jumped at his position by the register. "Jesus, Aldo! You scared me."

Aldo slammed himself against the counter. He was breathless, seeming to sense that the treasure was at last within his grasp. "I'm on the special list! You can give it to me!"

"Calm down," said Sam. "You know, that movie is bullshit. Zach and those guys are just pulling your chain."

A snowflake slid down a steamed glasses lens, leaving a smear of water. Aldo gasped some air. "What did you say?"

Sam repeated himself. "It's a joke, Aldo. A stupid joke. There is no DVD of the uncut *Greed*. The film was destroyed decades ago."

"What?" Aldo asked, and Sam told him a third time, and Aldo asked, "What?" and Sam told him yet again, and it went like that for a while, until finally, Aldo got it.

"Oh, man! Man!" The kid slapped the hips of his jeans several times. He staggered around in a little circle in front of the counter, dripping snowmelt on the carpet and bobbing his anvil-shaped head, as if trying not only to accept the idea that the ten-hour cut did not exist, but to swallow the idea, too. Aldo clutched his temple. "Well, what the heck am I supposed to do now?"

"Rent another movie?" proposed Sam, who wished with all his heart that he had not said anything.

"Rent another movie?" Aldo gaped. A plow growled by outside, blade screeching, and the ceiling banks of fluorescent light flickered. "You want me to just—*rent another movie?*"

The indistinctly damaged kid continued to come in after that, though when the other employees of Video Store asked if he was interested in renting *Greed*, he'd shrug and pick a *Three Stooges* compilation, pay, and wordlessly shuffle out. Aldo never fingered him for having broken the spell, and soon after, Sam quit to pursue weddingography full-time.

"Poor guy," Zach commented on the change in Aldo. "He must have realized that we were all bastards and life is a machine that skins guys like him alive."

The feeling he had on the Friday-morning drive north to Hasbrouck to see his dying father put Sam in mind of Aldo for the first time in years.

A forbidden door inside Sam, padlocked and drawn with chains and nailed over with plywood and braced by a jumble of furniture, had without warning come crashing open, and now he was gazing out beyond its step into the ultimate nothing of freezing, sucking space. He supposed this was how it was for Aldo when he learned that the uncut *Greed* didn't exist: as if his entire belief system had been called into question, making everything dizzy and inconceivable, and his brain couldn't seem to catch up. It was also like that time when Sam was a kid and Booth's mistress gave Sam her underwear, and Booth spun everything around somehow, and after the wheel stopped, it was Sam who was the culprit. His chest ached to remember it. The trees that hugged the shoulders of the Taconic Parkway smeared green beyond the windows, Sam's foot was a brick on the accelerator, his sister had beaten the hell out of everyone, and Booth was dying.

His father seemed even less like an actual physical being than usual. Sam was accustomed to Booth being way out there, in the deep background—undoubtedly conductive but invisible, like a satellite. To attempt to conceive of his dying was like imagining that gravity could die. "You want me to just—*rent another father*?" a voice in Sam's head asked.

But he was dying; Mina had said it was stomach cancer, an untreatable mass in his guts.

Relations between Sam and his father had, over the last eight years, not so much broken off as petered away.

Months had elapsed before Booth returned Sam's phone call of that rainy September night in 2003.

When contact was reestablished, his father explained, "I'm sorry it's taken me so long to call you back. I've had phone troubles. These cellphone companies are merciless in their demands for payment. But how did the picture turn out? What happened? Please tell me that you let a little bit of light into the room!"

At the time, Sam was sunk too deep in his own sorrow to say what he really felt, which was "You had your chance. Your last chance. Now: die." He would have liked to, but he couldn't make the effort to execute his relationship with his father. Instead, he told Booth, "It didn't turn out. End of subject. Don't ask again."

And Booth said, "Oh," and Sam said, "Really. I mean it. Don't ask me again," and somehow, miraculously, his father listened, and didn't.

A couple of years after that, once the cult of the film penetrated the mainstream media outlets—right around the same time, as it happened, Sam left Video Store to pursue a stimulating career in weddingography—Booth sent Tom Ritts as an envoy. "Your father wants to talk to you about what happened to your movie, buddy." Tom was so ill at ease about raising the matter that he avoided Sam's eyes.

"He shouldn't try to do that," Sam warned, and his godfather nodded and said no more. The message must have been conveyed, because his father never did mention *Who We Are,* not once, not to this day.

Booth had recently relinquished the Manhattan apartment that was his base of operations since the mid-nineties, and moved in with Tom, taking official possession of the guest room that his factotum had maintained for him for years. The money Booth made from voice-over work—such as the monster-truck rally pitch, for example—was apparently not bad. By all reports, he hadn't been late on a child-support payment since Mina was in elementary school.

Still, his sister's conception of Booth as some sort of rock struck Sam as either confounding or ludicrous, depending on the day. He never let himself get too curious, though. He couldn't see how, at this late date, it could benefit anyone.

If the old man had undergone some sort of Awakening, he at least had been decent enough not to proselytize about it.

The only concrete sign of his reform was a card that had arrived in Sam's mailbox in 2007. A late-seventies photograph of Orson Welles adorned the front of the card, the aging genius dwarfing a chaise longue and brooding over a backgammon board. Nothing was written inside, but it contained a money order for the amount of $587.34.

Hours elapsed before Sam registered that it was recompense for John Jacob Bregman's prosthetic nose. Initially, he felt chastened by the payback, but after that, he was irritated, more with himself than Booth. Because it wasn't as though his father had made Sam a great gift. All he had done was square a debt years after the fact. Sam went ahead and deposited the money, barely prevailing against the urge to use his cell phone calculator to figure what he'd been cheated of in interest.

Booth sent his son the occasional e-mail (from bdolan@celebrity-treasures.com), usually forwards of YouTube videos. (It had to be said, the old man had excellent taste in forwards; among other wonders, he sent Sam a video of a ragged black cat prowling around in a cage and, through the magic of CGI, reciting a portion of a Willy Loman mono- logue from *Death of a Salesman,* and it had been as moving as it was sur- real.) Occasionally, a short "Just thinking of you" or a "Too long since we got together" missive found its way to Sam's in-box. Usually, Sam didn't respond. Why should he? He wasn't thinking of Booth; he didn't think it had been too long since their last get-together.

Their last face-to-face meeting had been Thanksgiving at Tom's house, the previous year. Booth eulogized the turkey—"Let us remem- ber him *as the turkey he was,* not the turkey he became . . . a turkey in full . . ."—which was pretty funny, and he also spoke of his thanks that all the people he loved were present. Sam shook his father's hand, each attested that it was good to see the other, and the younger Dolan was back on the road before the second half of the Lions game.

Although he'd driven it hundreds of times, the pitted surface of the Taconic Parkway now seemed unfamiliar. Some brush along the side of the road split, and in a flash of brown and kicking hoof, an unknown animal—deer, dog, bear—disappeared, darting for cover.

It occurred to Sam that none of it would be happening if, instead of fleeing, he had gone home with Tess Auerbach, the nice, sad girl in the purple dress. They should have been having morning sex right then. If they were, he wouldn't have been in the apartment for Mina to wake him up, Wesley and the vagrant would have been unharmed, and though Booth would still be dying, Sam wouldn't have had to know yet.

Sam thought about all the times he'd wished his father didn't exist and suffered a pang of remorse—and then felt defensive and angry, because how many times had Booth let him down?

What was wrong with him that he had enjoyed the awful Grand Guignol of a show about a man doomed to die in a little room? They played those horrible things over and over. Kenneth Novey was going to keep killing himself for eternity in syndication. It didn't seem right, or fair. Why couldn't they give the guy a happy ending? Why couldn't a repairman came along and fix things, let Novey out, give him a chance to put his life back together?

Sam could feel himself bouncing around inside his own head, could almost feel the walls of his own skull:

Why shouldn't Aldo be allowed to see the uncut *Greed*?

How could Booth be sick?

What did you do, anyway, when both of your parents were dead? Sam knew well what it felt like to go to the movies alone, to sit with empty seats at either elbow. It felt like you weren't like everybody else, like you were strange.

It was all so hard to believe, let alone accept, and the best thing for everyone would have been a do-over, but the car was going forward, and Sam was going forward, and mile markers were passing by.

Sweat that had collected at Sam's hairline trickled into his eyebrow. He flicked it away with a thumb swipe. "Do you mind if I turn the air-conditioning on?" he asked his sister.

It had been hot and overcast when they stepped outside and had become more so as they drove, the cloud cover thickening and darkening, while the dashboard temperature rose steadily to a reading of 85. They had been driving for an hour and a half; Hasbrouck was two exits away.

"The noise that guy's head made when it hit the stone in the courtyard, God. It sounded like a tennis ball hitting a racket—that, like, *pop*. But meatier. I keep thinking about that sound. Somehow there's no mistaking the sound of a head hitting stone, you know?" Mina chuckled. "Crazy."

Sam found the dial, pushed it the wrong way—toward heat—and dragged it back the other way. The air came on, hissing cold from the vents. "Say that again? What you were saying before?"

"That *pop* the guy's head made. The knife guy. When it hit the stone."

Sam was cognizant of an odd euphoria radiating from his sister. Her boots were off, and she had put her bare feet on the dash, wiggling toes with black toenails to the music on the radio. For a portion of the trip, she had passed the time using a rag to polish the sword that she had taken from the madman in the courtyard.

Sam felt himself snap to somewhat. His sister was agitating him when he was already agitated. He punched off the radio. The car filled with the low tick and grumble of the parkway's patchwork surface.

"What are you doing?"

"Me? Nothing. Sitting." Mina tapped the point of the sword against the passenger-side window.

"You assaulted Wesley. We left him under a mountain of shit. And you practically killed that guy in the courtyard."

"Me? I practically killed him? You leaped onto his testicles."

"I did not—"

"Yes, you did! You leaped on that bum's balls when he was already down."

The testicle crushing had been reflexive, and Sam felt horrible about it. He wasn't even sure the man meant any harm. In the moment, it seemed like the vagrant had thrown the sword at Mina, and the next thing he knew, he was jumping on the guy's sack. The second-to-last exit streaked by on the right shoulder—Hasbrouck was a mile. "It was instinct."

"You did what you did. I did what I did. He could have shanked us both, you know." Her note of affront was feeble.

He glanced from the road, thought he caught the flash of a grin before she twisted to look out the passenger-side window. "Mina. This is serious. Booth—"

In the console cupholder, his cell phone rattled.

There was this, too: Tess Auerbach had called at least six times, and Sam wasn't picking up.

She was undoubtedly pissed, and with good reason. Sam yearned to placate her somehow, but he didn't want to tell her that his father was sick, and although he would have been happy to apologize, he didn't think that was what Tess wanted. What he thought she wanted was for him to hold still so she could dig her thumbs into his eyeballs for standing her up in such an obnoxious way. Sam also doubted that Tess would be assuaged by his admitting that it would have been better for everyone if things had gone as they ought to have gone—him, her, sex—and that, if given a second chance, he would make different choices.

Sam was ignoring the buzzing phone and, meanwhile, taking comfort where he could find it—in his vision of the different choice he would have made: him, her, sex, and none of this happening—for as long as he could keep his conscience at bay.

Mina had asked him why he wasn't answering this Tess Auerbach person's phone calls, and since Sam had told her it was private, his sister had been needling him. "Your girlfriend is persistent," Mina said. "Did you give her an STD or what?"

That people reacted differently to crisis was a given; Sam wanted to be accepting, to be a big brother and an adult.

"She's not my girlfriend. I know you're upset, Mina, but cut it out."

"Whatever. She's totally your girlfriend."

More from a desire to shut up his sister than to stop the ringing, Sam abruptly decided to bite the bullet. He snatched up the phone. "Listen, Tess, I know you probably—"

"Nah, dude. Nah. You got it wrong. This is Jo-Jo."

"Oh, hey. What's up?"

Up ahead, the Hasbrouck exit hooked off to the right. Sam piloted into the turn.

"What's up? Oh, that's comical." Polly's husband laughed. "What is up is: we got a problem, dude. Yah?"

"What? Is Polly okay?"

"Polly's fine." The telephone line buzzed faintly, like an insect trapped between screen and glass. "It's you has got me worried, Sam."

There was a famous photo of Jo-Jo snapped in the second before the collision in the 1998 World Series. Crouched in front of home plate at Yankee stadium, tree-trunk legs planted wide to absorb contact, catcher's mitt extended with both hands, the ill-fated runner, Esteban Herrera, inches away. (The twelve-year-old batboy is beyond the frame—and only a few hours away from the first of several osteoplastic procedures.) Drenched in stadium light, masked, the Jo-Jo of the image lacked any identifying features except his eyes, which were the color of ashes. There was no moving a man with eyes like that. If you wanted to score, you'd need a pickax to break him apart.

So Jo-Jo knew.

"I'm not sure I'm following you, Jo-Jo."

"I mean, you like to fuck men's wives, yah? Dudes don't like that shit, is the thing."

The truth was, Sam didn't like fucking other men's wives, it was stressful and in bad taste, and he was immensely regretful. He cared about Polly, and he thought she cared about him, too, but clearly, things had gotten out of hand. They had been careless and cruel. But Sam's father had stomach cancer, and as rightfully wounded as Jo-Jo was, and as unjust as it might seem, the whole matter needed to be tabled for the foreseeable future. In order of precedence, parental stomach cancer trumped adultery.

For a few seconds, Sam deliberated on how to compress this line of reasoning into the briefest, sincerest package. He sensed his sister, eyebrow raised, staring at him. They came to a stop in a line of cars at the tollbooth. He abandoned deliberations. "Jo-Jo, I'm sorry. We're going to have to talk about this later. I've got my hands full here."

"You've had your hands full, boy, yah? Full of my wife's ass. Well, now I'm going to cut off your hands. I'm going to keep them. I've got a special box picked out for them, yah?"

Down through the rest of his life, Sam suspected he would remember that, once, while he gazed upon an idling silver Subaru with a Cornell bumper sticker, a man had sworn to cut off his hands and retain them in a special box. "Pardon?"

"You heard me, yah? I got this wooden chest. Real nice, like an heirloom. Polished wood. And I'm-a have your hands to put inside it. Saw them off, yah? It's going to be ugly."

"I really am sorry, Jo-Jo, and I can tell that you're upset—"

" 'I'm upset,' he says?"

"Jo-Jo, my father is sick and I can't—"

"I don't care. Maybe I'll take your papa's hands, too, yah? Since I'm starting a collection—"

That was enough. Sam knew he was at fault, and he knew he deserved to be berated, but Booth was dying, and Mina was acting bizarrely, and it was way too much.

"You know what, Jo-Jo?"

"What?"

"Eat shit. Eat shit in your stupid pin-striped GTO. Eat shit in the fucking—in the fucking Deutschland."

"Oh, dude." The man on the other end of the phone made a blowing sound. Sam laid on the rental's horn; the guy in the silver Subaru was taking his time at the tollbooth. Jo-Jo kept repeating, "Dude, dude, dude, dude."

"Don't 'dude' me. I'm not your dude. You know what else? I fucked your wife the Red Sox way, and she loved it." Sam clicked off and jammed the phone back into the cupholder.

Ahead of them, the Subaru started to move.

Mina cracked her knuckles. She cleared her throat. Sam refused to look at her, but he could hear her grin. "I didn't know you were a base-ball fan, Sam."

He told her to give him a dollar, and she did. After the toll, they turned right onto Hasbrouck's central thoroughfare, in the direction of Tom's house.

The cell phone rattled again. Mina picked it up and peered at the digi-tal readout. "Here we go. This time it *is* your girlfriend. The Tess person."

2.

Having exhausted the horizontal bounds of his property, Tom Ritts had, like the ancient Babylonians, turned his ambitions skyward. The crawl-space attic where Sam had searched for salable items to raise cash for the movie had been opened up into two more bedrooms; atop these bedrooms, his godfather had stacked a loft and a fresh walk-in attic. The house's walls and roofs rose above the surrounding trees like some sort of rustic parking garage. Beyond exorcising Tom's boredom, these constructions had no purpose; Tom confessed that, having completed the third-floor additions, he rarely visited them because it was such a tiring climb.

The housing bubble had transformed Ritts Design and Construction from a merely successful business into a money-printing factory. (From 2003 to 2005, for instance, Tom's crew had built not one but *two* cas-tles in the southern Hudson Valley, one for a hedge fund magnate and one for the senior partner of a corporate law firm—actual castles, with actual parapets, actual drawbridges, and in the case of the hedge fund magnate, who had really blown his castle out, an actual oubliette.) It was this wealth that enabled Tom's renovations and expansions, though the endlessly swelling house was clearly not a compulsion based on van-ity. No one thought it was attractive; it spread upward and outward at sharp angles; you looked at it and imagined it ripping itself up from the ground, whirling and swiveling into a wooden Transformer.

But Tom just kept on building. Because that was the thing that he did—he built. Sam envied his godfather's resolution. Tom had found his groove, and he believed it, and trusted it, and just let it play. Tom built.

Nothing was ever that simple to Sam. For years he had done his best to reduce his relations, to indurate himself against the unforeseen, and he felt like he had done a pretty fair job of it. It was never a groove, however, because there came the last sixteen hours, and here he was, skipping and scratching again. It was disquietingly familiar: the sense of ambush, the drive in uncertain weather . . .

What a fool he was, he thought once more, not to go home with her.

The immediately striking aspect of Tom's house was the grand picture window that fronted the enormous sitting room off the front door. On bright days it filled with sunshine and shimmered like a magic portal. As they pulled up the driveway on that dim morning, the glass was pooled with blackness.

"Girlfriend, you have." Since exiting the parkway, Mina had been speaking in Yoda. "Call you repeatedly she does."

"I'm beginning to see why Sandra went nuts." As soon as he said it, Sam wished he hadn't. It was easy to forget sometimes that Mina was only a teenager.

She gasped. "What did you say?"

"Look. Can you stop? Remember why we're here, Mina? Remember Dad? Please?"

Mina's lips pursed into a real pout, and her eyes filled with tears. This was what she looked like when she was legitimately upset.

"Mina—" he started, and it was suddenly so obvious that he had been had, had been duped as thoroughly as Aldo. "Mina, this isn't real, is it?"

"I can't believe you just said what you just said." Mina turned and grabbed at the door handle, although the car wasn't yet stopped.

As Sam shifted the car into park, his sister's cell phone rang—a roar of guitar feedback—and two figures emerged from around the far side of the house.

The overhang of the roof threw a curtain over the duo and rendered them silhouettes: on the left was a short figure whose upright, narrow outline Sam identified as Tom Ritts's. Beside him, a step ahead, the other man was the size and shape of a refrigerator, poking along with a cane.

Booth emerged from the shadows, and Sam saw that his father was wearing a cape knotted around his neck with a piece of scarlet rope. It was a larger version of the garment that Mina sported.

"Shit. It's Peter. I should take this." Mina unsnapped her belt and craned over Sam to jab the button to open the trunk. The guitar ring blared again. "You can just set my stuff inside the door, fucker. Thanks." With that, his sister hopped from the car and ran toward their father.

It was bullshit, wasn't it? He felt light-headed in the moistness of the early day. It was bullshit. Sam was not relieved; he was astounded. His sister had told him the worst possible lie. He had driven all this way. It wasn't even ten in the morning.

Sam stepped out of the car. "Mina," he called after her, although he had no idea what he wanted to say to her, what he could say to her. "Mina—"

"My children!"

His father's voice was a bell clap; Sam flinched.

"Gotta take this, Pop," said Mina, waving her cell phone. She pecked the old man a kiss on the beard, gave Tom a quick one-armed hug, and spun away. Her boots thumped up the steps to Tom's front door, and she disappeared inside.

"All right." Booth shook his head. "Isn't she wonderful?"

"Yup. She's a cool kid," said Tom.

"And who is that alarmingly handsome young man standing over there beside the little red car?"

Tom said he looked familiar.

The soggy grass squished under Booth's heavy tread. His cane plunged and swung in a happy, vigorous rhythm. His beard was patched gray and white. As he moved, a slice of trembling belly peeked from between the flapping tails of his white shirt. Sam thought he must have crossed the three-hundred-pound threshold since the last time they were together. The old man was grinning, and his teeth were big and stained.

Sam rocked on his heels. Of course it was bullshit. He raised a hand. "Hi," he said, and found himself smiling numbly in return. Sam thought: When have I ever been happy to see him? "Hi," he said again, and his crackly voice didn't sound like his voice.

As his father's arms were raising, opening wide, Sam decided, I might as well, and he moved into them. He pressed his face into the massive chest, smelled the soap and hair and cologne and cigars and the fried eggs the old man must have eaten for breakfast; he let his mouth and nose slide across the shoulder of Booth's wrinkled white shirt. For a moment, he let go.

"I am so, so glad you are here, Samuel. When Mina told me you were coming, I was so pleased." Booth's breath was hot on his ear; along with the eggs, Sam smelled onion, pepper, and ketchup. "It's been far too long. I've missed you. I've wanted to call you, but—I love you, you know, Sam."

Sam imagined throwing it all into a fire: the absences, the lies, the betrayals, the disappointments, every bit of it, and watching the emotional junk melt and clench and disintegrate, until there was only a patch of scorched grass. Nothing would be the same; everything could happen differently. He wondered what it would have been like if Booth really had been dying, and for an instant, he regarded the idea with wistfulness. It would have simplified things. Sam saw himself holding Booth's elbow, helping him totter up a flight of steps to a pair of glass doors. He imagined saying, "I love you, too."

Sam took a breath. "You don't have terminal stomach cancer, right?"

"What?"

"Mina told me you had terminal stomach cancer."

A low sound rose up from the depths of Booth's chest, the rumble of large, unseen machinery. They continued to hold each other, swaying in the driveway. As long as he didn't know for sure, Sam didn't have to let go.

"Stomach cancer?" asked Booth.

"Stomach cancer," said Sam.

"No." His father sighed. "I'm sorry."

"Ah, fuck." Sam removed himself from his father's embrace. He retreated a few paces down the driveway. He guessed it might make him feel better to kick something, but there was just the car, and it was a rental. His head lolled back, and he gazed up into the thick ashen sky. "Fuck," he groaned.

"But I could die any second. I'm overweight," said Booth. "And old. I abhor exercise. I'm really, terribly fat."

"Hey. Don't say that," protested Tom, who was standing nearby.

Booth continued to tick off his ailments. "I have high cholesterol, bad circulation. Heart attack, diabetes, prostate cancer—I'm in the sweet spot for any number of potentially fatal afflictions, Samuel. I'm out of breath constantly. Something will take me out soon, I'm sure."

"I don't want you to die, Booth." A light drizzle began. Pellets of water pecked Sam's unwashed hair and hit his forehead. A bead of water dripped down his cheek where Tess had touched him with her hand. In bad Oscar-type movies, characters stood in the rain and were metaphorically cleansed. Sam didn't feel cleansed. He felt wet and crummy. "It's just been a rough morning, okay?"

"Factually, we're all dying, all the time. From the moment of conception, we are dying, " his father continued.

"I don't like this, whatever it is," said Tom. "I feel like I'm living all the time, goddammit. I don't care what you people say."

Eventually, Booth ushered his son out of the rain and into the shelter of the rental car. Sam was damp and drained. He wanted to go get his sister and shake her until she explained what was so hilarious about stomach cancer. This desire had competition from another, equally strong craving to find a cool, dark room and go back to sleep for another three hours.

(Tom had become about as grumpy as he ever did and stalked off. "I think there's something in there that needs hammering," he said, and retreated to the house.)

According to Sam's father, Mina had called late the previous evening to say that she would have to come and stay with him in Hasbrouck, in the wilderness, for the foreseeable future, because Sandra was in the loony bin, her boyfriend was gay, and Sam was a selfish asshole who didn't care about anyone except himself.

"But that's all I know!" professed Booth. "And the details are unimportant. I'm just so very happy to see you!" He was jammed into the compact's passenger seat like a football into a baseball glove. His chin rested on the backs of his hands, which were themselves planted on the bulbous brass head of his cane. The cane was somehow stuck between his gut and the dashboard.

Sam turned on the heat so they could dry out. The car filled with the must of his father's wet cape. Through the windshield was a view of Tom's airplane hangar/four-car garage.

"Why couldn't she just ask me for a goddamned ride? Why drag me out of bed at the crack of dawn and bring stomach cancer into it?"

"Your sister's going through quite a difficult time. You must try and be as forgiving as you can. You know the situation with Sandra's mental health, and I've not been as constant a presence as I should have been—as I plan to be—and she's run a bit wild. Also, bear in mind that Mina's seventeen. She's ankle-deep in the thicket of young adulthood. And look, I don't want to stick my nose where it's not wanted, and I'm not taking sides, but I think she may feel that, in the past, you've behaved a tad autocratically with her."

Sam asked his father if he was referring to the matter of Peter Jenks. "I wanted to scare him off." Sam couldn't believe that, on top of everything else, his sister had tattled on him to Daddy.

"I know, but the film you showed the young man . . ." Booth shook his head. To gain a better handle of Mina's outrage, he had rented the controversial film, the one about the saintly woman's grotesque trials—and eventual demise—at the behest of her demonic husband. "I have to tell you, I did not care for it. It was nicely made, but—I don't think 'disquieting' is too strong a word. Perhaps that says more about me than the picture. I don't know. It's hard to find the entertainment in martyrdom."

"I told you," said Sam. "I wanted to scare him off."

"It was a laudable instinct, too. She is young for a boyfriend. I'm merely trying to offer my sense of what your sister is feeling."

To have his instincts ratified by Booth did not make Sam feel better. It was well established that his father's instincts sucked.

"She pepper-sprayed two people this morning," Sam said. It seemed only fair to return the favor and tattle on her.

His father's expression turned rueful. "That does sound excessive. I'll have to speak to her about that."

"Wait, though. Mina is going to stay with you?" On its face, the idea shot straight past the impracticable up into the stratosphere of the impossible before plummeting like a lead weight to the fathoms of the bathetic.

"Yes." His father nodded on top of his hands. "You object?"

Sam ran his tongue around his teeth. "I'm sorry, Booth, but it's going to take me a little while to wrap my head around that one. You know you won't be able to get by, like, asking Tom to water her once a week? If she stays long enough, you'll have to get her enrolled in school somewhere. You'll have to drive her places and pick her up or else get her a car. You'll have to make sure she does her homework. All that shit."

"Yes. I know." There was a susurration as Booth turned the cane, working the tip lightly against the fabric floor mat. "You know, Samuel . . . I owe you a very large apology for—well, for a great many things. And I do apologize."

His father's neck, Sam noticed then, was skinny, an old man's neck. The skin was loose there, like pulled dough. There were a couple of liver spots, too. They resembled burn marks on paper. If you looked at it from another direction, the morning hadn't been a false alarm but a dry run. The old man's protests weren't completely hollow; sooner or later, he would die. *The relentless furnace of this world.*

"But we're not dead yet, are we? We have some life yet, don't we?"

"Booth." Sam heard the optimistic pitch in his father's voice and redirected his own gaze out the streaking windshield. "Let's just keep things moving forward."

"Fine, good," said Booth. "Ever forward."

"Thank you," said Sam.

The wipers ticked back and forth.

"So what are you doing now?" asked his father.

The way to the recording studio took them through Hasbrouck proper in the light drizzle.

Not a great deal about the town had changed since Sam's childhood. The head shop had slid a few storefronts southward on Main Street, but the canvas awning retained the same skipping Jerry bear, trembling in the wind and sweating streaks of rain; the record store was gone, but no new business had taken its place, and the yellowed album covers sat in the picture window. The library was where it had always been on a corner, and the bank was right where it always was, on the opposite corner. Likewise, in its accustomed place was the pawnshop, where Sam had cashed in his Nukies, among other valuables, one afternoon in the autumn of 2002. Although OPEN signs hung in most of the doors, the interiors of these places appeared dusky in the rain. The street had the destitute air of deck furniture left outside in winter.

How often had Allie driven this same way, in this same muddy weather? Sam found himself marveling at how many years she had been dead, as if it represented some sort of accomplishment, to be nothing. It was easy to envision how Allie would have responded to that idea: "Kiddo," she'd say, "I guess I've finally found my niche." Sam wondered what it said about her that he still knew exactly how she would let the air out of him; then he thought maybe it said everything.

Booth, sitting in the passenger seat, was taking snoring breaths, but he wasn't asleep.

In the cupholder, the cell phone rattled for the third time since father and son had left Tom's driveway.

His father had invited Sam to "attend" him in "the course" of his "rounds." Although the use of the verb "attend" was in the context predictably grating and Boothian, after he'd traveled such a long way, it seemed perverse to leave right away. If he were to do so, Sam had no idea where to go or what fire to attempt to put out first. Mina was mad at him, and he was mad at her. It was Sam's assumption that Tess was furious at him. Jo-Jo knew about the affair with Polly and wanted to cut off Sam's hands and put them in a special box. Wesley was probably all fucked up. Even Tom seemed irritated.

It was more proof, if any further had been needed, that people were hard to please and easy to hurt, and the problem was exacerbated, not lessened, by how well you knew them.

A couple of hours with Booth seemed for once to be safer than anything else.

They stopped at a red light. The phone ceased buzzing, beeped. His father cleared his throat. "Your communication device, it seems to want for some attention."

"Yeah." Sam picked it up, glanced at the readout: Tess Auerbach again. The problem, he decided, was that he was stuck in the wrong reality. In another reality, he had gone home with her, made love to her, convinced her to admit that she was wrong about the scene in *Dog Day Afternoon* being improvised, made love to her a second time, slept in, had breakfast, and made plans for the future. Sam was not a little envious of his other self. He noticed that his hand had crept from the wheel to lay fingers against the spot on his cheek where Tess had touched him.

"I saw an extraordinary French film yesterday, Samuel," said Booth.

The light changed, and the phone resumed ringing. Sam inhaled and returned his hand to the wheel. Booth said left, and they were moving again.

"It's called *Quel Beau Parleur,* which apparently translates to *What a Good Talker You Are.* It's about an unremarkable man who finds that all the women in Paris are absolutely desperate to screw him. I loved it."

"That sounds like every French movie, Booth. Sorry about the phone ringing. I'm trying to figure out what to do about that."

"I don't suppose you could just turn it off," proposed Booth.

"I could," said Sam. "I haven't decided."

His father tapped his cane against the seat well. "A woman, I assume? How serious?"

Sam hesitated, then figured, Why not? If Booth had anything going for him, it was that he was no one to judge.

"Hard to say. I like her. I mean, I don't know her that well. Or at all, really. But we had a moment. She's intelligent. Cranky, but in an appealing way. Physically attractive. We hit it off, but it got overly personal, and I sort of split on her. I'm pretty sure she's super-pissed at me, and justifiably so."

"Yes," said Booth. "I see."

"So she's been calling all morning, nonstop."

From Main Street, they passed into a series of sharply rising and dipping streets, shouldered tight with large, peeling houses that served as off-campus housing for SUNY-Hasbrouck students. After a few blocks, the road flattened and they were in the countryside. Sunken fields of browning vegetation filled the spaces between the occasional house, barn, or trailer.

"I see. This woman is menacing you. It doesn't happen often that one is menaced by an attractive woman." Booth gave an orotund chuckle. "But it can flattering and exciting. They go one way, you go the other, you want to be left alone, they want to know why you want to be alone, but how can you possibly explain it, and then someone tackles someone, and you end up rolling around on the floor. Sandra once buttonholed me into the restroom of a fast-food establishment, you know."

"I didn't know that," said Sam. "I'd rather I didn't."

"It was a Burger King. I can still picture, vividly, the wall above the toilet: painted on the tile was a sandwich dressed in king's garb—the crown and the jeweled mantle and so on—and how his visage glared upon me as I glanced over Sandra's shoulder. A stern burger emperor with a french-fry scepter." The reminiscence seemed to please Booth enormously; he spoke the words "stern burger emperor" with a zest that other men reserved for "ten-pound bass" or "blackjack."

"That's a wonderful story, Booth. Thank you."

"But you know," the old man continued, paying no attention to his son's sarcasm, "I've always felt that sex is a little pathetic if you take it too seriously."

Sam could grant that was not an unreasonable position. It was true that no one who had seen the satyr make sweet, steady love to an elm tree's knothole could ever again approach sex with complete sobriety, but he didn't think it made him a prude to not want to hear that from Booth. He had screwed around on Sam's mother. For that matter, he had screwed Sam's mother. It was creepy and too close.

"In fact," Booth wound up, "it's possible that everything is a little pathetic if you take it too seriously."

The wipers started to squeak. Sam switched them off. The rain had stopped again. The phone vibrated some more, beeped another missed call.

Five or so miles out of town, at a right-hand cut marked by two boulders, Booth said it was the place. The gravel lane rattled through the floor of the car. A few hundred yards in, they arrived at a farmhouse, painted red, with several smaller outbuildings of the same color and style huddled around it like offspring. Sam parked the rental in the small paved lot and turned off the engine.

"Did that come off sounding like an excuse?" his father asked. "What I just said?"

Sam was taken aback; self-awareness wasn't a trait he associated with Booth. "Maybe" was the cautious answer he settled on after a moment.

"I'm sorry, then. Again. Because I have no excuse. I made a joke out of too many things when you were young, and that is undoubtedly putting it far too gently. I was careless. Selfish. Stupid." The old man shook his head. He opened the passenger-side door but didn't get out. "I tried to resist saying something like that. It seems to me that it would be

awfully greedy to go asking you for forgiveness now. I just—I need you
to know that I feel sick when I think about that night you called me and
I didn't call you back. Sick, just sick."

The glance he threw his son was hooded, his beard closed over his
grimacing mouth. Was this what shame looked like on Booth's face?
Sam couldn't remember ever having seen it in life—or on film, for that
matter. It was shocking.

"Forward, Booth. Let's just keep things going forward." The words
were ineffectual, almost desperate-sounding, but they were all he could
find to say.

"I'm just glad to have a little time with you," said his father.

Sam rubbed a knuckle against his cheek and squinted at the dashboard.

The cell phone rattled. Fresh air blew in through the open door.

"Should you get that?"

"Yeah," said Sam.

3.

Celebrity Treasures was the name of the Santa Monica–based memo-
rabilia company with whom Booth had signed an exclusive contract.
Along with a number of other B-movie veterans and television personalities, Booth autographed posters and movie stills for them to sell, and
he licensed his image for other items such as T-shirts and coffee mugs.
It was a typical enough arrangement for old semi-famous movie types
and a decent source of income. What had turned out to be an especially
lucrative sideline for Booth was his more interactive work for Celebrity
Treasures—specifically, the recording of personalized messages.

For a fee, fans could have a celebrity from the Celebrity Treasures roster record a message. Each personality offered a list of messages based
on lines or catchphrases uttered by characters they had played in movies
or shows. Booth's messaging services were apparently in high demand, a
popularity that was easy to understand for at least two reasons: one, the
arresting quality of his voice—or rather, his Voice; and two, he had said
a lot of crazy shit in his movies.

Take, as an example, the script for the scene in the original *Hellhole* where Professor Graham Hawking Gould, Booth's renowned satanologist, sacrifices himself (though not permanently—Professor Gould is reincarnated for both *Hellhole II: Wake the Devil* and *Hellhole III: Endless Hell*) in order to destroy Satan's monkey, Anton.

EXT. NEAR THE PIT—BLOOD-RED TWILIGHT
Professor Gould grapples with the devil monkey, mere feet from the black chasm. The monkey SCREECHES and snaps at him and LASHES its hideous black snake's tongue.

ANTON
I'll bite your balls off! I'm the familiar of the Prince of Darkness!

PROF. GOULD
I don't care whose monkey you are! I'll be damned to hell before you use that tone with me!

The satanologist clutches the hateful primate to his chest and leaps into the impenetrable darkness of the hellhole.

When producing an answering-machine message for Joe Somebody, Booth adapted his immortal riposte to "I don't care whose monkey you are! You'll be damned to hell if you don't leave Joe a message!"

Inside the red farmhouse, Christine, the fortyish woman who ran the recording studio out of her home, gave Booth a hug and Sam a chuck under the chin. "Love the cape," she said to the old man.

"My daughter made it for me," said Booth.

"Aw, that's sweet." Christine winked at Sam. "You know your father's the Olivier of answering-machine messages."

Booth waved this away. "She's being facetious, Samuel. I'll never cease to hone my craft. The art of messages is a lifetime pursuit."

She inquired after Tom. "Is he lean and rugged?"

"Yes. The son of a bitch is as trim as a snake and as rich as Croesus and only a year younger than I am, though you'd never know it."

"Tom and Booth are besties," Christine informed Sam. Her bracelets jingled and clacked as she led the way to the control room. "Which makes it awkward that they're both so smitten with me."

The engineer pointed Sam to a leather couch against the back wall. There were silks tacked to the ceiling, and a stick of lavender incense was burning. The vibe was clichéd, but Sam liked it. Christine's daughter, introduced as Logan, a five-year-old ruddy-cheeked version of her mother, was huddled at one end of the couch in deep communion with a stuffed bunny.

On the opposite side of the soundproof window, Booth settled into a straight-backed chair with his cane across his knees. Pushed to the edges of the recording room were various off-duty musical instruments. Booth held a sheaf of scripts. The arm of a microphone stand was angled to a spot just in front of his face.

The first message was for a man named Alan. Speakers in the corners of the control room's ceiling reproduced Sam's father's voice in crisp stereo.

"It so happens that Alan, after a great deal of study—and a long sojourn in the deepest jungles of South America, where monkeys speak and where the wisest of men walk on their hands"—Booth paused for a couple of beats, his eyes widening clownishly and his cheeks swelling with malevolent mirth, so that through the soundproof glass, Sam saw an aged Horsefeathers Law flicker briefly into view—"*is still not home yet!*" He coughed. "Leave a message."

"Got it," said Christine into the intercom.

"No, no," said Booth, and he did a second take, and didn't cough, and it was better.

Sam's father performed twenty or so messages. The majority of these were adapted from the *Hellhole* trilogy, but there were others scattered across Booth's career. On behalf of someone named Pat, Dog, the sagacious cloud from *Buffalo Roam,* told a caller, "You must get right, my friend, and get along, and get yourself in the celestial way, *and*—get ready to leave Pat a message." Don Griese, Booth's mumble-mouthed, car-wash-obsessed mafia don in *Hard Mommies,* was more concise: "Vanessa's machine. After the beep, ya picaroon, youse."

It was odd for Sam to see his father express these different voices, inhabiting characters from obscure twenty- and thirty-year-old films. While the abrupt switches from voice to voice were unnerving, they were undeniably impressive. It was as though all of the characters lived inside his father, inhabiting some remote room of his mind. Sam imagined them in comfy compartments set into a wall, like upholstered morgue drawers. Whenever Booth wanted one, he could descend to this storage area, slide the character out, slap the dust off its shoulders, and pull the string that made it talk.

The old man was totally professional, requesting playbacks, ad-libbing multiple takes if he didn't feel like the message was punchy enough, redoing any stumble or slip. Probably this shouldn't have surprised Sam; it was, after all, the man's business. But what seemed remarkable to Sam was there was no sign that Booth considered the work beneath him. This didn't seem possible, that he should be able to approach the recording of joke answering-machine messages without giving away at least a hint of boredom, yet Booth seemed totally focused on the task. His son found his humility baffling—and interesting.

His father's movies ought to have been so much fun, all the mugging, the scares that weren't scary, the abundance of cheesecake, the papier-mâché sets, the stoned extras peering off in the wrong directions—and they were for other people, just not Sam. He had long understood that he was the exception, the grouch who refused to see past the boom in the corner of the frame, the spoilsport who couldn't find it in himself to care one way or another if a werewolf killed a bunch of Romans living in villas with grandfather clocks and speaking with Valley accents.

In the past it had dawned on Sam that in some cosmic sense, if you considered how many viewers had attended Booth's films, been relaxed and amused by them, and gone home to perform acts of procreation, there was an ontological argument (of a fairly undergraduate nature, but still) to be made for his father as the patriarch of thousands. While such a notion undoubtedly would have sent Polly into an uproar—Sam could hear her insisting that he needed to see a shrink, and in the next breath demanding that he tell her *more, more, more*—it left Sam feeling melancholy and reflective.

What had never occurred to him until this moment on this Friday was that Booth had gone to work on these movies like anyone else working on any other set on a "serious" movie. Had Sam thought that Booth went skipping onto soundstages, that he acted drunk? Sam didn't know. He supposed he hadn't ever dug that deep.

Out in the car, Booth had seemed sincere. Sam didn't know what to make of that, either, or what he wanted to do with it. The day had started dire and turned hazy. Sam sat on the couch and crossed his leg over his knee and observed his father's transformations.

When the day's docket of messages was accomplished, Booth recorded a pitch for a local deli:

"My name is Booth Dolan, and although I'm known as an actor, my first love is eating. And let me tell you, I've eaten a few sandwiches! Oh, yes! Torpedoes, heroes, subs, pitas—I've devoured scores of them!

"But something unprecedented happened to me the other day, at Bill's Bomb Shop on Route Seven in Devering. I met my match. I was humbled. By a sandwich! The mouthwatering, stomach-stretching Megaton Meatball proved too much even for me. Heavens! I had to take half of it home!

"My friends, at Bill's Bomb Shop, hunger is no obstacle. Visit us on Route Seven in Devering, directly opposite Lowe's."

Christine wolf-whistled into the intercom. "First take! First take!"

The actor was unmoved. He shook his head, shifted around on his chair. The creaking echoed in the control room. Booth puckered his lips and stared at the script.

Logan, still poised over her bunny, dabbed the stuffed animal's mouth with a strawberry. "Eat," she whispered, "please eat."

Christine shushed her daughter and ran a playback.

"What do you think, Samuel?" asked Booth.

Sam had thought it was shouty, one-note. He shrugged, told Christine to tell Booth it was fine, but the old man knew he was holding out. "Cough it up!" His father's voice bounced off the control room walls.

Sam sighed and pushed himself up. He went to the board, bent down to the intercom. "You could give a pause at 'by a sandwich.' Go softer, maybe. Like, you've had all these adventures or whatever in your films, but this amazing sandwich, it's—you know, it's bested you, sent you home on your shield, and you can't quite believe it."

His father nodded. "By a sandwich," he said. The profound hush of his delivery indicated shades of awe and incredulity; this sandwich was unlike any other sandwich, was somehow more than a sandwich.

The next take was better, and the third take was best.

■ ■ ■

Before they left, Booth requested a private conference with Logan. Propped by his cane, he leaned over her corner of the couch, and they exchanged whispers. The child did most of the talking. Booth gave the occasional nod. His expression was sober.

The other two watched from the door. Christine explained to Sam that there had been an incident with Bunny involving the driveway and a reversing car. Somehow the concept of gangrene had entered the child's head, and the stuffed animal was now expiring slowly and in agony.

"Logan's father," Christine said, "is useless in these kinds of situations. No imagination." Her arms were crossed, bunching her bracelets and bangles up to the stars tattooed on her elbows. "God, don't even let me start."

Sam overheard Booth say, "Hmm. Yes, yes. I can see that."

"Look at your father. It's not this big effort for him to relate to her. He's patient. He doesn't try to reason with her, you know? Drag her kicking and screaming. He goes along with it. Which is why she adores him. You can't expect a little kid to 'tough it out.' Because she's not tough. She's a little kid." Christine gnawed at one of her thumbnails. "I bet you had a wonderful childhood."

"I did. It was like Christmas," said Sam. "Every day."

The engineer rolled her eyes.

Next door to the studio was a bright, open kitchen area with a long dining room table. The old man swept off the morning papers and briskly set aside a couple of cereal bowls. He glared around; his eyebrows flared.

Sam bit back a laugh.

"Now, listen. If there's to be any chance of saving Bunny's life, I'm going to need a sharp knife, duct tape, cotton balls, a jar of ether, and above all else: *complete silence from all those present.*"

When the items were brought—a bottle of hydrogen peroxide was found to serve as ether—Logan kissed the stuffed animal and gingerly set it on the table. The creature's right leg was dirty and hanging from threads at the seam. It was a medium-size bunny with black eyes, furred in tight beige coils. The child's lower lip trembled, but she was brave and didn't weep.

Booth scrubbed up at the kitchen sink and made a production of holding his arms wide while Sam helped him into a red apron (a decal on the pocket showed an anthropomorphic egg in a chef's hat, frying bacon). The old man stepped to the surgical table where Bunny lay beneath a yellow dishrag.

"Nurse," he announced. "The scalpel—"

4.

Sam told his father he had never seen such a heartwarming amputation.

They were in the car, traveling back to Hasbrouck. After amputating the stuffed animal's leg at the hip, his father had patched the bunny with a massive wad of duct tape. To stem the risk of infection, he had prescribed a twice-daily regimen of potpourri misting.

"Do you suppose Bunny will live, Booth?" Sam asked.

"He'll live. Logan doesn't strike me as a macabre child. If she gives him his potpourri, he should recover nicely."

"He'll certainly never hop again, though. Is that any kind of life for a bunny?"

"Bunny never hopped before. He's a stuffed toy." Booth grumbled, playing along. "His sole purpose is to be loved by that little girl, and his handicap won't interfere with that."

"She'll probably grow up and marry a one-legged man."

"She'll probably grow up and marry a damned dashing surgeon. You get this from your mother, God rest her soul. She loved to razz me, too. That's fine, I can take it." He thumped his cane on the floor of the rental. "But I really think you'll like this movie, the French one. Here's the nut of the thing: why is this man who is so dull—almost belligerently dull—suddenly irresistible to women? I can't stress enough, there's nothing even vaguely impressive about him. The man used to be writer—which makes sense, because writers are the dullest people on earth besides bureaucrats—but this man, our protagonist, he came down with a terrible block, so now he bags groceries. And yet women are fucking him left and right. Fucking him insensate! Parisian women of every stripe are absolutely putting this schnook through his paces—"

"Okay, I'll see it! Jesus." It might even be good. Booth's taste in films—the ones he liked to watch as opposed to the ones that he appeared in—

was not inevitably horrible. However, as well as they were getting along, his father's musings and reflections on matters sexual nevertheless produced in Sam a feeling similar to that of being nosed in the crotch by a big, slobbery dog.

"Excellent. *Quel Beau Parleur*! We should see it while you're here. It's playing in Kingston."

A shuttered farmer's stall slipped by on one side of the road. The steeple of Hasbrouck's Catholic church sprouted over a rise. The rain had recommenced, falling in fat, irregular drops. Sam's cell phone jiggled around in the cupholder.

"Maybe you should answer it," said Booth. "If you'd like, you can pull over and I can get out while you talk."

"That's okay." Sam wondered how mad Tess was at this point, if her wrath could be quantified. Then he wondered if it wasn't cowardice that was keeping him from answering but the likelihood that once he did pick up, and she did tell him off, that was the last time he'd ever hear from her. His hand started to drift up to his cheek, but he redirected it to ten on the wheel. At least her other self was off enjoying herself with his other self. Where would they get together for a proper date, those alternate-reality lovebirds? If Sam's alternate-reality self were on the ball he'd suggest they go to a Segway store and test-drive one. Sam thought Tess's alternate-reality self would love that. The phone beeped another missed call.

Sam abruptly wished he could drop a brick on his other self's head, drag the smug prick into a panic room, seal it, and leave him to mummify. Some guys didn't appreciate what they had.

"You're thinking about her, aren't you," said Booth.

"Yeah." To Sam's surprise, the observation—especially coming from Booth—didn't bother him.

His father made an empathetic sound and, unexpectedly, didn't prod, or advise, or pontificate. He just let the thing be. It was the kind of steady, unexcited reaction a person wanted from his father; the kind of reaction that implied sympathy but, more important, confidence that Sam would figure it out. It was, therefore, highly un-Booth-like. He wasn't accustomed to his father being so—not normal, that wasn't possible—acceptable.

"What is this about Mina pepper-spraying two people?" his father asked.

"I don't know what you want me to tell you, Booth. It's what happened. She went on a rampage."

"Did they deserve it?"

In the hush of the car and the odd peace of the moment, Sam could summon a degree of sympathy for his sister's actions. While the vagrant's intentions might not have been violent, the guy had a large knife, and it was a second's decision. As for the attack on his roommate, although Mina obviously overreacted to a minor annoyance, if you did happen to be in possession of a canister of pepper spray, Sam could see how it might be hard to resist using it on Wesley. "Maybe. But she's on the edge of something, you know? And Sandra nearly burned down their apartment. The whole thing's a mess."

Booth grunted in an authoritative way. "I'll fix it," he said.

"What?" Sam laughed. "Mina? You'll fix Mina?"

"The situation," said his father.

"Okay. How?"

Booth admitted that he wasn't sure yet. Something about the set of his lips and the quiet, half-there quality of his voice caused Sam to withhold a further expression of disbelief; it wasn't like his father to be so contained.

They were downtown again.

"Where the Coffee Shop was, Samuel," Booth directed. "That's our next stop."

Before they left the studio, Christine had given Booth a couple of bulging plastic sacks. The contents—clothing—were intended for a group, Booth said, of "less fortunate local children." But when they pulled up across the street from the structure that once housed the Hasbrouck Nickelodeon, what Sam saw were some street people loitering under the eave.

Subsequent to its incarnation as the Coffee Shop, the theater building initially passed into the town's hands. The details had never been clear to Sam, but his rough sense was that once Allie gave up the café, Booth defaulted somehow, or was forced to surrender it for unpaid taxes, something like that. The town used it as a warehouse for the VFD and other local entities, then eventually sold it. For a short while after that, it was a restaurant, and later, it was totally abandoned for a few years. Now it was once again a café.

While the marquee had vanished, the building otherwise appeared relatively unchanged: glass double doors, the brick facade with cement rectangles for eyes where poster frames once hung. The only thing missing was Allie, her hair tied up in a purple bandanna, poking her head out the door to remind the smokers to pick up after themselves. "Hey, scuzzy," she'd say if she caught a person walking away from a butt on the sidewalk, "you forgot something."

What was more troubling, Sam wondered, how a place disappeared, or how it stayed the same? A veteran of the Great War returns to the buried trenches of the Eastern Front where his comrades died and stands in a field in the sun, while grass licks at his belt buckle, and it is fantastic for him to imagine the smoke and the mud and the thundering nights. Nevertheless: regrowth is a stage of the natural cycle. Everything flesh and bone is eventually fertilizer; we know this.

How are you supposed to be old in a place that knew you when you were young? It was disorienting, like shooting a film out of sequence, the end at the beginning or the beginning at the end.

A wooden placard on a hook clacked in the wind. The placard bore the name of the building's latest iteration: SMOKE ME DRINK ME. It was a hookah bar as well as a café.

Many of the bedraggled youths—tank tops, holey shorts, sandals— who clustered around the door were visibly unwashed to such a degree that they appeared singed. One girl strummed a guitar with a splintered casing. Another member of the group, a boy in checkered pajama pants, was stretching in slow motion and making circular motions with his hands, as if assessing the strength of unseen barriers. A few were smoking cigarettes. Present as well were several large, grinning, and collarless dogs that circulated among the company, nosing hands and sniffing pavement.

Booth promised that he would be only a moment. Sam watched his father walk across the street—the old man still led with his shoulders, but it was obvious that the huge body exerted a drag. His cane worked like an oar, appearing to pull him forward.

A lanky girl with chopsticks protruding from her nest of dreadlocks hooted and clapped and jumped up and down. She was barefoot. Some of the others clapped, too. Sam's father bowed slightly to the group and conducted a flourish with his cane and approached another young woman. Tattooed across this young woman's face was a spider-web, which made her features appear soldered together, yet she was star-tlingly pretty. Her hair was free and auburn-colored, and there was an intimation of mischief in the little smile she wore in the middle of her checkerboard face. She threw her arms around Booth.

They conversed for a minute or two, and he handed her the plastic bags. He bellowed something to the entire group, exhorting them, and jabbed his stick in the air. The young woman with the tattoo began to share out long-sleeved T-shirts and windbreakers taken from the bags.

Unable to hear the words, Sam put his own subtitles to the scene: *Ladies and gentlemen! Step right up and set your gaze upon the eighth wonder: Booth Dolan* as *a Human Being! Wonder at his sensitivity! Marvel at his responsiveness! Entirely stomach cancer–free!*

The phone rattled in the cupholder again. He felt an urge to answer it. In their brief time together, Tess had demonstrated a gift for observa-tion. Maybe she could explain what had possessed his father.

They were homeless, the "local children" who hung around outside the hookah bar–cum–café; or near homeless, squatting or splitting one-bedroom apartments four and five ways. Without doubt, there were drugs involved and probably a certain amount of petty crime, Booth said. College towns tended to draw such periphery youths. Shut out of secondary education by poverty, they were nevertheless attracted to its freedom and opportunity and romance, so they coalesced around cam-pus hangouts.

Hasbrouck had taken a particular dislike to its bunch, his father claimed, having returned to Sam's rental car and settled back into the passenger seat. The letters section of the weekly newspaper was a catalog of grievances against them, about the way they cluttered the street, and how their collection of stray dogs frightened pedestrians, and what they portended for the future, shiftless, stinking addicts destined to gobble at the public trough and leech from the public goodwill.

"And it's really over-the-top, in my opinion." As he related this infor-mation, Booth gradually became more exercised, but here he leveled off. "Because you know, they're not any different than the young men and women with whom I made *New Roman Empire*. They're not shiftless. They're disenfranchised. They're searching. They're waiting for their lives to start. For the lights to go down, the curtains to open, and the world to come up and the excitement to begin. They're underfed and uninspired, that's all. I don't know why people can't recognize that."

"Sure," said Sam, who thought he understood something about the disillusionment of the young. He'd made a movie about it.

"I got to know a few of them, became friendly with them, and now I try to make a little time whenever I can, speak with them, encourage them, hand around a few dollars. With summer over and the cooler months coming on, I thought it was time to bring them some half-decent warm clothes. I mean, look at that girl, running around on the sidewalk in her bare feet!" He threw a hand in the direction of the dreadlocked girl.

A picture of Mina came to Sam's mind. There couldn't have been more than two or three years between her and the barefoot girl, if that.

"That child doesn't need to pay more taxes, she needs our support! She needs some damned shoes, for God's sake!" Booth thumped his cane on the floor of the car. "It offends me, Samuel, how many so-called adults in this country reflexively think the worst of the young. These Tea Party people, for instance. They think everyone else is as greedy and fearful as they are, when it's the exact opposite. Whatever happened to optimism? Whatever happened to generosity? Never mind generosity, whatever happened to decency? Whatever happened to curiosity? Engage with the future of your species, you cranky old shits!" He thumped the cane again.

"They all have cell phone clips on their belts," said Sam.

"What?"

"It's something Tess said to me, that all the Tea Party people have cellphone belt clips. A lot of them, anyhow. That it comes off as incredibly self-important. That's what she said. I don't know for sure. Tess said to watch one of their rallies and I'd see."

"That's very interesting." Booth wiped at his beard. "Is Tess the young woman who keeps calling for you? Has she made any other observations I should know about?"

"She compared the president to a Segway."

"That fits. Segways are wonderful and underrated, just like the president. I already appreciated this young woman's taste in men, but now I'm really beginning to warm to her," said Booth. "Where was I?"

Sam didn't bother to correct his father on Tess's actual, rather more lackluster assessment of both the Segway and the president. "You were on the Tea Party."

"Oh, fuck them! Fuck them! It's not about them. They think it's about them, but it's not about them." His father produced a *what can you say?* raspberry. "You know, those kids over there, they're just a few years older than Mina."

Across the street, the girl with the bare feet had settled down on an egg crate to examine her T-shirt and, in what seemed to Sam a gesture of heartrending meticulousness, was smoothing it over her lap to study the image on the front.

"Yeah," said Sam. "I was thinking that, too."

Would Sam believe that, on their first date, Booth and Allie saw a movie at that old theater? "Quite a bad movie, I'm afraid," said his father. "But we had a lovely time."

They were on the way to Booth's last appointment of the morning. A car ahead of them was waiting for a break in traffic to make a left. For the sixty or so seconds that elapsed before they were moving again, one part of Sam's mind gently conducted another part of his mind to a private cubicle and set out a three-ring binder. Inside the binder were head shots: jut-jawed Professor Gould; Plato, brooding and nibbling on a fountain pen; sleepy-eyed, fish-lipped Don Griese; Horsefeathers Law in his smart boater, grinning creepily; President Lincoln, speaking for the sanctity of the Union; page after page of different characters, and in the last sleeve, Sam's living, breathing father, large and bearded and radiating self-satisfaction in a mustard-stained shirt.

The one part of Sam asked the other part, could he make an identification?

They were all familiar, but—no. The man in the passenger seat wasn't anywhere in the book.

"Booth," said Sam. "This isn't—a put-on, right?"

"No," said Booth. "No put-on."

"You're being you."

"Such as I am."

"What happened?"

His father shrugged. "I had an Awakening of sorts." He made a floating gesture with his hand. "The details don't matter."

The phone shook in the cupholder. The car ahead of them turned. Sam ran his thumb lightly back and forth over his cheek and cocked his head at his father. Booth gazed forward studiously. The car behind them honked twice.

"Stay on this road," said his father.

5.

The final stop of Booth's rounds was itself a final stop: Hasbrouck Horizons, a nonprofit hospice specializing in geriatric care.

While tossing around for rummage-sale items, a hospice administrator had discovered a projector in the basement. Word of the find had somehow made its way to Booth, owner of a small collection of reels (six of his own pictures—*Alamo II: Return to the Alamo: Daughters of Texas, Black Soul Riders, Fangs of Fury, Hellhole 3: Endless Hell, Rat Fiend!,* and *New Roman Empire*), and he had recently convened a regular Friday matinee.

In the facility's sweltering, squeaking rec area, two tweed couches were angled to either side of a drop-down screen and spaced apart to make room for a half a dozen residents in wheelchairs. Gold streamers, remnants of a party, drooped across a plate-glass window. The window provided a view of a weedy hill sloping to the interstate toll kiosks below. The lights had been lowered, and the air smelled like pine cleaner.

On the right-hand couch, a tiny man in a gray housecoat was tipped over against the armrest—drool had collected in the gristle on his cheek and dried into a chalky wave—but many of the attendees appeared positively lambent at the sight of Booth. A nearly hairless woman in one of the wheelchairs, her shoulders and arms draped in tubes and translucent bags of fluids, implored Booth to get the show on the road. "Dolan, I lived all week for no other reason except to make sure that stupid werewolf movie wasn't the last movie I ever saw. Plato, my bony ass."

"Good morning, Ms. Elstner. Glad to see you're feeling well today. You know how I cherish your thoughtful, measured appraisals of the cinema." The projector was set on a stand behind the wheelchair section. While Sam shone a penlight, Booth threaded the reel into the spindle.

"And the one about the devil's hole," Ms. Elstner continued, "or whatever it was, that was even worse. I am feeling well. I think your terrible movies might be killing my cancer. If you don't show something passable, I worry I may never get to die."

Sam remained at the projector while his father tapped around to the front of the audience.

"Ms. Elstner," Booth said, "let me reassure you. No one has ever survived to see all six of our features twice. The end is nigh, you have my word."

The hairless woman shook some of her tubes to show what a low value she placed on Booth's word. "If you can't show us a good movie, you might at least show us one where there's one woman who wears a bra."

"I asked my grandniece about the styles these days, and she says it's all down to the whims and preferences of one single rich lady in California who makes all the decisions," said another elderly woman intriguingly. Gnarled hands folded in her lap, she sat on the couch by the sleeping man.

From the rear row of wheelchairs, a rumpled pile of a man—his spine was kinked like a garden hose—gave a sulky boo. Whether to the bra-wearing initiative or the rich lady in California who decided on the styles, Sam couldn't be sure.

Before the pull-down screen—the sort that Sam associated with educational cartoons in elementary school—Booth leaned on his cane and addressed the terminal audience. "Today's feature is titled *New Roman Empire*. It concerns the machinations of a sulfurous charlatan, the corrupt political interests who employ him, and the young freethinkers who threaten those corrupt political interests. As it happens—"

Ms. Elstner tapped a ring against her wheelchair for attention.

"Yes, my dear?"

"Why in the hell are you wearing a cape? You're too old for dress-up, you know."

"My daughter made it for me. She has a great interest in design. I think it looks wonderful. It makes me feel like a gentleman. It goes with my cane."

"Gentleman." Ms. Elstner laughed as though this were the funniest thing she had heard all day, which caused Sam to laugh, too. "What's your cape made of, then?"

"I don't know," Booth huffed. "Wool, I think."

"It'd be better if it was made of silk," she said.

"Like fancy panties," elaborated the lady who had mentioned the supreme fashion goddess of California.

Booth raised a finger. "False. It's a fall-winter cape. That's why it's wool."

"Then it should be velvet," Ms. Elstner insisted.

"You are not the cape jurist, woman. There are all kinds of capes, and this cape is just the way it ought to be, because that's how my daughter made it."

"I didn't say I was the authority on capes, Booth." Ms. Elstner tucked her chin and glanced away as if injured. "It's merely my opinion. You don't have to like it. A true gentleman would allow a sickly woman to have her opinions."

Booth leaned more heavily on his cane. "I questioned your expertise in the cape area. I never said anything about denying your right to an opinion, dear."

She snapped back to face him and grinned. "Booth, you look like a Dracula that ate another Dracula!"

Sam, at his position at the rear of the room, behind the projector, broke out laughing again, along with several of the others. The rain must have stopped, because the antiseptic room seemed much brighter; a new diffuse light fell through the window and glimmered the leftover streamers. It was a show, obviously, an act. Booth was being a fool for them. He's making their day, Sam thought, and felt—proud?

Hunched over his cane in a pose of exaggerated forbearance, Booth glowered at the floor while he waited for the mirth to cease. When it did, he said, "Have I mentioned, Ms. Elstner, how glad I am that you've not yet expired? Would anyone else like to insult me before I finish introducing the film? Maybe we should have a roast instead?"

The patient with the kinked spine piped up in a faint voice. "No more flirting. I am ready to see a picture now."

Ms. Elstner told the man to hold his horses. She asked if that was Booth's son at the projector. Booth allowed that it was. Ms. Elstner opined that Sam was quite handsome and, luckily, seemed to have avoided the worst of the heavy gene.

"That's it!" His father crossed the room, bounced his cane off the floor, caught it, and nimbly slipped it under his armpit. He bent and planted a smacking kiss on her papery cheek. "Peace?"

"One more!" demanded Ms. Elstner, so Booth kissed her on the other cheek before returning to the screen.

Sam imagined performing the cane trick for Tess and impressing her so much that she stopped hating him. Maybe Booth could teach him. Or maybe, thought Sam, I'm lying on the floor of a sealed panic room, hallucinating this entire day.

"Other questions?" his father asked.

"Ah . . . Booth," said the woman on the couch with the locked hands. "I think Irving has passed."

The only sounds were of raspy breathing and the ticking drips of life-supporting fluids.

Irving, the man in the gray housecoat, sagged against the arm-rest. Behind the chunky lenses of his glasses, his wide-open eyes were unblinking. His pale lips, his white face, his small hands cupped at the knot of his housecoat had a desiccated appearance, like papier-mâché.

Sam felt a twinge of sadness, more for the moment than for the man. It had been a nice thing, to show a movie, and now this had happened. And Booth was doing so well, too.

"Should I go get someone?" Sam asked.

The crooked-backed man took a quavering sigh. "I don't suppose there'll be a picture now."

"Irving." Booth extended his cane and prodded Irving's slipper. Irving didn't move. Sam's father leaned forward slightly, peering close at the man's face.

Sam recalled how, at the funeral home, his father had stood coffinside in that exact position. Booth had appeared less sorrowful at his ex-wife's death than perplexed. The coffin and the body were in the room when everyone left, but later, someone rolled Allie away to the bowels of the funeral home, to the furnace, where they placed her on a steel table and pushed her into a fire. Meanwhile, Sam returned to his sophomore year of college. Booth went wherever Booth went.

Maybe what was really bewildering was not the abruptness of a death but the swift resumption of life. You came out from the dark, and the sun was so hideously bright, you feared you might go blind.

"Irving O'Dell," said Booth, for the corpse in the gray robe belonged to none other than that prominent member of the *New Roman Empire* ensemble, originator of the role of Mr. Jones.

The whistle of the cane through the air was followed by the twang of wood against aluminum as he dealt a wicked blow to the frame of the couch. "Irving! Wake up!"

His voice—the Voice—caromed around the room. Several patients in wheelchairs bucked, and someone's pole of bags and tubes crashed to the ground. There was a screech: "Oh-oh-oh!"

Irving blinked, yawned. He levered himself upright and clawed at his crusty jaw. He noticed Booth standing in front of him.

"What is it?" Irving asked. "Oh, criminy! Don't tell me I slept through the movie?"

Once the film was rolling, Sam and Booth remained just long enough to see the medicine wagon come creaking over a rise, then left.

6.

At Tom's house, father and son separated. In addition to his other duties, the old man was teaching a Film Appreciation class at the community college, and because there was a session that night, he needed to spend some time looking over his teaching materials. He also intended to have a quiet word with Mina.

"When the hell did you get so industrious, Booth? You know this is all kind of weird, right?" Sam asked. "I want you to tell me about this Awakening."

"Yes . . ." Booth shook his head and turned to open the car door. "Some other time. You're welcome to sit in on my class if you like."

"What's the topic?"

"*E.T.* I find the central characterizations, the parallels, very interesting. The sad little boy from the shattered home. The sad little person from beyond the stars who has been stranded. They're really in the same situation—brokenhearted in the same way. I want to highlight the way

Spielberg captures their bond. The magic, the flying bicycles and all of that, is simply an expression of the comfort they take from each other. Their friendship even brings E.T. back to life. It's about friendship. On top of that very elegant metaphorical content, there's a lot of excitement and adventure and cuteness, and that's exceptional, too." Booth threw his legs around and out of the passenger seat, hauled himself up. "And I'm sure, as usual, that I'll weep copiously when E.T. dies."

Sam scratched his head. He thought, This whole thing is literally making me scratch my head. He thought, I can't believe how good Booth makes that ridiculous sci-fi-fantasy piece of shit sound.

Booth leaned down and poked his head through the open door. "There's a rusted short sword on your floor."

Sam said he knew, and his father said, "All right," and shut the door. A second or two after that, the old man reopened the door. "Remember: *Quel Beau Parleur*! You're going to like it." He shut the door again.

The old man lumbered toward the house, slowly picking his way across the drive and the wet lawn, cane swinging and plunging.

The habit of mentally filming the odd moment never left Sam. His interior camera was a crisp 35 mm, smack in the middle range, very flat, very "real." He started close on the big man's shoulder. Gradually, Booth's figure expanded, head and back, arms and legs, ballooning into view before gaining shape. As soon as his whole form was visible, the camera began to withdraw. Booth diminished, sinking away off-center, as the walls and angles of the yard and the house rose around him. To the right, his father's reflection wavered across the surface of the picture window. The natural light was fine, sharper than it had been that morning but filtered and lending a dull shine to the wet surfaces. Sam pulled farther and farther back until Booth was a remote figure at the door. Then Booth passed inside, and all that remained was a nicely composed shot of the front section of the looming house.

A couple of times Sam rewound and watched it and liked it, but he couldn't figure out what sort of weddingography it could fit into—unless he wanted to build a new template, a Bergman Wedding, maybe.

If he were going on a one-way trip, never to return—rocketing into another galaxy, say, on a mission to discover other humanoids—and he could bring only one *whatever* along with him, what would he choose?

Allie had asked her son this question some afternoon not too long before the end of the century, when everything seemed basically okay. The towers were standing. Kenneth Novey was alive. Sam was eighteen, and it was the summer before he left for college. The subject arose somehow in connection with his imminent departure for Russell College, where, though it was only an hour north, he'd be on his own.

"I'd take my piano," said Allie. "It came down to either you, the piano, and I decided that I wasn't comfortable letting you blast off into the galaxy. Too risky." (With the help of Tom's pickup truck, she had rescued the neglected piano from the side of the road that day. Retuned, it had been living with them ever since.) "Also, you have free will. I didn't know whether you'd want to explore the Final Frontier with your mom."

"Sexbot," said Sam. He was sprawled on the living room couch. There was nothing to do. The movies at the theater—the closest one, across from FDR's estate in Hyde Park—were all stupid, and he had seen them anyway. "The latest model of sexbot. Slut 9000."

Allie told him not to be an imbecile.

"The graveyard, then. I like the graveyard."

"You can't take landmasses to outer space."

"Too late. You should have said that in the first place. I'm packed. They're coming with me: the bones of the Huguenots, their gravestones, the moss, all the little trees and stumps and everything. Space is stressful. I'll need someplace to relax."

Allie, who was seated on the floor, drew her legs up to her chest and hugged them. She peered at her son over her knees. "Can I ask you something, kiddo?"

"Fine."

"Does it have to be so serious?"

"Does what have to be so serious?"

"Oh, art and everything. You have a very serious outlook."

"I don't know," said Sam, but really, he thought that it did. There was the fake, and there was the genuine; the former was abhorrent, and the latter was everything.

"I don't want you to be disappointed, doll. People are erratic," said Allie. "Who's that Swede you're so crazy about? The one who made the movie about the kids and the theater people and the dink priest, and there was all the icy scenery and everything? And the freaky puppets?

303

Remember, it went on so long it was dark when we started and dark when we finished, and I had to pee six times?"

"Ingmar Bergman. *Fanny and Alexander*. Eight hours is not a lot to give to an immortal cinematic masterpiece. You didn't have to watch it if you didn't want to." For such a smart person, his mother could be irritatingly obtuse, and he had to work to keep from getting angry with her.

"That's not what I saying. Christ, Sam. Give me a chance. I'm glad I saw it. It was beautiful and romantic, and every time I see snow at night, falling past a streetlamp or a lit window, I think about it again. Every snowy night, I think about it. At the same time, I wouldn't want to live there, you know? I need a little more levity day to day. It can't all be snow in the night."

"Okay, then," he replied, feeling hurt and superior. He was almost old enough to vote. "What movie would you like to live in? *Hard Mommies*?"

Her response was a burst of near-hysterical laughter that made Sam flinch. "You know what? There have been more than a few times when I'd have been very happy to live in *Hard Mommies*."

Amusement was Allie's fallback position from the beginning to the end. Sam had envied her coolness and mistrusted her acceptance and, to this day, couldn't quite fathom that she was dead. It was so easy to picture her lying on the red heap of a settee that used to be in their living room, head propped on fist, smiling slightly, and listening to something on the record player, maybe a Scott Joplin rag, or maybe just the fuzzy skip at the end of a side. While the specific question of how she could reject Bergman in favor of a gleefully soft-core seventies artifact like *Hard Mommies* (in which a group of PTA mothers open a sexy car wash to fight back against an encroaching mafia kingpin—played, naturally, by Booth Dolan in a piggish nose, a ponytail wig, and an oceanic pair of red-checkered pants) was no longer relevant, his mother's resolute satisfaction with her lot remained an enduring mystery. Allie had never graduated from college and never had a real career. Her marriage had failed. The modestly successful business that she had built from the floor up was abruptly shuttered following the divorce. In the aftermath, she patched together a living from substitute teaching and giving piano lessons to children. She volunteered for Family of Hasbrouck, stuffing bags of necessities. Save for her ex-husband and her ex-husband's friend Tom Ritts, Allie had no close friends. Then she was dead. Her body was slid into a furnace on a steel tray. No one objected to Tom's plan to till her ashes into a flower bed.

Sam had seen his mother weep once or twice, and she was surely depressed a few times, but if she ever said "I wish—" or "If only—" or in any way indicated a deep and lasting regret, it had not been in the range of her son's hearing. His only possible conclusion was that Allie had been content.

7.

The leaden morning clouds had partly evaporated, and the off-again, on-again rain was off again. Sunlight poked through here and there, and the wind was mild. Sam decided to go for a walk. Whether it was from everything that had happened, or from being in the car so much, he felt slightly feverish and wanted air.

Somewhere to his left, against the right side of Tom's house, around the corner from the big picture window, was where Allie's ashes were interred. Yellow and purple echinacea grew from the bed, tough and bright and spindly—the absolute right flower for Allie—but they had been cut to the ground. Sam passed by the bed and continued across the side yard in the direction of the woods.

At the back of the house, below the redwood deck that extended out on pilings, the ground fell away steeply before flattening out into forest. Most of the trees were green, though a few canopies showed a spattering of yellow and orange. At the foot of the hill, one towering sugar maple, leaves already showing a dozen shades of heat, stood out from the rest, a forerunner of change. Sam gave the big maple a knock on the trunk as he walked past and forged into the woods.

The same rail trail that backed up against the Huguenot graveyard ran along the eastern margin of Tom's property. After about a quarter mile of wading through deadfall, Sam reached the railroad embankment and climbed it easily.

The gravel-bedded trail tunneled beyond sight. The branches of the neighboring trees did not quite cover the path; a zipper of pale sky hung directly over the center of the lane. Sam's sneakers crunched softly. Probably due to the uncertain weather, he saw no one else.

It had been nearly an hour since Tess's last call. Perversely, this made him worry. Although he couldn't have expected her to keep calling him indefinitely, he had begun to anyway.

Sam fished out his cell phone, thumbed up the recent calls, and pondered the long accusatory column of her name—

Tess Auerbach 212-555-6161
Tess Auerbach 212-555-6161
Tess Auerbach 212-555-6161

—and found he didn't have the gall. He hoped maybe he'd have it in another few minutes—or better, maybe in the meantime, she would call again and he wouldn't have to do anything.

It crossed his mind then that, really, when it came to telling Mina what to do about relationships, he was standing on a hell of a wobbly leg. On one hand, he was carrying on an affair with another man's wife, and on the other, he preferred a person he might be interested in to keep calling him but not to, you know, speak with her. All Mina wanted to do was date a nice gay guy whose parents' apartment had a view of the park. What was so objectionable about that?

The thought of his sister led Sam to Wesley. It was well past time to ascertain if his roommate had been killed by the avalanche of boxes.

Wesley answered on the first ring. "Hey." Sam was taken aback. It was uncommon enough for Wesley to bother to answer the phone under any circumstances. It was unheard of for him to pick up on the first ring.

"Are you okay?" Sam asked.

"Mentally or physically?"

"Wesley. Just tell me if you're okay."

"I'm a mess. But what else is new? I'm bruised, but I'm alive. Forget about me. How's your old man?"

Without getting too involved, Sam explained that his father was not dying, that Mina had scammed him, that he had spent the morning and early afternoon with Booth, and that during their few hours together, Booth had healed the sick, fed the poor, and raised the dead. "Anyway," he said, "I guess I'll probably drive home tomorrow."

"I'm relieved that Booth's not dying."

"Yeah."

"Don't sound so happy, Sam. We're just talking about the man who jizzed you into existence. No one important."

"I would give anything to unhear what you just said."

"Someone needed to say it."

Based on their shared enthusiasm for eating, watching television, and doing both while taking up a whole couch, it was no surprise that Booth and Wesley got along famously. Both were also big fans of *The Prisoner*, the 1960s BBC television series about a spy held captive in a nefariously quaint hamlet where all of the inhabitants are referred to by number (the Prisoner's handle is Number Six) and anyone who tries to escape is attacked by large gelatinous bubbles. During their junior year at Russell, Booth had dropped by the boys' suite and ended up camping out for the better part of a weekend to watch the entire run. Several loaded pizzas and dozens of beers were consumed, and late into the night, amid a haze of farts, the two men collaborated on a deranged theory wherein the Prisoner was behind the entire scheme, that his desperate attempts at escape were put-ons, and he was the true mastermind of the Village (i.e., Number One). It was an existential Möbius strip; the actual "prisoner" was the viewer.

"But what's the point?" Sam had asked, drunk, incredulous, suffocating. "Why would he want to mindfuck us through our television like that?"

"Isn't it obvious?" With a smug smile, Booth turned to Wesley to answer the question, as if they maintained a telepathic link.

"Because he can," Wesley said.

"Wesley, that is exactly right: *because he can*. On the nose!" Booth cackled abrasively, and they toasted each other with cans of Bud Ice.

The black dot of a jogger appeared a few hundred yards down the trail.

"I'm sorry my sister tried to kill you," said Sam to Wesley. He added by way of consolation, "She beat up a bum, too."

"It wasn't the coolest thing that ever happened, I'll be honest."

"I'm sorry. For what it's worth, the bum got the worst of it."

"It did give me a chance to reassess things."

"It did, did it?" Sam smiled. Wesley was heroically full of shit.

"After Mina whipped my ass, I'm lying at the bottom of this pile, you know, shrouded in utter darkness, and I have this flash: I get all this free stuff, I have a job I love and that I excel at, I make my own hours. My mother still does my laundry. You clean the bathroom. All the cuisines of the world are delivered to my door. It's the perfect life—but I have no one to share it with."

The jogger, a heavyset bald man in a pink T-shirt with the sleeves cut off, huffed by on Sam's left, his footfalls like fists hitting a heavy bag.

"What do you think?" asked Wesley. "Am I ready to be loved?"

Sam didn't like to be discouraging, but he had misgivings. Choosing one at random, it was hard to imagine the woman who could love a man who clung so tightly to his urine-scented Popsicle pajama pants. He tried to be gentle: "I feel like, by any fair accounting, you're a handful, Wesley."

"Am I too much of a people pleaser? Is that it?"

They talked for a few more minutes, and Sam invited his friend to come up. In light of the Jo-Jo situation, Sam had been thinking that it might be in the best interests of his skeleton to stay clear of Brooklyn until Polly's husband cooled off.

Wesley actually said he'd consider it, which was surprising, because to do so would surely violate several items prohibited by the "List of Seventy-four Things That Cause Unnecessary Fatigue." However, before he committed to anything, he needed to weigh the pros and cons of a computerized flyswatter that delivered bons mots when you smacked it against something.

"Hey, did you hear any sirens or anything? From downstairs? That bum I mentioned, Mina took him down pretty hard." Sam opted not to confuse the issue by adding that he had chipped in by pounding the guy in the nuts.

A pause indicated that Wesley was taking the phone to the window with a view of the small courtyard. "Nope, no body. Either he got up on his own, an ambulance came, or the elves took his corpse, which is probably the best scenario."

"Good."

"Also this Tess chick called. Very intent on speaking with you, had to settle for me. We talked about you for a while. I did my best to put her mind at ease."

"What did she want to know?"

"If you were gay, stuff like that. If you had a history of heart disease in your family. Smart questions. I liked her."

"What did you say?"

"What do you think? I made you sound like a combination of Jesus, Springsteen, and Buck Rogers. Give me some fucking credit."

A middle-aged woman in jodhpurs trotted by on a horse the color of chocolate milk. A light wind shook the trees in a continuous hush. Sam was working up a sweat from the walk, and it didn't feel too bad.

Wesley had cheered him somewhat, but he still felt guilty about Jo-Jo. Although the man had threatened to saw off his hands, Sam's culpability in the situation was as manifest and unpleasant as roadkill. He'd had sex with a married woman—a mother—and he had jerked off while exchanging dirty messages with her over his cell phone. Though telling the guy to eat shit wasn't the most cretinous act he'd committed against Jo-Jo, it was definitely regrettable.

For months Sam had been wavering about the affair with Polly. The good humor that always held between them had grown vampiric; what once was playful repartee felt, finally, more like they were needling each other. It was cheerless on top of wrong, and he needed to end it.

A fence appeared ahead on the left, and when Sam reached it, he stopped and sat down on the path's gravel bed. He leaned back against chain links and let the fence bow and absorb his weight. Avoidance, Delay—call it whatever you want—Hiding might have been most accurate—his general strategy was no longer working.

Sam took his cell phone, picked out Tess's name, took a deep breath, and pressed dial.

"Hi," she said.

"It's been over an hour since the last time you called. What's the problem?"

"I remembered that I had a life. I was about to dial your number again, had my finger on the button, and it dawned on me: I have a life. By the way, before it slips my mind: fuck you very much, Sam. What you pulled last night, that wasn't nice." Tess's mild tone suggested that she had passed through considerable exasperation but arrived on the far side and settled into a state of dismal acceptance.

"Listen, I owe you an apology," said Sam. "I'm sorry about that."

Until he said it, he wasn't aware of how earnestly he meant it. She had tried to play it tough and loose at the wedding, but he didn't think that was what Tess was about. He thought she was basically a sincere person. She didn't deserve to be treated like a member of his family.

"I don't know, Sam," said Tess. "I've had plenty of guys run out on me, but I've never *actually* had a guy run out on me, you know? It's kind of dispiriting. It kind of made me feel like a prison guard or something. Like you had to get away from before I ate you."

"Don't think that. You seem terrific. I'm just—a fucking idiot. And a bummer. You're much better off."

"Thanks, I guess. I guess I accept your apology."

A few seconds of dead air elapsed.

"Is that it?" asked Tess.

Sam thought he detected relief in her voice. He hoped he was wrong.

"Can I be a little forward?" Sam asked. He supposed that he didn't have much to lose.

"Jesus Christ. When you put it that way. Yeah, go ahead. Ignore the flapping noise in the background. It's just me fanning myself."

"I really wish I'd gone home with you last night."

"That's optimistic of you," she said. "Insulting, too, now that I think about it."

"Be flattered," Sam said. "I'm not done yet."

"Go on," Tess said, "I'm listening."

"I have this vision of an alternate reality: we spend the night. Talk. Sleep in. Bagels from H and H. You think I'm pretty cool. My taste in movies impresses you. We make plans to find a Segway store and test one out."

"Wait, wait. Is this the alternate reality where I've got the virulent herpes?"

"Uh-oh."

"Be careful here, Sam. You made me feel bad enough."

"I've been thinking all day about how you touched my face."

He heard her breathing, but she didn't respond. The fence links were starting to hurt his back, so he leaned forward.

"You talked to Wesley," he tried.

"Yeah, I did. He's funny, your roommate. I sort of like him."

Sam said he had his moments. Tess asked if Welsey was fat, and Sam said, "Not that fat." Tess said she thought he sounded kind of fat on the phone. She enjoyed him, though. "Nothing against fat people. I just wondered." Sam asked if he sounded fat on the phone. "A little, maybe. Nowhere near as fat as your roommate," she said.

"Hey. Let's try, you know, really talking," he said. Where to start, though? With his transformed father? His dead mother? His sister, the angel of war? The stupendously thighed German-American athlete and used-car pitchman who had threatened to take his hands? With *Secrets Only Dead Men Know,* the show Tess produced, the diversionary TV garbage about the man trapped in his panic room? With Sam's movie and Brooks and the Arcadian creature of desire? With Sam's spoiled dream that had entertained so many people?

"Really talking." Tess inhaled. "Do we have to?"

Sam chose to go with the subject of Mina. Maybe Tess, as a former teenage girl, could provide some insight. "When you were a teenager, did you ever tell an unforgivable lie? Like say that someone you loved was dying? Anything like that?"

She asked if he was talking about his sister, the one who had texted him at the wedding, and Sam said he was. "I don't remember. I might have done something like that," Tess said. "I was pretty starved for affection. I even tried pen pals."

"Do you think that's what that is? A cry for affection?"

"That's my completely uneducated guess." She paused, then added, "Or it could be the first sign of a psychopathic mind."

"Good one."

"Ask a question, get an answer. I'm starting to like really talking. Next topic."

"I saw your show," he said. "About the guy in the panic room on Y2K."

"Oh. Kenneth Novey. I remember that one. The part about having nothing to read for months except that one issue of *Newsweek,* that gets to me every time. Good episode."

"It was, it was . . ." If by "good" she meant "impossible to turn off," there was no denying it: Sam had been totally hooked.

"But?" He heard Tess sip something.

"What does it say about us, about who we are, that we should enjoy something like that?"

"Hmmm," said Tess. "Hold on, hold on." She shifted again, and he heard her feet hit the floor. He listened to her walk around. He wondered if she was in her underwear.

"Damn. You know, I've been waiting for someone to ask me that question, and I have an amazing answer all ready, but naturally, now I'm blanking. Let me get back to you, okay?"

Sam said whenever. He wasn't going anywhere.

When he stood up, Sam noticed for the first time the field beyond the fence: it was dotted with pine saplings, each furry green antenna stabbing up from its own little hill of mulch. He pondered the sight for some seconds before it came to him that what he was looking at was once a junky railroad yard. There were no specific details to match up to his memory, but somehow he knew, and it was amazing. The mess of years had been swept away and given over to baby trees.

8.

Before entering Tom's house, Sam stopped in the driveway to remove his computer bag from the trunk of the rental car. It was around four in the afternoon. Sam grabbed a couple of pieces of Mina's luggage, too, deciding whether he wanted to or not, he would probably need to make a peace offering.

The stairs to the second-floor addition were to the right of the front door in a closed passageway. Sam ascended with the luggage, stepped onto the landing, and nearly ran into his godfather's chest.

Before he could speak, Tom made a *shh* gesture. He tilted his head across the hall.

Visible through the open door of the first room on the right was a four-poster bed on which lay Booth and Sam's sister. Booth was flat on his back on the far side, snoring lowly, his body forming a range of hills and dales beneath the comforter. On the near side of the bed, Mina was on her stomach, an arm dangling loose, silver-ringed fingers twitching. Apparently, his father's class preparations had not been too demanding.

The long-ago afternoons at Booth's Manhattan apartment came to Sam's mind, the naps he'd taken against his father's shoulder while, on the television, black-and-white actors moved through black-and-white worlds. He was happy for Mina that their father was actually some kind of father to her. The thought made Sam melancholy, but it made him glad, too.

Sam set down her bags and stepped forward to shut the door, pausing with his hand on the knob. Between beveled windows overlooking Tom's front yard was an antique escritoire laden with newspapers, crumb-speckled plates, and empty wine bottles. On the wall above the escritoire was the framed thirty-eight-year-old letter from the Hollywood Foreign Press Association, announcing Booth's Golden Globe nomination. There was a hairy, salty smell and some woody cologne. A pair of conspicuously large blue jockey shorts lay crumpled in a corner, strongly resembling a deceased devil ray that Sam had seen in a nature program about the effects of nuclear testing on aquatic species.

He gently closed the door. "So it's a permanent thing? The two of you living together?"

"I hope so. House is lonely." Tom reached up to pat Sam's shoulder. "You look healthy, buddy. It's a treat to see you. Always."

"He's changed, hasn't he?"

"He might have put on a few pounds. Booth's never been slender, though." Sam's godfather frowned. "Still can't manage to plunge a john, I'll tell you that."

"No, I mean, he's—"

"Mellowed some?"

They had been whispering, but now Tom accompanied his godson up the hall to the bedroom that he used when he visited.

"So what happened?" asked Sam.

"Two or three years ago, he called me, said he was ready to come home. I said great, and the next afternoon he moved in. That's it. He's been here ever since."

"He called you, and that was it."

"Yeah, he said he'd just seen a movie, he'd been thinking, and then he called me."

"Come on, Tom, you're not giving me much here. Are you sure he didn't mention anything about being visited by three spirits on Christmas Eve?"

Tom said that wasn't the kind of thing they talked about, he and Booth. "We're a different generation, buddy. We're not open about our feelings. We're of the old school." They generally stuck to work and food and the people they had known in the sixties—comfortable sub-jects. "And the movies. We watch a lot of television and movies, and we talk about that. You know those director commentaries on the DVDs? Booth's like my personal–director commentary. We just had a good talk about *E.T.*, you know. That flick takes me apart." Tom ran a hand up his long, smooth-shaved jaw, his mouth lowering into a frown of solemn appreciation. "Booth says Elliott and E.T. have a 'shared sense of loss.' I thought that was a good way to put it."

To Sam, all of the things that Tom mentioned sounded feelings-related, but maybe that was his misunderstanding of the old school. He thanked his godfather for letting him stay and excused himself so he could check his e-mail and have a nap.

There were three e-mails in his in-box: a query from a wedding coor-dinator (Subject: "Peckinpah wedding?"), a going-out-of-business-and-everything-must-go e-mail from Video Store (Subject: "the internet fucked us and now it is time to leave"), something from Polly (Sub-ject: "oops"), and something from Wesley (Subject: "Not sure how you'll feel about this"). Sam dropped the wedding coordinator's e-mail into his business file for later, wrote a quick e-mail to Video Store to say he wanted to buy the store copy of *Chimes at Midnight,* if they hadn't already sold it, and then clicked on the message from Polly:

> hey dollface,
>
> big, big oops! i left my cell phone out and jo-jo read your mes-sages :(
>
> he was NOT HAPPY! he's like, "i can't believe what a pervert sam is!" and i was like, "neither can i!!!" :P seriously though i am handling the situation. do not worry. jo-jo is a big softie once you get to know him, which, come to think of it, is probably the reason i have to go to you to satisfy my filthiest urges, perv!! more grist for my therapist, right???
>
> anyhoo I have HUGE NEWS!!!! rainer rolled over for the first time!
>
> xoxo,
>
> P

Attached to the bottom of the missive was a photo of Rainer lying on a pillow, shot from above. Nearly spherical in a tiny Yankees uniform, he scowled out of the frame. A caption beneath read, *I want to be just like my daddy!*

Sam pondered a response, but Polly was at her most redoubtable when the facts of a situation disagreed with her. To watch her decline to accept the reality of a stormy day at the beach—and Sam had—planting her umbrella and lying under it with an issue of *Lucky* as clouds of rain and spray dervished across the sand, was to witness a display of pure, positive willpower that was not to be underestimated.

If, therefore, anyone could convince Jo-Jo not to cut off Sam's hands and put them in his wooden collector's box, Polly was the one. There was not much Sam could do at this point except put his faith in her ability to bend reality and hope for the best.

The next e-mail, from Wesley, was under an hour old:

I know how you feel about the movie wanks and their message boards and such, but this came across my radar and I thought you should know. Condolences?

WESLEY

There was an accompanying link to www.whoweargot.com, Who We Argot: The Official *Who We Are* Fansite.

Wild enthusiasm, let alone rabid fandom, had never been Sam's bag, even before the catastrophe of *Who We Are*. Movies meant a great deal to him; he had seen *The Apartment* so many times that he sometimes recited the dialogue to put himself to sleep. Billy Wilder's comedy of business and sex gave substance to Sam's instinctive belief that the most anonymous existence—i.e., that of Jack Lemmon's office drone—could be as dramatic, as droll, as genuinely afflicted with conflict and pathos as any space captain's intergalactic quest. And he was delighted to discuss the film with someone who wanted to discuss it. But he had no urge to harass people at parties about *The Apartment*. No question was more inane than "How can you not have seen—?" be it *The Apartment,* or *Breathless,* or *Solaris,* or whatever. Such fervor was immediately offputting, desperate and tedious and, he thought, fundamentally mindless. People should be cooler than that, he felt, and if that made him an elitist, that was fine. Better to be an elitist than to be an Aldo; or worse, to be the kind of person who belittled an Aldo by reacting with amazement because the Aldo had not seen such-and-such's immortal, incomparable, towering cinema classic.

Such caffeinated talk was the coin of the realm at Who We Argot, an all-purpose meeting place and database for discussions, tributes, and screening locations, and the hub of the camp industry that flourished around his blighted film. On a few drunken nights, Sam had succumbed to the temptation and clicked away into the morning, laddering down through the message boards. There were numerous debates about Sam, about what he had intended, about whether he was an idiot or a twisted genius. (The breakdown seemed to be about fifty-fifty.) Other threads concerned ideas for sequels ("Okay, so at the start of the first act, the satyr's in the magazine section at B&N, just chillin', flipping through a *Paris Review*. He looks toward the ladies' magazines, and there's this centaur chick, and she's giving him a very frank up and down. Next thing you know, they're in a tattoo parlor . . ."), Rick Savini, the other actors, how to make your own horns and hooves without spending a lot of money, Russell College, experiences watching the film while under the influence of certain drugs ("I took a horse trank on 4/20 last year, passed out during the satyr's first jackoff, and came to twelve hours later in a puddle of my own doo-doo . . ."), and so forth.

It was, therefore, with a deep breath that Sam followed Wesley's link to a discussion under the log "BREAKING: SAD HORRIBLE TRAGIC NEWS." An administrator with the handle Thunder Shanks—profile pic of a chipmunk in shades and a porkpie hat—had posted the following:

We at the Argot are majorly, majorly bummed to report that Costas Mandell, the satyr, the genius in the furry leggings, the man who brought us all so much joy, has passed away at the age of 64.

A second link carried Sam to a 150-word obituary from the *Quentinville Weekly News* website:

Costas Michael Mandell, son of Kalogeros and Melinda, born in the coastal city of Piraeus, Greece, on September 4, 1951, died after an extended decline from heart disease. After a long spell in the maintenance department at Russell College, he worked as an associate at Gander Mountain in Kingston before retiring in 2006 due to poor health. A fine fisherman, Costas loved to cook what he caught and to share a chilled bottle of wine with friends on warm evenings. He was an avid moviegoer. Those wishing to pay their respects are invited to attend a brief graveside ceremony at the Quentinville Acres Cemetery on Quentinville Acres Road on Monday. In lieu of flowers, it is asked that donations be made to the Boys & Girls Club of America.

No mention was made of satyrs, Brooks Hartwig, Jr., *Who We Are*, or Samuel Dolan.

The news of Costas Mandell's death was flummoxing. Like an unexpected traffic snarl or an out-of-order elevator, it was an obstruction for which there was no leeway in a tight travel plan. Although Sam had spoken to him once, on that long-ago morning on the lawn in front of the Russell Film Department, the man was, to Sam, almost as much a creature of fantasy as the satyr he played. Now Mandell was to be buried, but what he was every day of his actual life—the unfilmed days— had instantaneously burned down to the paragraph of his obituary. The man's very being had never made sense to Sam, so how was he supposed to process the demise?

The answer was that he didn't know, couldn't begin to know, didn't know if he wanted to know.

Sam abruptly shut his laptop and set it to the side and climbed under the covers of the bed. "Nope," he said to the room. "Not thinking about that right now."

The bedroom was nominally his because his godfather insisted that it should be. However, it lacked the sedimentary quality of a true childhood room. There were no movie or band posters, no bulletin board of photos from his teenage years; the drawers of the built-in desk were empty. The only proof of Sam was a bookshelf with some Vonnegut novels that he had read, some Pynchon that he hadn't, a few high school textbooks, and the parked model of the P-51 Mustang that Tom had helped him build and that had somehow survived the intervening decades. The wing decals were curling slightly, but otherwise, it was in good shape. The whole space had a vacation smell of wood and dust and stale air. Late-day shadows painted the floor.

Sam closed his eyes and pretended that he was in his right place—a boy in the old house down the street from all those dead pilgrims, safe and mothered—in the time when he might have made different choices, followed different interests, become some other, better self, the right self for Tess and for everyone else, too. The narcotic stupor of daylight sleep began to draw him under.

With the coils and meters of his brain ticking down, Sam's guard was lowered enough to allow a passing thought of Brooks, wherever Brooks was, whatever glassy ward or seaside sanitarium. The assistant director appeared to Sam in a thick white robe, tucked into a deluxe chrome-appointed wheelchair and parked in a sunny spot. There was a peaceful set to his dozing face, and his eyebrows were still.

Sam felt a flaring of rage at Brooks, but it quickly dissipated to pity. What he did to Sam was awful. What he did to himself—inside, where the animal heads cackled and ridiculed, and the satyr wept, and the invisible documentary crew jabbed their cameras—must be worse.

Now Sam felt a pang of envy. Brooks had checked out. Brooks was worry-free. Brooks was in a big wheelchair in sight of the ocean, dreaming, well doped.

Another wheelchair creaked up beside them. Sam was in a wheelchair, too, sitting beside Brooks. The ocean below was choppy and gray.

"Jezebels," said Costas, by way of greeting. A nurse had rolled him up and parked him between the other two. Hooves protruded from beneath the lip of the dead man's robe. "Looks almost like some kind of art, doesn't it?" He pointed at the ocean.

Sam called to the nurse that he couldn't be thinking about this and would need to be moved. The nurse rolled him to the Brooklyn Bridge and parked him in the river wind. She yelled that she'd be back when she remembered her answer, and left to hail a cab.

His cell phone chirruped. He dug it out of the pocket of his jeans. "You took a cab . . ."

"It's Tess."

He opened his eyes; the digital clock read 4:31 P.M. "You remembered your answer? Why we enjoy awful things?"

"No, not yet—but I saw the thing about the satyr guy, and I called Wesley, and he said he'd tell you, but he wasn't sure how you'd take it." She cleared her throat. "And I just wanted to say that I'm really sorry for your loss, Sam."

Sam tried to work through this statement. It was like attempting to grasp a lug nut with his toes. "Shit." He rolled the blankets tighter around himself, locking his hand and the phone into place by his ear. "You know about my movie?"

"Yeah," said Tess, "I know. At the wedding, I actually recognized your name from your business card."

"That's all right," said Sam, trying to get the lug nut. He preferred to hold off on explaining his connection to *Who We Are* until a second date, but the revelation was pretty much inevitable.

"How are you holding up?" she asked.

"I don't think I've absorbed it yet. I suppose that in some sense, he's been an important part of my life, but I didn't really know him . . . So it's . . . multifaceted. I'm mostly just tired out. I was up at dawn and ran around with my father most of the morning and afternoon, and . . . I'm just tired. Let's, maybe—let's talk about the guy some other time?"

She said okay. Sam tried to raise his eyelids, but his eyelids stayed closed.

"Would it be weird if we talked about the Segway, then? 'Really talked'? I mean, given the circumstances?"

"I guess," said Sam, wondering if he was partly dreaming.

"Did you honestly think the Segway was worth the hype, or were you just jollying me?"

"I'm not a big jollier, Tess." Sam shifted within his cocoon, relaxing into a new, more comfortable position. "I don't know if it was worth the hype. I was just saying . . . it seemed pretty cool." He paused to yawn. He abandoned the lug nut. "I'm not a Segway expert, though. Never even driven one."

"My family exhausts me, too."

"Yeah?" The cocoon was warm and deep.

She had grown up in Massachusetts, near Braintree. Her mom was a social worker, retired now. Her parents had met in college, at UConn;

both were in student politics, her mom more than her dad. Her mom got arrested for handcuffing herself to the doors of the university's ROTC chapter. She was that kind of woman, Tess's mother; if her mind was made up to go right, you would have to haul her kicking and screaming if you wanted her to go left. She was a bomb thrower through and through. Tess's father was more of a gaping bystander. Of course, he had a job, he was an entertainment lawyer, apparently, he kicked ass at that, but the rest of the time, he was an unbearable misanthrope. Maybe all Sam needed to know about her dad was that he had this fetish about lingering by the checkout aisles at the health food store to count how many people talked on their cell phones right in front of the sign that said PLEASE DON'T TALK ON YOUR CELL PHONE. It was revolting, the delight he took in observing incivility, how it gratified his lousy opinion of humanity. But for Tess, it was an incredible grind to be near him, all of the negativity. So Sam probably wasn't going to be surprised to hear that

"We're leaving." A creature had crawled on top of him and was tapping his forehead. The room was pitch-black.

"No," he told the creature.

Mina flicked his nose, and Sam jerked away, upending her with a thud, and used his free hand to pull the blankets all the way over himself and create a protective enclosure. The phone was in his other hand. "Tess?" Sam asked into the receiver. His heart was slamming; his pulse was jittering around inside his neck. "Are you there?" Something was wrong, something was lost, something was broken; he was hot and frantic. Sam didn't know her at all, not really, but he needed her to be there.

And she was. "Yes," said Tess. "I'm here, I'm here."

He breathed. His pulse slowed. He smelled fabric, himself, the wood, the dust. The world locked back together. The fear left as abruptly as it had flowered.

Beyond the seal of his blanket, he heard Mina call him a spastic and say he had to be downstairs in fifteen minutes if he wanted to come to Booth's class. "Or stay. Whatever." The door banged shut.

"I'm here, Sam," said Tess.

"Thank you," he said. "Thank you."

"Are you okay?"

"Yeah. I'm okay." He threw back the blankets to blink his sticky eyes at the red digits on the bedside table clock: 6:17 P.M. They had been on the phone for nearly two hours. He had slept through everything about her. "Ah, shit. Have you been talking—"

"No. Once you started snoring, I shut up. You only missed about a half hour of my life story."

"I'm sorry. I'm really, really sorry. I was tired and—"

"I know," she said.

"Hold on," he said, but the line was already dead.

Allergic as he was to obligation, Sam tried to be polite. He held doors for women and waited for them to order first. He didn't automatically hang up on telemarketers. Even when people were blatantly wrong, he made an effort not to talk over them.

And though he held no illusions about his prowess, he was diligent about giving head and open to direction. If he wasn't drunk, he generally made an attempt to get up for seconds. If a woman he had hooked up with wanted him to, Sam was happy to stay until morning and to foot the bill for breakfast. Polly had teased him mercilessly for asking her, after the first time they screwed in the changing room of the Bergdorf's at the Shining Hudson outlet mall (conveniently located right off I-87), whether she wanted to grab a bite at the food court. "Oh, that is so chivalrous of you, Sam. All of sudden I don't feel like I just got fucked in a mall changing room. I feel like a princess."

Canny film editors sometimes use actors' reaction shots out of place; take an actress's come-hither smile originally filmed for a scene in the first fifteen minutes of a picture; and appropriate it for a moment in the last fifteen minutes, when she confesses her affair to her husband. In the late scene, the come-hither smile adds a note of defiance to the performance. It was a technique that Sam once would have used without hesitation, but these days, he wasn't sure he'd have the gumption. It was stealing, really, to take a smile like that for your own ends. Maybe that meant that he didn't have the stuff anymore, if he ever did.

When Sam called Tess back, the first ring sent him to voice mail. He recorded that he was sorry, that he wanted to be a good guy, that when you got right down to it, that was probably the biggest reason why he tried so hard to avoid entanglements like the one he found himself in with her. It was damned difficult going when you couldn't do whatever you wanted. He'd finally figured that out, he said. "I really like 'really talking' with you," Sam added, and finally let it rest.

It took him a few minutes to get up, wash his face, and regain his wits. When he did shuffle downstairs, he did so only to issue his regrets and officially resign from the evening's festivities. The most ambitious plan he could conceive of was to make a sandwich, drink a beer, and head back upstairs for more sleep.

They had already left anyway. On the floor in front of the door lay a blue index card with a message from Booth:

> Rest easy, my son. Perhaps some other time I can elucidate the subtexts of *E.T.: The Extraterrestrial* for you. We shall return.
> > Sincerely,
> > BD

Once he had made his sandwich and uncapped a beer, Sam went to Tom's study and had a seat on the cracked leather couch. On the wall to his left was a framed copy of the *New Roman Empire* poster—Horsefeathers Law dangling the pocket watch. Sam thought about directing his father that afternoon, the little note he gave him on the radio spot, and how Booth had gone right ahead and done it perfectly. It was silly, nothing, really, an ad for a sandwich joint, but in retrospect, Sam appreciated the moment. It was nice to feel useful. He tipped his beer in the poster's direction and swigged.

There was a plasma-screen television in the center of the built-in entertainment center on the facing wall. Sam turned it on to watch something while he ate. Because it was the weekend, he wasn't surprised to come upon another rerun of the Kenneth Novey episode of *Secrets Only Dead Men Know* playing on the same basic cable channel.

Novey rises from his panic room cot on the first morning of the twenty-first century, walks to the keypad by the vaulted door, punches the release button—and nothing happens. Two more times Novey jabs the button, but the keypad is black. "Uh-oh," says the voice of the ghost, "this is . . . problematic."

Sam's cell phone rattled: it wasn't Tess, it was Polly.

The possibility of ten or fifteen minutes of pleasant stroking, of Polly whispering about her fingers and her nipples, of her making noises that started in her chest and emerged in kitten squeaks, unraveled before him. He thought about it, and the idea was as abruptly and flatly unappealing as cold, melted yellow cheese.

Sam glanced from the shuddering phone to the screen. Novey has developed a deranged beard and is laughing hysterically because his *Newsweek* with the picture of a double helix on the cover has come unstapled. The wings of pages drift to the floor. Soon he will kill himself.

It seemed to Sam that here, right here, through the snow of pages, is the moment when an escape hatch ought to appear—a crawl space, a loose floor panel, some cut in the world that could be peeled back and squeezed out through.

The phone stopped ringing, then a few seconds later produced the burble that alerted him that there was a message.

On the television, the show went to commercial: Jo-Jo's pin-striped GTO fishtails out in front of a family of nerds in a minivan. "Hold on, yah?" The ex-catcher jumps from the car and rushes at the minivan. "No money down, my friends!"

Aware that he had made a choice, Sam picked up his sandwich and took another bite. The phone began to quake again. He went ahead and turned it off. If he was going to find his way back into Tess's graces, it probably wasn't going to be tonight.

The commercials ended, and the show returned. For the second time that weekend, Sam was beguiled by the reenactment of the senseless tragedy of Kenneth Novey and his malfunctioning panic room.

9.

Maybe it was related to witnessing Novey's entombment again, but Sam felt a sudden urge to get out, go somewhere. He didn't want to see Mina or Booth, or even Tom, not right then. He hadn't figured out how to talk to his sister, and he didn't know what to make of his father. If he called Tess again, he risked making it worse.

Sam decided to drive the rental car across town, have a pass by the cottage where he had grown up.

At Main, he caught a red. While he waited, he heard the sound of fireworks but didn't see them. To his left and his right, the orange street-lights cast spacey, acid-looking pools on the concrete.

On the other side of Main, he drove a half-dozen side streets, none of which he could have named but that, put together, formed the way home.

He parked curbside under a familiar, heavy-headed elm tree. The tree stood at the edge of a brief rectangle of lawn, which also held a darkened cottage with a white door and pewter-colored shingles that shone dimly in the night. A pickup truck sat in the driveway.

When he tried to imagine himself inside the house, Sam kept bumping up against furniture he didn't recognize. It was a place where some other people lived now. He put the rental back into drive and pulled away.

Up the street a few hundred yards, at the Huguenot graveyard, he stopped again. Inside the enclosure of the low rock wall, a couple dozen earthen humps and rocky shapes were visible in the dark. There were no lights or reflectors to discern the specific hillocks, piles, and grave-stones. (Costas Mandell, soon to be laid down in his own oblong of rest, came to mind—but Sam stayed fast and hurried him out as suddenly as he'd appeared, directing him to clop off the set and get into his trailer. Someone would notify him when he was needed.)

As Sam's eyes adjusted he thought he discerned a few white flowers scattered on the ground, little peels of luminescence—or maybe it was a trick of moonlight. There was nothing else to see. The dead were well buried.

A little wired—the unexpected ease with which he had slipped past the stomping grounds of his childhood and adolescence had stirred him— Sam went to the hookah bar-café, Smoke Me Drink Me.

The establishment contained nothing like a traditional table-chair arrangement; couches and oversize pillows were littered around, along with a few low tables. Shelves on the walls displayed burnished hookahs of different shapes and sizes. Concealed speakers played jazz at a low volume. Pieces of translucent fabric hung in front of the track lighting to filter the room in aqua light.

Where double doors used to lead to the theater proper, there was now a solid wall. In circling the block for a parking space, Sam had discovered that the entire rear of the original structure, where the seats and the screen once stood, had been leveled to create a municipal parking lot. He recollected Tom mentioning this development, maybe as far back as four or five years ago, but somehow or other, Sam had never seen or noticed. Not that there was a whole lot to see or notice; it was just a parking lot.

Inside, Sam drew away from the groups of younger people sharing bowls on the rugged floor, and carried the herbal tea that he had purchased up the stairs, through thin, flitting clouds of acrid smoke. An arrowed sign on the landing pointed TO THE PATIO.

On the second floor, the double doors remained. Sam stepped through to the balcony.

Though the theater had been razed, the balcony yet protruded from the building, in the form of a patio with one open side. What remained were two decks—upper and lower—linked by a brief set of stairs. The movie seats had been cleared away except for the front row. A drape of thick plastic sheeting hung from the roof to fall down in front of the balcony railing, presumably to keep out the insects.

Sam descended to the railing and chose a seat in the middle. He turned on his cell phone; there were ten messages from Polly. Whatever else, the day was certain to go down in his personal history as a bumper one for women wanting his attention. He clicked the phone off before she could get through again.

Through the plastic sheet, he could see the parking lot, his rental car and some other cars, a Dumpster, the rear of another building, and a small cut of sidewalk with a streetlight. He had a vague memory of his father taking him up here one time, predivorce. It was like an old reel without the sound elements—Sam could see the outline of his father's face against a red wall, but the conversation was gone.

If the day had proved that his father was different somehow—worthier somehow—then what was he supposed to do with Booth now? He couldn't exactly see himself calling Booth for advice. Sam tried his tea; he had added a lot of honey, and it was delicious.

"How's the movie?"

The springs of the neighboring seat twanged as a girl dropped down beside him. Sam recognized her from that afternoon—she was the one with the spiderweb on her face.

In the gloom, her swan neck was particularly white and sinuous. The way the web carved up her face produced a multifarious effect that made it hard to meet her gaze straight on for longer than a second or two. It was like she was looking back from all her different sections; not that it was ugly or scary or threatening, but it was somehow insistent, strongly insistent. Immediately, Sam wanted her to like him.

"I'm not sure I get it. I keep waiting for something to happen, but so far, it's all parking lot. I do like the plastic drape—it gives the scene a cool little blur."

She had a careless grin that tiptoed right up to the edge of a smirk. "Oh, it's an arty film?"

"That's right. We should be seeing Europeans having sex any second now."

This earned him a throaty smoker's chuckle. She patted her stomach; there was a small bulge. "I hope you don't have any ideas. I'm taken."

"I'm Sam." Since he didn't know precisely how the so-called local children viewed Booth, Sam thought it safest not to mention their relation.

"Bea." They shook. "I hope you don't mind the company. My friends are communing with the spirits. It freaks me out. I'm afraid a ghost will get offended and I'll end up giving birth to a Satan baby."

Sam scratched his head.

"Ouija board," Bea added.

"Oh, that's dumb," said Sam, and she said, "I know, I know."

The new acquaintances sat in silence and stared at the parking lot. A skunk stalked onto the little stage of street between the buildings but didn't break pace, just continued off left.

"So that's it," she said. "The skunk survived. The end. Lame, dude."

Sam said that for some reason, the skunk had him thinking of the end of Antonioni's *Blow-Up*. She asked what happened at the end of *Blow-Up*. He asked if she was sure she wanted to know, and Bea said yeah, go ahead, and Sam said it was a classic, and she said, "Don't be a tease."

"Okay." He leaned forward, rubbed his hands together. "The protagonist of the film, he's been wrapped up in this kind of—I don't know, there's been a mystery, right? Let me see if I can remember. It's been a while. Right: so there's this guy—"

"Amazing so far. No way I'm getting up to pee—"

"Shut up. This guy, he may have witnessed a murder. He's a photographer, a very slick operator. He's the main character, and it definitely seems like there was a murder that he saw in this park. Seems that way, but it's actually not definite. And this is the sixties, the swinging sixties, London. But someone breaks in to the photographer's place and steals the photos that might be evidence of the murder. Also, there's a woman, Vanessa Redgrave, who has been on his case, and she's a big mystery, too. But still. It's not clear. He never figures it out one way or another what's truly happened, if maybe nothing's happened."

"And that's the end?" Bea grimaced. "Thumbs-down."

"No, no," said Sam. "Hold the fuck on. The end is that the photographer, he finds himself by these tennis courts. A group of mimes happens along. And they all start playing mime tennis."

"That's it? Mimes playing tennis?" Bea rubbed her webbed forehead as if it ached. "Mega-thumbs-down."

Sam shook his head. "That's still not quite it. There's one more thing: *he hears the tennis balls*. He hears the balls bouncing, hitting rackets. That unmistakable tennis sound. And so the guy, our hero, he joins in."

"It's meta-tennis," said Bea.

"It's an acquiescence to the unknown."

The girl with the tattooed face sprawled back in her chair. "So deep." She pretended to make herself barf.

Sam couldn't restrain a smile. "You haven't even seen it!"

"I don't mean to sound like a philistine, but it's a cop-out. 'Oh, I can't figure out an ending! Mimes playing tennis! Life's a big old mystery!' You could quit on any story at any time and use that ending. Seriously, what's the point? Mimes? Mimes are everything that is wrong with everything."

"I guess the point is that we can't ever be sure that something is exactly what it seems, and—mimes. Huh. I might not have done it justice. I haven't seen it since college." The ambiguity once appealed to Sam, the unsettled quality, the lingering question of what was real and what wasn't real and whether there were invisible forces at work. Now, through her eyes, it was, well, a bunch of mimes playing tennis.

"So what was the connection with the skunk, Mr. Movie?" Bea laughed. And how long ago was he in college—a hundred years?

The amiable tattoo-faced girl asked Sam to come down and meet her friends. "I need some backup in case they got possessed while they were fucking around with the Ouija. It's always the pregnant woman that the ghosts most want to get their hands on."

Sam agreed; he was curious to meet her friends, and he wasn't afraid of spectors. If, to take an example, ghosts were real, that meant Brooks Hartwig, Jr., was the sanest person he had ever known; and to take another, if there was a way for the dead to communicate with the living, Sam had no doubt that he would have heard from Allie by now, to offer her opinion on a whole range of issues from his grooming habits to his brooding to, most recently, his shoddy treatment of Tess Auerbach. "Sure," he said, "I'll come say hello to these spiritualists."

Downstairs, the boy in the checkered pants, the girl who had been strumming the guitar, and a couple of others were gathered around a coffee table covered in a drape of silky yellow fabric and situated in a small alcove at one side of the lounge's main room. The Ouija board had been set aside, and they were sipping from steaming, widemouthed ceramic cups. Sam and Bea brought over a couple of pillows to sit on.

Bea introduced him to the group, and everyone said hello. He noted right away that the boy in the checkered pants was wearing what must have been one of the T-shirts that Booth had given away: it bore a reproduction of the poster for *Buffalo Roam*, showing a white buffalo standing in a line at a hot dog stand along with a Native American in a feathered headdress, a hippie girl in fringe, and a boy holding a red, white, and blue balloon. A teaser read, "A Legend of America!" Sam knew if you looked closely at the credit block at the bottom that Booth was the last listed actor: "and Booth Dolan as 'Dog the Cloud.'" It almost made Sam laugh, not because of the movie—an inarguably tedious stoner epic that made the overrated *Easy Rider* look like *The Rules of the Game*— but because he was imagining all the street kids uniformly dressed in Booth's T-shirts. It was as if Booth had adopted his own fucked-up Little League team. The girl, who had been strumming the guitar, Elsie, had the *Devil of the Acropolis* poster on her shirt.

"I thought you were communing with the dead," said Bea.

The boy in the checkered pants rolled his eyes. "Elsie kept screwing around."

"I did not!" Elsie objected.

The boy, whose name was Josh, explained that they had been contacted by a ghost named Sarah. Sarah had said she was waiting for the bingo to start, and it was sweet of them to say hello, but she hoped they understood that she would rather just sit quietly and read her James Michener novel. After that the pointer had gone still. "And by still," said Josh, "I mean that was when Elsie stopped making up random stuff."

Elsie protested. "Don't be a shitnose! I didn't make up anything!"

Everyone at the table offered an opinion on the legitimacy of the Sarah ghost. The general consensus was that it was awfully mundane; haunts were supposed to be, well, haunted, not waiting for bingo. Bea asked Sam where he stood.

He had been thinking the opposite, that it made more sense that a soul might get stuck in a habit as opposed to turning into some window-rattling, mirror-breaking poltergeist out for vengeance. If he imagined himself as a ghost, Sam couldn't picture himself doing anything except what he usually did—eat, watch television, fantasize about women. "I guess if I believed in ghosts, yeah, I could believe that they were hung up on bingo," said Sam. "People get in ruts, right? They get stuck."

They drank tea and joked about their hang-ups. Josh said he couldn't sleep without a fan; he was a slave to his fan. Elsie said she was addicted— no, seriously, addicted like a crackhead is addicted—to ChapStick. For Bea, the problem was her boyfriend's butt: "I just have to pinch his ass. It's so lowbrow." When it was Sam's turn, he said it was difficult to pick a single hang-up, he had a whole bunch: he found it difficult to think of his sister as a young adult; he was hung up on an accident that had happened years ago, still felt it almost every day, like fingers on the back of his neck; there was a friend he had a hard time saying no to; his father drove him so nuts that when he actually didn't drive him nuts, it was confusing; and there was this girl, Sam wasn't sure what that was about, but he couldn't stop thinking of her.

10.

In Tom's driveway, he listened to 1010 WINS—"Give us ten minutes, and we'll give you the world"—until the news wrapped around. The economy was teetering, the polls were negative, football players were injured, the weatherperson hoped they had enjoyed the official last day of summer because real fall weather was on the horizon, and after that the economy again. Wesley had said to him once that when 1010 WINS flipped over, he suffered a pang of existential sadness. "Like, that's everything. I'm abreast of everything of significance. I can fit the whole planet in my pocket."

Sam found reassurance from the compaction and aggregation— here was all the important stuff, nothing but important stuff, selected and pruned by professionals. And the news could be worse; the economy wasn't definitely sunk, and fall weather was better than summer weather. He would take it.

His own uncertainties—whether Tess was going to give him one more shot, or when it would be safe to go back to his apartment, what he might do tomorrow—remained uncertain. But just admitting out loud that he wasn't doing so wonderfully made him feel like maybe he was already doing better, or about to. The urge to call Tess to share the feeling was not easy to resist. Had she remembered the answer to his question yet, the reason why it was okay for Kenneth Novey to die again and again, and for viewers to take pleasure from it? Sam really wanted to know, wanted to "really talk" about it. She had to give him another chance, didn't she?

The only lights he saw on in the house were from the second-floor hall. Somewhere behind the rental, out in the street, a car rolled past making those growling, popping, barely restrained sounds that racing-type engines make.

Inside, he removed his shoes and started up the dark stairs. He assumed everyone was in bed. A few steps up, however, Sam heard a thumping. There followed a terrible hacking, as if some animal were fighting to regurgitate a large chunk of meat. Sam went back down the stairs. It was a busted-dishwasher sound; he wanted to be sure that nothing was running broken and making a mess.

The kitchen was empty, the lights off, nothing running. The noises grew closer, wetter, and more disturbing. "So wrong," someone half-spoke, half-moaned. Sam identified the voice: Mina.

Off the kitchen, a wide hall ran the right wing of the house: first there was a room with nothing in it but an armchair and a dead fern, then a room with some boxes and a pretty window seat, then Tom's bedroom, then Tom's study, and finally, a door that led out to the redwood deck. Sam poked his head around the doorway of the first room. The fern's withered leaves were briefly electrified by a splash of headlights from out in the street, but there was nothing living in the room.

His sister said, "So, so wrong." The sounds were coming from the study.

"Hm-hm-hm." This noise of assent belonged to Tom.

Several quiet paces carried Sam by the next two rooms and to the entryway of the study. The door was half open. Sam spied his sister, his godfather, and his father seated side by side on the leather couch. Because they were facing the plasma screen in the entertainment center, his view was of the back of their heads: on the left, Mina's jagged, glossy shoulder-length hair; in the center, the trim yellow-gray reverse beard at the bottom of Tom's skull; and at the right, Booth's bushy white curls.

Who We Are was playing on the television.

Roger is on the footpath to the parking lot. He is talking to his father on a cell phone. "What are you talking about?"

"Your mother. There was an accident." The voice-over takes a harsh breath. "She is . . . She's gone."

Roger lowers the phone and scratches his temple, considering. When he raises it, the cell is a newer, smaller model. "Nice try, fatso. You nearly had me." He hangs up before his father can reply.

"Who was that?" asks Claire, catching up to him.

There is a cut to the forest.

The late Costas Mandell, in his hooves and leggings, is on his knees, in flagrante delicto; he is ramming a hollowed log. His ass is very pale and loose-skinned. It slops up and down in time to his thrusts. He huffs and snorts. Around him the greenery is verdant, punctured here and there by pipes of sunlight winding with motes. An oblivious sparrow perches on a birch branch and preens its wing.

When the satyr speaks, his delivery is full of foreboding, cracking with strain. "I am—your—darkest hour, my friends. I am—your—hardest feelings—come to flesh."

God, he was good. It always startled Sam, momentarily made him forget and just marvel, Mandell was so damned good. He was otherworldly and brokenhearted, and his commitment was incontestable. He was fucking a dead tree.

There was another thump—Booth's shoe pounding on the floor. His hands flailed upward, waving and flapping, like a sinner's at some old-time tent revival, reveling in the glory. The breathless regurgitate sounds were coming from him; they were the sounds of laughter. The laughter was the kind that looked like agony: turning the face purple, accompanied by tears and kicking and thrashing. It was the kind of laughter that felt like agony, too—suffocating—and also felt wonderful, untethered, mad in a way, mad-happy. That was how Booth was laughing, like he was nearly choking on his mirth.

Sam edged away.

The sense of betrayal, the simple horror of the scene—of the three them watching it and Booth laughing that way—numbed him. He was angry, but somehow too angry to inhabit the feeling. He could see it, though, his anger, tall and burning and growing taller.

He retreated through the kitchen, continued on to Tom's massive living room, and sat on the couch in the dark. His vague thought was that he could sit there, concealed, and bide his time. When Booth eventually came around the corner, he could jump out and confront him. Whether Sam was going to hit him, or yell at him, or simply stare at him without speaking—stare and stare and stare—he couldn't know yet.

Framed photos hung on the walls: of Tom and Booth on a beach in California; of Booth dressed as a buccaneer; of adolescent Sam in an apron, playing baker at the Coffee Shop; of Mina wearing sunglasses; of Allie grimacing with her hands on her hips and a licorice string dangling from a nostril. Moonlight through the picture window spilled emulsion across the images and made ghosts of the figures.

The living room stretched the length of one side of the house, like a bowling alley. Another picture window spread the far wall, opening onto the deck and the woods. Darkened branches hatched across the view.

Sam had known better, or he ought to have. That was what he kept thinking, what his anger said. Hadn't it happened over and over again? Why should tonight be unlike any other time? Why should it be different than when he was ten and Booth had turned on him on the train? Why should it be different than when he was eleven and Booth said he was coming home and didn't? Or when he was thirteen, or fifteen, or sixteen, or twenty-three? It dawned on Sam that Brooks had just been a stand-in for Booth. Brooks had wrecked the movie nearly as well as Booth wrecked everything else.

Sam sat on the long couch under the street-side picture window. The room smelled like vacuuming.

Headlights raked across the wall: Tom and Booth had sand in their chest hair, and the ocean in the background was indigo; there was a gold hoop in the buccaneer's ear; frosting streaked the front of Sam's apron; Mina's movie-star sunglasses covered almost half her face; and what looked like a grimace before was, in the headlights' beams, clearly a smile that Allie was trying to hold at bay until the shutter snapped.

Sam rose, raised a forearm to shield his eyes, and looked out the picture window. A GTO idled on the lawn, perhaps twenty feet away. The vehicle's headlights insinuated the barrel of a shotgun. The combination of the glare and the dark reduced the driver, Jo-Jo Knecht, to a vague, blurry shape behind the windshield.

The headlights flickered high-low-high, causing Sam to jerk and twitch involuntarily. The GTO's horn yelped and the engine revved.

He was telling Sam to come outside.

Sam thought about Jo-Jo, and about Jo-Jo's thighs, and about the detailed description Jo-Jo had given of his "special trunk." Sam thought, Certain death. He thought, There is no way I am dying until I tell Booth whatever it is I need to tell him. He thought, Tess.

High-low-high, the headlights flickered for a second time.

Sam shook his head slowly back and forth: No.

The car leaped forward a few feet and stopped, like a frothing attack dog brought up short by its chain.

They were causing his eyes to water, the GTO's headlights. In an automatic reaction, Sam put up his other hand and gave Jo-Jo the finger.

The GTO shot ahead—chain snapping—and Sam dove left.

A torrent of glass, wood, and chunks erupted behind him as the GTO exploded through the picture window, accompanied by a monumental tinfoil rip and the prehistoric roar of a V-8 engine. Sam, asprawl near the sitting room's entrance, twisted to see the sports car shoot past, and saw the couch he had recently been sitting upon melded to the fender like a plow. For a second Jo-Jo was perfectly profiled in the driver's-side window, and then he was gone. White dust snowed down. Reams of plush beige carpet, torn from the floor, shot out and up in the wheels' wake, scrawling through the air like streamers. The pictures dropped from the wall, their breaking glass muted by the engine's backwash. Only one picture stayed—Allie, holding back her smile—dialing around on its hanger by some trick of centrifugal force. The pin-stripes on the car's flank lingered a moment on the surface of Sam's vision in faint waves of distortion.

The GTO blew the length of the room, coated in debris, echoed by the undulating carpet fragments. There was a shrieking of brakes, but it lasted a quarter beat at most before the car hit the far picture window and went through, out into the night. An immense crackle followed, the thudding of heavy objects falling from heights, tinkling glass, and last, a short, impotent burp of horn.

Exhaust and dust mingled in Sam's nose and mouth. Bits stung his face. The room stormed, and Allie spun.

11.

The GTO was netted in the crown of the great sugar maple, thirty or so feet off the ground. In the wash of the deck's powerful floodlights, the car was plainly visible, suspended at a slight front-end-up diagonal, its single working headlamp beaming a fuzzy white cone into the night sky. Resting in the branches a few feet below the car, on the other side of the maple, was the couch. It was broken in the middle but evidently held together by its fabric covering. Pieces of siding and tufts of insulation littered the branches. In Sam's eye, the scene inspired an unending stream of images: a woman with a bat in her beehive hairdo; a Christmas tree decorated with garbage; a fearful boy hiding up a telephone pole from bullies searching below; and so on.

As far as Sam could figure, what happened was this: as Jo-Jo's car exited the picture window, shooting outward from high on the hill, its downward arc had been swiftly interrupted by the lofty maple, which rose from the bottom of the slope. There was a faint, plopping drip. The GTO's engine was mortally pierced in the smashup, and the maple's trunk was coruscated with black ooze.

Sam and the others clustered on the flat ground near the tree. The overcast summery day had faded to a cool fall night. Above and to their right, around the deck pilings and on the slope that led down from the house, chips of broken glass lay everywhere. Where Jo-Jo had made his exit was a roughly star-shaped puncture in the side of Tom's house.

Mina had taken a spot on the grass with her knees drawn up, hugging herself and rocking against the chill. Booth was leaning on his cane, periodically shaking his head, and then rubbing hard and deep at his beard, as if he meant to flush out a gnat. Tom, characteristically, had reacted without heat to the attack on his house. Once he had inspected the hole, he announced rather cheerfully, "Okay, I can fix this," and went to fetch a beer, which he stood drinking.

Sam yelled up to Jo-Jo: could he hear them? The vehicle's body was hammered and veined, stretched in places like taffy. The driver's-side door creaked open, and Jo-Jo Knecht—World Series hero, proud Yankee, cuckold—leaned out.

A dark fork of blood leaked from his nostrils. Although his face was wide and rounded, his features were pinched so that even under normal circumstances, he tended to look mildly nonplussed. Currently, his eyes were so huge that they were nearly knocking together. He blinked at his wife's lover. "I'm in a car in a tree," he said.

"Are you badly hurt?" asked Sam.

"I'm in a car in a tree." Jo-Jo made a high-pitched noise. It was not a giggle or a sob but contained aspects of both. "I'm not, you know, super, yah?"

In the five or so minutes since Polly's husband had attempted to make him a hood ornament, Sam was surprised to find that he was not more surprised—maybe it was shock? His chief sense was of wonder. As Jo-Jo had pointed out, he was in a car in a tree—along with a couch and many fragments of Tom's house. Also, it was heartening to encounter someone who was an even greater disaster than Sam himself.

"We're going to get you down," said Sam.

"Cool!" The man in the car in the tree found this sidesplitting. "I'll just hang out, yah?" He beeped the horn and flicked his one remaining headlight high-low-high across the treetops.

Mina, who had been silently staring up and pondering the hole in the wall of the house, yawned. "It looks like Mr. Kool-Aid broke through, doesn't it?"

"It does, doesn't it," said Tom. "I haven't thought about Mr. Kool-Aid in years. Is he still around?"

"Oh yeah, he's still around," said Mina. *"Oh yeah."*

"I really feel that we should call the police, or at least the fire department." Since he had come outside, Booth had yo-yoed sharply between fury and tears.

"No. We're not calling anyone," said Sam. What had happened was, at least partially, his fault. Jo-Jo had not been justified, but he had been wronged. If the accident ended up in the papers, it was hard to believe that the Yankee organization would look kindly on one of its employees taking a shortcut through someone's living room. Add in Sam and Polly's affair, and the headlines in the *Post* practically wrote themselves: GOOD GERMAN, BAD DRIVER; THE CATCHER WAS A CUCKOLD; ICH BIN EIN WHACK-JOB; AUTOBAHNED! YANKS YANK KNECHT AUF AIR!

Booth rushed at the base of the tree. "Fine! Then why don't we leave him there! Let him try to survive the winter up there! Let the owls pick his bones!" He whacked the maple's trunk several times with his cane as if to shake the car loose, like a wasp's nest.

"You're going to give yourself a heart attack, Booth." Tom gently hooked his friend's elbow and drew him away.

"Hey," said Sam. "Everybody. Be quiet." It wasn't a yell. It was a simple command, spoken clearly and firmly. Adrenaline had its limits. The mess had to be sorted before everyone was too tired. "I need you, please, to be quiet and listen."

"That fucker tried to kill my son, Tom!" Booth dabbed a piece of his cape at his eyes. He turned to Sam. "He tried to kill you, Sam." A fragment of yellow leaf had gotten stuck in the old actor's beard.

"Dad," said Sam. "I'm okay. I promise. Are you okay?" He spoke to his father as gently as he could. Right then he couldn't be concerned with what he had seen in the study; for the sake of everyone, right then he could worry only about what had to be done.

His father frowned, blinked several times, and allowed a reluctant nod. Sam patted him on the shoulder. "Thank you."

In the next couple of minutes, Sam swiftly directed the members of the crew to their respective tasks.

Mina was charged with gathering up the couch cushions scattered about the backyard. Tom was sent to fetch the two blow-up mattresses that Sam had seen tucked in the coat closet. Booth was told to station himself at the foot of the driveway to intercept any police. It was late, and the house was set fairly far from the road, but it wasn't inconceivable that someone might drive by, notice the Mr. Kool-Aid hole in the wall, and call the cops.

"What do I tell them?" his father asked.

"You'll think of something."

"Hmm," said Booth. "Very well."

As soon as his father disappeared around one side of the house, Sam heard shoes tromping around the other side. There was the crumble and slide of dirt and gravel, a baby's burble, a sneeze.

Tess moved into the light. Behind her was Wesley, and last was Polly, bearing Rainer in a Björn.

"Sam!" cried Polly, rushing ahead of the other two. "You're alive! For God's sake, will you please answer your phone the next time my husband is planning to assassinate you? I know it's partly my fault, I told him this is where I thought you'd be hiding, but as soon as he got all his weapons together, I called to warn you."

Sam apologized. "I was watching *Blow-Up* with a friend."

"You were ignoring me, is what you were doing." Polly threw a surreptitious thumb back toward Tess and winked at him. She mouthed, "She's so great! Go you!"

The GTO's horn bleated. "Get lost, whore!" Jo-Jo screamed. "Get away from my tree!"

His wife walked within a few yards of the maple to gaze up and address her husband. "Jo-Jo. Look at you. You're hung up there like a kite. What are we going to do with you?"

"I don't know," he said. "Fuck you. You broke my heart."

Rainer chattered in baby and shook his tiny fists.

Jo-Jo was heard to blow his nose on something. "Hello, *sohn*," he called down to the child.

Tess touched Sam's elbow. She wore a puffy green vest, and her black hair was loose around her shoulders. The pebble of a gem at her nostril was flickering between pink and purple, and her mouth was tight. She was gorgeous and perturbed. "I called Wesley, and he mentioned that he was thinking about taking the train up, and I was worried about you, so I tagged along. Our taxi dropped us off just a second after your mistress and her infant pulled in."

An apology would have been worthless, and an excuse would have been offensive, so Sam was blunt. "I'm glad you're here," he said. "I hope you'll stay."

"I know you are, and I know you do." Her tone made it clear that she herself was less sure.

She jammed her hands in her vest pockets and walked over to stand beside Polly. Their talk made puffs in the air. Sam was simultaneously curious about their conversation and relieved that he couldn't hear it.

"Evening, fuck-snot." Wesley was wearing a wrinkly red button-down with a frilly napkin thing tucked into the collar. The frilly napkin thing looked like what French kings wore when there were French kings. "What can we do?"

Sam gestured at the napkin thing. "You forgot to take off your bib."

"It's a jabot," said Wesley.

"It's a bib," said Sam. "Now go help Tom with the mattresses, and maybe grab an armful of blankets, too."

"No problem." Wesley yelled over to Tess to run up to the house and help Tom with the mattresses and to try and find some blankets, too.

By one in the morning, they had the couch cushions and the inflated mattresses laid out to create a crash pad, with blankets and some movers' quilts from Tom's garage piled on top. Jo-Jo tested the pad by dropping some objects that he had in the front seat of the GTO: an oversize roll of black garbage bags, a bone saw, and an ornate wooden chest about as wide and deep as a milk crate. All three items were reasonably heavy, thumping down into the plush surface and bobbing up with no problem.

Sam asked Tom what he thought.

"So long as he doesn't miss, he should live." Tom was halfway through a six-pack. Grinning, he added, "Probably break his legs, though."

Jo-Jo, thinking along similar lines, hollered to the people below: "I'm going to get paralyzed!" He had swung his legs around to dangle out the open door. With one hand, he gripped the upper edge of the door, and with the other, he had hold of a branch. The GTO appeared remarkably secure in the clutch of the tree.

The ex-ballplayer's mood had shifted erratically in the course of his ordeal. His fury at Polly had preceded a sullen period during which he hurled coins from the GTO's console in an attempt to wing Sam and instead nicked Wesley in the cheek with a penny. Lately, Jo-Jo had become fatalistic. "Get Rainer out of here, yah? I don't want him to see me die."

"It doesn't matter. His declarative memory isn't there yet. Whatever happens, sweetheart, I promise Rainer won't remember any of it," Polly replied, perhaps not as helpfully as she might have. (Rainer was actually asleep in the Björn, drooling, his crown and ears snugly encapsuled in an orange hat with a green stem that was meant to suggest either a carrot or a pumpkin. Either way, it was darling.)

Now, with the extraction nearly at hand, Sam worried that Jo-Jo's next shift would be into a state of panic. Sam cupped his hands around his mouth and called, "Jo-Jo! I need you to take a few deep breaths, man. You can do this."

"No, no. You can do this, dude. You can do this, yah? You can jump without a parachute and get paralyzed."

Sam was tired. His nose was cold, and his body was sore. Wet had seeped through his sneakers and soaked his socks. They were all of them wrung out from running up and down the slope. It was late, time to wrap it up. Sam squeezed his fists and pressed his tongue hard against the back of his teeth.

Tess came to stand beside him. She was regarding him in an expectant way. The arc lights traced violet waves in her hair. Her attention fortified him. Sam nodded to her and redirected his attention to the man in the tree. "Jo-Jo, you're going to be fine! All you have to do is let go and fall."

"It's not so easy, dude!" Jo-Jo was shifting around at the open door, swinging his feet, trying to work himself up to it.

"If you just jump straight, everything will be okay."

Jo-Jo kicked his legs back and forth and seemed to inch forward slightly. After a few seconds, he visibly slumped. "Ah! Can't do it, dude."

Tess groaned. "We're never getting this Kraut out of the tree, are we?"

"Hey," Sam called up. "Hey, hey." He inhaled.

Sometimes you needed what you needed. It wasn't about you, though. It was about the crew, about all the people who worked to make it possible, and their effort, and their belief in the common goal. The director's responsibility was to that shared investment. When persuasion bumped up against necessity, the director had to make sure that necessity won. Sam had been wrong to leave Brooks out in the rain all those years before; but he had been absolutely right to whip Wyatt across the face with the rolled-up script.

He made a bullhorn with his hands. "Jo-Jo! Thunder thighs! If you don't come down out of that goddamned tree in the next three seconds, I am coming up to get you!"

By the last word out of Sam's mouth, Jo-Jo was flying. Arms spread, legs tucked, his silhouette was awesome, superheroic. He resembled a frog uncoiling. As he fell, his scream lengthened into a screech, then cut off sharply as he struck the crash pad, the resolute thump like the sound made by a hard ball settling into a soft mitt.

Whether because of the dual impacts—the crash and then the fall—or because of the situation in general, Jo-Jo emerged from the pile, deflated. "I see what you did," he said.

Sam reached out and pulled him upright. "Sorry." Jo-Jo said it didn't matter.

Sam walked up the slope alongside Jo-Jo, while Polly ran ahead to put Rainer into his car seat. "You feel all right?" Sam asked.

Jo-Jo said yeah. He'd been in worse crack-ups. "I just want to go home, yah?"

Sam wanted to say something to cheer or divert the man, whose discouragement was made manifest by the heavy sighs that accompanied each step up the hill. It was dicey, though, trying to find the right morale-boosting approach for the person whose wife you'd fucked and who had attempted to murder you. Sam settled for repeating that he was sorry.

"Yeah," said Jo-Jo. "Me, too."

When they arrived at the driveway, Jo-Jo lifted a hand in vague fare-well to the assembly and, without speaking, accepted the keys to the Knecht family SUV from Polly and climbed into the driver's seat. Seconds later, the Knechts were on their way home to Westchester County.

That left the rest of them in the driveway, a few yards from the GTO-size opening in the street-side wall of the house. Booth had walked in from the street—no sign of police—and stood propped by his cane. Wesley and Tess leaned against the hood of the rental car. Mina had lugged up the bone saw in its hefty plastic case and taken a seat on it.

"Good job." Sam's godfather clapped him on the back.

"You guys ready?" Sam turned to his friends. It was time to split. What he'd needed to do, he'd done, and he didn't feel it was safe to stay around Booth another minute longer than necessary. Now he was exhausted, but later, Sam thought—and it was a dispassionate realization—when he had more energy, he might feel compelled to inflict an injury on his father. It was best to leave before it came to that. They could find a motel.

Tom spread his hands in a show of dismay. "What's this? Don't leave. We've got room for everyone. Hell, we can set up a tent in the hole room if we have to. I was going to hang some plastic sheeting to keep out the elements anyhow."

Sam said thank you, but he needed to be going. "Love you, buddy." Before his godfather could respond, he wrapped him in a hug.

"Don't go, Sam." Mina was seated on the bone saw case. The damp air had smeared her eye shadow into purple blotches. It made her look more than ever like the child he needed to quit thinking of her as.

A stray realization had descended upon him, and it was this: his sister was not the only child of Booth Dolan with a less than admirable tendency for taking drastic measures. Sam himself had been abruptly cruel to Tess and to Jo-Jo, and that was just this weekend. Mina, meanwhile, at least had her age for an excuse.

"I'm sorry about what I said this morning," he said. "Your mom's being nuts has nothing to do with you."

"Okay," said Mina.

"I'm not mad that you made up that shit about Booth having stomach cancer. I'm not mad that you kicked everyone's ass. I've been pushy, and I'm sorry about that, too. But you do need to calm down."

"I do?" She picked at her bangs, running her fingernails along the silver strands.

"What do you think?"

Mina shrugged. "Probably." She looked at him. "I love you, Sam."

"I love you, too," said Sam. He hugged her and whispered into her ear. "Give me a couple of days to get my act together, and I'll find a way to show that a little better. All right?"

He felt her nod.

Sam released his sister and tossed the keys to the rental to Wesley. His roommate caught them, shrugged, but didn't ask any questions. "Take it easy, gang." Wesley saluted the group and climbed into the driver's seat.

"Nice meeting all of you," said Tess. "Sorry about your house."

Off to the side, Booth had been quiet, hunched above his cane. The old man cleared his throat, and Sam thought, Yeah, he knows that I saw what they were watching, and that I heard him laughing. Booth knows.

When he spoke, he didn't look up from the ground.

"Where are you going?" Sam's father asked.

Sam thought for a moment. "There's a funeral," he said.

CONCESSIONS

(2000)

1.

"I am such an old lady." Allie tucked a loose tendril of gray hair behind her ear. "Pooped at one in the afternoon."

They were right on time: her son's Trailways bus—making stops in Kingston, Saugerties, Quentinville, and other points north—idled in the parking lot, tinted windows shimmering in the sun. It was Sunday, time for him to go back to college with his bag of clean laundry and make it dirty again.

Sam hopped out, grabbed his duffel from the back, and walked around to her window. She was about to roll the window down, but he told her through the glass not to bother. "If we kiss, you might get your old on me," he said, a little smirk on his face. Never did it cease to fascinate her how, in Sam, her expressions sat on Booth's face. It was better than science fiction.

"You're a little shit."

He leaned forward and sealed his forehead against the glass. "I'm your little shit."

"I want you to do two things for me: one, call me when you get in; two, put on your damn coat when it gets cold. It's November, kiddo."

"Hmm-hmm." There was a small suction pop as he peeled his forehead from the glass.

Allie rolled her eyes. "And if you see a vegetable, kill it and eat, okay? Now I'm going home to take a nap and dream old-lady stuff."

"Okay, cool. I'll have my people call your people." Sam knocked the window, spun on his heel, and walked away.

Then he turned and backpedaled a few steps. As he did this, he raised his fingers, making a camera frame, and drew it out, focusing on her. Allie had seen him do it a thousand times—the gesture acquired from his father before Sam had twenty-five words in his vocabulary—but it never failed to stop her heart.

On the drive home, Allie called Booth, and as usual, her ex-husband's cell phone was disconnected. She had wanted to share her realization that children were the ultimate special effect. It was probably banal, but she liked it, and she thought her ex-husband would, too.

So she conducted their conversation herself, alone in the car, while the streets of Hasbrouck wound their way toward home:

"Booth, I've had an insight."

"Marvelous. I'm sitting. Let's have it."

"Children are the ultimate special effect."

"Yes, that's right. That's absolutely right."

"Do you know that movie, the one where you get your legs bitten off by the giant rat?"

"You're thinking of *Rat Fiend!* Not a personal favorite, Allie, if I may be honest."

"Well, children are way, way more amazing than that. Than giant man-eating rats or whatever."

"I actually think you're giving children short shrift. Those rats were just rats running around in rat-size sets. They were neither special nor effective. They were plain rats. Again, while few of my pictures are in danger of being confused with Beckett, that one is not a personal favorite. Children, Allie, and our child in particular, are really quite tremendous, whereas everything to do with that picture is fairly shitty. I don't feel as though the contrast you've arranged is quite satisfactory."

"They're of us, but they're not us. There's this alien quality to them. In a good way, though. Am I making any sense?"

And she would be able to hear his smile—whether he was in California or Mexico, New Orleans or Saskatoon—hear it in the wet crackle of his lips and that satisfied intake of breath as he said, "Perfect sense, sweetheart."

Stopped at the intersection of Main Street she leaned her head against the driver's-side window and giggled. She was in a funny, reflective mood. Everything was—okay. Allie supposed she had always expected that—for everything to turn out all right—and yet it struck her as a wonder. She was divorced, and that was okay. Her son was alive and healthy, so that was okay. There was no reason why she might not live another fifty years, and that was A-okay. She did what she liked, and that was okay, too.

Speaking of which: she rolled down the window and pressed the gas, let her arm drape out, and felt the air blow in.

It surprised some people—and actively disgusted her son—that she remained close to her ex-husband. At first, maybe, it took her aback, as well.

For one thing, it wasn't as though divorce had changed anything about him. Booth was still blithe, and selfish, and blithely selfish—he missed trains and he missed flights; he forgot to call on birthdays; he said way more than he should; he said anything that came into his mind; he was capable of behaving deplorably in situations involving his dick. You couldn't count on Booth for anything.

But she was always—always, always—glad to see him. What kind of sense did that make? It was a question she pondered for years. In the meantime, she continued to sleep with Booth on occasion, to call him when she was bored, to chat with him when he wasn't around, and when he was, to tamp down the rumpled cloth at his shoulders.

At home, Allie decided to sit at the piano and make some noise. She could do that. It was her house, and there was no one else there. Before beginning, she opened a window. The early afternoon was unseasonably warm; you could get by with a light jacket or sweater.

"The Entertainer" was her warm-up. She liked to play it really slow and woozy, what Sam called the "cough syrup version." From there she proceeded to "The Easy Winners," "The Maple Leaf Rag," and a few others. These she played as correctly as she knew how, skipping lightly along. Scott Joplin wasn't Bach, but his music pleased her in a simple, particular way, made her feel she was getting away with something, like she was on an escapade. The songs reminded her of Booth and of being young.

The melodies went drifting out the window, along on the sweet air, and, Allie fancied, maybe tempted those old Huguenots, snug in their coffins, to wiggle their dried little toes.

When she closed the café, she took up music again, some substitute teaching but mostly private lessons. While in retrospect, few careers were less rewarding than hustling java for student Communists, the contentment she found in this new-old pursuit was considerable. The student-teacher transaction appealed to Allie immensely. She liked to help. She liked their faces when they mastered a part.

One of her favorite students, a fifteen-year-old girl named Beatrice Nillson, had recently proffered a theory about love to Allie. "It's what makes us truly pathetic, isn't it?"

She was a punk, this Beatrice, and had an adorable habit of tattooing her own face with Magic Markers. In her flannel shirts and motorcycle boots, she'd drop onto the bench beside Allie and slam away at Chopin as if he'd stolen her diary, chewing purple-smelling gum the entire time, identical pretty pink kittens inked on her cheeks.

"I'm intrigued," Allie said. "Can you elaborate?" It was after a lesson; Bea's left hand was finally coming together. They were waiting at the foot of Allie's driveway for Bea's boyfriend to pick her up on his scooter.

The girl thoughtfully scratched a pink kitten. "A while ago, these cheerleaders, they did this poster for homecoming. It said, 'Freak out on Hudson!,' which I guess is who we were playing in some game. But under the word 'freak' they had pasted this, you know, crappy likeness of me."

Allie put her arm around Bea. "Kiddo."

"Thanks, Ms. Dolan. It was a bummer, I'll be honest. So, a little after that, I was at my gran's, right? And you have to picture my gran. She's like a baby doll, all tiny and round, reeks of potpourri, and just super, super old. You want to give her a bottle, she's so sweet and puffy.

"And we were playing a game of Scrabble. Nothing unusual, not talking about anything special, and out of the blue, Gran says, 'Lovey, would you give me an angel?,' and she's pointing to her cheek."

"I think that's beautiful," said Allie.

"It was. It was insanely beautiful. And pathetic. That to cheer me up she'd let me draw on her lovely old face. To me, that's love."

According to Bea's standards, had anyone ever been more loving than Booth?

When there was a review saying that Allie looked "lobotomized" in *New Roman Empire*—which she sort of did, because she was so scared to have a lens pointing at her face—Booth rode a train to the city and buttonholed the critic, insisting that they visit Bellevue together and meet some actual lobotomies. The critic later printed a retraction, offering that perhaps "anesthetized" would have been a more suitable adjective.

At her father's funeral, he had wept so much that Allie's mother snapped from her own grief-stricken stupor to lead Booth away to a stone bench. In the frosty sun of that northeastern April morning, they had made an odd, moving tableau: squeezed together on the low ornamental bench, the elderly widow and her mountainous son-in-law in his navy leisure suit, his face pressed to her thin breast. The smile at the corners of her mother's mouth was the first Allie had seen on her face in months.

How many bluesy evenings did he rescue, calling from who knew where, from whatever roach-infested soundstage, to ask Allie if he could be of service? "I was just sitting here," Booth would say over a crackling long-distance line, "perched on my large ass, and wondered if I could do anything at all to please you." If she wanted to hear Ethel Merman recite the Gettysburg Address, Booth did not hesitate. If the only way to raise her spirits was to hear Kermit the Frog explain in clinical detail how he planned to service his pink plush paramour, Booth could be counted on.

For God's sake, had any man ever given more head than Booth? If there was a more sweetly wretched sight than an enormous nude hairy man bunched up against a footrest and squeezed between a pair of thighs, Allie was not aware of it.

And when that apologetic doctor—a wen on her second chin, glasses dangling on a silver chain—had told them that Sam would be Allie's last child, Booth held her hand and said nothing, because there was nothing to say. He let her see that he was, finally, helpless. She would always owe him for that.

None of which changed the obvious: there was no justification for the man, for Booth.

She thought maybe Sam had scared him—from the beginning, at the hospital, when the nurse placed the bundle in his arms. The neediness of the child was something altogether different from the desire of a lover. She thought maybe that unnerved Booth.

Booth never seemed to understand, when it came to your kid, you were working from a surplus. You were big, and you knew things. They were already impressed with you.

What made him so funny in films—the wide-eyed pantomiming, the speaker-popping proclamations, the ravenous smiles that stretched from one theater wall to the other—could be discomfiting in person. The harder he tried, the more Sam recoiled. It had been a depressing cycle, and it had taken Allie far too long—until after the divorce—to make her own sense of the situation.

The fact was that Booth was not quite three-dimensional—or if he was, his third dimension was very small and very shy, a blinking, inexpressive creature born of ten thousand blacked-out movie-theater afternoons.

"What did your parents go to do when they were leaving you at the movie theater every day?" she asked once. "I don't know," he said, and on his face was a quizzical look. It was as if the question had never occurred to him. "Maybe they went home?"

Booth was all love and all hurt. He was, when you saw him fully, pitiful.

Which meant that, in violation of the basic parent-child rules, it would be up to Sam to accept his father instead of the other way around. Sam still had the potential to be a grown-up. Booth was already a total Booth.

Right in the middle of "Swipsey," Allie decided she'd had enough. Of late, her left hand had developed a lazy tendency. Maybe she really was getting old. Anyway, that was enough for the dead Huguenots.

It was such a beautiful day. The air from the open window was rotten and sweet. What a shame she couldn't tell Booth about Sam filming her with his imaginary camera, how he was the ultimate special effect.

So she did the next best thing—she called Tom Ritts.

"Tom, why doesn't your best friend pay his phone bills?"

"Do you know how little kids don't like to quit playing even though they've got a load in their pants?"

"Yes."

"My theory is that Booth's like that with bills."

"Does Sandra call you, too, when she can't get him?"

"Yeah."

"What does she want?"

"Let me see. This last time she told me that Israel owns all the oil companies and all the football teams, and that it's all managed through offshore corporations and Switzerland and . . ." Tom went on: there was something about beer distributors, and government townships in the Nevada desert that were mysteriously erased from maps printed after 1957, the Kennedys, and just a week or two ago, the unexplained death of a hedge fund manager named Kenneth Novey, whose corpse had been discovered in the panic room of his Saddle Brook, New Jersey, mansion, where it had been rotting since New Year's Eve. These various elements formed a monstrous web, Sandra claimed, and the rest of us were trapped in it.

Allie was impressed by how much of Sandra's craziness Tom had retained. She didn't hate Booth's second wife the way Sam did—in fact, Allie thought she had a terrific sense of personal style, not to mention a fascinating imagination—but it was obvious that the woman needed medication.

"I read about that guy, the panic room guy. Didn't the door mechanism malfunction because of Y2K?"

"I'm pretty sure Sandra thinks that's a cover story, but if you're interested, I'm sure she'd be delighted to fill you in," said Tom. "I'm probably leaving some important stuff out. She kept saying it was all 'bread and circuses.' I guess that's the bottom line. Frankly, I don't see the proof. Talked to Mina, though. She seems peachy. She's got an invisible friend named Inchy. Inchy's good, too."

"I like that kid."

Mina was cool. Allie had gone to the city with Sam, and they had taken the little girl for ice cream. The meeting had made Allie anxious; there was a special feeling of displacement—of familiar furniture in an unfamiliar place—that came with the sibling of your child who was not your child. But it turned out fine, natural, even.

"You play the piano?" the four-year-old asked, peering blue-eyed over a scoop of pistachio ice cream. Allie said she did, and Mina said, "You won't when you're dead, you know." Allie burst out laughing, and Mina, too. Sam propped his feet on a nearby chair and seemed to relax for a change.

They were going to be great friends someday, Allie thought, she and Mina.

"But listen," said Allie, and told Tom what she had thought, how kids were the ultimate special effect. "*Jaws* is horseshit compared to kids!"

"Yeah. That's true," said Tom. "Okay. I'll buy that."

When he didn't add anything more, Allie poked him. "That all you've got, Ritts?"

"What else do you want?" asked Tom.

2.

There was still a whole Sunday afternoon spread out in front of her.

Allie went for a walk to the Huguenot graveyard.

There had been a few other men over the years—several of them better, if you got right down to it, than Booth.

Her old friend Paul Grandpierre had been one of them. Paul worked as a printer and lived in Woodstock and was the coach for a youth soccer team he sponsored, the Fightin' Fonts. He was so easygoing and self-effacing, Allie decided that she couldn't possibly add anything to his life. "You're already perfect," Allie said, and Paul said, "If you say so, sister," and she thought that he was at least partly relieved. But they still got together every once in a while, smoked dope and listened to records, talked about things that happened when they were kids.

She casually dated an amusing, sack-bellied electrician and bar-band drummer named Diarmid off and on for two years, until he abruptly announced that he'd met his true love. "At the Staples in Kingston, of all places," marveled Diarmid. "Just laminating, she was."

Allie punched Diarmid in his fat shoulder. "I thought you were talking about me!"

"Heavens, no!" he said, making a face as if she'd traded his drum kit for some magic beans. Allie punched him again, much harder this time, and they'd had a final go, tickling each other the whole time. It was less than a year later that she played the piano at his wedding to the woman from Staples, and he sat in with a bongo for a few songs.

The best had been Rick Savini, an old actor friend of Booth's. She'd run into him at the movie theater in Hyde Park one afternoon. They were both there alone to see an animated movie about a pharaoh cat in the time of Moses, and they ended up sitting together. Rick had voiced the cat's chief adviser, an ornery but wise mouse in gold parachute pants, Qasim.

"The thing is, someone has to be the cranky mouse sidekick, you know? Not everyone can be the brave cat," Rick said to her as they strolled back to their cars in the humid dusk. His explanation of the supporting player's lot had struck Allie as profoundly incisive, and she nearly grabbed him right there.

The younger actor was, in every way, the antithesis of Booth. It was no accident, for instance, that professionally, Rick Savini specialized in reaction shots. He was a listener. If there was something he wasn't, it was avid. While she talked, Rick watched her with those damp saurian eyes of his and never seemed to blink. Rick could sip ginger ale and listen to her play rags for hours. He was patient and curious and sad.

She enjoyed his quirks:

He held a grudge against the summer, hated the heat and the length of the days, and associated the season with serial killers: "People get sweaty and rashy, and the next thing you know, bodies are turning up in parks with their livers cut out and somebody's writing letters to the police saying, 'I won't stop killing until the government stops pouring absinthe into the water supply.'" To identify his cookie-cutter Westchester McMansion, he kept potholes in the driveway. The actor's great hobby was to shop from airplane catalogs, and he had a large room filled with the gadgets, toys, and decorations that he bought from them: a miniature solar-charged windmill, a LEGO Empire State Building, a row of scuffed plastic seats from a demolished baseball stadium, several metal detectors, leather-covered editions of famous books, fancy movie replicas, a knee-high robot that could perform a range of rigid dances, and a plethora of other marvelous ephemera.

Rick wanted Allie to fly around the world with him. They could drink champagne at forty thousand feet and order things from airplane catalogs. The two black-and-white cats who lived with him cycled quietly in and out of the McMansion's rooms like maître d's, checking to make sure the service was adequate.

But Rick was too sweet, somehow too giving, too much a reflector. She didn't want to be the complicated one in a relationship, to play the Booth part.

"I'm used to loud, difficult people," Allie said.

"I can be loud and difficult," he replied, but she didn't want that. She liked who he was.

"Booth's more fun, isn't he?" Rick asked.

A little bit, she admitted, and Rick, with a thin smile, conceded that he agreed.

Even Booth had been crestfallen by this last breakup. "Goddammit, Allie, what are you looking for? You can't do better than Rick. He's a nice man. He's interesting. He's wealthy. He gets cast in everything, the bastard. Is it all the gadgets and crap? I've warned him about that."

"No, it's not his toys."

"Well. What possible excuse do you have, then?"

The café had been Booth's idea. He wanted her to have something, and he wanted to hang on to the movie theater, and it came together very simply. What was apparent later—almost twenty years and a divorce later—was that Allie never cared about coffee or pastries or business, but she cared about Booth a lot, and wanted to make him happy, so she spent years working at something she didn't care about. She still wanted Booth to be happy, but other priorities came first: Sam, always—and herself.

"I don't need an excuse," said Allie.

A gang of children, six blondes scattered between the ages of four and twelve, were yelling and chasing one another around the graveyard. Allie sat on the retaining wall beside their mother, a woman in her early fifties whose long gray hair was frizzy and uncombed.

"So today I took my kids to play in a graveyard," said the mother.

Allie laughed. She told the woman that her son loved to play here when he was young.

"Did it make him eccentric?" asked the weary woman.

"No," Allie reassured her, "I think that's something we did to him ourselves. Can I share a theory with you?" Allie asked her, and the woman said, "Please do." Allie explained how kids were the most incredible special effect of all. "They just go and go and go," she finished.

The mother agreed that she might be on to something. "But have you seen that *Titanic*? Seriously, I'm not sure if it's more incredible than kids, but it's definitely close."

It was almost hot in the sun that fell in an unbroken stream onto the wall. Allie closed her eyes and tipped her head back. She couldn't get enough of the air. It burned the insides of her nostrils, and she loved it.

The woman put a hand on the small of her back; Allie was about to slip off the back of the wall. "Careful," she said.

"Aw. Do I have to be?" asked Allie. The mother said yes.

Booth was more fun. Booth was the most fun. Booth was a monster of fun.

She recalled the visits she used to make to see him in California.

One time they drove to Sonora and drank too much and rode donkeys around a weedy field. Booth looked so funny sitting on a little donkey that she pissed herself at the sight, pissed all over her own poor donkey, and then cried because she felt so bad about what she'd done to the animal. Booth paid the donkey man extra, though.

On another trip, they went fishing and caught nothing but had memorable, sunburned sex on a boat.

Booth had a deranged landlady at the place he rented in Tarzana. She was obsessed with lemons. By the end of any trip to California, the mere mention of the word "lemon" was enough to send them into hysterics.

Allie went to sets with him a few times. The soundstages smelled like pot and ozone, and there were tentacles of ropy black cord everywhere, like some kind of alien infestation. Everyone seemed to get a kick out of Booth. They treated him like a star. He had his own little camp chair, the canvas backing labeled simply BOOTH.

If only, she thought, Sam could catch his father just right, trap him between the four walls of his camera. If only he could see Booth the way she saw him, from his good side.

At the end of their marriage, it had been, perversely, up to her to comfort him. Booth cried, and she soothed him. It wasn't fair that it should be that way—he was the cheat—but that was how it was between them. She had made her peace.

Allie came to the sharp curve at the far end of their street; this was where she usually turned around. In the middle of the curve there was a turtle. The turtle was about the size of her largest mixing bowl; indeed, the animal looked like nothing so much as a dusty green mixing bowl with legs. It was a snapping turtle, and to judge by the pissed-off expression on its wrinkled bulb of a head, not a nice one. "Get off the road," Allie said, and made sweeping gestures at the side of the street that the animal was facing.

The snapping turtle spat at her a couple of times and withdrew into its shell.

"You're going to get squished," she told the turtle.

There was an echoing hiss from inside the shell.

"Fine. Be that way." Allie turned around, scattering pebbles of pavement as she scuffed along.

As she passed the graveyard, the gray-haired mother spotted her. "Can't get enough of us?"

"No! I'm on the way home now!" Allie yelled, and comically threw up her hands. "There's a suicidal turtle over there!"

"Oh, those are the worst kind!" the mother hollered back.

Sam had used the camera that Tom gave him to make a stop-motion film, *The Unhappy Future of Mankind*. It starred these creepy, maimed plastic figurines he collected—Nukies, they were called—and Sam spent weeks and weeks meticulously inching them around on his bedroom floor.

The final product had astonished Allie. The tiny people were so urgently striving and heroic and doomed. Sam's bookshelves towered over them in otherworldly promontories, like the cliff faces in cowboy movies.

"Do you think you'll make one with real people next?" she asked him.

Sam lifted his shoulders in a noncommittal shrug.

"I'd act for you," Allie said. "If you wanted."

"I don't want to be disappointed in you," he said, making it sound inevitable—which it was.

Disappointment was the real common cold. Allie's students disappointed her when they didn't practice. Her cooking disappointed her. People she didn't know—politicians, especially—disappointed her terribly. Award-winning films weren't interesting. Surveys put you in the minority. Long-settled plans fell apart at the last second. Beloved sports teams were defeated in impossible ways. You forgot things that you cared about, and when you remembered them, they were gone. Machines couldn't be relied on. Service was slapdash. Mostly, your friends came through, but there were those times when they didn't. Parents never ceased to be your parents, which was both disappointing and frustrating. Sex was mostly just okay. It rained.

Disappointment was predictable and disappointing.

Allie could hear her semi-adult son's response to this declaration. "Which means what? I should wallow in my dissatisfaction?" he'd ask. "Make friends with it? Feed it chicken?"

"No," she'd reply, "it just means you should be less—*you know*—that thing you are sometimes." At this, Sam would probably hurl himself onto the floor and lie there, six feet one of him in bare feet, as if her wisdom had literally bowled him over, the little shit—her little shit.

This was a person she had birthed. She had tended his shitty ass. He had bitten her and passed her hideous childhood sicknesses and kept her awake. Allie's money had bought him books, tickets, sports equipment, trendy clothes, and disturbing figurines.

But Sam had had a propensity toward dourness for about as long as he'd had agency. For his second birthday, they visited a petting zoo. Sam frowned and pointed at a baby goat. "Our food," he said. Sam didn't look on the bright side. She had wanted a child and she had gotten one, and she was the furthest thing from sorry, but he wasn't easy.

One afternoon, though, he had touched her cheek with his fingers.

No blockbuster's fleet of spaceships, their thousand seamless gunmetal prows blotting the western sky, collective silhouette transforming the desert into an ocean floor, could have amazed her more than that—more than Sam's fingers at her face that afternoon. The piano was wretchedly out of tune. Cars whipped past behind them. There was a char stink in the air and on everything. And her son comforted her. They turned into people, your kids. It wasn't better than science fiction. It was science fiction.

Now if he could just get it through his head that Booth was Booth was Booth was Booth. Booth was a dreadful disappointment. Allie was sorry about that. He had not been much of a husband, either. The particulars had been established, and the record stood. Sam needed to let that be all right.

Sometimes you had to let yourself be absolved of every mistake and every resentment and every other fixation large and small, and breathe in and breathe out a few times, and say, "Okay, this isn't the apocalypse—and so what if it is?" and take it from the top, fresh.

3.

Inside, Allie poured a glass of water and went to the table. The phone rang, and she let it go. On the fourth ring, the machine picked up.

"Allie, I have negotiated a cease-fire with the cell-phone people," said Booth. "In so doing, I have discovered why our once great nation is in such a shambles. We still have the innovators, the creators, and the geniuses. What we don't have are the ass breakers. The public sector lacks ass breakers, and it is because the cell-phone companies and the insurance companies have gobbled them all up. They have contracted all of our top ass breakers, and the nation is suffering. Additionally, this is why there are no good movies anymore. All of the great directors were ass breakers. Welles must have snapped a thousand asses over his mighty knee."

Allie thought about standing up and getting the phone, but oftentimes it was as fun to listen to Booth as it was to speak with him. Another day she could tell her ex-husband how their son was the best special effect in the world.

"Anyway, I placated them, and here I am, my coccyx shattered but my cell phone restored, and I was thinking of you, and the many wonderful times we've had, and thought you might want to talk," Booth went on. "Are you sure you're not home, dear?"

"Should I go save that stupid turtle, Booth?" Allie asked, although he could not hear her. It was sitting out there in the middle of the road. She absently flexed her left hand—arthritis?

"Well, call me, darling. You are adored. Your attitude and your decency set a wonderful example for all of us, and I feel lucky to know you. Goodbye, Allie."

Allie sighed. She sat up straight, stood, and left the house. This morning, life was a snapping turtle in the middle of the road. She had an example to set!

They were safe; a few seconds after Allie placed the turtle on the grass at the side of the road, a gray pickup truck passed around the curve, tools rattling in its bed. That thing would have punched your ticket, she tried to tell the turtle. The animal was a few feet from where she was lying, gazing at her with amber eyes. Allie didn't remember falling down—perhaps she had passed out for a moment—but there was no pain, just a vague heaviness where the left side of her body used to be. She could smell the warm pavement.

The turtle hissed at her. It shuffled away, and she never saw it again.

You're welcome, she tried, but couldn't. She laughed, and it sounded like someone was crying.

Sam, she thought.

Before Allie, a small pothole at the edge of the street expanded into a wide and bottomless pit. A movie screen slid up from the tear in the earth, and there was no more turtle, road, or truck. There was just the movie screen and the circular darkness beneath it. A blocky credit appeared:

A Sam Dolan Picture
The Unhappy Future of Mankind

Her favorite! Bergman, eat your heart out!

I'm in the middle of a movie, she told herself, but knew it wasn't true. She was on the side of the road. Something had happened to her—heart attack, stroke, fit—after she moved the stupid turtle, and now she was partly stone. A pavement smell was in her nose, and a movie screen was in the street.

The movie commenced:

A red man with a smile for a head, the grinning mouth shaped like a watermelon wedge and stuck atop a body in a trim business suit, stands at the foot of a column of other scarlet-colored individuals. They are grouped against a backdrop of gray rug in the vast oblong shadow of a humongous bed.

Various considerations bobbed and sank: Allie didn't want Sam to be upset. She wanted to remind Booth to take care of his little girl. She had a lesson scheduled with Bea Nillson Monday morning, which would need to be rescheduled for eternity. A puppet string drew her right eyelid closed.

The man who has a smile for a head twitches forward. Row by row, the others—twisted, lumpy, and red—echo his movements. The bed's shadow ripples across them.

It came to Allie then, very clearly, that she was not going to be watching this movie to the finish, and that was too bad. She liked what she had seen.

PART 4
THE LONG WEEKEND

(2011)

Saturday and Sunday

1.

At the Days Inn up the street from Russell, they shared a room. Tess chose the big chair in the corner, leaving Sam and Wesley to share the bed. It was dawn by the time they turned in, and Wesley went to great lengths to block out the band of light at the bottom of the long window, using the phone book, the Bible, and all the towels from the bathroom to plunge the room into darkness.

When Sam awoke, he felt around on the bedside table until his fingers found the digital clock. He thumbed the button to show the readout: 11:21 A.M.

"You're awake." Tess was somewhere to his left.

"How long have you been up?" he asked.

"Since eight."

Sam blearily calculated that Tess had been awake for three hours. "Jesus. Why?"

"It's my body clock. I have a job. They make you get up early for those."

"That seems harsh."

As his eyes adapted to the dark, he could somewhat make her out in the big chair, a cloud of dark hair over the edge of a blanket. He was amazed and, in the awareness of a new day, sharply embarrassed that she had stuck around. He was glad, too—it would have been a punch in the stomach if she'd sneaked out—but on top of everything else that had passed between them, now she had met his family, too. Her continued company was making him feel increasingly naked.

"You really didn't cry during *E.T.*?" she asked. "I still find that hard to believe. I was just trying to make a mental time line of all your lies, and I want to put that first." He had expected her to ask him "What's the deal with you and Polly?" or "Do people try to kill you often?" or even "Was your father in movies?," so *E. T.* came from the left-field bleachers.

"What else did I lie about besides meeting you for a drink outside the Stables?"

"So you did lie about *E. T.*"

"Yes, I cried at *E. T.*," Sam admitted. "But it made me mad, too."

"Why?"

"Maybe it hit a little close to home," he said.

"You were friends with a space alien when you were a kid, and the government tried to steal him for experiments? I think I understand you better all of a sudden."

"My parents were divorced. My personal experience was more depressing than exciting. No space aliens. I never saved anyone, I never had any adventures, I didn't have a cool big brother. We didn't live in California. The movie made me intensely aware that my reality was disappointing and a lot more complex."

"Yeah, but how was that the movie's fault?" asked Tess. "That your reality was disappointing?"

Sam could see a little more of her now, the hollows of her eyes, the line of her jaw and neck. Tess couldn't have clocked over 120 pounds at the outside, but her presence was weighty. He had no explanation for why it was *E. T.*'s fault that his childhood had been disappointing. It was kind of an obvious point, so obvious he couldn't conceive of even a token defense. "I don't know," he said.

A duck call—the pitch starting low and rising to a poignant whine— came from his right. Like a thunderclap, the smell of Wesley's fart was delayed for two or three seconds before it materialized into a palpable force. The stench was crappy and beery, with notes of fried meat.

"Oh my God." Tess pulled her blanket over herself.

"Gotta chuck a shit, folks." Wesley thumped down from his side of the bed. A moment later, the entryway light flickered on, affording Sam an unwelcome glimpse of his roommate's hairy ass before the bathroom door shut.

"Oh my God," said Tess again, voice muffled by the blanket. "That is so horrible."

"So what's the appeal, then?" Sam was still on *E. T.* Years of living together had rendered him largely immune to Wesley's farts.

"Of *E.T.*?" asked Tess. "That it's not supposed to be your reality. It's about what might happen to a kid like you. Not you but like you. If there was an alien he had to save. If he lived in California. If he had to rise to the occasion." The blanket rustled. "It's not supposed to be complex. It's a fairy tale. It's supposed to appeal to your sense of possible impossibility."

The men left Tess the room and descended to the lobby. Beyond the registration counter was a tiled space with a carpeted island in the center and a pair of catercorner plastic-covered armchairs. Each man took a crinkly seat. Hung on the wall above Sam's head was the gilt-framed photograph of travelers enjoying the complimentary breakfast. Rich afternoon sun poured through the glass walls of the reception area.

"Beautiful," said Wesley, chinning at the photograph.

Sam inhaled and shut his eyes.

"How are you doing?" asked Wesley.

"I'm magnificent. I feel like a lumberjack."

"Like Paul Bunyan."

"Just like Paul Bunyan."

"You don't look like you feel like Paul Bunyan. You look like a scabby old homeless man just took a hot, leisurely piss in your mouth."

"My sister kicked your ass, Wesley. You got pummeled by a teenage girl."

"You look like you guzzled whiz, and not by choice."

"Go fuck yourself."

"I take it that it's over with Polly?"

"Yeah. I'm glad. I think she is, too." Sam, eyes still closed, explained how she'd confessed that she was the one who tipped Jo-Jo to where Sam might have gone. In this light, it seemed as though maybe she, too, had had enough of the affair. Naturally, since she was Polly, a breakup note couldn't suffice—she had to release her steroidal husband from his kennel so he could go on a hand-chopping rampage.

"If it's for the best, why the glum 'tude?"

Sam opened one eye. His friend had adopted a psychiatric pose, elbow planted on the arm of the chair, chin on fist, gaze placid, lips pursed. Once again Wesley was wearing the jabot, along with a dingy Russell College sweatshirt and a pair of wrinkled Dockers.

"Don't," said Sam.

His friend shrugged and sat back.

The lobby doors opened. A middle-aged woman, dressed for some kind of function, crossed to the front desk, the thin gold chains draped around her boots jingling in step. A son, ten or so, wearing a black suit, trailed behind her.

While she was filling out a form, the boy strolled to the carpeted island. He scowled at the men from behind long black bangs. Sam was reminded of the recent vogue in horror films for evil ghost children.

"What's up?" asked Wesley.

"Just checking out a couple of dirtbombs," said the evil ghost child. "Dirtbombs in chairs. Illing in the hotel lobby. Being dirty. Nice napkin, dirtbomb."

"It's a jabot."

"Whatever."

"You know what?"

"What?"

Wesley flicked a hand. "Go away. That's not how you talk to people."

The evil ghost child's mother called to him, and he departed without further comment.

Sam peered at his friend, studying for signs of irony.

Mildness and maturity were qualities that no one had ever attached to Wesley Latsch. Wesley had made a pastime of worrying at a large cauliflower-shaped plantar wart on his right foot. He had conserved and accumulated the dead skin until he amassed a full canning jar of fawn-colored shards. It was something he "felt compelled to do." The jar of wart pieces lived on the shelf above Wesley's bed, like a religious icon. In the years that Sam had known Wesley, he had never left a room by saying merely, "I have to go to the restroom/bathroom." It was apparently incumbent upon Wesley to say specifically what it was he was going to do in the restroom/bathroom (i.e., "chuck a shit," "tinkle the ivories," "cast a cum spell with the flesh wand," etc.). Not only did his mother make frequent visits—*from Maryland*—to do his laundry, he had no qualms about bitching her out if she couldn't remove the stains from his favorite shirts.

To see him behave like an adult caused Sam apprehension. "What was that?"

Wesley made a *what can you do?* gesture with his hands. "Kids act out."

Sam craned his neck as if a bit of extra distance might reveal his friend's game. Wesley yawned and scratched the puffy unshaved chins piled atop his jabot.

"I call bullshit," said Sam.

"Whatever." The other man shrugged. "Are we going to get something to eat before we go to the cemetery?"

"No, no," said Sam. "I don't believe you. What's the scam?"

"No scam. I'm not here to make a scene. I'm here because someone tried to grease my main man."

A television was buried in the wall directly in front of the armchairs. It was set to the news and muted: there was a crowd of elderly white protestors, and at the bottom of the screen, a ticker read, TEA PARTIERS RALLY ON THE MALL. Sam noticed that the protestors were, to a one, armed with cell-phone belt clips.

"I saw Booth watching it. *Who We Are.* He was laughing his ass off."

"I'm sorry, Sam. That sucks." Wesley picked at the fabric of his armchair. "But . . ."

His friend of many years—dissolute, blithe, a jokester whose best joke was perhaps on the verge of not being so funny any more—met Sam's eyes. He had a wide-open smile on his face. Wesley's teeth were so awful, they looked singed—and yet for an instant, his expression was completely earnest, and he was Mrs. Latsch's bright little boy. "But she came here for you," said Wesley. "Sam, you know, I don't think there's a person in the world who would so much as cross the street for me. I don't know if I'd cross the street for me. And this girl, she's laying it all out there for you. She came all this way. She thinks you might be worth it. That's something to be happy about."

The elevator bell dinged. Tess stepped out into the lobby.

2.

At a diner, they ate lunch and received directions to the Quentinville cemetery. The route took them a couple of miles east of the little college town, along a winding, hilly road between stands of birch trees. Near the hilltop, their progress was abruptly stayed at a high wrought-iron gate. Sam stopped the car, and they piled out.

A laminated sign on the gate read CLOSED. A chain was padlocked across, and on either side of the road's raised bed, the ground crumbled away into mucky gullies and a stretch of swampy forest where the standing water was carpeted in fluorescent green algae. Through the bars of the fence, they could see the road hooking into another turn, and farther on, the edge of the cemetery, where a few newer-looking headstones stood.

"I thought the funeral was scheduled for noon," said Wesley.

Tess touched a fence bar. "Guess it got canceled."

A floral arrangement had been propped against a corner of the gate: it was of a penis and testicles. The shape was edged in red roses, and the interior was filled with white roses. A substantial tribute, the arrangement came about as high Sam's hip, and the balls had the circumference of a truck tire. The penis was definitively erect. On the rear of the arrangement was pinned a card: *In loving memory of Costas Mandell from his fans and admirers at Who We Argot.*

Perhaps because of the headstones in the distance, or the flowers, which managed to seem convincingly funereal in spite of the design, a somberness fell over the group. That Sam hadn't really known him was unimportant. The guy, Mandell, had lived, and now he was dead. You had to respect that.

"I'll shimmy under and try to deliver these," said Tess.

Sam thought again what a serious, straight-ahead person she was, and he appreciated that about her. There was a gap between the bottom crossbar and the pavement, which, with a fair amount of wriggling, she slipped underneath. Once Tess was on the other side, the men squatted down, but it was obvious that they weren't going to make it.

They carefully slid the flowers through to her. Tess tucked the arrangement under her arm and started off in search of the satyr's final resting place. The sight was one of those that you know you'll never see a second time: a woman on an empty road, carrying a huge flower penis under her arm, sort of like a guitar without a case but not a guitar without a case—a huge penis made of flowers. What was surprising was the melancholy of the composition: the lone figure and the vulgar flowers and the headstone-dotted field. The sun ducked behind a cloud, and the green grounds turned pewter.

As Tess disappeared around the bend, Sam found himself wishing yet again that he had a camera.

Wesley wandered off the way they had come, searching for a bar of reception for his BlackBerry. (On the drive, he had drafted a judgment on Brooklyn Aristocrat's Basic Jabot, and read it aloud to Sam and Tess: "This anachronistic neckwear made me feel both powerful and dissolute. You cannot wear this accessory without feeling a yearning to smoke opium and sex it. Jabot flouncing in time with your thrusts, pants around the ankles, ramming the petticoated woman of your dreams—can you imagine it? People, I can't stop imagining it! YEAH, I'LL TAKE IT!!"

After Wesley finished reading, Tess said, "Looks like somebody just figured out what to get her dad for Hanukkah this year.")

Sam leaned against the hood of the car and breathed the cool, fresh air and considered Costas Mandell. He was a puzzle. What did you do after you ran around in the forest in furry chaps, jerking off, screwing knotholes, pissing on leaves, massaging your taint, popping thigh zits, waving your humongous cock at the world, and never cracking a single smile? Sam could only suppose that you did what anyone else would do: went home, guzzled a beer, relaxed, watched a movie on cable. The obituary said Mandell had been an avid moviegoer. It also said he liked to fish and had emigrated from Greece. He certainly had a colossal penis. That was about the extent of what Sam had to go on. There was no way to know if Costas Mandell had been entirely proud of what he had done, or if he had been entirely sorry, or something in between.

In the years since his film was vandalized by Brooks Hartwig, Jr., Sam had often reflected on the day before the catastrophe struck, the afternoon when Tom and Mina visited and the movie seemed best. Earlier that day, Sam had watched the movie by himself; he hated it, disbelieved it, was sickened by it. Then, while Mina sat and wrote dismal prophesies on the head shots of the cast members, he had watched the movie with Tom and thought it was not bad. What was evident to Sam these days was that an honest accounting of his movie—the one that Brooks incinerated, that no one else would ever see—lay somewhere in between. His beloved conceit, for instance, the speeding-time effect that blended four years into a single day, was still, at least in theory, a visually appealing idea. The evolving clothes and hairstyles, the backgrounds that had no continuity, the erratic lighting, these shifting elements aggravated the eye—in a good way, because they made you want to keep watching. What was less successful—was downright juvenile, in retrospect—was the idea that those four years were the sum total of anything. The sunrise at the end of the film was blatantly symbolic: the Dawn of Adult Understanding. Sam hadn't felt like an adult after college graduation, and he didn't feel like one now. He felt like himself, and understanding in general remained generally elusive.

If, therefore, you added up each column, the sum was an independent film like a lot of independent films: some interesting ideas, gestures at profundity, and actors who looked like real people as opposed to movie stars. You could easily find worse ways to expend eighty-four minutes than by watching *Who We Are,* and if you would get off your ass, you could easily find better ways.

But Sam's version of *Who We Are* didn't exist; Brooks's version did. And the movie that Brooks had cut was not like any other films. It was truly different. Mandell's performance was singular. Mandell disturbed and he astounded and he sold every baffling word. He was magic, unreal—he was a satyr. If not for Brooks, and Mandell's performance that Brooks had captured, *Who We Are* most likely would have gone unnoticed. It was Brooks and Mandell who had made the movie special. This reality might have relieved Sam, but instead, it made him a bit envious. Sam wished he had been less sure of himself when he was twenty-two and twenty-three.

Like a siren, the memory of Booth's crazed, guttural laughter from the night before rang in his mind—and to Sam's surprise, even amazement—like a siren, it dispersed as suddenly as it arose. He knew that he had to be angry, yet he felt absolutely still inside. Sam didn't know what the feeling—the lack of feeling—meant, but he was glad of it.

Tess slid the flower penis back through the gap and then herself. Although there had been a couple of fresh graves, either of which might have been Mandell's, they had lacked headstones. "I didn't want to risk leaving a cock-and-balls arrangement on some random person's grave."

Sam complimented her instinct.

They knocked around the possibility of taking it with them, but where? Another option was to leave it against the fence where they'd found it. It was hard, though, to believe that it would ultimately pass muster with the graveyard authorities. Someone would throw it out.

Sam suggested the swamp. Tess thought that was an okay gesture. Wesley was still off down the hill somewhere.

Sam gingerly descended the embankment six or seven feet, reaching the platform of a few large, slick rocks at the water's edge. Tess handed him the arrangement, and he held her hand while she picked her way down the uneven declivity. He squatted to lay the flowers on the water's scummy surface. "Here goes." He shoved the arrangement off. It began to drift, cutting a wedge of clear water through the green fur.

They watched as the flowers made it through the strait between two spindly trees.

"Okay, here's the reason," said Tess. "Are you ready?"

"Kenneth Novey, we're talking about? Why it's not evil to enjoy his pain and suffering?"

"Uh-huh."

The arrangement was about a half dozen yards out now, rotating slightly. A beard of frothy green scum had already collected around its hull. Sam put on his listening face. "Let's hear it."

"Don't fall asleep, okay?" The sharp angle of her right eyebrow implied that she wasn't attempting to lighten the mood.

"I'm really sorry about that." There was no defense for the window escape or the ignored phone calls, either. Then there was everything with Polly, which wasn't a direct affront to Tess but didn't exactly cast him in a fulsome light. While they'd known each other only a couple of days, he had already racked up a karmic debt that could take years to whittle down. He had behaved poorly. She made him feel more than naked; with Tess, he didn't even have any skin. "Really sorry."

"You fucking should be." Tess rubbed her index finger around an eye. Her visible exhaustion was attractive. There was a wrinkle at one corner of her mouth that he wanted to kiss. The top of her head came parallel to his chin. A single shimmering white hair ran to the left of her middle part.

"Did you hurt anybody because of it?"

He waited for her to continue, but she let the question hang until he responded.

"Pardon?" Sam asked.

"When you watched the show? When you watched the reenactment of the awful way that the man died? Kenneth Novey."

"I guess not."

"Then it's fine. If it's not hurting anyone, then it's fine. Who does it hurt? Kenneth Novey doesn't care. He's history. The rest of us have to keep ourselves amused somehow."

"What if it hurts my soul?"

"Uh-uh. If you want to travel that street, best of luck, but I'm staying right here. We're blood and bones and organs. We don't have souls. When our bodies stop, we're gone."

Sam didn't want to make her angry, but he wasn't persuaded. It was too simple and too easy. "I feel like I have a soul. Or at least like I have to proceed on the assumption that I have a soul."

"Look, something terrible happened, yes. The guy got a bad, horrible, nasty deal, and he died. And we made a frivolous, trashy show about it. We sensationalized a tragedy, and you were captivated by it. But did it inspire you to go out and kill someone? Did you go out and burn down an orphanage? Did you go out and punch a kitten?"

Sam shook his head.

"Of course you didn't. Because it was a diversion. It was an entertainment. It was a fantasy, a cheesy reenactment that probably didn't so much as scrape against the reality of the guy. Maybe it was a travesty. Probably it was a travesty. But it was just a show.

"So it struck you funny. So what? Can't you laugh? Why shouldn't that be okay? Did you laugh at the man's misery? No. I'll tell you why you laughed: you laughed at his predicament. You laughed at how unfair and stupid and grotesque his predicament was. You laughed because you had to. How else are you supposed to react to exhibit number ten trillion and one that however random and mean you think life can be, it can always be far more random and way, way more mean than you could ever imagine? By curling up in a ball? By hitting yourself in the face? By kicking furniture? What would that achieve?"

She jabbed her hands deep into the pockets of her vest. He couldn't tell if she was furious with him or with herself. "You want something to feel guilty about? Let me help you. Feel guilty about people living beneath underpasses. Feel guilty about shortchanging some poor waitress's tip. Feel guilty about throwing out plastic bottles. Feel guilty about something real, something current. Don't feel guilty about some freaky, unlucky, terrible fucking thing that happened, and that no one could have seen coming, and that's over and done with. Give to charity. Tip appropriately. Recycle.

"Listen. Sam. You're allowed not to feel shitty about everything. You know? If you want to have a soul, fine. I have a soul. Care about something you can change. Get over yourself, man."

The flowers had stopped about twenty yards out. The arrangement's scrotum was snared against a half-submerged, splintered log that jutted at a forty-five-degree angle from the swamp.

"Yes," he said, and thought of his father's wild laughter in the study, and felt his heart continue to beat, steady and unconcerned. She was right, obviously. His priorities were a mess.

Sam raised his hands in surrender. "I got it. Point made."

"And you know what else?" Tess looked at him as if she wanted him to explode. He thought she made a beautiful Fury. "If it's such a bad show, why don't you make one that's better? If you think it's cavalier about death, that it makes a joke out of something that's sacred, that it lets the audience get away with something, then make your own. Punish us. Give us the truth."

"Okay."

"Thank you! Christ!" Tess inhaled. She blinked. She made a brisk *come here* wave. He moved closer, and she wrapped her arms around him, and he put his arms around her. Her hair smelled like coconut. He could feel her breath between the buttons of his shirt.

"Sorry to change the subject, but are you at all surprised that there was a florist around here who does penis-shaped arrangements?" Tess's voice was muffled by his chest.

"No," said Sam, but then again, he supposed there wasn't too much that surprised him anymore.

3.

Since there was no pressing reason to go home, they drove back to Quentinville, to the Russell campus, with the idea that they could walk around, maybe peek in the windows of their old dorm rooms. But as soon as they parked (in the same overflow lot where Sam had filmed Roger and Claire's handle-pulling fallout), Tess objected. "What are we doing? All the people here are so young. Do we really want to expose ourselves to that?"

"They can't hurt us," said Wesley.

Sam asked if they could at least drive around. While Tess didn't seem thrilled about that, either, she acquiesced.

The campus loop hadn't changed; the narrow road still wound in meandering circles through the college grounds. Nor was there any detectable difference in the faces of the dorms: the bloodred stone of their facades was as fresh as ever. When the car passed through the crosswalk near the cafeteria, Sam spotted the tree where the freshmen girls had hung the condoms. Today its branches were black and undecorated—or wait, was it a different tree? He wasn't sure. There were four or five nearly identical trees in a cluster.

On the sidewalks, students walked with messenger bags slung over their shoulders and bare skin showing in spite of the cooler weather. Though it didn't make any sense, Sam kept expecting to see someone he recognized.

"Still no black people," observed Wesley.

"See!" Tess stabbed a finger in the direction of a group of students loitering around the steps of one of the dorms. "They're kids!"

"You would not believe what a hard time I had getting laid here," said Wesley.

"I might believe it," she said.

"Hey, are these Chinese figures?" Wesley, in the backseat, had unearthed the rusty short sword that the vagrant had been wielding before Mina disarmed him and Sam squashed his balls. Wesley handed the weapon across the seat to Tess. She wasn't impressed. "They look like bullshit runes to me. Elvish or Romulan or whatever."

At the stop sign where the loop intersected with the drive leading out to the front entrance, Sam craned his neck to try to see the lawn of the Film Department. Sometime since the fall of 2003, a pine tree had been planted at the corner of the lawn, and its dark green bell largely obscured the view. He supposed that the sinkhole at his former apartment complex was gone, too. Someone had surely come along with a machine, filled it with stuff, sealed it up.

"The building where I took all my classes is over there somewhere." Sam gestured in the direction of the pine tree.

"Uh-huh," said Tess.

A tall boy in a poncho glided by the car on a Segway.

"Check out this numbnuts," said Wesley. "I'd like to poke him with this shitty sword."

"Oh, wow." Tess plastered her face against the passenger-side window in the manner of a young child. "I've never seen one in person. A Segway."

When she went to college, Tess said, she had used a Trapper Keeper and written letters to her high school boyfriend, who turned out to be gay and broke her heart into a thousand tiny shards, shards that had also shattered, and so on. "I needed a Dust Buster with a special existential setting to suck up the millions of fragments of my heart, that's how busted it was."

She could remember hunching across the quad—on foot! in the rain! with a sinus infection!—Trapper Keeper pressed to her chest, as if to somehow hold in the trillion pulverized specks of her destroyed heart. "I was so miserable." Tess hadn't moved her face from the window. "And now college kids get Segways." Steam from her breath whitened the glass.

"See? It looks like a good time, doesn't it?" asked Sam.

The kid on the Segway glided forward. He looked like a young man with a future—a young man of the future.

"Yeah," said Tess. "It does."

There was a honk behind them. They were still at the stop sign. Sam began to swing the wheel left, to follow the loop past the pine tree and make a pass of the Film Department, but changed his mind. There was no reason why anyone else should care, and suddenly he wasn't sure he cared that much, either. It was a hell of a long time ago.

So they turned right and went out through the college gate.

. . .

After two flat-out busts—a closed cemetery and a familiar place where everyone was a stranger—the only sane response was to blow the afternoon at the movies. Auspiciously, Tess had had the foresight to bring along a baggie of marijuana. In the parking lot of the multiplex in Kingston, they smoked it, using the tiny, faux crystal–encrusted pipe that was hooked to her key ring.

Sam, who loved getting high, hadn't done it in two or three years, primarily because he had never managed to make the transition from college, where you went to the drug dealer's dorm room and bought some schwag mixed with catnip, to city living, where the drug dealer came to your apartment door and laid out a dozen different vacuum-sealed packets from which to choose. It made getting stoned formal, like drinking fine wine, which for Sam defeated the purpose.

Tess ran the lighter's flame over the leaves while he held the pipe. Sam made intense hypnotist eyes at her. "Less staring, more smoking," she said.

He took a rip, his second or third, and held it until he thought he could feel the smoke crawling over the backs of his eyeballs. Sam exhaled out the top of his window, which was cracked an inch.

For privacy from any mall fuzz, the rental car was tucked in between two minivans. An ocean of parking lot lay beyond the windshield, strewn here and there with cars and shopping carts, reefed with cement islands.

"You know who you remind me of? You remind me of the Monopoly guy," Sam said to Wesley. He handed the pipe to Tess.

"Tell me more."

"It's the aristocratic veneer that you share. The five-day growth of beard, the little hairs sticking from the top of your nose, the jabot with the maple syrup on it, the angry cold sore. I look at you, and what I see is a man who knows the rules of whist."

"There is a Rockefeller-ish quality to me. It's something I've never been entirely at peace with. I think you know that as well as anyone, Sam. You've seen me play croquet. You've seen me eat caviar with my own platinum cocaine spoon."

"I've fed you caviar with your platinum cocaine spoon."

Thin streams of pearl smoke emerged from Tess's petite nostrils. Wesley told her she was a dragon, but she didn't respond. Her expression had become distant and frozen.

Sam asked if she was okay.

"I counted seven teddy bears." Her speech was a near monotone. "A rhino and one kind of—I'm not sure what it was—some kind of avian—at the cemetery, and I didn't even come close to walking the whole place. Graveyard stuffies. It was dreadful, the way they were left reclining against the headstones."

"Were they weathered?" asked Wesley, accepting the pipe and the lighter.

"Yes. Terribly weathered. One of the bears, he was in overalls, but he was barely a bear anymore. His nap was all pilled, and his overalls were streaked, and his head was sort of sunken into his neck. Awful. Bad. Sad. Who wants to be a graveyard stuffie when they grow up, you know?"

"Was it an owl?" Sam asked Tess.

"I have no idea what you are talking about," said Tess. Then she said, "Oh, right. Yeah. It could have been an owl."

Wesley released a cloud of smoke. It rolled from the back of the car to the front, slowly, like a tiny bank of mist. The other two were sufficiently baked that they ceased talking in order to observe the phenomenon. Through the filter of the pot cloud, Sam met Tess's eyes, and he grinned at her. She blinked.

They should rescue them, suggested Wesley, the graveyard animals. "Or not," said Sam, but Tess was a "maybe." First thing was first: she needed to see this movie about the hole that eats Las Vegas, needed to see all the fake monuments crash down. Tess felt like she needed to not think about anything for ninety minutes, not the Monopoly guy or the stuffies of the dead or whatever, not think about anything, and be peacefully stoned and eat yellow popcorn.

The Pit was a blockbuster multistar extravaganza, the last holdover from the summer season.

The premise was that, on a random beautiful spring day, the land beneath Las Vegas abruptly craters, dropping the entire metro area eighty feet below what had been the surface. In the aftermath of the disaster, a contrasting band of survivors—a gambler on a losing streak, a teenage supermarket cashier, an IHOP hostess, an animal trainer and her cat circus, a little moppet named Ari, and a mysterious man in a wheelchair—try to escape the burning, choking, violent wasteland that used to be America's playground.

"Oh my God! It's a sinkhole!" murmured Sam as the camera withdrew to a satellite view to reveal the fullness of the collapse: the acres of shining city plummeting into the cracked earth like a loaded platter falling down an elevator shaft. The image excited and thrilled him. He was awesomely high.

"Shhh," said Tess.

The three of them had claimed the handicapped stadium seats fixed in the broad horizontal aisle at the waist of the theater. Sam was in the center.

While the reasons behind the titanic sinkhole were left devilishly unresolved (there were hints at environmental factors, at black magic, as well as at some ambiguous higher power, but nothing was definitive), the spectacle was undeniable, the action taut and astounding. Along with the expected pleasures—the screeching Eiffel Tower and the splitting Sphinx, a vicious pimp squished beneath the toppled Big Boy statue—there was a wit and a peculiarity that kept Sam's attention from drifting.

At one point, the band of survivors walks through the shattered hall of a casino. Among the smashed tables, broken beams, and corpses, an old woman in a soiled bathrobe is blandly pumping quarters into a (miraculously operational) slot machine. She doesn't so much as glance up as the group goes by. It was not quite profound, but it was definitely creepy.

The filmmakers also made brilliant use of the cat circus. The heroine, a trainer named Wylie, gets her circus cats to help the group out of all sorts of dastardly fixes. When they need a car to escape from a gang of end-times cultists in a cracked-up parking garage, she uses the cats' training to get them working together to retrieve a ring of keys from the body of a dead man lying out in the open. It was tense bordering on nauseating, watching this team of intrepid cats darting out in a martial little line, bullets biting into the concrete around them. Sam wanted to hug whoever had decided to go as kooky as a cat circus for the representative element of Las Vegas entertainment instead of something typical, like a magician, or Cher.

The inevitable death of the oldest, bravest circus cat, Frank—there were five of them, each named after a member of the Rat Pack: Frank, Joey,

Sammy, Dino, and Peter—caused Sam's eyes to blur with tears. Peeks to the left and the right revealed that his friends were weeping, too, their faces streaked in the candied screen light. Tess was sniffing and clutching her pipe. Wesley was outright bawling, lips shaking, cheeks trembling. The only other person watching was a theater attendant who had wandered in halfway through and sat down on top of a flipped bucket in the right vertical aisle. She was not crying but appeared mournful, face pressed against the pole of the mop that she held upright between her feet.

At the end of the film, the survivors escape the pit of Las Vegas by ascending a tipped missile silo that has created a perilous ramp to higher ground. The gambler, a Bogart-esque reluctant-hero sort, equal parts blasé and capable and irritably ethical, fights a militia warlord as his friends scrabble up the scary incline of the silo.

Sam imagined how silly it would look in script form—

EXT. MISSILE SILO—HIGH NOON
Captain Poul holds Carver by the front of his shirt. The drop yawns beneath his kicking feet. A flap of skin has torn away from Captain Poul's blistered cheek, exposing the raw tissue beneath.

                         CPT. POUL
Degenerate!

Poul is about to throw Carver off. Carver's hand darts into his jacket pocket.

                         CARVER
Joker.

The gambler riffles his lucky deck of playing cards spraying into the madman's face. Poul staggers. Carver falls—and catches a rung. Playing cards snow through the air. Captain Poul slips over the side and falls, HOWLING.

CLOSE-UP: ON CARVER'S DANGLING HAND: WHERE HE STILL HOLDS THE DECK'S JOKER.

—but on the screen, it was gangbusters: hand-to-hand combat on top of a missile silo! The survivors reach the surface of the earth with only moments before the missile blows. When the credits roll, Wylie, the cat-circus ringmaster, her remaining cats, the moppet, and the gambler head into the sun while, behind them, the nuclear fire rises higher.

The lights came up. Sam blinked dry, gritty eyes.

It was all so inorganic—crane shots, copter shots, shots from the point of view of statuary falling on people's screaming faces, an orchestral score that sounded like it had been written for a thousand pieces and performed by ten thousand, explosions from multiple angles, breathtaking stunts (many involving cats), actresses so beautiful, actors so cool. It was antithetical to everything that Sam recognized from life. It was totally impossible, aggressively meaningless—and, in its way, perfect. He liked it. It had been a great show. "That was fun."

Tess smiled. "It wasn't *E.T.*, but . . ." She leaned her head against his shoulder. "I want a circus cat so much."

Wesley was on his feet. He adopted the Heisman pose—forearm stiff, invisible football tucked—and uncorked a thin, screechy fart that sounded like a sneaker digging for purchase against hardwood. "Double feature?"

Sam and Tess carried the motion.

Wesley hollered to the attendant, who had started to wheel away her bucket: was there a place in this theater to buy weed?

The best place, it turned out, was Farah's locker. Farah was the theater attendant. She led them up to the roof, and they all hunched down against the tarpaper-walled rectangle that contained the upper landing of the interior stairs, taking turns with her bong.

The movie theater, which Sam had visited literally hundreds of times in the course of his childhood and adolescence, was your basic sugar cube, a cement square planted in a field of pavement. Through the years, various other boxes had sprouted up around it—a Best Buy, a Circuit City (RIP), a Lowe's, a PetSmart, a Dollar Store, a medical group—and the vantage point of the roof was dour.

But there was a sense of home, too. Other people, he supposed, had family memories of trips to the Grand Canyon, Niagara Falls, the Mediterranean. Sam remembered walking with his parents, together and separately, across the theater parking lot. It was a good memory, better than he'd ever realized.

A navy blue darkness wiped out the last of the daylight. The open air made Sam's buzz crisper, more austere.

The only thing missing from *The Pit*, he thought, had been Booth. Booth would have fit right in. He could have played some bellowing local yokel. That was it: the shady-cowboy used-car salesman who, after hemming and hawing, does the decent thing and hands over one of his Winnebagos to the sinkhole survivors, so they can quickly traverse a particularly dangerous section of the decimated city. Allie would have loved that, Booth as a used-car salesman. She wouldn't have hesitated to give him his proper share of shit for it, and Booth would have taken it.

Sam accepted the bong from Wesley and took a belt.

They were seated shoulder to shoulder, Tess, Wesley, Sam, and Farah.

Wesley leaned forward to address Tess. "Raise Farah's awareness of the tragic plight of the graveyard stuffies."

Farah was a short, broad-hipped young woman who spoke in the sedated manner of the perpetually stoned—as if words were cars and she a roadway construction worker, waving them through a few at a time. "Yeah, fill me in."

Tess did. "They're out there right now," she finished, "even as the darkness gathers."

Farah fiddled with her vest's single gold button. For a woman who exuded mellowness, the theater attendant was also surprisingly engaged, an appealingly professorial combination. Earlier, while she packed the bong, it had emerged that she was saving the money she made from dealing drugs for college and health emergencies. Right now Farah was thinking urban planning, but she wasn't committed.

"I doubt that the guy in Laos," said Farah, "on his assembly line, gluing bear eyes—by candlelight. Or whatnot. I doubt that's what—he envisions. That his bear is ticketed—for a cemetery. I'm sure he'd be—bummed."

None of them proved capable of responding to this observation. It was a very heavy deal, the stuffed animals in the graveyard.

Wesley took a cell-phone picture of a purplish growth on his chest and sent it to the WOUND database. While the response was loading, he gave the phone to Farah and asked her to tell him what it said. Wesley was worried it was cancer.

The phone burbled; the message had loaded. Farah stared at the phone. "It's a—an ingrown hair."

"Thank God," said Wesley. He raised his shirt and petted his growth.

"We saw a guy on a Segway," Tess said brightly, changing the subject. "He was just—" She cut slowly and smoothly through the air with her hand.

"Yeah." The theater attendant nodded. "Just—" She echoed Tess's gesture, cutting slowly and smoothly through the air.

Tess reached out for Sam and took his hand. "It made me pretty excited for the future," she said.

4.

Before they checked in to the early-evening show of *Fair Share*—Farah threw in free passes with any purchase of weed—Tess drew Sam into the alcove off the theater lobby. The last time a girl had taken him into the alcove, he was sixteen and her braces had slashed his lips. Within the small maroon-tiled space was a Flash Gordon pinball machine that had been dead since he was in high school.

Tess pressed him against the wall beside the pinball machine. Her mouth clamped over his mouth. Sam tasted pot, salt, and spit. His hard-on was terrific, but insensitive from the dope. It wasn't a disagreeable feeling. He knew it was down there, his penis, doing its level best.

After a minute or so, Tess pushed off to wheel around in a circle, letting her hand scrape over the walls of the alcove, giving the flippers on the darkened pinball machine a whack. Then she dashed back to kiss some more and swerved off. This pattern repeated itself several times.

"What are you doing with me?" Sam asked.

"You're cute," she said. "I liked your weddingographies." She kicked her left foot and slowly spun around on the toe of her right sneaker, like a wind-up ballerina. Her eyes were fevered. "You seemed miserable."

"Is that a plus?"

"With me, it tends to be, I'm afraid."

"What if you make me happy?" asked Sam.

Tess leaned against the pinball machine. Seconds elapsed. Sam's heartbeat was steady but unusually reverberative; it was like he was made of wood, and hollow, like an acoustic guitar. He couldn't remember being ever quite this high.

"I don't know," Tess said. "That might spoil it. Have to take the risk, though." She stepped to him, and they kissed some more. She stopped, and they stood there and held each other.

"Have you seen it?" he asked. Tess nodded. He didn't need to tell her what it was he was referring to. "Did you think it was funny?"

"In a sad way." They were holding hands with both hands, like people at a wedding altar.

"So you liked it?"

"I did," she said. "I do."

Sam studied her hands. They were a girl's hands, with fine, tapered girl's fingers and chewed nails. Who wouldn't laugh? It was funny, wasn't it? He kissed Tess's fingers. He kissed her mouth. She asked him if he was sad. He said he didn't think so. "Not too sad, anyway."

Fair Share was a thriller replete with macabre deaths—a career IRS agent snaps and goes on a serial-killing rampage against a supercilious tax cheat and his investment firm of blueblood CPAs, the first of whom the agent burns alive on a pile of gasoline-soaked bonds—but Sam found himself only periodically checking in to the narrative. The second round of pot had dispersed what the first had gathered, and his attention toggled freely between the screen and any number of unrelated thoughts.

Did Tess have any tattoos or scars. Would he ever see them, or would she come to her senses when the drugs wore off. Was she right about everything. Was she bossy. Did he like that, really like that, in a nonsexual way. He thought she probably was right about everything. Did that make it okay that she was bossy.

The IRS agent absently slides around the beads of his ornamental desk abacus and listens to a radio report about a thrill killer.

Was Tom's maple tree going to have to come down. What a shame that would be.

A terrified banker huddles atop a platinum-plated toilet seat in his private executive john and sweats and shakes. The psychopathic IRS agent unzips to take a leak in the platinum-plated urinal on the opposite side of the partition. The hand that isn't holding his dick is holding a NYSE replica gavel. Bits of bone and brain speckle the hammer's head.

Where was Sandra now. Had they put her in a room with windows. Maybe he hadn't given her a fair chance. God bless Mina, but she was a handful.

The coroner says he's never seen or heard of anything like it: there were over sixty thousand dollars in bonds in the victim's stomach. "The killer forced the poor bastard to *eat* a small fortune," he says.

Rick had a sword-knife thing like that, with elvish runes. Sting. Brooks stole it.

Brooks with a beard. Brooks dueling with the air, strangling the air. It made sense in a Brooks kind of way. He'd stomped Brooks's balls and made him cry.

Brooks? Could it be?

"What's wrong?" asked Tess.

Sam was shaking his head; it had been him. It had been Brooks.

"I'll be right back," he said, and she appeared doubtful, but he added, "Really this time. I promise."

Out in the main hall that ran between the multiplex's four auditoriums, he did some pacing and deep breathing. He started to feel better, less busy in the mind, like he could manage.

There was stiff brown carpet under his feet and peppered drop-ceiling panels above his head. He hadn't known it was Brooks; he wouldn't have hurt Brooks, or anyone else, on purpose.

Sam told himself he was okay. He was baked, but he was going to make it.

Across the hall from *Fair Share* was a family movie, *Cheeks,* about a little girl whose parents are in a nasty custody battle but who inherits a magic talking pig from her eccentric grandfather. The pig, Cheeks, can be mischievous, but he's ultimately a very good-hearted pig. The little girl convinces Cheeks to help her show her parents how much they still love each other.

In the preview, there was a part where the kid exclaimed, "Cheeks, if you don't help me, who will?" and the potbellied pig gulped. "You do know I'm a pig, right?"

Anthropomorphism was maybe not the best additive for the freak-out he was trying to come down from, but Sam thought it might at least be quiet.

He entered the theater and slipped into the back row. While there were a few tall-people-short-people combinations toward the front of the theater, it was, as he'd hoped, a fairly sparse house.

On the screen, Cheeks was trying to get a farmer to give him a ride. "Why, you're just a pig!" said the farmer.

"A pig with money to spend!" exclaimed Cheeks.

Sam leaned his head against the rear wall of the theater and passed out.

When he awoke, it was the climax. There were a hundred potbellied pigs scampering around in the gallery of Grand Central Station. Cops with nets were trying to catch the pigs, ladies in fur stoles were screeching, tourists were hanging on to their luggage, pigs were boarding trains to Rochester, the stars who played the estranged couple were looking around desperately for their daughter, and it was bedlam.

"Jesus," said Sam. His mouth was dry, and his vision was smeary.

Tess was crouched down beside him, shaking his knee. "Are you okay?" she whispered.

"I had an episode. Too much pot. Too much everything. I got overwhelmed."

"Does that mean you're going to be a bitch and not smoke some more with us?"

"Yes."

"Hmph." Tess unzipped his fly, fished around, grabbed his penis—the cold of her hand caused him to stiffen almost instantaneously—tugged it out, and put it in her mouth.

Sam straightened, and the seat back clapped against the wall. The swabbing sensation of her tongue over the tip of his penis caused his breath to catch and his toes to curl inside his shoes. The seat clap seemed to echo; the echo seemed to announce, "Blow job back here!" While it was happening, his thoughts alternated between I'm being blown in a movie theater, and Please don't turn around anyone. It was scary. When he was on the edge of orgasm, his eyes fell on the screen: the reunited family—father, mother, daughter—are locked in a group embrace while Cheeks the potbellied pig looks on with tears in his eyes.

Tess released him with an inhalation and rocked back onto her haunches.

He doubled forward over his exposed penis.

"You said you'd come back."

"I was going to." Sam stuffed his wet hard-on into his pants. His high had evaporated, he was famished, and his penis ached.

She had crossed her arms. She was still down between the seats, addressing him from below. Damp shone on her cheeks and forehead. "You need to be better. You can't be overwhelmed by me." Her position gave her words a particularly plaintive aspect.

"I thought I didn't have to feel shitty about everything anymore?" He was annoyed.

Tess frowned at him. "You don't have to feel shitty about things that are over or made up. But I'm real. You can feel shitty about letting me down. I listened to you about the Segway."

"What does that have to do with anything?" asked Sam. He was feeling abused. "I told you it was probably better than you were giving it credit for, and that you should give it a chance, and you saw that I was right. This has nothing to do with the Segway."

She took a ChapStick out of her vest pocket and applied it to her lips. "No. I believed you. I haven't even tried one. I let myself get swept up in your conviction because I want to believe in you. And you need to start justifying my belief."

Sam thanked her for her candor. She said he was welcome.

5.

He gave her the car keys because she said she needed to go with Farah and Wesley on an "operation," whatever that meant. Sam suspected it was something adolescent, and he was weary. Where Wesley had unearthed so much energy, he had no idea; the man regularly slept fourteen hours a day and had the bedsores to prove it. Sam brooded sulkily on the conjunction of Tess's appearance and his roommate's resurgence before discounting the thought for the excuse that it was. Wesley was his friend, and although Tess had given him what could only be called a mean job, he supposed he deserved it.

He had been careless with her. He had been selfish and unreliable. He had been a lot of things—and he did need to be better.

When *Cheeks* finished—Mom and Dad renew their marriage vows, and Cheeks gets a banana split—Sam purchased a large bucket of popcorn and a ginger ale.

The lobby area of the multiplex was glass-walled on three sides. He found a bench opposite the longest wall and gazed out on the parking lot at night. It looked like a parking lot at night. There were cars traced in reflected light. There were acres of pavement. Shopping carts stood stranded, looking picked clean. The popcorn tasted like butter and squeaked between his teeth.

He wanted to believe that if the patch of ground beneath him dropped out and the whole world fell, he'd be the hero who'd rally the troops and come up with a plan for getting everyone to the top. But Sam couldn't believe that; directing a movie was one thing, death-defying adventure was something else.

Allie had gone for a walk, suffered a massive heart attack, and expired on a semi-suburban roadside. How was that for banal? You wanted to die spraying the bad guys with machine-gun fire or sealing the crack in the hull of the space shuttle, running face-first into an inferno or slashing a scimitar at zombie hordes, but in all likelihood, you went for a walk on a Sunday afternoon and ended up sprawled on the shoulder of the road.

Was there any way to be a hero in plain old life, parking lot/box store/multiplex life? Sam didn't know. He needed to try and be more thoughtful. There might be a touch of heroism in that. To give another person the benefit of the doubt was about as difficult an everyday task as anyone faced.

Maybe next time, he could be a tad more circumspect before jumping on an incapacitated man's balls.

Could that really have been Brooks? It had been. He knew it. Sam hoped someone had brought the man to a hospital. Sam hadn't meant to hurt him.

What made Sam uneasy, what made him run the jagged nail of his right thumb up and down between his teeth, was the possibility that, conversely, Brooks had very much intended to hurt Sam. Rick Savini's Sting was rusty, but it could kill. How many weeks had Brooks been following him, lurking around, gathering his courage, waiting for the right voice in his head to tell him the moment to finish Sam off?

"I wanted to see *Quel Beau Parleur* again," said Booth from behind him.

"Funny meeting you here." Sam had observed his father's reflection in the window, approaching from the opposite side of the theater lobby, cape flicking around his heels. He turned. "Where's Mina?"

"She claimed she had homework. Though I do not like to accuse your sister of gainsaying, my suspicion is that her true intention was to talk on the phone with the young gay man she's in love with." Booth inquired as to the whereabouts of his son's friends. Sam said he didn't know. They'd taken some drugs and the rental car and abandoned him.

"I'm sorry that we laughed. I know you saw us." His father placed a light hand on his shoulder. "I'm suddenly always sorry, aren't I?"

"Ah, forget it. It was funny. The movie's funny. It just is. Why should everyone else laugh and not you?" Sam dug up a handful of popcorn.

"Because I am your father."

"You have my permission."

If Tess was right and he didn't have to feel shitty about everything, it followed that neither did anyone else, not even Booth. Also, it was exhausting, being pissed off all the time. He'd felt that way before Tess said anything; he just hadn't wanted to admit it. He offered the popcorn bucket.

Booth sat down and helped himself. They chewed. Booth used the tail of his cape to dab around his mouth.

"What if I don't want permission to laugh about that?" asked Booth.

Sam rolled his head around. "Shit, Booth. I don't know. I guess that's your problem."

His father grunted.

A few kids were horsing around in the parking lot, kicking trash, surfing the hoods of cars. Out of sight, an engine hacked, wheezed, wheezed some more, finally turned over. The two men continued to lower the level on the popcorn in the bucket.

"You know that movie *The Pit*?"

"Yes. I saw it. Las Vegas falls into a big damn hole. I enjoyed it very much."

"Do you think I'd be able to survive? If I were there? If I lived through the initial fall, I mean."

"With all the militia and end-times cultists and gas fires and unstable structures and so on? You're no fighter, Samuel. You'd need protection. You'd need a skill to barter. Do you have any abilities that would help start a new civilization?"

"Mina taught me to a knit a little bit once."

Booth shook his head in grave apology. No one would need knitwear after the apocalypse, not in Las Vegas.

"My head would end up mounted on the hood of some warlord's all-terrain vehicle, wouldn't it?"

"If it's any consolation, I'm certain I'd suffer some variation of the same fate. Men like us aren't built for post-apocalyptic adventures. If there was anyone who would have performed well under such conditions, it was your mother. Your mother was not merely intelligent, she was cunning. She was also tough. I think she would have fared well in a post-apocalypse. If we could stick with her, we might manage to survive."

The thought of Allie in the apocalypse, directing them through their paces, ordering them to boil water and board the doors, amused Sam. He had an idea it would have amused her, too. "I like that, Booth."

A mall cop car pulled up, and the juvenile delinquents scattered. There was only a little popcorn left in the bucket.

"Your girl's lovely. Is Tess her name? She seems to have a fine head on her shoulders, too."

"Tess. Yeah. I'm not sure what she sees in me."

"A thought to keep in mind: just as it is a mistake to count on the generosity of a woman, it is also a mistake to underestimate her capacity for pity."

"Okay," said Sam.

They finished the popcorn. The parking lot was broad and dark.

Booth cleared his throat. "Should we go in and get our seats?" He hated to miss the previews.

A bony, dark-eyed middle-aged man trots up the walk of his apartment building, carelessly swinging a bouquet of roses. A few petals drift onto the ground unnoticed as he goes. The camera lingers long enough to show passersby, how their shoes flatten and tear the petals.

(In the foyer of the building, a pensioner greets him, and we learn that the man's name is Marcel. "Written any good books lately?" asks the pensioner, leaning over a battered walker and grinning a spittle-flecked grin. More information is gleaned: the man we are following is a writer.

"Keep bothering me and I'll take your walker, old man, and give it to my wife for her art," says Marcel.

The pensioner waves a hairy hand: *bah!*)

Marcel enters his apartment and discovers a note tucked in the frame of the hallway mirror. As he unfolds and reads the missive, as his face falls, our view inches wider, revealing the pale square on the opposite wall where a painting used to hang. His fiancée has left him.

The bouquet is deposited in the garbage and quickly buried beneath empty wine bottles . . .

Furry dust lies on the keys of a typewriter. Marcel is blocked. Day after day, he slumps in the window seat of his apartment, sucking brown cigarettes.

From the window seat, he sees a white shirt on a clothesline that traverses the air above the street, connecting his building with the building opposite. The garment grays and stretches through autumn, stiffens and freezes in the winter, thaws in the spring, and begins to fray as summer arrives.

An anemic mustache has germinated across Marcel's upper lip, and the dark circles under his eyes are pits. No matter how often he smoothes the hair at his temples, it fans up. He is transparently, quietly frazzled.

One day men in white suits transport a body bag from the apartment building across the street. The clothesline's owner apparently was deceased for months, but no one noticed . . .

At the local grocery, Marcel gets a job bagging groceries.

A queue develops on his first morning. Marcel arranges the contents of his grocery bags with artistic judiciousness. The baguettes are tucked into one corner of the bag and braced by the boxes of pasta; bricks of cheese are pieced together in another corner; potatoes fill in the center; parcels of sugar and flour are added; a carton of eggs tops off. Some people yell at him to pick up the pace. An outraged man actually uses a beret to strike Marcel. The blocked writer is so numbed by his own troubles that he ignores the abuse. Even when the beret briefly awakens him from his stupor and he invites the man to suck his ass, it's obvious that his heart's not in the insult.

A few days later, Marcel realizes that a young woman—a customer we recognize from the grocery queue—is stalking him on the streets. She wears a yellow scarf knotted in her black hair. Her expression is fierce. When their eyes meet, she snarls, bares her pretty teeth and growls; a close-up shows her pupils dilating.

Marcel, alarmed, tries to shake her. As he darts up a department store escalator, she darts up behind him. He slips into the second-to-last car of a Métro train, but she manages to dive into the last car. On the street again, Marcel dashes for a bus, grabs the back railing, and swings himself up just as the vehicle is accelerating, leaving the woman in the yellow scarf behind. She shoves a man from the seat of his Vespa—the man had been leering at her, flapping his tongue—and leaps aboard, and comes roaring after the bus.

Marcel disembarks in front of his building. He steps out into the street to face the oncoming Vespa. In a gesture of absolute surrender, he shuts his eyes and spreads his arms. The Vespa shows no signs of slowing, its narrow wheels flickering around like snapped reels, its engine hum rising to a whine, the obsessed woman tucking low over the handlebars, scarf drawn out behind into a fluttering antenna. Marcel stands mere feet away, eyes tight, unmoving, and—

—the film slam-cuts to the writer's bedroom. He's lying nude except for the yellow scarf, which is knotted around his neck. The young woman sits on the edge of the bed and slips on her stockings. She is very beautiful and tranquil; the unexpected range of freckles above her bare breasts make her appear unusually naked. Marcel asks, "Why me?" He's forty-nine. He bags groceries. His most recent novel is already out of print. The view from his window is of a tattered shirt. "What about me attracted you?"

"You're a very good talker," she says insensibly. Until that afternoon we know that Marcel has hardly ever spoken to her except to tell her how much she owes for her groceries. *Quel beau parleur . . .*

The woman in the yellow scarf is the first in a patternless series of lovers—young and middle-aged and quite elderly, all female customers from the grocery store. The blocked writer is initially aroused, then annoyed, and finally exhausted by the stream of lovers. When he asks them to justify their attraction, they refer to his handsome face, which isn't handsome—or his physique, which is scrawny—or his kind hands and gentle fingers, which are nicotine-stained and bitten to the quick. Most frequent are references to his verbal savoir faire.

Much of the movie's second act chronicles Marcel's efforts to evade these ravenous females and, failing that, to convince them that they could make a far better match.

"I'm not even a successful bagger of groceries," he says to the willowy red-haired wife of a diplomat as she winds around the doorway of his bedroom. "Blah-blah-blah," she says.

After a long chase, a cheerfully corpulent middle-aged woman tracks him to his hiding place in the showroom shower stall of a department store. "Okay, okay! But be careful!" cries Marcel as the enormous woman presses in on him, her bosom swallowing up his face, her hands digging into his hair. "I never could resist a sweet talker," she confesses.

A cut removes us to the exterior of the stall, where our perspective is largely occluded by the shower's frosted door. What we can see is reminiscent of a lava lamp: through the pebbled glass, the woman's paisley-print dress swells and heaves against the scarlet of Marcel's grocery-store uniform.

An elderly widow tricks Marcel into delivering groceries to her luxurious motel suite. Upon opening the door, he finds her seated in a wing-back chair, nude and smoking a pipe. Marcel, startled, drops his armful of groceries, where they explode against the floor—eggs, milk, meat, apples. "Um," says Marcel.

The elderly widow uncrosses her legs. "Enough with the fancy chit-chat! Tell it to the box, Don Juan!"

Dutifully, he approaches . . .

Marcel arrives home to find a skinny, mohawked, giggling stranger in his bathtub. He is unsurprised. "Whenever you're ready," he tells her.

She is riding Marcel on the window seat—the ghost of a shirt fluttering in the background—when the pensioner bangs into the apartment, thudding down the hall with his walker.

"Papa!" cries the woman.

"I'll kill him," shrieks the pensioner. He is fumbling with an antique pistol.

"I warned you, you old fart," says Marcel.

We cut to the apartment landing. The pensioner has a bloody nose.

He's on the floor, leaning against the wall, wheezing and clutching the pieces of his destroyed pistol. His granddaughter walks past him. "I'm not sorry for you," she says . . .

"What's this?" asks Marcel's ex-fiancée.

Marcel has come to the art gallery she curates. He has the pensioner's battered walker. "I thought you could use it for an installation."

The ex-fiancée asks, "Did you take this from a cripple?"

"He was an asshole first and a cripple second," says Marcel. "I want to understand what went wrong between us, Selene."

"So you bring me a walker?"

"Everyone loves me except for you," Marcel says plaintively.

Selene shakes her head—and guides him to a nearby painting.

Before the wall-size oil, Marcel's ex-fiancée scans one way, then the other: no one is watching. She grabs the frame and hoists herself up and into the artwork. Marcel follows.

They stroll around a cubist jungle scene, alive with boxy parrots and jumbled-looking monkeys, distorted palm trees and crooked clouds. The distances are unstable, single elements broken into close-up pieces and faraway pieces, as if seen through a shattered lens. Marcel isn't interested, though. He doesn't want to wander around the sweaty, jagged world of the painting. What he wants is their life back. They were comfortable. They made sense. "What is your problem?" he asks.

"What is your problem?" Selene replies.

Marcel becomes furious. He kicks the sharp grass and punches the sky; several blades snap, and one of the crooked clouds fissures. She smiles sadly. It's evident that Marcel has spoiled any chance he might have had to win her back.

Together, they do their best to repair the painting, gluing the grass, applying some powder from her handbag to the cracked cloud. Eventually, Marcel climbs out of the frame and offers a hand to help her down to the floor. The curator accepts it with a sigh. "Time," Selene observes, "makes us imprudent with what we love."

"It's because I'm mortal, isn't it?" Marcel lights a dented cigarette.

His ex shakes her head. She looks at him and manages a half-hearted smile. "No, you stupid man. You don't see. That was my favorite thing about you."

At the door, he tells her she doesn't have to take the walker if she doesn't want it. Selene kisses him and says thank you. It was a thought-ful gift. She won't use it for art, but maybe for magic . . .

The next day the first young woman, the one with the yellow scarf who chased him on the Vespa, comes to the head of Marcel's queue. "Marcel . . ." she whispers. He groans and shoves a bottle crunching down on a head of lettuce in her bag. The woman slaps him and dashes out, ignoring his belated cry that she should take another lettuce.

That evening he walks home instead of using the Métro. His path carries him past a housing complex whose central feature is a wrecked fountain in a crumbling courtyard. There is a boy in the courtyard. He is a child of seven or eight, dressed in high-water overalls. The young fel-low has collected an impressive pile of rubble, pieces snapped off of the fountain's bowl, spout, and figures.

For a while Marcel watches as, with great precision, the boy in the overalls sets one piece of broken masonry after another back into place, using wads of chewed bubble gum for adhesive. A crowd of young girls standing nearby provide the chewed gum. When signaled, the girl whose turn it is steps forward and drops her wad into the boy's waiting palm.

Before the unhappy man's eyes, the fountain gradually, impossibly reforms.

Marcel breaks into a full sprint toward home.

Instead of returning to his own building, he enters the apartment building opposite. Marcel careens up the stairs and finds his way to the apartment that parallels his own. He bangs on the door. A dark-skinned man in a dashiki answers. Marcel lurches around him, through the kitchen, and out onto the balcony. By turning the rusted pulley attached to the railing, Marcel reels in the remains of the dead man's shirt. He takes it down and carefully folds it.

When he steps back into the kitchen, the immigrant family—mother, father, two daughters—is huddled in a corner. Marcel's mouth moves, but he can't seem to find the words. He is finally crying.

The patriarch of the immigrant family steps forward. He gestures to the table, where there are platters of food and an empty seat. "Will you stay and share our dinner?"

As the credits roll, the camera adjourns to a stationary position to watch the family eat. The father asks his daughters about their day. While the children begin to relate the details of several interlocking neighborhood conflicts and scandals, the three adults circulate the platters, and listen and nod, and are still listening when the screen blacks out.

Afterward, Sam walked with his father out to Tom's truck.

Sam admired the movie, particularly the lead performance of his former collaborator Rick Savini. Besides speaking in what was not his native language, Savini played his part with a degree of outrage that Sam wouldn't have thought the actor had in him. While the film's subtext—that what women want above all else is a man who is careful with their groceries—seemed to him both dubious and too cute, he thought it was a heartfelt attempt. It was interesting that his father liked it so much. No one could ever accuse Booth of being careful with the groceries.

"Tremendous," said Booth. "Simply tremendous. Did you enjoy it?"

Sam said he did. They had come to the driver's side of the truck. The air was cold enough to make Sam wish for a coat; the summer was really over. The CINEMA sign above the theater doors cast a red nimbus.

"What do you suppose happened next, Samuel?"

"They had dinner?"

"Smart-ass. After that."

"I honestly don't have any idea," said Sam.

"I would like to believe that Marcel took a chance at redemption, at change. I would like to think that he did something marvelous for the woman he loved. His great gift was for organization, wasn't it? Maybe he organized something for her, made it so she could access it in a way that made her very happy, and won her back that way."

Sam thought of the women he knew and the wildernesses of their closets. "Maybe," he said, "but I think they ended it in the right place."

Booth assented. He blew a puff of white steam. Sirens burbled somewhere in the dark. "Welles cut me."

"Say again?" Sam had no clue what his father was referring to.

"I won't bore you with the grubby details, but a couple of years ago I managed to finagle a viewing of the assembly of *Yorick*. The Welles movie. I wasn't in it. He cut me out."

His father glanced at him with a raised eyebrow. Sam didn't know whether to read the expression as a challenge or a bid for sympathy or what. He was momentarily tempted to ask for "the grubby details," but in the next instant, he decided it might be better not to know.

"I'm sorry," he said.

Booth shook his head. "You shouldn't be."

"I shouldn't?"

"No, you shouldn't. It hurt terribly because I loved Orson. He was my idol, and he told me I was great. He took me seriously. When the takes were over, he clapped for me. So when I saw the picture and I never appeared, not even for a frame, it felt almost as if I'd been edited out of my own life.

"And that scared me terribly. For then, if indeed *that* was my history, what had been filmed, then what was *this*"—Booth circled around with his index finger pointing, indicating the cavernous parking lot, the cement box of the movie theater, the distant interstate, and beyond— "what was it that happened here, with your mother? With you? With Mina and with Sandra? That was the start of my Awakening."

"Then I had a toothache."

"You had a toothache," repeated Sam.

"Yes, a toothache." His father slumped slightly. He peered into the middle distance. His beard jutted. "I went to the dentist, and while I was waiting, I picked up a wrinkled old issue of *The New Yorker,* and I read a poem. It was about our obligation to enjoy ourselves and engage in frivolity in spite of the world's many cruelties. And when I read it, I suddenly felt validated, Sam. I felt that my work meant something. Would you like me to recite it to you, the poem? I have it memorized."

Sam had to bite back a smile. The ruthless fire of this world consumed everything—everything except dentist-office back issues of *The New Yorker*. "If you'd like."

"'Sorrow everywhere,'" Booth began, and the poem unreeled. There was horror and there was joy, and before the fire consumed us, the sufferers obligated us to our joy. Sam's father spoke the words without a lilt, without projection. He let them be. At the end, after the oars drew through the water, Sam clapped politely. It was a pretty poem. The sound echoed faintly in the parking lot.

Booth responded with a dip of his head and finished the story. "And so, feeling greatly reassured, I decided to hang up my pistols and to return home for good to reacquaint myself with my family and perhaps, in some minor way, make amends."

"I'm happy for you, Booth." Sam stuck out his hand, and they shook.

■ ■ ■

An hour later, there was no sign of Tess, Wesley, and Farah, and the projectionist needed to lock up the movie theater. Sam called for a taxi to return him to the hotel in Quentinville.

Booth had invited them to a party the next day; an old mutual friend, none other than bilingual actor and Westchester resident Rick Savini, was holding a celebration for the end of summer. It sounded like a decent time, particularly for a Sunday—and it so happened that Sam had something belonging to their old mutual friend that was long overdue to be returned. He said he'd talk to the others, promising to do his best to convince them to put off the drive back to the city in favor of the get-together.

They'd left it in a good place, Sam thought, probably as good a place as they'd ever left it—maybe as good as they ever could. The exchange had somehow diminished his father, shrunk him down to a size such that Sam could see all his edges. It seemed amazing that he had spent so many years brooding over Booth, over what he had and hadn't done, over what was true and what was untrue. He had long believed that his father was full of shit, but he had never comprehended what was as obvious as his own nose: Booth was as confused as anyone.

In the backseat of the taxi, while the interstate carved between rock walls and fields, Sam conceived of a movie: about a man—call him, Jim—who finds himself stranded in his Chevy Malibu in a vast parking lot. Jim goes out on a quick trip to pick up an extension cord only to find, when he tries to leave, that his car won't start; it's out of gas. Jim then waits—surreally, obstinately—through several seasons for his no-account brother to bring gas so he can return to his apartment. Sam thought the idea had potential; God knew there must be a parking lot somewhere that could be used for short money. A few scenes sprang up: the marooned driver using the demonstration barbecue set up on the sidewalk in front of the Lowe's to cook a pigeon he'd caught; the mailman bringing Jim's mail to the window of the disabled vehicle; the kindly checkout girl from the Dollar Store across the parking lot coming over one night with some chintzy battery-powered Christmas lights to make the car more homey. The castaway Jim, when Sam saw his face, he saw Wyatt Smithson. Wyatt had that flummoxed yet resolute look. Maybe he'd be willing to give it another go. Maybe Sam could convince Anthony to quit his father's lobster boat and give it one more shot, too.

In his mind, he was pulling them all back in, his old crew, and this time it was better, it was fun.

Then again, it was also possible that he was still a bit high, and in the light of day, the parking lot movie would present itself as somewhat less promising.

In a single long afternoon, he had observed as Las Vegas fell into the ground, as an IRS agent coolly murdered several bankers and traders, as a potbellied pig helped a little girl, and as an aggrieved man learned that consideration was romance. His head felt dopey with fantasy lives. There were worse ways to kill a day. Polly asked him once what it was that drove him to want to make movies, if it was about his father, and he told her that he wanted to surprise people with a movie the way they were surprised in real life—something along those lines. He didn't know about that anymore. It seemed overly ambitious. If he ever made another film, Sam thought he could settle a bit. The movie would just need to be fun enough and good enough for a few laughs and maybe a moment or two of grace. Fun enough and good enough to chip a few hours off a day.

The taxi rolled along. The driver asked if he minded the radio, and Sam didn't.

6.

The others showed up at the hotel room around two A.M., briefly waking Sam. "Where have you been?" he asked.

"Some questions are better left unanswered, coxswain," said Wesley, and flopped onto the bed, reeking of dope and jostling Sam.

"Plausible deniability," said Tess. She bumped off a few pieces of furniture on the way to the armchair in the corner and collapsed into it.

Farah, apparently attached to the group, waved a hand, said, "Hey—Sam," and disappeared into the bathroom to sleep in the tub.

A few hours later, Sam woke up for good. He lay under the prickly hotel comforter, and his first thought was that he needed to e-mail the wedding coordinator who had written him on Friday and tell her he couldn't take the job. He was going to quit making weddingographies. It was a dreary job, and he didn't like doing it, and if he was going to be less dreary and more likable, or at least more bearable, quitting was a place to start. How he was going to pay the bills going forward, Sam didn't know, but at a minimum, he needed to find something where he didn't fantasize about the people around him being covered in boiling lava.

Errant thoughts about the parking lot movie—a row of pigeons on a light stanchion as the protagonist barbecues their comrade; a long shot of the checkout girl, draped in the battery-powered Christmas lights, walking through the dark to the stranded car—made Sam smile.

Beside him, Wesley's snoring was like the idling of a piece of old and unreliable machinery, a grinding of rusty gears and a deep gurgle.

Tess, curled up in the chair, cleared her throat. "Good morning." Sam could see her bloodshot eyes in the dimness. "You look very pleased with yourself."

"We got invited to a party." He grinned at her.

Tess gingerly prodded her jaw first one way, then the other, apparently confirming that it still moved. "Oh, goodie."

To the question of attending the late-morning party, no opposition was registered from the other two members of the group. So the four piled into the rental, Sam and Tess in the front, Wesley and Farah and the half dozen or so memorial stuffed animals liberated from the Quentinville Cemetery in the back.

They drove to Farah's apartment in Kingston so she could change out of her uniform. Tess and Sam went to purchase coffee and bagels from a diner across the street. Wesley stayed in the car to fart.

Once the waitress brought the bagels they'd ordered, Sam carefully loaded them into the paper bag open on the counter, one at a time.

"You're very painstaking with those bagels," said Tess. It was hard to read if she was being sarcastic, because her eyes were shielded by a pair of opaque sunglasses, but then she took his hand and leaned against him as they walked back to the other side of the street.

The sun had come out. The air was dry, and although they were on an urban block, it smelled like the earth. The street trees showed vibrant new patches of color. A couple of boys were kicking around a soccer ball in the drive between buildings. The step and crunch of their sneakers on the gravelly pavement seemed especially autumnal.

"How are you feeling?" he asked.

"The way I always do when I smoke ten bowls and run around all night stealing toys from graves. Poor."

"I ended up going to the movies with my old man last night," said Sam. "It was actually remarkably okay."

"Let me guess: you went to the French movie with all the tits."

"Hey. I liked it."

"Shocker." He sensed her rolling her eyes, but her face against his shoulder was angled away. "I'm glad you had an okay time with your dad, though."

The trip was slow going, the road clogged by city drivers heading home from their country getaways. The two in the backseat had promptly passed out, leaning in opposite directions, the ratty stuffed animals mounded between them.

"Can you finish telling me about your parents?"

Tess had been quiet for a few miles, tucked behind her sunglasses. "You really want to know?"

Sam said he did. If they turned into something, she'd hear enough about his parents. "When I fell asleep, you were saying how your mother raged and your father needled."

"Okay." Tess yawned. "When I was, jeez, about seventeen, the situation started to get really itchy because my mom, she decided she wanted— Oh, Christ, Sam, can I tell you this another time? I'm enjoying the drive."

"Sure," he said.

"It's like, 'He spends all day writing insurance binders for theater producers so their asses are covered in case a piece of scenery falls on one of the actors. She retired at fifty and spends her days buying ceramic creatures and organizing the ones that she already has in little tableaus on the windowsills. At night, they make drinks together and then go drink them in different rooms. They make me insane and they make each other insane. The End.' That's the CliffsNotes version. Are your parents any different?"

"My mother's dead."

"See. Now I feel bad."

"Don't. Honestly, don't."

"By the way. If you made that up, you're going to hell."

"She's dead, I swear. Totally, totally dead. When I was in college, she had a heart attack out walking."

"I'm sorry, Sam."

"Thanks. Our friend Tom tilled her ashes into a bed of his echinacea. You walked by the spot when you were at the house."

"I like echinacea. They're tenacious."

"And my father. He's—a lot."

"But see, Sam? Do you really want to go there today? Right now? It's already been a long weekend."

The rental car was in the second of four packed lanes. In front of them was a smoke-colored SUV that had a bicycle belted to the top. The SUV's passengers were keyhole-shaped silhouettes. The bike's wheels spun. Sam wanted to pass the SUV—the turning of the bike's wheels seemed to hint that it wanted to break loose from its straps and shoot back into their windshield—but the traffic was tight.

For a few quiet moments, Sam placidly contemplated a vision of the bike slipping its tethers. He saw it plunge backward into the windshield, the glass splintering and folding, and their bodies enveloped and shredded by debris. As was nearly always the case when he imagined bad things happening, his thoughts spun off to Brooks, to the movie, and to what it had been before the AD put a match to it. Much quicker than usual, the thought gave way, snapped over like a slide, and what replaced it was a small hairy man, spitting and moaning on the ground.

Sam checked his mirrors, signaled, slipped into a space in the passing line, and pulled around the SUV.

"Nice maneuver," said Tess. "What's the hurry?"

"I was worried that the bike on top of the SUV was going to fall off and kill us."

"That's a hopeful thought."

"I am hopeful," he said. It was the truth. The blatant fantasies of his youth, the ones that his father had performed in and the ones that his father had committed, had made him suspicious of make-believe, and Sam prided himself on his sense of realism. To suspend disbelief had always been a problem for him. But if the last few days showed anything, it was that truly improbable things did sometimes happen. He wasn't thinking of Jo-Jo driving the GTO through Tom's house, either, or even of how he and Booth seemed to come to a détente. What he was thinking of was Tess, of her putting up with him, of her coming all this way—for him. It wasn't a miracle, exactly, but it was damned generous of her.

And from there, it struck Sam that he needed to balance the scale, to make his own gesture of goodwill, to get in the passing lane and make some time. He needed to try and do something for Brooks Hartwig, Jr.

"Do you think your father could help me sort out the residuals on *Who We Are*? You said he was an entertainment lawyer." The unopened checks back at the apartment in Red Hook—by all rights, at least half belonged to Brooks.

"Probably," said Tess. "What's in it for me?"

"Dinner and a movie."

"Dinner and a movie?"

"No. Better still: two movies."

"Two? Wow."

"Uh-huh. Later this week. A double feature of *E.T.* and *Dog Day Afternoon*. And sometime after that, we're going to make our way to the nearest Segway store, take a test spin, and settle things once and for all. Which, I'm optimistic, you'll see is pretty neat, even if it's not a jet pack."

"You'd take me to test-ride a Segway?"

"I'd take you anywhere."

"Aw." Tess touched his knee.

7.

A mighty lion reared across a maroon background. The wind turned the flag lightly back and forth, an oar dipping in and drawing out, and the blue sky like water.

"Gryffindor," said Farah. "That's the emblem—of Gryffindor."

"Awesome," said Wesley. "I'd totally take that."

They parked the car alongside the walk that edged Rick Savini's long driveway. There were already a half dozen or so vehicles lined up, Tom's truck among them.

As they walked up the driveway, Sam was pleased to see that his fills had held over the eight-plus years since that spring morning in 2003; Rick Savini's driveway was in excellent shape. He further surmised that the Gryffindor flag, which flew from a pinnacle at the top of the house, was the actor's solution for differentiating his house from the others in the neighborhood—and an elegant, magical solution it was, too.

As they were getting out of the car, Tess noted that she thought she'd seen it in an airplane catalog not too long before.

Rick Savini embraced Sam in the doorway. "Kid, you don't call, you don't write, you don't show up unannounced and perform house repairs. I was starting to worry you'd forsaken me." The actor appeared the same as ever, as if he'd spent the preceding night trying to sleep while someone stood outside his window banging trash can lids.

"I'm sorry," said Sam. He held out the rusted sword.

Rick took the weapon and turned it over a few times. "My Precious." He stuck it through his belt, grunted in apparent satisfaction, and glanced up at Sam. "You should be sorry. You goddamned should be." The actor inspected him with a pursed-lipped expression of disapproval. "What's your next movie about? I need work."

Sam couldn't hold off a smile. The guy really was a hell of an actor. "I was actually just working through an idea. It has to do with a guy who gets stranded in a mall parking lot."

"Shit, Sam, that sounds like a blockbuster," said Rick. "Okay, send me the script when you're ready. I'll do it." He waved the rest of the group inside. "Come on in, we're celebrating fall and getting drunk."

Sword clacking at his hip, he guided them down a long hall toward the rear of the house. As they approached, there was the tidal sound of lots of people talking at once. Tess squeezed Sam's hand.

About twenty people were gathered in Rick Savini's parlor, a high-ceilinged room outfitted with a large television, a couple of leather couches, some armchairs and oak occasional tables, and French doors that gave onto the lawn. In the crowd Sam spotted his father, Tom, Mina, Christine the recording engineer, and Christine's daughter, Logan, who was dragging her amputee bunny by an ear. An aromatic spread of barbecue had been set on a table, as well as some ice buckets. There was a basket of apples. Running along the entire length of the French doors was an elaborate navy-carpeted scaffold, vaguely resembling a model roller coaster, which must have been for Rick Savini's cats to play on. Somewhere out of sight, a stereo was playing Motown. It wasn't too warm or too cold. Laughter came from all directions.

Tom spotted him, put up a hand, and waved. "There's beer!"

Sam realized that everything was going to be okay. He bent down to Tess and whispered in her ear, "Everything is going to be okay."

"Why wouldn't it be?" she asked, and detached herself to go and chat with Mina.

A broad-shouldered figure rose from one of the couches. Johannes "Jo-Jo" Knecht strolled over. Rick introduced him. "Sam, this is my neighbor, Jo-Jo."

Jo-Jo said they'd already met. "Sam's a friend of Polly's, dude."

They shook hands. Jo-Jo's hands were large enough to palm Sam's head.

Polly approached holding Rainer. "It's Uncle Sam!" The baby glared from the depths of its face fat.

"Hey," said Sam.

"Did I interrupt something?" asked Polly. "Oh, dear. Were you boys about to compare penises, and I came over and made it awkward?"

"No. We already did that," said Sam.

"Mine was bigger," said Jo-Jo. To demonstrate, he put out his enormous hands and spread them apart about seven inches, parallel.

Sam reached over and readjusted one of Jo-Jo's hands to widen the gap another inch. "There."

"My stars." Polly fanned herself.

After he'd helped himself to a beer, Sam milled around and talked with the people he knew and introduced himself to some of the ones he didn't.

Tom said he'd already started reframing the broken walls of his house. The car, he observed, could have been a lot bigger. Sam nearly pointed out that the car could have caused more damage if it had been an aircraft carrier or a neutron bomb, but he wished his old friend a happy autumn and told him how glad he was that he was here, and that he loved him. Tom blushed.

Over by the French doors, Sam chatted with Christine, Logan, Polly, and Rainer. Christine said she didn't want to offend Rick, but she thought that summer had a lot to say for itself. Polly nodded; she liked summer, too. "And I've never murdered anyone," she said, "let alone a whole string of people." The little girl slid her hand over the sloping surfaces of the cat conduit and observed that it must be pretty nice to be a famous person's pet. Rainer pooped.

Rick Savini's UPS man, Rick Savini's agent, Farah, and Wesley were clustered around an occasional table spread with the laminates of Wesley's list of "~~Seventy-four~~ Seventy-five Things That Cause Unnecessary Fatigue." They resembled generals around a battlefield map. Loud sounds of appreciation were voiced. The UPS man said it was like seeing a printout of the inside of his mind. "I can't tell you how glad I am to see someone stand up to grapes with seeds," he added, referencing item #59. The agent said, "This is wonderful. I mean, it's really all here, isn't it?" Farah gave Wesley a thump on the back. "Thank you," said Wesley. "Thank you."

Seated on a couch, Booth held forth for a group that included Rick and Jo-Jo. Sam's father had a sweating bottle of beer in one hand and was leaning forward, all of his bulk piled on his thighs. His cape was draped over the back of the couch, and he was raising and lowering his free hand as if relating a story about weights and measures. Everyone was smiling.

Sam was feeling good. It wasn't often, he thought, that you could cast around a crowded room and feel nothing but generosity toward the assembled—maybe at your wedding, or perhaps at your funeral, on the unlikely chance that some remnant of you was able to look on. Sam wished he'd felt that way when he'd wrapped his movie, but he'd been too sick, and too young.

He made his way over to Tess and Mina. They were standing by the fireplace, commiserating about boyfriends who turned out to be gay.

"You want them to be a little gay," said Tess. She was wearing Mina's DOOM watchcap.

"Yeah." Mina grimaced. "But not totally gay."

"No." Tess shook her head. "That's when you've got a problem." She turned to beam at Sam. "Mina gave me her hat! She's making a whole line: doom, plague, wreck, and toxin. Isn't that great?"

"I'd wear any of those," said Sam.

Mina, looking past Sam toward the rest of the room, inhaled sharply. When he swung around, he saw Sandra shuffling in on the arm of a lanky teenage boy whom Sam recognized by his skinny tie as young Peter Jenks. Sandra appeared even more wind-whipped than usual, her eyes large and her cheekbones drawn sharply. She wore a clashing ensemble of purple sweatpants, plaid shirt, and fringy scarf. Behind her came a man in a doctor's coat—a filled-out version of Peter, wearing a grown-up tie—and behind him, another teenage boy, this one wearing a Killers T-shirt.

"I'll go talk to her." Sam had no idea how Sandra had found her way to Rick Savini's party—he sensed Booth's errant hand—but he was prepared to drag her right out the door if she started to make a scene.

"I hope you don't expect to get much out of her," said Mina. "Dr. Jenks dosed her. She's real mellow. I guess she's going to be crashing with Tom and Booth for a while, too."

"Really?"

Sam's sister nodded. "The whole happy family. Think about it: you know how convincing Booth can be. If anyone can get her to take her pills, it's Booth."

"Are you okay with this?" Sam thought she sounded mostly resigned.

"Eh," said Mina. "I could go either way. We'll see. It ought to be interesting, anyway." With this, she snorted. "I just can't believe Peter brought *him.*"

Tess slid an arm around the girl's shoulders. "Whatever. He's not that cute."

Sam went over. Sandra had settled in beside Booth, and her head was resting against his shoulder. The sight was surprising but sweet, the comfort between them, and the feeling that Sam had—of wanting only the best for everyone—expanded to a point where he felt almost dizzied by it.

Sam squatted down alongside his stepmother. He asked how she was feeling.

"Glum," Sandra said. "And so stoned. I'm trying to smile now. Can you tell?" A corner of her mouth twitched.

"Oh, yeah," said Sam.

"Liar," said Sandra. Now one corner of her mouth did curl up.

"Mina loves you," Sam said. He took her hand. It was thin and dry. It felt lifeless. "Try and concentrate on that."

"Maybe that's it," she said. "I'm already thinking of later, of the disappointment. I'm always going to be disappointing. Even if I'm not crazy, I'll still make mistakes. There's no medication for that."

"No, there's no medication for that," said Sam. "But Mina loves you. And there's no medication that can take that away, either." He squeezed her hand, and she squeezed it back.

His father, meanwhile, was speaking:

"And here was this boy. He peers up at me with this little scalded face and does not cry, does not make a single peep. And the nurses have swaddled him in a rough brown cloth, such as an extra will wear in a biblical production, so that he resembles a tiny leper. And he makes no fuss, no fuss at all. He just squints at me with these hot blue eyes. Looking so aggrieved, so deeply aggrieved. Can you picture it? It was most disquieting." Booth shut his eyes and nodded, and the bare skin above his beard was hatched thick with wrinkles. When he opened them, he spotted his son nearby. The old man gave his nose a sly tap. "I mean, really. Allie was so happy. And I was so happy. You could not look at him for more than a moment and not love him."

A hand touched Sam's elbow, and Dr. Jenks asked if they might have a word in the hall.

8.

Although the enormous coincidence—that Peter Jenks's psychiatrist father should be, along with treating Sandra, already engaged as Brooks Hartwig, Jr.'s, therapist—overwhelmed the better part of the case history in Sam's mind, he was able to catch and hold a few of the major details.

Brooks had never been particularly adept in a social sense. When he was a boy, his fascinations had an eerie trend. The seven- and eight-year-old Brooks did things like ask other children to go to sleep so he could watch them, and approach strangers and offer them dollar bills if they would allow him to peruse their car glove compartments; he had a horror of empty playground swings that he refused to explain; when he was eleven, Brooks watched *E.T.* every day for six months, and kept the videotape under his pillow, and once threatened to kill a housemaid who attempted to dust it. Somewhere around this time, there was an afternoon lightning storm, and preadolescent Brooks, at a window of the Hartwig family estate, witnessed a bolt of lightning strike a gardener. The man's hair exploded into flame, his clothes burned off, and he went naked and screaming into a hedgerow. Though the gardener lived and recovered, this was understandably a traumatic, affecting experience for Brooks. It was then, Dr. Jenks had learned, that the invisible film crew manifested.

"My theory is that the documentary crew is a coping mechanism, a convenient explanation for everything bad that happens to Brooks," said Dr. Jenks. From inside his coat, the doctor had produced a ballpoint pen and clicked the button at irregular intervals.

In college, the film medium perhaps initially allowed Brooks to exorcise some of his torment, but his work on *Who We Are* had been too stressful. He'd become a danger to himself and to others. It was only with years of therapy, experimentation with different drugs and dosages, and lots of peace and quiet that they had managed to bring Brooks into some kind of balance.

Sam found himself thinking of *Psycho,* of the half-assed epilogue where the shrink appears to explain that Norman and his mother were the same person. He had a feeling from Dr. Jenks's little smile that the man was thinking of the same reference point, or of something similar—maybe an episode of *Scooby-Doo* where a particularly dastardly villain was unmasked—and relishing the chance to be the one who explained the mystery. Sam felt irritated on Brooks's behalf. If anyone deserved a chance at the glory of reenacting a classic movie moment, of being allowed to pretend that his own life rose to the level of cinema, it wasn't Dr. Jenks or even Sam—it was Brooks. He was the one who had put up with the anxiety of living inside a continuous production for over fifteen or so years. If there was a purer notion of hell than that—of being trapped in a film shoot that never ended—Sam didn't want to know it.

"Can you not do that?" Sam pointed at the doctor's pen hand.

"Oh, sorry," said Dr. Jenks, as if he had just woken up. He stopped clicking the pen and stuck it back in his pocket.

"You know Brooks was hanging around outside my apartment building with a sword?" asked Sam.

The doctor shook his head. "I didn't know that, though I can't say I'm terribly surprised. There was a mix-up with his medication, and

Brooks skipped the reservation for a few months. We only got him back because he was viciously attacked." Dr. Jenks lowered his voice. "A mugger crushed his left testicle."

"Ouch," said Sam. He noticed a fascinating knot in the grain of the wood floor.

"People can be very callous. Only the other evening, one of my private patients—an elderly gentlemen, a widower, a man of letters—some hooligan left him lying in a puddle of feces."

There were several interesting knots in the wood floor, some larger than others.

"But I can assure you that we've got Brooks settled down," said the doctor. In fact, Dr. Jenks had made the (admittedly aggressive) move of attempting to advance the poor man's treatment by bringing him along to the gathering in Westchester in hopes that Sam would meet with him. "I know it's asking a great deal, but I assure you, Brooks is no danger. He's given me full permission to tell you all of this, and I feel strongly that it would be of immeasurable therapeutic value for him if you'd consent to go out and have a friendly word with him." The doctor nodded, ratifying his own thought process, before adding, "It might even have some small positive benefit for you, Mr. Dolan."

Parked in his wheelchair by the circular flowerbed at the center of the driveway, swaddled in a gray blanket with a freshly shaved face, Brooks was like a pale spot at the opposite end of a tunnel. He lifted a thickly bandaged hand an inch or two as Sam approached.

"Hey, Brooks," said Sam. The padding of his sneaker soles was the only noise. The sky was a deeper blue than before, and it was warmer.

The puffy figure in the wheelchair was basically a stranger to him. Otherwise, what had happened never could have happened, because Sam would have stopped him, and both their lives would have been changed unfathomably. Brooks had given Sam money. They had not had the same ideas about movies. At times Brooks had annoyed Sam, and at other times he had unnerved him. They used each other in different ways, and now, seeing Brooks again—diminished, hobbled, alone in the middle of the long driveway, on a day pass from a hospital where you weren't allowed to have shoelaces—Sam thought it was fairly obvious who had gotten the better of the deal.

Sam stopped a foot or two from the wheelchair.

Brooks blinked. The hollows under his eyes were nearly black. He lifted an eyebrow and held it steady. "So . . . this is, like, a fall party? I've never been to one of those."

"Uh-huh. Me either. Happy fall, Brooks."

"Yeah. Yay, fall," said Brooks.

"I'm sorry," said Sam.

Brooks angled his head quizzically. "About what? I'm the one who stole Rick's sword, right?"

"I meant about the movie," said Sam. "For picking on you to get what I wanted. I should have treated you with more respect. I was a bastard. I'm sorry about that."

"Oh. Whatever. Long time ago. We did what we had to." The little man in the wheelchair waved his hand to shoo the apology away.

Sam decided to let Brooks's use of the first-personal plural pass. If nothing else, it was proof of what he should have known all along: Brooks was a director in his own right, possessed of his own vision and his own fierce drive.

"It was just such a great sword. And sometimes I get afraid. But it was wrong. I needed to give it back."

That was what Brooks had wanted. To give Sam the sword so he could return it. "I gave it to him."

"Oh, good. Like, yay." Brooks's head bobbed down and up. The slackness of his features made Sam sad. The current that had run through him—twitching eyebrows, fluttering eyelids, leaping hands—had been tied off. His gestures were sluggish and half formed. He was like a toy whose batteries were nearly spent.

A battered forest-green compact turned in to the driveway and parked at the end of the line of cars.

"You hear about Costas?" asked Brooks.

"I did."

"He was such a great satyr."

There was no question about that, Sam admitted. Costas had been committed. He told Brooks that he'd always wondered how they'd hooked up.

"I saw him at the library one time, one of the viewing stations, you know? With the headphones? And I noticed he was crying very quietly. This old guy in his maintenance uniform and his Santa beard. So I peeked around and I saw that he was watching *The Wizard of Oz*, the very end. Where Dorothy wakes up back home, in black and white. And I knew just how he felt."

Brooks's head drooped again. While he was speaking, his gaze had drifted from Sam's to fall on the mulch of the flower bed so that he seemed to be addressing the ground. "Like, where did all the colors go?"

"Sure," said Sam. He tried to imagine what it was like inside Brooks's head, and the picture that came to him was from the previous night, of the shopping cart stranded in the middle of the huge parking lot, looking like the bones of something.

"So we became friends, and he was very supportive. He got it immediately. What it was about. Our movie, and he saw that it was missing that thing, that one thing, that brought it upward to the next level. And it must have been fate, because the guy was—you know—suited for the part." Brooks grinned. "But satyrs, they're the saddest, right? They're the soul of the party and everything, but then what about after the party, after the storm or whatever, you know. No one cares who they are, really are. 'Who we are'—like the title? And they, satyrs, they—" Brooks raised a hand and used it to push at the air above the armrest. A frown tightened his mouth. "I hate these fucking cameras."

"It's okay, Brooks," said Sam. "Let me." He ran his own hand through the bothersome space.

The man in the wheelchair sighed. His hand settled back on the armrest. "Costas loved movies, though. He said that in Greece, in the city where he grew up, it was really crowded, so they had outdoor movies. Like drive-ins but way better. They showed them in people's backyards, against walls and under the stars. He said you could smell the flowers and everything, and the sea, and what the neighbors were cooking, and everything. Great, right?"

Brooks looked at Sam. His eyes were glassy and full. His nose was red.

Sam could picture it: the sweet summer air, the smell of butter warming in a pan, the stars above, the grass between his toes, the projector whirring, a window of light opening on the blank wall. "That sounds wonderful, Brooks."

A car door slammed shut.

■　■　■

Bea, her pregnant stomach tenting the lower portion of her anorak, called hello to Sam. He pushed Brooks's wheelchair over to meet her halfway. They hugged.

"What are you doing here?" he asked.

"My boyfriend is friends with the guy who owns the place."

A realization lay just beyond Sam's reach. He could hear it, though, snickering around like the tail of film at the end of a spinning reel.

"Hey. Nice face tattoo," said Brooks.

Bea gave him a once-over and determined that the compliment was unironic. "Thanks."

The three of them stood for a moment, nodding all around. "Should we go in?" she asked.

They started toward the house. The sun was high, glazing the gabled roof and the windows of the big house, and spilling gold across the pavement. Sam pushed the wheelchair and blinked. It was right around noon. "God, it's so bright suddenly," said Bea. "Is this what they mean by the magic hour?"

No, he said, that came later.

CREDITS

There's unfortunately not space here to acknowledge all of the texts that informed this novel, but I want to make special mention here of two especially crucial ones: first, Bret Stern's *How to Shoot a Feature Film for Under $10,000 *And Not Go to Jail* provided Sam with his lighting solution for shooting the rave; and second, Richard Shepard's *I Knew It Was You: Rediscovering John Cazale,* which in its focus on the "Wyoming" exchange between Al Pacino and John Cazale, and in its interviews with Sam Rockwell, Sidney Lumet, Carol Kane, Israel Horowitz, and Pacino, undoubtedly influenced Sam and Tess's respective viewpoints on the scene.

The character of Booth Dolan is, in many ways, inspired by the great Orson Welles. David Thomson's *Rosebud* and Peter Bogdanovich's *This Is Orson Welles* were invaluable resources. Specifically, Thomson highlights the passage quoted from *A Touch of Evil,* and Bogdanovich's heartbreaking story of watching *The Magnificent Ambersons* with Welles helped to inspire the moment when Sam discovers Booth, Mina, and Tom watching *Who We Are.* In general, both men's books helped me get to know Orson Welles a little bit better, a providential introduction for any person who aspires to make-believe.

ACKNOWLEDGMENTS

I was immensely lucky to get feedback on this manuscript from film industry professionals like Peter Askin, Scott Tuft, and Glenn Kenny. You guys are nice.

Tom Bissell was my first, and most frightening critic, and I adore him for it.

I can't overstate the value of the input extended to me by my early readers: spiritual advisors Elizabeth Nelson Bracy and Timothy Bracy; Mr. Big Deal himself, Sean Doolittle; Timothy Schaffert, the sweetest person in Nebraska (which is saying something); the totally super David Yoo; Drew Ervin, who barely knew me, and was generous and enthusiastic when I badly needed for someone to be generous and enthusiastic; and Professor Nathan Hensley, who has put up with more of my foolishness than just about anyone save my wife and a few medical professionals. Sorry that Craft Services never showed up, gang.

Anne O'Neil Henry and Emily Bragg turned my prose into French. They are both excellent talkers.

My editor, Brant Rumble, is a beacon of good taste and calm. He's also the man to speak to if you need a new title in a pinch, or information on the mid-nineties roster of the Braves. I'm proud to call him my friend.

Amy Williams has been my agent for years and tears. She's the best.

I'm grateful to Nan Graham and Susan Moldow for believing in me and for believing in this book that has so many penises in it.

I have never met Beth Thomas, but she is one hell of a copyeditor, and I am tremendously grateful for her efforts.

The following individuals helped, commiserated, encouraged, listened while feigning interest, or otherwise assisted in the long and generally agonizing process of this novel's development, oftentimes without even knowing they were doing anything except being their usual terrific selves: Julie Barer, Frank Bergon, Holly Bergon, Jim Braffet, Theresa Braffet, Michael Cendejas, Norm Elrod, Joshua Ferris, Megan Forbes at The Museum of the Moving Image, Benjamin "Son of Swoop" Freeman, John Glynn, Matt Grebow, Lauren Grodstein, Elizabeth Kennedy, Jennifer Krazit, Binnie Kirshenbaum, Christina Baker Kline, Shane Leonard (leader in the fight against the scourge of handle-pulling), Lawrence Levi, Danielle Lurie, Bridget McCarthy, Kelly McCormick, John McNally, Kevin Newman, Stewart O'Nan, Daniel Pipski, Lynn Pleschette, Mark Poirier, Paul Russell, Brenda Shaughnessy, Daniel Silver, Scott Snyder, Amanda Spielman, Brittany Statlend, Peter Straub, Craig Teicher, Jimmyjack Toth, and all the people at Scribner who have been so kind to me.

I'm sure I've left off some people who belong in here. Please know that I appreciate you, but sometimes I'm stupid and forgetful.

William Gay, I really wanted you to read this, my friend. You are missed.

My mom and my dad, my sister and my brother: thank you.

Kelly Braffet, sometimes I think I can't love you any more, and then the next day happens.

WESLEY LATSCH'S LIST OF
~~SEVENTY-FOUR~~ SEVENTY-FIVE THINGS
THAT CAUSE UNNECESSARY FATIGUE

1. Rushing
2. Exercising
3. Children
4. Pets
5. Pet-sitting
6. Cooking
7. Dating
8. Laundry that must be air-dried
9. Analysis
10. Shopping in stores—clothing stores in particular and malls in general
11. Parties—hosting or attending
12. Hiking
13. Preservation—framing artwork, storing and displaying mementoes, maintaining photo albums
14. Recycling
15. Investing
16. Air travel
17. Contact lenses
18. Holiday celebrations
19. Gift giving and gift receiving
20. Writing thank you cards and receiving thank you cards

21. Bachelor parties
22. Weddings
23. More than seven close relationships/friendships (*including immediate family*)
24. Overnight visitors, visiting overnight
25. Memberships
26. Discount cards and coupons
27. Libraries
28. Jazz
29. Opera
30. Criticizing people face-to-face and being criticized face-to-face
31. Political talk
32. Voting
33. Effort to obtain illegal narcotics
34. Prying into the affairs of strangers
35. Empathizing with people you don't know or don't know well (*empathy should ideally be limited to the seven close relationships*)
36. National pride
37. Music on vinyl
38. Noisy environments
39. Crowded environments
40. Driving in urban areas
41. Driving a standard shift vehicle
42. Driving a motorcycle
43. Giving driving directions, copying down driving directions, following driving directions
44. Owning property
45. Gardening
46. Telephone landlines
47. Petitions
48. Rooting for sports teams
49. *Risk*
50. Conspiracy theories and discussion with people who believe in conspiracy theories
51. Religious worship
52. Gambling
53. Waiting in lines

54. Going to concerts (particularly when there is no seating)
55. Dining in restaurants
56. Eating at tables
57. Morning appointments
58. Re-sealable packaging (does not work)
59. Grapes with seeds
60. Zappa
61. Inkjet printers
62. Pencils
63. Use of semi-colons
64. Pynchon
65. *The New Yorker*
66. Science Fiction (especially all the different versions of *Blade Runner,* totally unnecessary)
67. Science
68. Book Clubs
69. DVD Easter Eggs
70. Anime
71. Freelance anything
72. Collaboration, partnership (fair share of labor impossible to determine, plus other obvious problems)
73. British-style crosswords
74. Museums
75. Hugging a mummy